The Great Stink

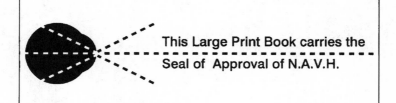

This Large Print Book carries the
Seal of Approval of N.A.V.H.

The Great Stink

Clare Clark

Thorndike Press • Waterville, Maine

Published in 2006 by arrangement with Harcourt, Inc.

Thorndike Press® Large Print Mystery.

The tree indicium is a trademark of Thorndike Press.

The text of this Large Print edition is unabridged.
Other aspects of the book may vary from the original edition.

Set in 16 pt. Plantin by Ramona Watson.

Printed in the United States on permanent paper.

Library of Congress Cataloging-in-Publication Data

Clark, Clare.
     The great stink / by Clare Clark.
        p. cm. — (Thorndike Press large print mystery)
     ISBN 0-7862-8321-1 (lg. print : hc : alk. paper)
     1. Crimean War, 1853–1856 — Veterans — Fiction.
2. Underground areas — Fiction.   3. London (England) —
Fiction.   4. Ragpickers — Fiction.   5. Sewerage — Fiction.
6. Large type books.   7. Psychological fiction.   I. Title.
II. Thorndike Press large print mystery series.
PR6103.L3725G74 2006
823'.92—dc22   2005029351

For Chris, always

As the Founder/CEO of NAVH, the only national health agency solely devoted to those who, although not totally blind, have an eye disease which could lead to serious visual impairment, I am pleased to recognize Thorndike Press★ as one of the leading publishers in the large print field.

Founded in 1954 in San Francisco to prepare large print textbooks for partially seeing children, NAVH became the pioneer and standard setting agency in the preparation of large type.

Today, those publishers who meet our standards carry the prestigious "Seal of Approval" indicating high quality large print. We are delighted that Thorndike Press is one of the publishers whose titles meet these standards. We are also pleased to recognize the significant contribution Thorndike Press is making in this important and growing field.

Lorraine H. Marchi, L.H.D.
Founder/CEO
NAVH

★ Thorndike Press encompasses the following imprints: Thorndike, Wheeler, Walker and Large Print Press.

I

Where the channel snaked to the right it was no longer possible to stand upright, despite the abrupt drop in the gradient. The crown of William's hat grazed the slimed roof as he stooped, holding his lantern before him, and the stink of excrement pressed into his nostrils. His hand was unsteady and the light shuddered and jumped in the darkness. Rising and rushing through the narrower gully, the stream pressed the greased leather of his high boots hard against the flesh of his calves, the surge of the water muffling the clatter of hooves and iron-edged wheels above him. Of course he was deeper now. Between him and the granite-block road was at least twenty feet of heavy London clay. The weight of it deepened the darkness. Beneath his feet the rotten bricks were treacherous, soft as crumbled cheese, and with each step the thick layer of black sludge sucked at the soles of his boots. Although his skin bristled with urgency, William forced himself to walk slowly and deliberately the way the flushers had shown him, pressing his heel down hard into the uncertain ground before unrolling his weight forward on to the ball of his foot, scanning the surface of the water for rising bubbles. The sludge hid pockets of gas, slop gas the flushers called it, the faintest whiff of which they claimed could cause a man to drop unconscious, sudden as if he'd been shot. From the little he knew of the toxic effects of sulphuretted hydrogen, William had every reason to believe them.

The pale light of his lantern sheered off the black crust of the water and threw a villain's shadow up the curved wall. Otherwise there was no relief from the absolute darkness, not even in the first part of the tunnel where open gratings led directly up into the street. All day the fog had crouched low over London, a chocolate-coloured murk that reeked of sulphur and defied the certainty of dawn. In vain the gas-lamps pressed their circles of light into its upholstered interior. Carriages loomed out of the darkness, the stifled skitters and whinnies of horses blurring with the warning shouts of coachmen. Pedestrians, their faces obscured by hats and collars, slipped into proximity and as quickly out again. On the river the hulking outlines of the penny steamers resembled a charcoal scrawl over which a child had carelessly drawn a sleeve. Now, at nearly six o'clock in the evening, the muddy brown of afternoon had been smothered into night. William was careful to close the shutter of his lantern off beneath the open gratings, as furtive as a sewer-hunter. It was bad enough that he was alone, without a lookout at ground level, in direct contravention of the Board's directives. It would be even harder to explain his presence here, in a section of the channel recently declared unsafe and closed off until extensive repair work could be undertaken. William could hardly protest to be innocent of the decision. He had written the report requiring it himself, his first official report to the Board:

Within the southern section of the King-street branch deterioration to interior brickwork is severe, with the shoulder of the arch particularly suffering from extensive decomposition. While tidal scour can be relied upon to prevent undue accumulation of deposits, the high volumes of floodwater sustained within the tunnel during periods of full tide and heavy rainfall

9

pose a grave threat to the stability of the interior structure. Underpinning of the crown is urgently required to prevent subsidence. DANGER.

The precision of the words had satisfied him. Within them was contained the evidence of a world where method and reason strapped down chaos. On their very first day as assistants to the Commission the group of young men had been taken to meet Mr Bazalgette himself. One of their number, eager to ingratiate himself with the master, had begged him to disclose what he considered the characteristics of a successful engineer. Bazalgette had paused, his fingers against his lips. When he spoke it was quietly, almost to himself. The great engineer, he said, was a pragmatist made conservative by the conspicuous failures of structures and machines hastily contrived. He was regular in his habits, steady, disciplined, methodical in his problem-solving. He was equable and law-abiding. Carelessness, self-indulgence, untidiness and fits of temper were foreign to him. From the turmoil of his natural instincts he brought order.

'How unutterably tedious he'd like us!' one of the pupils had hissed at William as they were dismissed. William paid no attention. In the months that followed he had held on to Bazalgette's words, repeating them to himself until their shape acquired the metre of a magic charm. William no longer trusted in prayer.

Where the floor of the tunnel levelled out once more William paused, holding his lantern up to the wall. The water tugged impatiently at his boots. Where the light caught it, the masonry bulged with overlapping wads of fungi. They sprouted fatly from between the spongy bricks, their fleshy undersides bloated and blind, quilting the holes that pocked the walls. They were the closest that the tunnels came to plant life but William could find no affection for them. He ducked further, pulling in his shoulders to avoid brushing against their pallid flesh. Their cold yeasty smell rose above the privy stench of the filthy water. William's throat closed. For a moment he felt the tilt of the ship and his hair crawled, alive with vermin. Men moaned all around him, crying out for help that never came. He had a sudden urge to dash the glass of the lantern against the wall. A shard of the broken glass would be as sharp as a knife. It would slice through the stinking fungi until their flesh fell away

11

from the wall. Would it bleed or would it simply yield the yellowed ooze of a corpse too long in the sun? The craving quickened within him and his breath came in shallow dips. He imagined his fingers closing round a dagger of glass, tight and then tighter until his blood ran in narrow black streams between his knuckles. The hunger pressed into his throat, and crowded his chest. He stared into the lantern, watching the worm of flame curl as he swung it slowly backwards and forwards. Just one hard blow. That was all it would take. He pulled back his arm . . .

No! The lantern swung dizzily as he snatched in his hand and a pale fragment of mushroom swirled away in the stream. A fine crack ran upwards through the glass of the lantern but the light did not go out. Unhurriedly the flame stretched, shivered and then steadied. Sweat trickled from beneath the brim of William's hat. He gripped the handle of the lantern tightly, angry at his imprudence. Without the lantern he would never find his way back to the shaft. Forcing his mouth full of saliva he licked his lips. *Regular in his habits, steady, disciplined, methodical in his problem-solving. Equable and law-abiding.* He repeated the words to himself as he moved further into the tunnel. His knees were unsteady.

Once again the tunnel narrowed. Here there was barely room to accommodate the spread of William's shoulders and the water rushed over his knees. At high tide the flow would fill the channel almost to the roof. Where the stream scoured the walls there were no more mushrooms. Instead the walls were slick with a fatty dew of nitre that gleamed silver in the lantern's light. In the darkness beyond, a row of stalactites hung like yellowing teeth from a narrow lip of brick in the curve of the roof. This was the place, the place where young Jephson had finally gone to pieces.

It had not come quite without warning. Jephson, a gangly surveyor with the raw oversized knuckles of the not-quite man, had been discomfited for at least a half-mile, the perspiration standing out on his forehead as he complained of stomach aches, headaches, of difficulty breathing. He had insisted that the ganger pause every few yards and hold out his lantern on its pole in the darkness, checking and re-checking for the presence of choke-damp. While the measurements were being taken his hands had trembled so violently that William had taken the spirit level from him, anxious it might be lost in the underground sludge. But it was not until they reached this point that the boy finally lost his head. His fear had travelled backwards through the tunnel like gas, poisoning the other men, but not William. William had watched with a detached disinterest as Jephson flailed, screaming, in the filthy water. He had noted the lettuce-green tinge of his pinched face as his hat was carried off by the current. He had observed the spots of red flaring on each of his sharpened cheekbones, the bony white fingers clutching at the crumbling walls. He had felt nothing but a faint impatience as Jephson thrashed and shrieked in the restraining grip of the ganger and his assistant. The flushers were stout as butchers and their great fists encircled Jephson's arms as easily as if they were axe-handles but for a time the young man's movements were so violent that it had been as much as they could manage to hold him at all. At last Jephson's wild legs had kicked out with such force that he had dislodged a welter of bricks. *'Get 'im out of 'ere!'* There had been no mistaking the edge of warning in the ganger's habitually lugubrious tone. When finally they bundled him up into the street, the rest of the surveying party following in subdued silence, Jephson's hair was clumped with filth and his nails had been quite torn away.

After that Jephson had been transferred to Grant's department. These days he was making studies of Portland cement, experimenting with the weight-carrying potential of beams of varying dimensions. It had been left to William to make the required assessment of the tunnel's condition to the Board. Since then Lovick had placed him in charge of the review of the existing system on the north side. Reportedly he had emerged from the Jephson incident as a man capable of retaining a cool head in a crisis.

The recess that remained in the brickwork was clear of the water and almost a foot across at its widest point. If this was not the work of Jephson's boots then it would do just as well, although William would have to open it up further. The space needed to be large enough for him to sit in, and to accommodate his lantern. He could not do it one-handed. William shone light into the space. The wall was patterned with grooves, inked with shadow. Most were shallow, short and clustered in fours and fives, like the ones carved by prisoners to mark the passage of time;

some were broader and blunter and showed up only in pairs. Rats. They had tried to burrow here, presumably seeking refuge against the rising current, grinding their claws and even their teeth into the masonry. But they had been confounded. The brickwork was soft enough but the putrid black stream that surged around William's knees had once been a river. Once, a long time ago, there had been a bridge here and large blocks of the Portland stone that had supported it remained embedded in the brickwork of the tunnel. The rats' efforts had achieved no more than chalky scratches on its unyielding surface.

For a moment William let himself imagine what it might have been like to stand here in a different time, the warmth of sunlight on his face and clear water playing over his feet. He pictured prosperous gentlemen in their powdered wigs promenading with their wives along its grassy banks, dipping their hands to drink its sweet water, or leaning from bridges and boats to admire their contented reflections in its mirror. As the pollen drifted across the brook, the silvered fish stretched lazily and offered their mouths to the waiting hook. William was not to know

16

that this particular stretch of the stream had been little better than an open sewer for centuries now, lined from the time of Queen Elizabeth with slaughterhouses and tanneries that poisoned the fish and turned the water red so that Ben Jonson himself had written of it as eclipsing in foulness all four rivers of Hades. Perhaps the rats had sensed the river's grim past. Thwarted by history they had gone elsewhere, leaving William alone in the darkness. His unshed tears ground into his eyes, hard as stones.

The screams were starting to build beneath his diaphragm, pressing up and out of his ribcage so hard it seemed they might force the bones through their covering of skin. William's hands shook. Strapping his lantern to the front of his leather apron he fumbled in the tool pouch he kept slung around his waist. His fingers were cold and clumsy and, as he pulled out the knife, he almost dropped it. Wrapping both hands tightly around the handle he swore at himself, a stream of quiet, intense obscenities as rank as the river he stood in. It was the first time that day that he had spoken and his unaccustomed voice creaked over the words. He cleared his throat. The curses surged forth, smoother and faster, asserting themselves over the rushing of the water. Their simple contours calmed him a little.

Once again William felt the stirrings of purpose in his belly and then the cravings began to swell as they always did, scouring him with their voracious heat. In the frozen mud of the nights that William did not let himself remember the men had circled uneasily in the darkness and complained loudly of their unsatisfied desires. Nothing, it seemed, not the gnawing hunger, nor the vicious cold, nor even the sheer paralysing terror of the night-watch, could strip these lusty London boys of their yearnings. Women had done for them good and proper, the soldiers had lamented again and again, raking at the skin beneath their verminous uniforms; for a man would do almost anything to scratch an itch that fearful ticklish. Night after night they had passed the long hours describing Her, the fantastical amalgam of all their wild dreams and narrow experience, her feather mattress unrolled across the ridged mud of the trench and her white legs spread. In the beginning William had considered their rough talk an affront to gentlemanliness, to decency, most of all to Polly herself, but long after that was gone he found himself comforted by it. At least it was always the same.

Those exchanges came back to him when at last he and Polly lay together once again and on the many nights afterwards when he lay awake listening to her soft snores. Before the war he could barely so much as hear her voice without wanting to touch her but since his return from Scutari he had been unable to summon up for her anything more than a vague disoriented kind of affection. She touched his face with her tender fingers, kissed the corners of his mouth, flickered her tongue over his neck and his nipples and his belly but he could feel none of it. His penis hung as wrinkled as a discarded stocking between his legs. He saw the fingers, the lips, but they were no more than pictures to him, random plates torn from a book. When Polly spoke to him, adjusting the tilt of his head so that his eyes were forced to meet her own gay twinkle, he had to recall himself, so far had he drifted from the place where they were together. Words lost their meanings. Colours faded or blurred. He had difficulty recognizing everyday objects. Sometimes he was unsure of who he was. There were days when William was certain that he was simply disappearing, fragmenting and disintegrating until he was nothing but dry sand, trickling away between the floorboards.

Except when the cravings came. They licked him with their flame tongues and whispered of ecstasy. Their power overwhelmed him. He had no hope of resisting them, nor any wish to do so. They were the closest he came to hope. When the cravings began to burn inside him the frozen darkness thawed a little. In their flickering light he could finally sense the shape of a man, of someone who, despite everything, was still alive.

William's breath came quickly and his heart sucked at his chest. His head felt empty, a balloon attached to his body only by a string so that he seemed to observe its movements from a great distance. But his skin was frantic with dread and anticipation. Quickly he worked around the slabs of stone, prising bricks out with the point of his knife. It did not take long. The mortar in this part of the network was soft as gangrene. As he removed each one he threw it into the narrowing mouth of the tunnel. The black water swallowed the bricks without a splash. Beneath the loose fabric of his shirt the skin on the soft underside of his arm prickled and burned.

When the space was large enough he sat, placing the lantern beside him. The blade of his knife quivered as he held it up to the light. Crumbs of mortar clung to the fret-work of tiny scratches left by the whet-stone. Sewer mortar would carry infection. His work in Scutari had taught him that. Carefully William wiped the steel with a large clean rag. Holding it close to his face he stroked the ball of his thumb over the blade to test its sharpness. Abruptly the cravings rose in him again, this time with such intensity that the hairs on his arms and neck pulled taut away from the skin. His fingers tingled. Clamping the knife be-tween his teeth he folded the rag in half and then in half again and laid the pad of fabric across his lap. Then he unbuttoned the cuff of his shirt and rolled his sleeve to above the elbow. His fingertips skated lightly over the underside of his forearm but he did not look down. It distracted him to see it. It muddied the purity of the first moments. There was always a time, after-wards, when he felt completely purged, whole, happy even. For a while it was pos-sible to persuade himself that he would never come back, that it was over, finished with. But there was always a part of him that knew that it would never stop.

It was time. He was ready. He slid the shutter on the lantern.

The darkness closed over him. It no

longer mattered if his eyes were open or closed but he closed them all the same. Behind his eyelids, no longer connected to the movements of his own fingers or the ghost of his white-tipped nose, he separated from himself. In the darkness he could feel the quickening of life within him. Up there in the unending press and clamour of the city its light grew faint, its circle of heat so infinitesimal that it was possible to believe it had been quite snuffed out. But under and away, in the darkness, beneath the wheels and the hooves and the hobnails, knee-deep in the effluvia of the largest city on earth, his spirit found freedom. Here, where there was no light, no warmth, nothing but the sickening stink of shit, somehow here it found its own oxygen so that it might reignite and brand its living form on to the frozen surrender of his flesh. Here it mutinied. It forced itself to be heard. William May was not dead! He had only to purge the blood in his veins, the air in his lungs, ridding them of the black putrefactions that poisoned them, infecting all that they touched. If he could only flush away the filth, the poison, and establish in its place a spring of sweet clean blood, sweet clean air, that would bring with it health and life . . .

Dreamily William raised his knife. Gripping its bone handle, he cut into the flesh of his arm.

The ecstasy exploded within him. William wanted to laugh, to cry, to scream out loud. At this perfect moment of climax he occupied himself once more. He was whole. The relief was exquisite. He cut again, deeper this time, and felt himself filled with a calm that was at once peaceful and exultant. Blood gushed from the long gashes, spilling on to the rag on his lap. He smeared it across his skin. It was warm, real, wonderful. On impulse he held his arm up to his mouth and licked it. It tasted beautiful. He licked again. The pain was on the outside now, held safely where he would manage it. It was real at last, defined. Something he could hold on to, something he could control. The disintegrating sand of his self no longer slipped from his fingers. Instead its particles began to pull together, asserting themselves back into a solid whole. Inside his head the shadowy twilight darkened and tightened to reveal at its centre a single vivid pinprick of light. The muscles in his thighs tautened as his feet pressed against the jagged brick floor. He felt strong, clear-headed. He cut one last time, the pain singing out from his flesh in triumph. The blood filled the palm of his hand and he clasped it so that it ran between his fingers. He wanted to cry out with the sheer joy of it. *I'm alive!* he wanted to shout until the darkness echoed and the bricks shivered in their sockets with the categorical certainty of it. *I, William Henry May of 8 York-street, S., am alive!*

II

Long Arm Tom tipped back his grizzled head and sniffed. Once, a long time ago now, Joe'd reckoned it a lark to take the rise out of Tom about the sniffing, had liked to call him Long Nose Tom or Lurcher Tom or just Dog, on those days when his words came out in ones. Joe hadn't reckoned it was worth a farthing, the sniffing, not till they came out early that time on account of Tom's certainty that it was going to rain and those other coves had gotten themselves drowned over King's-cross way. After that he'd seen it different. He could never get hold of how Tom did it though, how he pulled the smell of the rain clear of all the others. To his mind all the smells just mixed themselves up together so as you got one big soup of a stink that smelled like London. Tom didn't think much of that. It wasn't just that every part of London had its own flavour so even with your eyes closed you could tell to the nearest street where you were. It was that the stinks came in layers, each one thick and sticky as the river sludge on the soles of your boots. If you only used your nose you could pick them out neat as fleas.

At the bottom of the stink was the river. It stretched a good few streets back from the banks, in fact there weren't many places in the city you couldn't catch a whiff of it on a warm day but in Thames-street it was certain as the ground you stood on. You couldn't see so much as the surface of the water through a fog like this one, not even if you hung right over the river wall, but you couldn't miss knowing it was there. The smell was solid and brown as the river itself. The water didn't know nothing of any modesty or shame. It wasn't going to hide its filth among the narrow alleys and rookeries in the lower parts of town like them in the Government might wish it to. It grinned its great brown grin and kept on going, brazen as you like, a great open stream of shit through the very centre of the capital, the knobbles and lumps of rich and poor jostling and rubbing along together, faces turned up to the sky. The rich ladies could close their doors and muffle their noises all they wanted; theirs stank same as anyone else's and out here was the proof, their private doings as clear to see as if they was on display at the

Crystal Palace. There were times, mornings and evenings in particular, when there was twenty steamers at least churning their great wheels below London Bridge, when the water was so dense and brown it seemed that it should bear a man's weight, so as he could walk clean across it without so much as wetting his feet. On a hot day the stink could knock you flat. Through the windows of hansoms on London Bridge Tom had seen ladies swoon dead away and white-faced gentlemen cover their mouths with handkerchiefs. But on a November afternoon the salt-water tang of the sea ran in silvery threads through its thick brown stink, at least up as far as Southwark. Sometimes, when Tom came out on to the river bank at night down Greenwich way, he swore he could see the salt rising from the river, glinting and dancing above its muddy plough like clouds of silver midges.

The next smell you got, when you was done with the river smell, was the sour soot-smudged stink of the fog. London's fogs came in all sorts and each one smelled only of itself. This one was a slimy yellow-brown gruel that sank and crawled along the streets, skulking into courts and cellars, looping itself around pillars and lamp-posts. You tasted it more than smelled it. It greased itself over the linings of your nostrils and choked your chest, distilling in fat droplets in your eyebrows and whiskers. When Tom breathed through his mouth it coated his tongue with the taste of rancid lard, faintly powdered with the black flour of coal dust. It had mouldered over the city for close to a week, rusting iron and smearing soot over all it touched. Through its gloom the buildings looked like grease stains on a tablecloth.

South of the river, of course, the fog got itself mixed up with the smoke. There were parts of Bermondsey where the sky looked like it was held up by nothing but chimneys and the same again in Southwark. Each smoke had its own particular flavour, so as you could always tell where you were. The smoke from the glue manufactories had a nagging acid smell that caught in the back of your skull and made you dizzy, while the soap-boilers, their stink had the sickly flavour of boiling fat. The match factories' chimneys pissed a kind of yellow smoke that reeked bad as the alley behind a public house. Then there was the particular drugging smell of hops from the breweries, which didn't smell nothing like the reek of leather and dog shit from the tanneries. South of the river you could smell the change in the neighbourhood when you crossed the street.

Here in Thames-street the smell was all of its own. In a fog like this one the market was no more than a dirty smudge looming out of its moat of mud, the everlasting clamour of the hucksters muffled even thirty yards off. But the reek of fish, stale and fresh, that was stately and self-important as a church. At its base, for foundations, was the seashore smell of seaweed and salt water, and upon these smells were built, layer by layer, reek by reek, the pungent stinks of smelt, of bloater, of sole, herring, whiting, mussel, oyster, sprat, cod, lobster, turbot, crab, brill, haddock, eel, shrimp, skate and a hundred others. The porters that hustled between the boats and the stalls carried them from shore to shop and back again, every inch of them given over to the intoxicating brew of stinks. The stallholders swung their knives in it and sent it splattering across their bloodied wooden boards. Their leather hats and aprons were dark and stiff with the contents of a thousand fish stomachs. Streaks of blood striped the fish-women's arms, their faces, the hems of their quilted petti-coats. Fish scales caught in the mud on

29

their boots and glinted like scraps of silver. Melting ice slid from their tables, shiny and thick with fish slime. Beside them wooden crates packed with straw leaked salt and fish fluids into ditches and gullies. Even if you was only in Billingsgate an hour or less the stench caught in the pelt of your greatcoat so that you carried a whisper of it with you the remainder of the day.

Tom stood aside as a fish fag bullied her way through the crowd, a dripping basket of flounder on her head. When the stalls finally were shut up for the day and the fishwomen went home, the flattened mess of their bonnets and caps and hair would be lush with the stink. In Thames-street the everyday every-place smells of London, smells so common you had to remind yourself to smell them at all, crept into the nostrils for no more than a moment before being straight-ways knocked out again. Tobacco, the rotting straw and dung of a cabstand, hot bread, the pungent gush from an uncovered sewer, the occasional surge of roasted beef and spilled porter from an ale-house door, the hot red heart of a lit brazier, none of them were any match for the fish. Not even the sharp sour odour of unwashed clothes and bodies and breath, a smell that had occupied Tom's nostrils without pause for all the decades of his life so that he no longer took any account of it at all, not even that could make more than the faintest scratch on the proud edifice of stink that was Billingsgate Market.

Tom sniffed one more time. He could not be certain, not top to bottom certain. A city so full of tricks and dodges as this one could get the better of even him but to his mind there was no hint of the metallic edge of rain. The fog made things unpredictable, of course. Its swirls and flounces could hide pockets of rain that fell sudden as a boot tipped out on the street. And then the waters down under rose in the blink of an eye. If you were in the wrong place then you didn't have long to get yourself out. Still, the tide was right. They had eight or nine hours straight, he reckoned, maybe longer. And the fog had its advantages too. Now the law'd started offering rewards to people who reported any goings-on in the sewers, the johnnies on the water were vigilant as spiders. But in the fog they couldn't make you out so easy and, what with the streets all blind clamour and confusion, the traps had other things to concern them. In the fog it was harder to make out a light through the grating too. If people chanced to see it they were like to take it for a trick of the mist.

Joe was set to meet him at the cellar. There was a hidden place there where they stowed the necessaries, the crates, the shovels, the hoes they'd rigged up with hooks for the lanterns. Tom could still remember the way the old man had taught him how to thrust the lantern into the tunnel ahead of him to test for the gases. If the flame didn't go out it was safe to go on. It was Brassey who wanted the rats this time, no less than one hundred and fifty of the buggers for a big fight at his place in Soho. It had been a great day for Brassey, the day the law'd come in banning the dog-fighting. Suddenly there were all these coves looking for sport any which way they could get it, their pockets fair springing with money. Course everyone said there were still dog fights aplenty in the big houses. The nobs could get away with it where the traps weren't exactly like to come barging in. But the dog-pits at Westminster had been closed a good long time and only a few of the public houses dared to go on with the dog-fighting after that. The dogs had gone, and into their place had come the rats. It hadn't taken Brassey long to smell the profit in it. He'd set up a pit in what had once been his upstairs parlour and, though it was a long time since Tom had been one for the fight, there was no doubt the publican's business was booming. There were weeks when he'd be at you for fresh supplies two, even three times in as many days so as you could hardly keep up with the call for them. Not that Tom was complaining. There was money in it and no shortage of the devils. The usual arrangement was two for a penny but Brassey had agreed to pay a penny a rat this time, on account of being particular about the size. Five pounds, all told. These days the rats was worth ten times the tosh, whichever way you chose to look at it.

The fog darted ahead of Tom as he ducked beneath a low archway no wider than a door. It opened into a kind of court-yard, twenty feet long and no more than two across, surrounded by tall wooden houses with so many rooms jutting out from the upper stories that they formed a roof across it that quite hid the sky. The courtyard in turn drained into a narrow alley and then another and another, each one twisting away from the other. All along them the broken-down houses jostled and pushed for space, sagging against one another like drunks.

The lanes swarmed with ragged children, some of whom tried to clasp Tom's hand or tugged hopefully at the hem of his coat. Tom shook them off without so much as looking at them. He walked quickly, slipping easy as an eel through the confusion of the rookery until he reached a corner where two walls of crumbling brick met. An iron bracket rusted on the wall above him, the glass globe of the gas-light long smashed. Even the fog struggled to penetrate this far. Only a thin slice of blacker shadow revealed that one wall was in fact set slightly ahead of the other, concealing a tiny courtyard no wider than a man's outstretched arms and, set low in one corner, a rotting wooden door that slumped between the fingers of its hinges. Tom eased the door to one side and, stooping, went down a shallow flight of steps into a low windowless cellar.

In the mouldering gloom he slung his lantern from a nail and reached into the wall for his wire crates. They were broad and flat, of the kind used to take chickens to market. At a pinch you could get a hundred rats to a crate, stacked one over the next like bowls. His fingers worked into the corners of the cages, checking for holes. You didn't want to find a rat had worked his way out, not once you were in the tunnel. The rats were more skittish in the fog, more likely to turn nasty. It rattled them, though for the life of him Tom couldn't see why. Surely when you was underground it made not the least odds whether twenty feet up it were possible to see nothing but your hand in front of your face or clear to the golden flames of the Monument. It wasn't like the buggers didn't know their way around down there blindfold, well as he did. But then there wasn't much future in trying to understand rats. They might have a vicious bite on them but they were too stupid for sense. He and Joe had been trapping them the same way three years now and they'd never cottoned on. Not that he was complaining of course. Without the rats times would be bad. The work might not have the excitement the toshing had, when you never knew what was around the next corner. But it was a business and you had to be grateful for that. There weren't many men of his age could learn a new trade, even if there was one out there for the learning. If he'd been pushed to guess he'd have reckoned himself to be a few years long of sixty, although he was strong still and had some of his own teeth. He was lucky to have the rats and he knew it. The speed with which everything was changing these days it seemed like there was a new dodge come along every day of the week to knock the bread out the mouths of ordinary men.

The rats could still give him the creeps, though, even after all these years. Rum, it was, when you thought about it. Above ground they'd never bothered him. Where he came from, the constant scrabbling, the darting movements across the floor, the taking turns to watch over the newest infant as it slept so it might not be bitten or snatched, they were as much a part of life as the mud. But down in the tunnels it was different. Gathered in great shifting swarms in their caves in the brickwork, some of them big as dogs, they had a whole different air about them. As though it was them that was in charge and the only reason they let you alone, for now, was that they couldn't be bothered with you. Some days Tom'd been certain they followed him, thousands of them, their cold rat feet scrabbling in the darkness, waiting for him to falter, to fall in the rising water or to stray down the wrong tunnel. Once or twice he'd tried to turn on them but they were quicker. He never caught them at it. But he knew they were there. And when he made his mistake, they'd have him. They would swarm over him then, their claws and teeth tearing at his flesh, eating him alive. It would take no time at all. When the old man finally found him he'd be nothing but yellow bones. The old man would click his tongue and shake his head and put the bones in his bag. The glue works at Bermondsey took every bone they could get.

Tom'd never said nothing to the old man of course. It was the best thing that had happened to him, Tom reckoned, nearly drowning that time at Cuckold's Point. In the mud there you were lucky to happen across more than ropes and bones and the occasional spar of iron. Coal didn't turn up there too often and if you found a coin you could barely believe your luck. It wasn't much of a living even for a young lad. It was his third winter doing the Point when he sank. Afterwards the only thing he had remembered about it was the sense of bewilderment he'd felt as he was sucked into the mud, his feet struggling for a solid purchase that wasn't there. He'd always boasted he knew that stretch backwards, the places where you'd go over head and ears in the mud, and the solid slices of ground just alongside them where you could walk safe as you liked, the dirt beneath your bare feet steadier than granite. Other boys went in groups, fearful of the place's reputation. Not Tom. It was his patch. The mud was up around his armpits when the old man saw him. Tom had stopped struggling by then. Instead he had laid his head back in the mud and stared at the sky. Even if he didn't sink deeper the tide would get him when it came. Two hours, he'd reckoned, and he'd wondered if the mud would taste the same as it smelled.

After the old tosher'd hauled him out they had worked together till the old man died. Aside from the rats Tom liked it well enough. The stench of the channels never bothered him. He had found it roughish at first but it was nowhere near so bad as the others said, especially not if you were used to the river as he was. And the old tosher had taken to him, he'd been kind. He hadn't always shared the spoils fair as Tom might've liked but he'd taught him the tunnels till Tom knew them as well as the alleys of St Giles. The old man reckoned there was near on a thousand mile of sewers in London if you cared to follow the length of them but they stuck to the centre where the pickings were richest. In the open rural sewers the best you was like to find yourself was watercress. South wasn't so good either. Under the sugar bakeries the steam poured into the drains as hot as vapour from a kettle so that a tosher could be boiled alive. Under the gasworks was worse still, for all that the law said clear as day that they wasn't meant to use the sewers at all. Word was, the air under the Gas-Light and Coke Company could set a man aflame before he knew what hit him. Tom'd never been there. The one time he had seen the gas catch, there had been someone up ahead of him got a whiff of it so they was down on their backs before it could get them. He still remembered it. The blazing gas had rushed over them like a firework, a glorious whoosh of flame along the crown of the arch. It had been beautiful.

Tom's favourites were the sewers beneath Mayfair and Belgravia. It satisfied him that beneath the fanciest homes in the city the drains were the worst of the lot. Beneath the snowy new stucco of Belgrave-square the sewers were crumbling so bad that any attempt to flush them would have brought them clattering down altogether. There were always riches to be found there amongst the kettles and the rags and the bits of broken stoneware. Young Tom could get into small places where the old man couldn't and when he got up near the grating in a street he'd stretch into the sludge and search about in the bottom of the sewer. It was his reach that had given him his nickname. There was usually penny pieces and often shillings and half-crowns. There were metal spoons, iron tobacco boxes, nails and pins, bits of lead, boys' marbles, buttons. Once he had found a silver jug big as a quart pot. They had celebrated that night, good and proper.

Those had been the glory days, when toshing was a business passed down father to son. In those days, the sewers had opened straight on to the banks of the Thames and at low tide them that belonged there could walk in bold as brass. That had changed years ago. Now they had reinforced the arches with brick and hung iron gates over them that opened and closed with the tide. The notion was that the water could flow out but the people couldn't get in. For some of the sewer-hunters it was the end of things. The gates were treacherous and they didn't know no other way in. Of course there were still lads who thought it a lark to take the gates on, catching them when the water had raised them far enough open to slip through but before it was coming so fast they couldn't stay on their feet. Tom didn't trust that. There had always been other safer places to go down, although he wasn't in a hurry to tell about them. Long ago the old man had shared with him his secret map of traps and gullies, some of them used from time to time by the flushers, others so ancient and hidden away that likely no one else but he and Joe even knew they were there. Most of them you could only use after dark. It would have roused suspicion if anyone saw you. But they had used them all the same, even before the Thames doors were put up. There was only so far a man could get in the eight or nine hours the tide gave him and it didn't make sense always to start at the river, not if you wanted more than someone else's leavings. Besides, there were days when you were wrong about the rain. Those days you needed to be able to get out in a hurry.

They were putting in more gratings and manholes these days, some to serve as vents, others iron-covered flues with bolts rammed into the brickwork for ladders. They were supposed to be kept locked although you could get them open if you knew how. The flushers forgot to lock them anyways, or perhaps it was easier not to bother with it now they was going down so much more often than they used to. Some sewers they went into as much as two or three times in a month, forcing water through the tunnels to scour away the mud and the sludge. Joe had said they was doing it to ruin honest men, so that the riches of the mud would be delivered to no one but the sea, but Tom knew it was on account of the cholera. It had run through the city like slop gas, the fever coming so sudden upon a man that he went from bright at breakfast to stiff at supper. Soon they were running out of room to bury the dead and out of gravediggers too, on account of the numbers. You could see the piles of them sometimes, uncovered, their eyes still open, heaped up on wagons outside of the graveyards waiting their turn. It was then the doctors told the Government that it was the stink of the sewers what did for folk and there it was, decided. They flushed more often after that. When people stepped over gratings or passed above the places where the sewers emptied themselves into the Thames, they tried not to breathe. They still died. Whole families sometimes, all together, so there was no one even to go to the pump for a dipper of water. It was best not to think about it. If you thought about it too much you might be next.

Now there was talk of Parliament rebuilding the whole entire sewer system, top to bottom. Tom would not have believed it if he hadn't seen it with his own eyes but in recent months gentlemen had started coming down the drains with the gangs of flushers, their silk hats and shiny shoes exchanged for the fan-tailed leather caps and high boots of the tunnel men. The men stayed down only an hour or two but they went into the tunnels like explorers to the other side of the world, their guides laden down with lanterns and packs and countless instruments for measuring and inspecting and whatever else. It wasn't hard to tell when they were down there. They left a trail of men posted at street level along their route, ready to give warning should the rain begin to fall. Sometimes Tom could hear it, the distant echoing clang of a dropping sewer cover that signalled the need to retreat. Once or twice Tom had got himself out on account of it but it'd never been nothing to worry about. Perhaps, Joe'd said with a glint in his eye, the gentlemen didn't like the feel of the water when it rose over their delicate white ankles. They weren't exactly rushing at it, that much was for sure. So far all they'd managed was a single new sewer tunnel, built beneath the new Victoria-street that ran north from Holborn Bridge. It had taken more than a year to complete and wasn't more than one hundred feet long. At that rate Tom would be long buried before they made it as far up as Clerkenwell.

Still, it meant you had to be careful. There wasn't much hope for mercy from the beak if you fetched up nose to nose with a string of nobs slap under the Old Bailey. It might be worth it though, Joe'd sniggered, just to see the look on their faces when the pair of them loomed up out of the darkness like a couple of ghosts. Tom hadn't laughed. Joe didn't know what he was talking about. He'd not done time inside. Tom had. He had no wish to do it again.

Up above Tom's head the door shifted a little in its muddy base. Tom whistled softly and the answer came back in an echo before he heard the clatter of boots down the stairs.

'What ho,' Joe muttered, raising his lantern to his face. The sudden flush of light caught the twin bushes of his whiskers so that they looked as though they were on fire. It was tradition to give toshers something in the way of a nickname, always had been, and some of the handles the men fetched up with took a bit of explaining, but it didn't take much to see why they called him Red Joe. When he took off his hat, which wasn't often, mind, his hair sprang up from his head in a veritable explosion of ginger. If you thought of life as a stretch of rope you had to admit that Joe, like Tom, was considerably nearer the end of it than the beginning, but so far there was not so much as a single strand of white to dampen the blaze. Not soot, not grime, not even the filthiest of sewers could contrive to put that fire out. Stiff and matted it might be but it still glowed bright as a brazier as soon as it managed to catch itself the faintest streak of light so that you almost thought to warm your hands against it. Above his pale eyes his eyebrows sprawled like a pair of fiery caterpillars, each one thick as a thumb, and, beneath the fire of hair that licked along his arms, his skin was splattered with copper flecks. Out there on the main streets there were the brasses on the big houses and the harnesses of the horses and gaslight in shop windows and sunlight glinting off polished glass but here in the rookery nothing shone

45

as bright as Joe. Beside Joe, Tom reckoned he looked like something knocked up out of ashes and dust.

'We off then?'

Tom nodded. Joe was nearly a head taller than Tom and, where Tom was lean, Joe was thick-legged and strong as a bull. He hoisted two crates easily on to his broad shoulders as Tom lashed the lantern to his hoe and checked the hidden pocket of his apron for his gloves. The sewer-rats, coats were poisonous and when you grabbed them they twisted and turned like street boys, screaming and lashing out with their yellow teeth. You didn't want to get bitten, not if you could help it. A rat's bite was three-cornered, like a leech's, only deeper, and the devil to stop bleeding. Tom had seen a man once swing a rat by the tail, more in the way of showing off than anything else, and before he knew it the creature had flipped itself round and bit him in the arm. Next day it was blown up big as a ham and black to boot. Tom didn't know what had happened to him after that. He'd not seen him again.

Gripping a short thick stick in his right hand and his hoe in his left, Tom led the way across the sodden floor of the cellar. The house had once had a cesspool beneath it and at its far end the cellar led out into a small open sewer. If it had been under anything but the rookery it would have been built in brick with a roof too low for a child to get under, but beneath the crumbling padding-kens it was largely uncovered, the wooden roof nothing but the floor of the room above it and often pieces missing so that if you straightened up you could stare right into the blank eyes of women and children squatting there on the floor. More often there were just holes in the planks so that as you made your way through the tunnel you caught snatches of a hundred families shrieking and squalling and snoring. Sometimes tufts of dirty straw and rags poked through to stroke the crown of your hat. One time Joe had stood under such a place and listened. Winking at Tom, he had boomed out in a voice so deep it could have been the voice of the Devil himself, *'You think I don't see you there when you are so close to Hell?'* The squeals and the scrabbles that followed would have put the rats to shame. Tom thought that Joe might choke himself, he laughed so hard.

After about a quarter of a mile the tunnel fell away in a giant step down into a wider brick sewer. Tom and Joe slid down

and headed east. It was easier going under-
foot but with the gratings overhead they
had to stop from time to time to shut off
the light. They didn't talk as they walked.
They'd already agreed on Newgate as the
place. It was a ticklish spot to get to, seeing
as you couldn't enter the tunnels anywhere
close to it and had instead to make your
way there underground, but Brassey's
order had not been in the usual way of
things. At Newgate they'd get the numbers
and they'd also get the size. Brassey
wanted them big. Directly beneath the
meat market the stream was thick with
blood and muck and lumps of discarded
flesh. Sustained by a diet of such richness
the Newgate rats were fat and ill-tempered
as beadles. On one side of the tunnel they
had succeeded in excavating a cavern as
wide as a room and more than two yards
high where the brutes bred their young.
There had to be more than four hundred
pair there, Tom reckoned, scrambling and
crawling over each other like a live mountain of soot. No one had ever seen the toffs
from Parliament at Newgate.

They were almost there. The stink of
rotting meat crammed the skull and a fatty
brown foam curdled on the water. At the
point where the tunnel began to sheer off

towards the north Joe let the crates down. Tom untied his lantern from the hoe. Propping the pole against the wall, he fixed the lantern to a loop on the front of his canvas apron. That way he could have full use of hands and eyes. He pulled on his cuffed gloves. They were so stiff with age and dirt that they contained within them the perfect cast of his hands, each swollen knuckle finding its own hollow. He gave them a final tug, took up his cudgel and nodded at Joe. They were ready to start work.

III

The offices occupied by Joseph Bazalgette, Chief Engineer to the Metropolitan Board of Works, and his team of engineers, surveyors and draughtsmen, were located at 1 Greek-street, Soho. It was from these modest premises that Bazalgette planned to execute possibly the most ambitious feat of civil engineering ever attempted, the construction of a completely new underground drainage system for the entire city. There was no disagreement about the urgent need for such a system. While improvements had been attempted by previous administrations they had led only to new problems. At the beginning of the century, each household had disposed of its waste into a private cesspool in its cellar which was regularly emptied by nightsoil men. However, as the population of the capital grew this system was decried as impractical and unsanitary. Instead all cesspools were to be connected to a local sewer which would conduct the flow, by way of a main sewer, to drain directly into the river. In the rotting and inadequate sewers, human excrement mixed with refuse from the slaughterhouses and knackers' yards, and waste from the tanneries and factories. Every day it drained into the Thames. It was not long before the river itself became the great cesspool of the city. At low tide the effluvium clung to the pillars of bridges or piled itself into stinking mudbanks and fermented.

London, the largest metropolis in the world, was poisoning itself. That was the consensus reached by doctors and scientists as the century passed its midpoint. As the filth pooled and putrefied in local sewers, many of which were hardly more than open ditches, it exhaled highly poisonous gases. When these poisons were diffused into the atmosphere and carried by corrupted air and water into the lungs and stomach, they entered directly into the blood, spreading deathly disease. In twenty years London had been ravaged by three brutal epidemics of the cholera. Each time the disease had attacked the city most savagely in the places where the air and the water was foulest. No one doubted that something would have to be done.

It was considerably less easy to reach agreement on a solution to the problem. Bazalgette's plan was for a new network of tunnels that would intercept the existing system of cesspools and sewers and take their vast polluted cargo to outfalls far downstream of the city. According to his scheme there would be required something in excess of eighty miles of new interceptory sewers, to be laid from west to east, three north of the river and two south. Since gravity in the low-lying basin of the Thames was inadequate to ensure the efficient flow of the water, Bazalgette had devised the tunnels on artificially steep gradients, placing at key intervals steam-driven pumping stations that would raise the flow by upwards of twenty feet and then release it once more, so that it might recommence its energetic downward course. As for the existing sewers, they were to be not only rebuilt but supplemented by tens of hundreds of miles of local sewers to feed these main channels, in order to enable the system to carry the half-million gallons of waste passing through the bowels of London every day. To complete the system, Bazalgette estimated, would take five years and cost the city in the order of three million pounds.

The funds were not forthcoming. While Parliament provided the monies to maintain the Board, fiscal responsibility for structural improvements fell to the local vestries who dithered and debated and delayed. But Bazalgette refused to be disheartened. Slowly he assembled a team of junior engineers and surveyors who, content with the necessarily low wages, worked tirelessly alongside him to prepare the countless plans and drawings necessary to perfect his scheme. He begged his friends to appraise him of any suitable candidates. And so it was that in the spring of 1856 his friend Robert Rawlinson, a distinguished engineer recently returned from a posting with Sutherland's Sanitary Commission in Scutari, recommended to him a junior surveyor by the name of William May.

May had been in Scutari for almost two months when Rawlinson arrived in the Turkish outpost at the end of the first savage winter of the Russian War. Although he had read the newspaper reports and had considerable experience of sanitary engineering in the poorest parts of Liverpool, the conditions he found in Scutari shook Rawlinson profoundly. The rotting Turkish barracks that served as hospitals were little more than slums, overcrowded, filthy and unspeakably ill-ventilated, and nearly half of the soldiers who contrived to survive the miserable four-day voyage from the front died in hospital when they got there. In the Barrack Hospital alone fifty men were lost every day, the bodies stitched up in their blankets, thrown into open carts, and laid in layers in hurriedly dug trenches. One nurse told Rawlinson how she watched as Turkish soldiers threw corpses into a shallow square ditch. When one soldier noticed a head protruding beyond the rest he jumped into the hole and stamped it down with an impatient boot. The burial had taken place less than sixty feet from the entrance to the hospital. Within four days Sutherland and Rawlinson had inspected all four hospitals and submitted their report. Within a week Rawlinson had begun to assemble a team of men to implement his improvements.

The starched and sponged gentlemen of the Commission could not have stood out more starkly amongst the ragged soldiers of Scutari if they had arrayed themselves in bonnets and crinolines, but William hardly saw them. He had survived the horrors of Inkerman, only to be bayoneted six weeks later by a Russian foot soldier who had crept up on him as he stumbled, alone and half-asleep, along a frozen trench while on night-time duty. When the dawn relief discovered him, face down in the scarlet snow, he was barely conscious. He was disorientated for days afterwards. When pressed to talk he stuttered, vomited, and managed only a childish gibberish. Despite his weakness he was frequently violent. Angered by a glancing blow, an exhausted doctor had knotted William's hands together with a length of rope. It was in this state that he endured the long voyage to Scutari. When he finally arrived at the General Hospital his dressings had not been changed for four weeks. When she lifted the rag covering the wound to his stomach the nurse was obliged to remove a quart of maggots before she could bind it again.

Although the wounds to his chest and stomach began to heal, still William remained weak, unable to stand or to feed himself. The nightmares continued to convulse him in fits. In his tortured sleep he tore at his flesh with his nails and bit through his lips until his mouth was rough with scabs. The nurses and the other patients learned to approach him cautiously as any unexpected noise or touch could cause him to lash out. On one occasion he smashed his fist into the face of a newly commissioned private from the 2nd ———, blackening his eye. Afterwards he had clutched desperately at the man and begged his forgiveness, weeping into the ragged fabric of his uniform. Reluctantly, for men were dying like flies in the glacial conditions of Balaclava and the need for replacements was acute, it was agreed that Private May was not yet fit to return to the front. Instead he was diagnosed with 'low fever' and transferred, shortly before the Commission's arrival, to one of the two convalescent hulks moored in the harbour. As Rawlinson's later report was to note, it would have been impossible to conceive of two worse places in which to attempt to restore a man's health. Both ships, ancient Turkish warships in lamentable repair, were so jammed with men that the fever and the filth raged uncontained, while the bilge water they spewed turned the water in which they floundered into an open sewer.

Doctors came rarely to the convalescent ships. Most of the time William lay motionless on his straw pallet. He was no longer violent. Instead he lapsed into a kind of petrified half-sleep which the noises and motions of the other men penetrated only in random fragments. Around him, with dry throats and quiet courage, his fellow soldiers muttered to themselves, accepting the will of the Almighty and committing themselves to His everlasting care. In his infrequent moments of lucidity William despised them for their wilful blindness. Could they not see that their loving God had abandoned them in this filthy place, had turned His face against their suffering with disregard, His attentions distracted by more pressing and glorious matters? The men of Her Majesty's Army had stared into the face of Hell and it had stripped away their souls. There was no substance to any of them now, nothing but dry bones wrapped in a shroud of lice-infested skin. There could be no forgiveness for men such as them, no possibility of Heaven. Without souls they were worth nothing. Death was a blank darkness, an eternity of nothing. Once it would have appalled William to think in this way, but no longer. Throughout the endless Scutari nights he derived from his thoughts a strange and terrible comfort. In death he might finally find rest.

And so he lay, day after day, waiting for Death's hand upon his shoulder. He would not have risen to eat had it not been for a gentle Irish subaltern called Meath who occupied the pallet next to his and who had lost his leg at Alma. The pitifully inadequate stores at Scutari, which were unable to provide necessities as basic as plates, knives and forks, and linen to the men, had run out of crutches before the fighting had begun. Since those on the convalescent ships were expected to be able to fend for themselves, what scanty rations there were available were distributed on the foremost deck. Every day Meath coaxed William to get up from his bed so that together, with Meath's arm slung around William's neck, the two of them could make their slow passage through the mass of palliasses to the eating area. Sometimes the warmth and solidity of Meath's body leaning into his made William stumble.

'The food here is almost as plentiful as it was when I was a lad,' Meath liked to joke. His family had been tenant farmers in Skibbereen; all but Meath and his brother, who'd both enlisted to escape the famine, had starved to death. 'If I'd known I'd get the same mud for coffee here as I used to get at home I'd never have come.'

At night Meath wept silently for his mother and for the unbearable cramps in his missing leg. William did not sleep either. Night after night he lay with his eyes open, his arms wrapped around his chest, motionless as the tomb of a medieval knight. He permitted himself no recollection of the horror that had brought him there. On the few occasions that a fragment of memory slipped into his conscious mind it was as unreal and indistinct as a blurred daguerreotype. It was when he slept that they came alive, the rows upon rows of the rotting dead, the black terrors of the frozen trench, the shadows and the stinks and the shrieks of accusation. One night he dreamed that he killed Polly, plunging his bayonet repeatedly into her throat. She continued to scream long after her head was quite severed from her neck. When he woke he vomited for hours, convulsed with guilt and horror. His wounds were healing but he never considered that one day he might be required to leave Scutari. The thought of returning to Polly, of stepping back into the ordinary contentment of their life together in London, was beyond imagining. That world, where meanings held solid and people reached out for one another in the darkness, that world was quite lost to him. His place was in this overcrowded dormitory where he lay packed in with the others, all of them weakened, unshaved, unwashed, shivering beneath their greatcoats. A doss-house for the half-alive, a place unburdened by affection and expectation, where yesterday and tomorrow meant nothing and passed unnoticed. This was where he belonged.

It was an overcast afternoon in the middle of March when May was sent for. Rumours of a fresh push for Sebastopol had circulated amongst the inmates of the hulks for weeks. Any man able to stand unsupported was to be sent back to the front. May staggered as he was marched by a sharp-faced officer across the frozen mud of the compound and the officer shoved him contemptuously with the butt of his rifle. There was no need for amateur theatricals, the officer informed him, his face compressed with distaste. May was not to be returned immediately to active service. Following the recommendations of the Sanitary Commission, extensive rebuilding had been mandated and all men with engineering or surveying experience were to be mobilized to execute their recommendations. As the chief engineer to the project Mr Rawlinson would remain in Scutari to supervise the work. He enjoyed the full support of the British Army at the highest levels, the captain instructed May, and his mouth twisted as though the words tasted unpleasant. While Rawlinson held no official military rank, May would be expected to understand his instructions as orders. That, the captain barked, was an order.

Rawlinson glanced over his half-moon spectacles at the private in front of him, conscious for the thousandth time of the smooth sheen of his own black coat, the starched white of his collar. He had been in Russia almost two weeks and still it shocked him, the deplorable state of the men he encountered here. This one was a particularly sorry specimen. He was so spare that the bones seemed to shine white through the skin of his face and he trailed the thin sour reek of sickness and squalor. From what Rawlinson knew of the hospital arrangements the man would have been lucky to have seen a bath more than once in his three months at Scutari. His uniform fell in rags from the knobs of his shoulders, and his sandy hair and beard stuck out in grimy tufts around his face. He had, thought Rawlinson, the appearance of a lion too long in captivity. Beside him the rigid captain in his scarlet coat made a reluctant keeper. No doubt he would prefer an animal more reflective of his impeccable military bearing, a fine Arabian stallion, perhaps, or a Bengal tiger.

'Private May,' Rawlinson continued,

suppressing a private smile. 'You worked with the Ordnance in London, I understand.'

He looked expectantly at May. When the private failed to reply the captain cleared his throat sharply before thrusting an elbow into his ribs. Slowly May looked up, blinking as though the gloomy room were startlingly bright, his dirty fingers plucking and twisting at the remaining button of his coat. Rawlinson reproached himself for his reflexive shiver of distaste.

'Well?' Rawlinson demanded, more brusquely than he intended. 'Speak up, man.'

'Yes, sir,' May murmured. 'I was with the Ordnance.'

'I am told it was your section that were responsible for the survey of London's drains requested by the Metropolitan Commission of Sewers. Five feet to the mile, that's right, is it not?' Rawlinson peered at the soldier. He seemed to be swaying on his feet and the only colour in his white face came from the dark purple smudges beneath his eyes. 'Are you quite well?'

May lifted his lion head and gazed towards his interlocutor. His sand-coloured eyes were neither friendly nor hostile. Instead they appeared to be focused not on Rawlinson or even the wall behind him but inwards, so that Rawlinson had the peculiar sensation of looking not at two coloured irises but at their raw unpainted backs.

'Private?'

'No, sir,' May murmured at last. 'I shouldn't say quite well, sir.'

Beside May the captain permitted himself a sharp intake of breath and pressed his lips together beneath the points of his waxed moustache. Rawlinson ignored him. Instead he sat back in his chair, his fingers steepled together, and studied May gravely. The papers on his desk informed him that the soldier had been decorated for valour at Inkerman. *The Times* correspondent had called Inkerman the bloodiest struggle ever witnessed since war cursed the earth. Rawlinson had read the report over breakfast in Portland-square; he remembered the words precisely.

'No,' he agreed, his intelligent grey eyes not leaving the man's face. 'Not quite well. I can see that.' He paused thoughtfully. 'But you are well enough to work? I urgently require a surveyor. You would begin tomorrow.'

May's breathing quickened and his fingers tugged more frenziedly at the button on his coat. He passed the tip of his tongue over his parched lips.

'I would be of no use to you, sir,' he stuttered. 'I — I — there will be someone else. Someone better suited. Better. Sir.'

Under the pressure of his wrenching fingers the final rotten thread attaching the button to his coat gave way. May stared at the loose button in his fingers, his face twisted with distress. For a moment Rawlinson hesitated and then he leaned forward, his elbows propped on the mahogany desk.

'Do you mean to die?' he asked May very softly.

The captain's eyeballs swelled as he drew himself up almost to the tips of his toes, and his nostrils flared white. May blinked at Rawlinson. Surprise brought a faint gleam of amber into the flat wood of his eyes.

'Most men wish to live, I think,' Rawlinson continued in the same soft voice. 'It seems probable to me that, during the dark nights of the arduous voyage here from the front, sick and wounded men like you are sustained by the belief that, once safely delivered into the care of our hospitals, they will be made well. They will be safe. And yet, in the past months, tens of hundreds of men have died in Scutari. The hospitals that sought to save them have not done so, indeed not. They have killed them, more quickly and more assuredly than the enemy could ever hope to with all the power of their cannons and their rifles.'

In the early twilight the knuckles of the captain's clenched fists shone like peppermints. It seemed that further outrages to his military propriety might lift him clear of the floor altogether. Had he managed such a feat it was unlikely either of the other men would have noticed. May stood quite still, faint smudges of colour dusting his white cheeks. Like the flame of a candle the pale light in his eyes flickered and steadied. They were extraordinary eyes, Rawlinson thought, the irises almost gold and encircled by a greenish rim that looked like it had been finished in ink.

'There is nothing glorious, no honour for Queen or country, in dying from dysentery or from the cholera,' Rawlinson continued. He spoke so quietly that the captain could barely hear him above the seashell roar of indignation that filled his ears. 'I cannot undo the damage that has already been done here. But I can and I will do everything in my power to ensure that it no longer continues. From this point forward I am responsible. If men die needlessly in Scutari, I am to blame. I do not intend to have men's deaths upon my conscience, Private.'

Rawlinson paused. May stood very still, the forgotten button cupped in his hand.

'The work has already begun. But with every additional assistance it will progress more quickly. You are not quite well, I see that. But you are well enough, I think. Every day the work that we do will save lives. Perhaps it will save yours. Will you help us?'

There was a long pause. May continued to gaze at Rawlinson. He swallowed once, and then again, and his teeth chewed at his ragged mouth. And then abruptly he closed his eyes. Through his loosened fingers the button from his coat dropped silently to the floor and rolled away. The captain gained a measure of relief from crushing it beneath his boot.

'Yes,' May said at last, without opening his eyes. The words were almost lost in the effort of making them. 'Yes, sir. I will help.'

The next day May was transferred from the convalescent ship to quarters within a converted barracks half a mile from the harbour. Meath took his hand and, shaking his head and smiling, called him a secretive bugger; it had never occurred to the gentle Irishman that May could read or write. Later that day Rawlinson brought him to the General Hospital where, on cracking the pipes that provided drinking water to the hospital, the men had uncovered the decomposing remains of a horse. It explained why, in the glass, the water had always looked like barley water and tasted like mud. May was to provide sectional drawings of the current sewerage system to a depth of ten feet so that a new one could be devised as a matter of urgency. The Purveyor's Office showed none of its customary reluctance in furnishing him with the tools he required. Alone, the paper set upon his drawing board, May stared at the shiny spirit level in his hand. It felt both startlingly familiar and quite strange, and for a moment he was certain that he would never know how to use it. This made him so uneasy he hurriedly dropped the level on to the table and pushed it out of sight. Had his memory not failed him he would have remembered feeling exactly the same way a few months before, the first time that he held a rifle.

There had been dawns in the hills above Balaclava when William, relieved at last from night-long trench duty, had returned to camp so thoroughly frozen that he dare not remove his boots in case he should take his toes with them. His icy fingers would anyway have proved unequal to the knotted laces. Instead he huddled in front of whatever meagre fire the company had managed while his feet and his hands and his ears throbbed and screamed back into life. The shifts were twelve hours long; before the first hour was complete, the warm, alive parts of William's body had retreated to a place deep within him where they huddled for the remainder of the night, like children hiding out in an abandoned building. When finally they were found they were quite savage. His hands and feet swelled until the stretched, shiny skin split like overripe fruit. His fingers and toes became stiff and useless with pain, the inflammation inside his joints forcing them into white and purple bulges the size of chestnuts that maddened him with their constant burning and itching. The pencil skidded between his fingers as he completed the watch log, the marks on the page so faint and clumsy they were barely legible. His ears bled. There were times when the pain of becoming warm was so unbearable that William wished he could sleep in the snow, so that later that day he might return to his icy post without enduring the agony of thawing out.

In the days after his meeting with Rawlinson, William again knew the anguish of those mornings but not in his hands or his feet. Since his arrival in the Crimea the only certain way to be safe had been to feel nothing, to care about nothing. It had been easy. The war had frozen him. He had only to hold on to that chill, to maintain in his chest a permanent deep winter. Until the Commission came he had found it easy.

Rawlinson was not a warm man. While he was much preoccupied with the humanitarian significance of his work his interest in people was theoretical rather than particular. He treated all the men with whom he worked with the same grave and considered distance. But the work, the work was different. When he worked he shone with the pure and unconstrained passion he felt for his subject. His enthusiasm carried the men with him, presenting them daily with sensations that had become as unfamiliar to the soldiers as fresh meat: curiosity, inventiveness, conviction, optimism, purpose. William watched Rawlinson as he went about his work, memorizing the absorbed expression in the engineer's thoughtful eyes, the triumphant flare of recognition at a solution to a tricky problem. At night he practised them but, although his own face could twist and lift just so, nothing connected those facial expressions to a point within him that made sense of them. Even when he drew his treasured botany journals from the pocket of his greatcoat and gazed on their worn pages for the first time in months he felt nothing. Nothing at all.

But despite this Rawlinson's enthusiasm worked like a warm breath on him, clearing tiny air holes in his carefully preserved ice. The holes appalled him. The searing pain of them was not the worst of it. More terrifying to William by far, they showed how much more pain would have to be endured, now that winter had set so bitterly within him. Rawlinson's arrival had changed everything. Before he came, William had been quite sure he cared little whether he lived or died. Part of him had wondered if he was dead already. Now he knew he had been wrong. He was not just alive. He wanted to live.

The cutting began almost by accident. As one of Rawlinson's working party, William was given weekly access to hot water. One morning one of the junior sanitary inspectors offered him the use of his razor. Carefully, William stropped it across its length of leather before holding the blade up to the light. Something was welling up inside him, clenching at his heart like a fist. Biting his lip he placed the razor shakily on the washstand and reached for the soap, fixing his eyes on the rising foam as the brush swirled round and round inside the cup. But the pressure inside him didn't stop. It swelled between each of the knobs of his spine, pressing out between his ribs. It felt as though he might explode at any moment. His hands jerked and his eyes burned, his eyelids scouring them as though they were lined with sand. Frightened, he gripped the edges of the porcelain basin of water, trying to force the feelings back, but on and on they came, stronger and stronger. He could not calm down. The pressure swelled in his head, forcing itself against the fragile cap of his skull. It roared in his ears, filling his throat and nostrils till he could barely breathe. William dug his fingernails hard into his wrist, leaving white half-moons in the flesh, but he felt nothing, nothing but the blackness that he could not hold back. Desperately he hurled the soap-cup across the room. He saw it smash against the wall but he heard nothing. And then distantly, as though he were suspended above his own body, he watched his hand reach out for the razor. The pressure inside him was different already, its clotted darkness streaked with a growing sense of purpose. Very slowly, his hand not quite steady, he drew the blade down his unsoaped cheek, pressing it quite deliberately into the flesh until it sliced into the skin.

The cut was shallow but it worked with the perfect predictability of a valve on a steam engine. The release was exquisite. As the blood flowed out so too did the terrible blackness. The rush of the blood soothed him, purged him. And it showed him that he was alive. He felt elated but at the same time quite calm. Tenderly, he pressed a clean rag against the wound. When he returned the razor to the inspector he was able to joke quite casually about his lack of practice, the clumsiness of his fingers. He obtained iodine and carefully cleaned the cut. For the first time in months he felt conscious and in control. He smiled. Smiling made the cut sting, which made him smile again. And when in time the numbness returned there was a new calm quality to it. It felt simple. Rawlinson commended him for the quickness and the accuracy of his work. William was a fast learner and he found himself increasingly involved in the engineering details of diameter, gradient and angle that grew, vital and solid, from the paper of his plans. One afternoon William even proffered his own tentative solution to a problem with the flushing apparatus on the west side of the Barrack Hospital, a solution that was agreed upon and duly implemented. For two long weeks William was absorbed in his work. Slowly, very slowly, he began to imagine himself once more, not as Private May, casualty of the Russian War, but as William Henry May, mapmaker and surveyor. The future did not stretch far ahead of him, perhaps only as far as the concerns of the following day, but it was a future. There had not been one of those for many months.

Two weeks. And then once more the pressure began to rise. This time William cut his thigh with a meat knife. The wound was much deeper and afterwards William was unable to recollect even the faintest detail of the cutting. The lapse of memory troubled him but not nearly so much as the prospect of not cutting. The next time it was his other thigh, and then his arms. Each time there were blackouts. He learned not to fear them but to rejoice instead in that moment of perfect ecstasy when he came back to himself in a glorious scarlet scream of blood. After that it was always his arms. He was glad of that. The arms were easier to bind and they were quicker. He could cut by simply rolling up his sleeve. When he rolled it down again only he knew the precise shape of the pattern upon the underside of his arm, the thin pink ridges of scars laddering the crusted scabs and the split lips of the freshest cuts. It spread across his skin like a fishing-net, holding him in. He kept a knife in his pocket. Sometimes, when the pressure began to rise but before it became unbearable, he would stroke the pattern softly with the blunt side of the blade.

The weather grew warmer and then oppressively hot. The mud melted and then baked into high ruts. In July, Rawlinson gathered together his team. Their work, he informed them with quiet pride, was almost complete. Thanks almost entirely to the improvements in hygiene and sanitation made possible by their work, losses amongst patients had been reduced from one in two to no more than two in every one hundred. There was no longer any need for Rawlinson to remain in Turkey.

He would be returning to England in due course but, before he did so, it was his intention to make a trip to the front line to see for himself the conflict that had brought so many men to Scutari's hospitals. He was due to sail for Balaclava within the week. Perhaps, he said, nodding gravely at the men, some of them would be cleared fit for a return to active service while he was still at the front. He hoped that, should duty and circumstances permit, they would do him the honour of paying him a call.

William cut more frequently after Rawlinson's departure and his sleep was more disturbed. His nightmares took on a particularly vivid quality. He dreamed he was in the basement room beneath the General Hospital where a colony of soldiers' wives had, until recently, lived on the beaten mud floor, their beds and bodies no more than heaps of filthy rags. One by one, by a rasping voice he recognized as his own, the women were ordered to line up against the wall. In the basement it was snowing. A man in the grey coat of a Russian soldier, his face obscured by a scrawl of beard, turned and, bowing slightly, asked in the unmistakably crisp accent of an English gentleman, 'Now?'

'Now!' the hidden voice barked. The Russian attached his bayonet and lifted it towards the first woman. The blade caught the light. The woman covered her face and shrank against the wall. Immediately her body shrivelled, her corpse as black as a sweep. The Russian turned towards the voice and smiled. The smile shifted his beard, curving it into a shallow spade striped with grey. His grave eyes twinkled.

The Russian was Rawlinson.

'You killed me,' he observed conversationally, his hand upon his breast. Blood ran in thick red ribbons between his fingers.

And then again, 'You killed me!' The second time the words were thick with fury and disgust.

William woke as Rawlinson fell. His shirt was soaked with sweat. For the rest of the night he sat bolt upright, his arms clutched around his knees. A few days later word was sent from the front. Rawlinson would not be returning to Scutari. He had been wounded by stray round shot in the trenches below Sebastopol. His injuries were significant but not severe; the doctor at the field hospital had recommended he be taken directly to England and for his personal belongings at the hospital to be sent on to an address in London. That night, William cut so deeply he severed a tendon. He was forced to seek assistance from a nurse who frowned and bit her lip as he explained how his razor had accidentally slipped in his hand. At the beginning of August William was given news of his own travel arrangements. He was deemed unfit for a return to active duty. He was to be invalided out of the army with a small pension and sent home.

The ship that would take him home docked in Scutari on a sunny morning in September. It had brought out to Turkey a new draft of soldiers who would undertake maintenance work in the Scutari base before being moved up to the front line. Despite their long voyage they looked neat and bright and extraordinarily young as they disembarked and moved in smart columns up the hill towards the base. William avoided them, but on his last afternoon he found himself walking behind two of them as they made their way up the dusty track to the mess. As they walked they sang together, their arms swinging back and forth to mark the metre of the verse.

Cheer Boys Cheer
No more of idle sorrow
Courage, true hearts, shall bear us
 on our way
Hope points before and shows the
 bright tomorrow
Let us forget the darkness of today.

IV

The public house they called the Badger was to be found down the back end of a muddy alley, one of a straggle of lanes winding out of the lower corner of Broadstreet. For all it was a long one, the lane'd always struck Tom as being of a weakwilled disposition, being unable to settle itself on going to the right or to the left, on being broad or narrow, straight or crooked. Aside from the sluggish ditch, a spine of sludge that dawdled along its length and lolled on patches of flatter ground, the only thing the lane could be depended on for was its unchanging stink, the sweetish reek of rotting refuse spattered here and there with the hot grease of fried fish and the fart smell of boiled cabbage stalks. Harsh blue curls of tobacco smoke rose from the dustheaps as women picked them over for rags and bones, their short black clay pipes clamped between their teeth, their skirts hitched up over their bare feet. Crouched in doorways their husbands dozed, their faces palsied and swollen and blotched so purple with the gin they were almost black. Tom's nose caught a hint of fresh porter above the stale breath of the old just a moment before the two can-boys elbowed him to one side, the pots in their wooden harnesses heavy with refreshment for the navvies labouring on Dean-street. Tom guessed it was something close to four in the afternoon. Since dawn the boys would have shuttled back and forth on their course between tavern and construction site, regular as looms.

The Black Badger crouched low at a crook in the alley where, as if the lane were all of a sudden scared half to death by its own boldness, it narrowed so sharply that Tom and Joe could no longer walk side by side. The tavern must once have been painted white but for as long as Tom had known it its face had been poxed and peeling, black with soot. It scowled out from between the battered hat of its low roof and the beard of mud that bristled round its chin. The windows were grimy and dark. Several were broken and patched with scraps of wood and old slate. From the front you would have been hard-pushed to discover a way into the place. Where a door should have hung there was only a thick sheet of metal, speckled with rust, secured by a slat of stair-rail held in position by iron brackets and buried a foot deep in the muddy ground. If you didn't know better you might have reckoned it quite deserted.

All in all there was not a single feature in which the Badger did not differ completely from the splendid drinking-house that dazzled the eye at the eastern end of Broad-street. The glittering plate-glass windows of the Golden Hind were garlanded with stucco rosettes and lit by a mass of gas flames that blazed with such sumptuous lack of restraint in their rich gilt burners that they turned the windows to fire. The magnificence of such a palace: the lavish ornament of its parapet and the illuminated gilt clock that sounded out the quarter hours; the brilliant mirrors carved with bunches of fat grapes and bowers of jasmine; the polished mahogany of the counter and the gay sparkle of the glasses; together they shrilled out their high-pitched song of welcome to all who passed by, so that no one might suffer the burden of a coin in their pocket for a minute longer than necessary. And many was the man tempted, only to regret it after. The Black Badger, instead, skulked in the darkness and the mud, hands thrust deep into its pockets. It didn't whistle or clear its throat. It had no intention of calling attention to itself. Its customers knew full well where to find it and what it was they came for. Those who wished to trade with the Badger understood its plainness, they appreciated it. They fancied it was the way they did business themselves, when they weren't on the dodge at any rate.

And to the Black Badger they came, in their droves, from all manner of directions. When they were admitted through the slip of a door buried in the tavern's right flank they were impervious to the smoke-grimed paper of the parlour and the dullness of the dented pewter pots. They came to drink, naturally enough. Every evening their arms moved their pots of beer or their glasses of gin and hot water like the pistons of a steam engine, up to their mouths and down again. But here, their eyes and their interests weren't directed only towards the bottom of their mugs. These men, be they costers, soldiers, coachmen or tradesmen, came to the Black Badger with one purpose. These men were sporting men. They came for the fight. These men were the Fancy.

Tom and Joe entered through the side door without knocking, stacking the crates at the foot of the staircase. They used the smaller ones for carrying the animals about, they called less attention to themselves that way. The narrow vestibule smelled strongly of dog, braided with the paler strands of dust, dry rot, tobacco and stale beer. Pushing and trampling over one another for a taste of it the rats squeaked and scrabbled behind the wire. Beyond the staircase was a closed door that led into the main parlour. The paintwork was scuffed and, at the bottom, scratched clean away. From behind it came a faint rumble of voices, like wheels over cobbles. Tom knocked, three short raps, as Joe settled himself on the bottom tread of the stairs, tipping his hat over his eyes and leaning back on his elbows. There were teeth marks in the newel post. Tom propped himself against the wall, watching the door. At precisely the moment he knew it would the door opened a crack and then closed again. Tom caught the familiar glimpse of crumpled cap. Joe yawned and stretched out his legs. His whiskers glowed copper in the gloom.

It was another ten minutes before the proprietor emerged from the parlour to greet them. Frank Brassey was a barrel-chested man with a flattened nose and a head that seemed to sprout directly

from his shoulders without bothering itself
with the trouble of a neck, but his legs
were slender and he walked with a curiously dainty gait, bouncing on the balls of
his tiny pointed feet as though he were
Monsieur Blondin himself treading the
high wire. Brassey took great pride in his
feet. While his black coat was turning
greenish and the elbows had an oily shine,
on his feet he wore only delicate slippers that
he had had hand-made in the finest Italian
leather. A plank propped against the wall of
the hallway served as a pontoon across the
mud so they might not be soiled should he
have to venture out. He scowled at Joe.

'You better've got the lot,' he barked,
jabbing at the bottom crate with a pointed
toe. His wide mouth was notably short of
the natural allowance of teeth.

'One hundred and fifty on the nose,'
Tom assured him quietly.

'Some right big 'uns too,' Joe added
from his sprawled position on the stair.
'Them dogs'll have their work cut out.'

'They better had,' the publican threatened. 'The Fancy's expecting something
singular here tonight.'

Joe jerked his hat at the large notice displayed on the wall and his eyes glowed
with mischief.

'You sure they ain't going to be disappointed, Mr B?' he drawled. 'Word is your so-called gent's already gone and stowed his precious watch over at Uncle's.'

The watch Joe reckoned pawned was a gold repeater, a drawing of which was provided on the notice for the number amongst the Fancy whose schooling hadn't stretched to letters. To those who could make them out the words on the poster, assembled in a mix of slanting hand and bold capitals, confided this reward to the first dog under eight pounds in weight to kill more than fifteen rats within a single minute. The generous benefactor of the timepiece called himself A SPORTING GENTLEMAN, Who is a Staunch Supporter of the destruction of these VERMIN. Dogs were TO GO TO SCALE AT Half past nine KILLING TO COMMENCE At Half past ten PRECISELY.

To Tom it was nothing but a jumble of lines.

'Don't you fret, Mr Brassey,' Joe went on. 'I hear business is booming over the King's Head. We'll just take this little lot on there directly, will we, Tom?'

Languidly Joe pulled himself up by the splintered newel post and placed a hand on the top crate. Squealing, the rats pressed their noses against the wire, paring their lips back from their yellow teeth. Tom looked away.

Brassey glowered at Joe and his tiny foot flexed in its slipper.

'That watch ain't in hock,' he snapped angrily. 'And even if it was it wouldn't be of no consequence. No more than a taster, that is. Them over the King's Head might consider it something special but the Fancy what frequents *this* establishment don't set their sights near so low.'

'Is that right? So it's a high-class lot you get in here?'

'The finest.' Brassey puffed out his chest.

'Right gentlemen, are they?'

Tom put out his hand. Experience told him, whatever direction Joe meant to take the publican, it weren't likely to be a journey that'd flatter Brassey's vanity. Tom had no wish to lose a customer.

'You pay us, we'll be off,' he said, disinclined as ever to say more than what was necessary.

Brassey glared at Joe and dug into his pocket.

'There,' he said, counting out money with considerable ceremony on to Tom's outstretched palm. 'A penny a pair.'

Tom took the money, stowing it in a hidden pocket within his canvas coat, and then held his hand out once again.

'A penny a beast. As agreed.'

'For that mangy lot?' Brassey flapped Tom's hand away. 'Ha'pence is generous.'

Tom shrugged. He nodded at Joe, who hoisted the first of the crates on to his shoulder.

'You won't get more than ha'pence over the King's Head, I can tell you,' the publican blustered.

Joe lifted the second crate. Brassey didn't move but his slippered feet flexed in agitation. Nodding towards the two cages that were left, Tom moved towards the door. Inside the flaps of his pockets Brassey's fingers clattered his remaining coins as though they were red-hot coals in a brazier.

'All right, all right,' Brassey burst out at last. 'A penny a beast, though it's out-and-out thievery. You'll have to come back for it, though. I ain't got sufficient right now.'

Tom paused in the doorway, his eyes narrow.

'I'll have it tonight,' Brassey promised him. 'Come back then. After nine. You got any nose for profit you'll put it on the fight.'

Tom thought for a moment and then nodded.

'Tonight, then.'

'Well, go on. Put them down,' Brassey demanded of Joe. Joe smiled but he made no move to put down the crates. They shifted a little on his shoulders as the rats scrabbled and jostled for position.

'Tonight. They's yours when they's paid for,' Tom said quietly and pushed open the door.

Brassey hesitated. Upstairs wood scraped on wood as, in what had once been the drawing-room, his boy dragged chairs across the floor. Although he was accustomed to provide tables and forms for most of his customers, Brassey had that morning ordered the boy to construct a low wooden fence around a small recess in the wall. Within its confines Brassey intended to offer the Captain and his associates all the comforts of a private box. The Captain was a gentleman of considerable refinement. On his last visit he had vowed one hundred guineas for a dog if it could kill twenty rats within a minute. There was no telling if he would have remembered so lavish a claim in the greyer, colder light of morning. Brassey licked his lips. Beyond the billow of his stomach he could just glimpse the polished curve of his slippers. Outside in the alley the mud was worse than ever. Raising himself on to the tips of his toes, he extended his shoulders out of the door and called to the men to come back.

Without the heavy cages Tom and Joe made quick progress back through Soho, while the new-found burden in their pockets was lightened by several lively hours at a public house behind the Strand. It was almost nine o'clock when Tom emerged into the darkened courtyard, his belly tight with beer and roasted beef. The plaintive creak of a fiddle drifted up from a basement window. Tom had his own private lodgings, no less than the luxury of a room to himself, but he was in no hurry to return there. He had never found himself a wife, wasn't sure why except that he'd always been one for liking his own company. There'd been girls washed up with him over the years, time to time, but none who'd not drifted away again, caught by a stronger tide. When he'd first come to London he supposed there might have been a few chances if he'd been quicker off the mark but one way or another he never saw them till it was too late. He'd always been awkward in company, tongue-tied and restless, and the bawdy talk that warmed the girls' cheeks and lifted their petticoats rattled him and made him blush. The other lads had thought him soft. Most of them were set up with a girl by the times they was twelve or thirteen. In the house in Flower-court, where he'd lived when he first started up with the old man, nine couples shared the one room each night, give or take, and he was always the only one sleeping by himself. He shouldn't rightly have been in there, only there was nowhere else. Even on the nights the other boys declared themselves tired of their arrangements and changed the girls over between them, sometimes more than once before dawn, Tom never seemed to find himself matched up. Instead he lay in the darkness and listened to the rustles and the giggles and tried to find a place on his damp straw mattress where nothing itched or bit. In the mornings he ducked his head to avoid the girls' curious stares.

'Wallop 'em,' one of the lads had advised him. 'That's the way. The gals don't fall for a feller till he gives 'em what for but after that, for as long as the bruises keeps hurtin', they's always thinking on the cove as gived 'em her.'

Tom had listened but he'd never heeded the advice. Not that he wouldn't have taken it, had things worked out different, but he never seemed to get that far along with a girl. Time he thought to thump her she was already up and off. So Tom kept his fists for the sewers. In them days, with the competition so fierce, you had to protect what was yours or you'd find it gone in the twinkle of an eye. Take Red Joe, for one. As a younger man Joe had been a pure finder, gathering dog dung for the tanneries. Good at it, he'd been, knowing the yards that liked it moist and dark and the others that preferred the chalky kind and would be prepared to pay the extra for it. He had himself what was almost a little workshop, mixing up the trophies he bagged with mud or mortar, depending on the customer, and rolling it out into fat little cigars or looser lumps to produce whatever blend the tanner liked to declare perfect for the dark glossy morocco of a gentleman's wallet or the delicate calf of a lady's glove. He was even in with the kennels for a time, before the tanners refused it on account of the quality being so poor. For a while Joe'd had himself a right little enterprise.

It weren't to last. Once the railways

came London started to bloat and swell and all of a sudden there were more people looking for work than there was ever work to be done. It wasn't long before there was so many after the pure that they was fighting over every last scrap, sometimes two or more waiting while a dog crouched in order to pounce on what it left behind. The tanners weren't stupid neither. They knew there was a hundred people out there if there was one, all scrambling over one another for their trade. Where once Joe might have got himself two shillings for a pailful and at least a pail a day, in the years after the Irish swarmed into the city like locusts he was lucky to win himself tenpence a pail five days in a week. There was nine children by then. If it hadn't been for the old man dying and Tom looking for a partner on the tosh, Joe would have found himself in serious trouble. He knew it, of course. They didn't talk about it, they didn't talk much at all, come to that, but Tom always knew he was grateful. If he ever needed a favour he knew Joe'd be first to oblige him. Tom hadn't tried to call it. Strange though it sounded, he was grateful to Joe too, in his own way. With no family of his own, Joe's family had become Tom's to fall in with when he chose. He'd even lodged with them a while before the tailor's family took up with them and they'd needed Tom's space for him to work in. It was the only time he had ever felt a pang, sitting in that crowded room in St Giles, a plate of supper on his lap and the clamour of family life racketing around him, and watched Joe's littlests, a pair of girls crowned with their father's flaming hair, as they entwined their arms around his neck and covered his great freckled face with their kisses.

They were all growed-up now, of course, the youngest one nine or more. Eleven of them all told, not counting the ones that had passed on, God rest their souls. Two of the boys were already transported and one there'd been no word of for nigh on ten years, but they took Alfred or Jem, who was Joe's fifth and eighth respective, down the tunnels sometimes, when they needed the extra pairs of hands. Joe had hoped one day there'd be something of a business to hand on, father to son, but it didn't look too likely no more. Times were changing fast and not for the better. At the docks, where Alf waited for work at fourpence an hour and the employers asked no questions, there were hundreds of men of every calling offering themselves for hire. They waited for the ships to come in like children waiting for their dinner, holding their thumbs and hoping they wouldn't go to bed hungry.

The night was clear and stars drifted across the black sky like ash. Tom felt restive, not yet ready for sleep. Slowly, barely noticing where he was headed, he walked back up towards Soho. His head tumbled with memories and it was with a start that, sometime later, he realized he'd found his way back to the arched entrance to Hawker-lane. Behind him on Broad-street the Golden Hind dazzled and blazed, her glass doors parted in invitation. Coins jingled inside Tom's hidden pocket. At his feet a ragged boy with a blackened eye turned cartwheels and demanded pennies for his trouble. On one foot he wore an ancient shoe knotted around its broken instep with a grimy length of ribbon, on the other a woman's old boot. Ignoring his petitions Tom ducked into the alley and made his way to the Black Badger.

It was a long time since he'd been to the fight but the place hadn't changed any since his regular days. The front of the long downstairs bar was crowded with every kind of man, all of them smoking, drinking and talking about dogs. Dogs fretted on tables and benches so as the Fancy might look them over, feeling and squeezing their feet, peering into their eyes and mouths. An omnibus driver, his round hat tipped over one eye, banged his fist upon a rickety table, glaring violently at a costermonger in a plush skullcap and a green neckerchief patterned with flowers in mustard yellow. Each of the buttons on the coster's sandy-coloured corduroy waistcoat bore the raised head of a fox and under his arm he clamped a Skye terrier that thrashed like a fish. A pair of coachmen dressed in fancy livery leaned against the bar and made quiet enquiries of the barman as to the proprietor's favourites for the night, holding their position despite the attack of a company of soldiers whose eyes were as red and dishevelled as their unbuttoned tunics. Throughout the crowded parlour grocers and ironmongers, their evening frock-coats thrown over their working clothes, jostled with red-capped sailors and grey-faced dustmen and hollow-eyed tailors. Tom found himself crushed against an old man wearing a patched frock of a type that might have suggested him a countryman except that his uncombed hair was thick with soot. He had sold his coat that morning, he told Tom, for two shillings. Tomorrow, if the dogs and the gods were kind, he'd buy himself a finer one.

The first fight was for the gold watch. If Brassey had been obliged to rescue it from Uncle's he didn't say so. The men muttered to one another, jabbing blunt fingers at fresh scars and on occasion drawing comparisons, not all of them favourable, with celebrated champions now retired or dead. Indignant owners bridled, their greatcoats bristling like the pelts of peevish tom-cats as they countered with glowing accounts of their dogs' triumphs. The grand match of the evening, for which heavy wagers were already being taken, would pit the dog Butcher against forty of the beasts. Voices were dropped. Money changed hands, sometimes in large amounts. One coster, whose face resembled nothing more than one of his own potatoes, backed Butcher for twenty pounds on a forty for three. In a chair beside the door, one soft slipper resting on his knee, Brassey stroked the sleeves of his shiny black coat and drew a large watch from his waistcoat pocket.

The dogs were running short of patience. One, a bulldog with eyes the colour of raw liver, snarled at Tom as he passed, straining so viciously at his chain that it seemed certain he would snap his neck in two. His muscular body was livid with scars and his forehead bulged dangerously as he peeled his lips back from teeth yellow and greasy as spikes of tallow. Drool looped from his jaws. Set wide apart on his flat head his ears were ragged with bites, one almost torn in two. Grey markings spotted the deep channel between his powerful shoulders. The famous Butcher. In the shadow of the champion, a bull-terrier with a black patch over one of his crafty eyes and legs as bowed as a groom's growled and flexed and scratched his autograph deep into a flaking table top. The chorus of barks and yelps rose steadily above the din of voices and clatter of pots.

Only one dog stood quite still, its eyes fixed on the sawdust floor. Secured by a loop of rope to the leg of a chair it seemed deaf to the clamour that surrounded it. Tom watched it out the corner of one eye. Despite its smooth white coat the animal had a raw and tender appearance to it, being peculiarly pink about the edges of its eyes and nose and belly. Its tail might have been chewed by a fretful child. There was no telling the breed from the look of it. While it had the stocky body of a bull-terrier, its legs were long and finely boned. And although its forehead sloped directly into its nose in the manner of a bulldog's, its ears owed nothing to the bulldog design. Indeed the pair of them were such a poor match they seemed cut from two quite different patterns and pieces of cloth. While the left ear stood stiffly to attention, the pink veins traced clear as the veins on a leaf, the other, soot-black and ragged, fell over the animal's right eye. This might have given the dog a rakish air had it not been so diffident an animal. As it was, the overall impression was of a creature assembled in the dark. On a whim, Tom thrust the toe of his boot under the animal's snout, tipping its face up towards his. Resting its chin on his foot the dog blinked its pink eyes and gazed up at him. Tom gazed back.

'I dunno what the old fool's on about, bringing that bitch 'ere,' a hoarse voice disparaged from behind a pewter pot. 'Ain't no self-respectin' rat wouldn't 'ave it for breakfast and want more besides.'

The dog blinked again and its head seemed to droop a little more heavily on to Tom's boot.

' 'E'd 'ave more chance in there 'isself!' another rejoined, bursting with mirth, as a bent old man with a goblin's mutter pushed past Tom and delivered a sharp kick to the dog's ribs.

'Get up, you good-for-nothing mongrel,' he hissed, yanking hard on the dog's rope. The dog stumbled to its feet. 'Worthless carcass.'

'Kicked out, is yer?' the hoarse voice enquired. 'And there was me fearin' the old Badger'd gone and lost its standards.'

The old man's face twisted with rage. Yanking again at the dog's rope he spat into the sawdust and was gone, leaving the voices to snigger into their beer.

Tom's boot felt cold and flimsy without the warm weight of the dog's muzzle. He pushed his way towards the fire where an ancient mastiff sprawled, its wheezy snores rumbling in its chest. The walls were crowded with trophies. Clusters of black leather collars with brass rings and clasps and framed engravings of famous dogs engaged in combat jostled for space with dusty glass display cases containing stuffed specimens the worse for moth. Tom peered into the one displayed above the mantel. It housed a brutish-looking dog with brown markings and a haughty expression. Around its thick neck the dog wore a flaking yellow chain of paste that resembled a lady's bracelet and between its blunt jaws it clamped a large stiff rat. The rat's glass eyes were round with bewilderment.

'You ever saw her fight?' asked a man standing at Tom's shoulder. He wore a mole-coloured waistcoat and his cropped mole-coloured hair was worn away in patches like old velveteen.

'Once or twice.'

'They've spoiled her in the stuffing, haven't they, though?' the man observed happily, showing his missing teeth. 'Made her far too short in the head. But what a dog! There was one occasion, years ago now of course but not long after I took up with —'

Tom never found out who the man'd took up with. Abruptly, as if a sluice had been opened, the men drained from the parlour. Tom followed them as they clattered up the splintery staircase. At the top each dropped a shilling into the box held out by Brassey as he entered the upstairs room. Tom posted his shilling and nodded at Brassey but the proprietor was distracted and flapped a hand, urging him onwards.

In the upstairs room the shutters were closed and lamps burned so ardently in every corner that the brightness hurt your eyes. In the centre of the room was the pit, a circular wooden structure about eight feet across and elbow height. It was painted white. In the centre of the pit was a chalk circle of perhaps a foot in diameter. Otherwise the boards were bare. The audience hung themselves over the sides of the pit or clambered up on to one of the tables behind it for a clearer view. Dogs whined and slavered. The room was full, the men restless. Voices rose above the clamour, shouting for the fight to begin.

In the open doorway Brassey hesitated, rotating his feet in anxious circles. His eyes flickered uncertainly over the empty alcove in the wall in which three diverse carvers had been arranged in a manner, Brassey fancied, as stately as thrones. But there was no sign tonight of the Captain and his friends. Brassey's lad looked at his master expectantly. Brassey frowned. Once again he brought out his watch. Someone at the back of the room began to chant. There was a chorus of impatient clapping. With a final reluctant glance down the stairs Brassey nodded at the boy and closed the parlour door.

As the lad brought out the first of the crates there was a deafening roar of approval from the company. The boy made a great show of setting the crate down in the pit, dancing around it and whipping up the crowd into a fever before flinging open the trapdoor in its lid like the conjuror on Epsom Day. For a moment nothing happened. Then like a wave, all of them moving together, the rats swarmed from the crate, streaking across the white floor of the pit before piling themselves up together in a shifty mound against the far wall of the ring. They were big ones and no mistake, Tom thought with a twitch of satisfaction. From their heaped-up bodies rose the hot stench of summer privies. As soon as they caught the scent of it the dogs went wild, baying and thrashing in their owners' arms. The noise was deafening.

Shouting for silence Brassey stood himself upon a table to state the rules of the house. Each dog would be permitted a second but seconds could stand only within the marked area of the pit. Any man touching dog or rats, or acting in any way dishonestly would have his dog disqualified. Time must be strictly observed. In a questionable situation it would be the umpire's decision whether a rat was alive or dead. By the time Brassey had finished his short speech the room was once again lost in an almighty racket. Brassey nodded at the boy as he took his seat at the top end of the pit.

Immediately a man leaped into the pit holding a large terrier. Both the dog and its second sported hairy coats of a rough texture in an uncertain shade of grey. The dog writhed so ferociously it was all the second could do to keep a grip on it. He muttered something into the dog's ear. Then, gripping it round the chest, he squatted, the dog clamped between his knees. The dog stared at the rats and it drooled. The second murmured a final word and let it loose. For a moment the dog stared wildly about it, its head twisting like a snake's. Then, giving a little bark as if it were clearing its throat, it hurled itself into the heap of rats, burying its nose in the mound. When it pulled out its head its jaws clamped a large brown rat by the neck. Squealing like piglets, the other rats ran in frantic circles around the pit or tried to squeeze between the narrow spaces in the floor. The terrier paid them no attention but gave his trophy one violent shake and then another, sending feathers of blood across the white walls of the pit. Imprisoned in his chalk circle, the second punched out his arms, bellowing at the dog to get back to business. The terrier shook the animal one last time before dropping it reluctantly to the floor. The rat gave a shudder and its tail twitched. Then it was still. Blood shone bright as fresh paint on the ripped-out meat of its neck.

In a moment the terrier was setting about dispatching his next victim. He was quicker this time, tossing its body aside before pouncing on another and another. By now the audience was in a storm of excitement and the second was fairly boiling over. The sweat poured from his forehead as he roared his commands and the rough hairs upon his coat stood out like the spines of a hedgehog. Steadily, rat by rat, the terrier pursued his slaughter. Only one of the devils gave him any trouble. Struggling desperately in the terrier's jaws, it twisted its body around and clamped its teeth on to the dog's nose. The dog faltered then, taken by surprise, but only for a moment. With a brusque swing of its neck, it dashed the rat as hard as it could against the wall of the pit. As the rat fell to the ground it left a dark scarlet stain on the paint as shameless as a birthmark.

'Time!'

The second clicked his fingers. Immediately the dog slunk to heel, its whiskered face beaded with blood. The second handed him over the rim of the pit to his owner, who pulled his ears and cuffed him gently on the head as a cluster of men crowded around them, beating the both of them on the back. The dog panted happily and licked his master's cheek. Fragments of fur and raw flesh were lodged between its teeth. In the bloodied pit the dark bodies of the dead rats littered the floor like clods of manure. Amongst them the rats left alive sniffed idly at the walls of the pit or sat back on their hind legs and set to cleaning their faces with their paws.

As the uproar subsided around him Tom looked down at his hands. They had gripped the wall of the pit so hard that its sharp edge had scored two long grooves along the balls of his thumbs. His palms glittered with sweat.

'Look who's here. Enjoy the fight?'

Brassey stood at Tom's elbow, his hands caressing his stomach and his feet neatly arranged in a V. Behind him the boy flung the corpses by their tails into a corner.

'Your rats didn't exactly put up a resistance, though, did they?' Brassey sneered. 'May as well've lain down and cut their own throats for all the trouble they gave that 'un. If you think I'm paying a penny apiece for —'

Brassey broke off, his attention distracted by a commotion in the doorway. Immediately his little eyes grew round and bright and the scowl on his face melted into a treacly smile. Pushing Tom aside, he scurried to greet the newcomers.

'Captain,' he declared, skittish as a girl. 'I am glad to see you, my dear friend. And you, sir,' he added to a second, unfamiliar, gentleman. 'We've some right pretty performers for you tonight. Are you set to wager?'

The Captain nodded impatiently, craning over Brassey's shoulder towards the pit. He was a thickset man of middling age, with dark whiskers crowding in on his slit of a mouth. He had the sneering look of a man accustomed to issuing unreasonable commands but otherwise he gave no indication of military association, wearing not a captain's uniform but a black coat over a high and stiffly starched collar that seemed from the irritable jut of his chin and the scarlet flush of his complexion to be causing him considerable discomfort. His friend's collar was higher and stiffer still but his neck was so thin and his face so narrow that it seemed he could have slid it on without untying the knot of his stock.

Brassey led them over to their box, his

head bowed so low Tom wouldn't have been surprised if his forehead'd borne the imprint of his buttons. The Captain made no remark upon the box provided for his comfort. Instead he flung himself into one of the carvers, his feet slung over the pit's wall, and abruptly demanded that the dogs be brought to him for his inspection. He examined them closely, his eyes half-closed against the smoke from his cigar. One man wished to sell him a bulldog and he looked at this one particularly closely, holding out the lighted end of his cigar to the animal; the dog sniffed and recoiled with a yelp of pain. The Captain smiled.

'Chuck him in,' he commanded.

'He'll pay all of a fortune for a champion, that one,' muttered a voice next to Tom. It was the mole man from the parlour. 'Mad for the sport, 'e is. Never seen 'im when he don't drop more in a wager 'an us reg'lar coves sees inside a year.'

The Captain clearly did not consider the bulldog a champion. The dog was given only minutes before the Captain waved a hand to dismiss it from the ring. Brassey scuttled off to fetch the next competitor. There was strong support amongst the Fancy for this dog, a fierce little terrier barely larger than the rats he set about, and a roar set up about the room the moment its whining was heard on the stairs. Tom had thought to put a shilling or two on this one himself but he was suddenly weary. His head ached. By the time the dog was set in the ring the clamour was louder than Tom could stand. In his box the Captain leaned forward and placed his elbows on the wall of the pit, sucking greedily at his cigar. Tom slipped out.

Outside in the darkened alley there was a thin wind blowing. It was cold. Tom shivered and thrust his hands into his pockets. He had gone near as far as Compton-street before he fancied he was being followed. He turned around. The pink-eyed dog dropped into a sitting position behind him, its chewed tail making patterns in the dust. It made no sound but it stared hopefully up at Tom in the darkness. A frayed loop of rope trailed from its neck. Tom looked at the dog. From Compton-street he could hear the shrill and splintered owl-shrieks of a woman hurling curses. Slowly he pulled one hand from his pocket and let it hang loosely at his side, the fingers uncurled. The dog watched him, its pink eyes travelling down his arm to his hand, and then back up again. Its erect ear quivered in the breeze. And then, quite silently, it got to its feet, took three careful steps towards Tom and placed its muzzle in the palm of Tom's hand. It was a good fit. They stood like that for some time, the dog's whiskers stitched between Tom's fingers. Then Tom bent and picked up the rope and together they made their way homeward.

V

The war against Russia was expected to last no more than a month or two. As troops from across the country massed in Southampton, their brilliant uniforms and glittering ornaments the incarnation of the majesty of war, the newspapers thrilled with accounts of heroic battles at the seat of war on the Danube, and the triumphs of the Napoleonic Wars were trumpeted gloriously down the decades. Crowds paraded the streets delirious with excitement, intoxicated with national pride.

In the doctor's house in Clapham Polly went placidly about her duties, her freckled cheeks dimpling as easily as ever to accommodate her wide smile. She had little idea of where William had been dispatched and certainly none of the reasons for the war he was fighting, but she knew that it had been his duty to go and that, when it was over, he would return to her. Polly had always had a knack for contentment. She had no capacity to dwell upon unpleasant things; it was not in her nature. Her life had not been without its hardships — her farmer father had died when she was a child, leaving the family penniless and requiring her to abandon her schooling and go into service before her eleventh birthday — but it had never taught her the habits of anxiety or introspection and she refused to learn them. There was no purpose in wishing night was day. William would return home in good time. Meanwhile she had a comfortable position in a kind household, she was fond of the children and she sang as she tidied the nursery, laughing with unfeigned pleasure at the perfect fury on the painted face of a toy soldier, the lopsided solemnity of a stuffed rabbit's button eyes. The unfathomable gravity of seriousness never failed to touch and amuse her.

She had always laughed at William's seriousnesses too, smoothing away the lines from his forehead with her hand and standing on tiptoes to kiss his lip where it caught between his teeth until he laughed too and took her in his arms. With her, he told her, one finger tracing the curve of her cheek, he could never be unhappy for long. If she had not silenced him with a kiss he would have told her more. He would have told that with her he stepped out of himself, leaving behind, like a chrysalis, the grocer's son with two left feet who took things too much to heart. That with her he forgot that life was unpredictable and cruel, that fathers died and fortunes changed so that everything that had once seemed certain was all of a sudden beyond your reach. He forgot that he'd promised himself to be careful, to always stand apart and alone where the ground was solid and familiar and moulded like old shoes into the shapes of his feet. With Polly he forgot he had feet at all. He spun and somersaulted through the days with her, so dizzy with astonished joy that upside-down felt much the same as right-way-up. He felt as though he had flung open a window in the middle of winter to find summer sprawled upon the lawn. Her warmth seeped into him like sunshine. For Polly's part, William's thoughtful gravity made her feel safe. Although she could never have turned the feelings into thoughts or words, she understood somehow that the weight of him tethered her like the ropes that secured the hot-air balloon above the pleasure gardens at Cremorne. He would never let her drift away.

Every morning in the month after William's departure Polly sang as she tidied the sunny nursery and readied the children for the day. And every morning a cold sweat gathered on her forehead and beneath her arms and sickness tumbled giddily in her belly until she vomited into the basin set ready on the washstand. When George remarked with some distaste upon this ritual to his father, the doctor had summoned Polly to his study. Her conduct was inexcusable, he told her sternly, but while he sincerely hoped that she felt ashamed before him and before God, there were things that might be done. The doctor had long specialized in those particulars of medicine peculiar to the female sex and he had established something of a reputation, amongst those who knew, for assisting ladies who found themselves in positions of difficulty. He was willing to offer Polly such assistance.

But Polly had politely refused. She was certain things would come out well. It would be months before the baby showed. When the war was over, and everyone said it must soon be over, William would come home. They would marry and the baby would be born. They would be happy. Beyond this she did not allow herself to think. At night she sat beside the fire in the nursery, her mending untouched in her lap, and smiled into the stuffed rabbit's anxious face. She knew that she was taking a terrible risk, that having the child could be ruinous, but she knew it vaguely, as she knew from the globe in the children's nursery that the earth was not flat but round, without having the least instinct for it.

It was a beautiful summer. In the long pale-blue evenings before she put them to bed, Polly sat with the children, one in the curve of each arm, and told them of the life that she and William would share together when he returned. Her caramel eyes softened with conviction as she described the home they would live in together once he was free from the army, the flowered china they would eat from, the names they would give to their children. The doctor's children listened, their faces rapt. Their previous nursemaid had favoured stories of an instructive bent, such as the tale of the girl who, unable to reach a shelf, had trodden on the big family Bible, fallen and died of her injuries. There were no lessons in Polly's tales. The children would demand again and again to be told the story of how Polly and William met in Kew Gardens, even though they themselves had been present. They could not get enough of the shy young man with the botany books who had stopped to help George free his hoop from a bush, flushing awkwardly when Polly had thanked him for his kindness. They laughed gleefully at the suggestion that, smitten with love for the pretty nursemaid, he had secretly followed them into the Great Conservatory and at last summoned the courage to approach them and to stammer out his name. Indeed they were so fond of that part of the story that they had chosen to quite forget that it was Alice who had first spotted him sketching in the tropical glasshouse and pounced upon him, dragging a reluctant William over to join their party and insisting that he show them the precise and beautiful illustrations in his journal.

'And then George said, "By the way —" '

'Polly!' protested Alice. 'You said you wouldn't skip.'

Polly grinned.

'All right, madam, keep your hair on. So I says to him, "The children's always telling me I'm a right ignoramus when it comes to flowers," and he says, "I only know about them because I had a good teacher." And I says back, "Perhaps you could teach me?" and he says, "Oh yes!" all in a rush and then, "If you liked," all gentlemanly only a bit too late and then he blushes scarlet, right to the roots of his golden hair.'

Alice clapped her hands together.

'That's right. And then George said, "By the way her name's Polly" and he said —'

She looked at George, the laughter already beginning, and together they chorused, ' *"Polygalaceae."* '

When the children had giggled William had been covered in confusion. He had never meant to say it out loud. It was just that the name Polly had set him thinking, first of *Polygonaceae,* the dock family and then *Polygalaceae,* the milkworts. Both short and tough, herbs that flourished on heaths and waste ground, but the milkwort flower was surprisingly dainty, the delicate white corolla peeping from the bell-shaped flower like lace-edged petticoats. Polly had broad strong shoulders and wide-set eyes, caramel brown and dusted with golden flecks like pollen, but her waist and her wrists were fine and neat. She had smelled of rumpled bedclothes and grass and salt and, very faintly, of carbolic soap.

It was Polly who suggested that William call for her at the doctor's house on her afternoon off. After that they spent every Sunday afternoon together, although Polly resisted with blithe determination William's early attempts to teach her a little of botany. She refused to see a flower as an arrangement of calyx, corolla, stamens and the rest, to be classified and noted along with the particularities of their habitat and distribution, its likely flowering time and frequency. She said such dry examination spoiled a simple pleasure. For Polly a flower was a thing of passing beauty to be pounced upon and plucked and placed behind one ear in the here and now of a hot summer afternoon until its petals wilted against a creamy cheek and its fragrance mixed with the scent of hair and the salty bedroom smell of skin. Then William's heart pressed so hard against his ribs he was certain it would snap them like matchsticks. Against such an argument his books made only the faintest of impressions. They remained unopened. Instead he walked with Polly along the banks of the river, their hands clasped, and, while she held her face up to the sky like a sunflower, he prayed silently that the Sunday sun might never set.

On one of those enchanted Sunday afternoons William asked Polly to be his wife. Within two years, he calculated, they would be able to marry. His work on the Ordnance, though tedious and repetitive, had equipped him with the kind of skills that were increasingly being sought amongst civil engineering practices. As they walked they planned their life together, arranging rooms, stoking fires, naming children. To William's delight Polly favoured flower names for a girl: Violet, Daisy, Rose. Fleabane, William teased. Goosefoot. Cudweed. Or milkwort after her mother. *Polygala amarella,* dwarf milkwort, baby milkwort. Polly laughed and tweaked his nose. My little milkwort, he called her then. He ached for her, the desire rising and rising within him until he could barely breathe, and, to his astonished delight, she responded to his tentative approaches with an ardour that inflamed him yet further. They hid themselves in dark corners on the common, out of sight, her fingers fumbling with his buttons, his breathless mouth upon her neck. He could not smuggle her into his lodgings — the boot-faced landlady kept watch over her staircase with the impassive rigour of a Royal guardsman — but on the occasional Sundays when the doctor's family went out to pay calls they crept up through the darkened house and into her narrow bed. Her breasts gleamed in the dusky light. My darling, he whispered, as she arched her back against him, her hair tumbling from its pins, and she bit her lip to stop herself from crying out. My own precious milkwort flower.

Summer passed. News began to leak back from the front, slowly at first and then in furious torrents. For the first time ever several newspapers, most notably *The Times*, had their own correspondent filing reports directly from the front line. They bore witness to a miserable and ramshackle campaign presided over by aged incompetents, crippled by chronic lack of supplies and decimated by disease. Before the armies reached Balaclava ten thousand lives had been lost to cholera. The bloody battles at Alma and then at Inkerman claimed thousands more and yet they brought the Allies not one step nearer to taking Sebastopol. The conflict that had begun with such jubilance stretched interminably ahead into the harsh winter, lodged in snow and suffering.

In London, as in the Crimea, the year shrivelled into bitter winter, the harshest in England since records had begun. The ice on the Serpentine grew six inches thick and fishermen were forced to beg dynamite from local laundrywomen to blow it open. At the stage in her confinement when he feared her condition might no longer be easily disguised, the doctor summoned Polly to his study once again. He had long prided himself on his radical principles and had determined upon regarding the situation as one of folly rather than depravity. Polly was ignorant but she was sweet-tempered and the children were fond of her. If, as he suspected, her sweetheart was already dead then she might be passed off as a widow. Although his wife would require considerable persuasion he was confident she would allow Polly to remain with them after the child was born, so long as no mention of it was ever made to the children. There was a woman he knew in Battersea who ran something of a foundling home with whom the infant might be lodged for a small fee. Few in her position would have dared to hope for such kindness but Polly accepted the doctor's terms without surprise. After all, did luck not favour those who trusted in it? At the end of her seventh month she took the coach to her brother's modest cottage in Kent where she completed her lying-in. The snow drifted thickly against the casement window so that even at noon the room was muffled with frozen shadow. When the baby was born her sister-in-law, who was barren, offered with grudging sanctimony to take the child as her own. Polly only laughed.

As soon as she was fit to travel Polly returned to the doctor's house and resumed her duties. She refused to listen to news from the front. In London the snow was finally melting, leaving the unpaved alleys of Battersea soupy with treacherous sludge. But every Sunday afternoon she picked her way through the mud to the old woman's crumbling cottage behind the railway line. She rarely took him out. Instead she cradled the infant William in her arms, inhaling his sweet milky smell, gorging herself on the sight of him. He stared up at her with her own round caramel eyes, their centres dusted with gold. Sweet William. He was a robust baby, with little of the flower about him, but when he screamed his face grew as purple as a foxglove. Polly soothed him, holding his soft cheek against hers and whispering of the perfect happiness that would be theirs when his father came home from the war. Then they would be together once more. He would gather them up, his precious flowers, in the circle of his arms and hold them close to him. He would keep them safe.

Polly barely recognized the gaunt and

haunted man who returned to her as the year 1855 drew to a close. Their son was almost a year old. William accepted the child without question, as Polly had known he would, sometimes staring at him for hours as he slept, his thin fingers pleating the edge of the infant's knitted blanket. But when Polly stood on her tiptoes to kiss his lips he blinked at her in bewilderment. He barely spoke. He no longer called her his flower, his precious milkwort girl. He no longer talked of flowers at all, although he carried his thumbed botany books, as he always had, tucked into the pocket of his coat. The leather binding of one bore a ragged dark stain. Sometimes, when Polly placed his son in his lap and he looked down into the child's muffin face, his arms would stiffen and he would thrust the infant back to her, his face averted and his eyes wild with panic. His cheekbones stood out upon his face like elbows.

On the last day of January 1856 they were married. Polly arranged everything and refused to be discouraged. He needed time to adjust to being a father, she told them both. He needed rest and wholesome food to put the flesh back on to his bones. Most importantly of all he had to find work so that they could live together as a family. The stipend from the Army was barely enough to support William himself, let alone to allow for Polly to leave the doctor's household. She encouraged him to look for map-making work, engineering apprenticeships to build upon his work in Scutari. Secretly, her tongue poked out between her teeth in concentration as she laboriously formed the words, she wrote to William's Mr Rawlinson appealing to him for help. He replied with great courtesy that he had considerable respect for her husband but, convalescing himself, could offer her no suggestions at the present time. She did not show William the letter, telling herself it would only discourage and disappoint him. As it was he had little stomach for the search for a position. He was exhausted, of course. He moved slowly and slept little. He grew thinner and sometimes when she spoke to him he had difficulty hearing her. Soon after his return from Turkey she insisted upon bathing the wounds on his forearms. She examined them briefly and then briskly bandaged them with fresh rags, commenting only that she supposed it was his weak condition that meant they were taking longer than they should to heal. After that she let him dress them himself. In the Grainger

123

nursery her voice was shriller than usual and her temper shorter. On one occasion she slapped George so hard that his cheek bore the red imprint of her hand. When she begged his forgiveness they both wept.

The letter arrived in late June. The Metropolitan Board of Works wished to offer William a position on the surveying team of the Metropolitan Main Drainage Scheme. The letter informed him that Mr Rawlinson, previously of the Sanitary Commission, had recommended him for the post personally and with considerable warmth. The salary would start at one hundred and twenty pounds a year. When William told her Polly laughed and cried together, pressing his hand against her cheek. When he took his hand away he stared in confusion at the tears that glistened upon his knuckles. She paid him no mind. Instead she threw her arms around his unresponsive body and kissed him. One hundred and twenty pounds a year! There could be nothing wrong with a man who was thought by so eminent and important a body to be worth one hundred and twenty pounds a year. They could afford to take a small house, perhaps even to have a girl come in to do the heavy work. They would be respectable; they would be happy. Just as she had always known they would be. The unfamiliar black shadows that had lurked in the unseen corners of her heart in the previous months vanished quite suddenly in the dazzle of her restored spirits. She had never acknowledged them; now she forgot them altogether. Each of her hopes was safely back in its place. It was no more than anxiety about their future that had caused William to be withdrawn since his return. As a man of honour and conscience the responsibilities of a wife and son naturally weighed heavily upon him but, steadied by respectability and a regular and robust wage, and soothed by the loving attentions of his wife and son, he would be soon restored to health. It was thus with a light heart that Polly took her leave from the doctor's household and settled with her family in a small terraced house in Lambeth at a rent of eighteen pounds a year.

VI

Dogs were a curse in the sewers, everyone knew it. There were two lessons you learned straight off if you were on the tosh: walk slow and steady, and no dogs. It was true, dogs might be worth something against the rats if the beasts set their minds on attacking you, but that wasn't much good when you couldn't get within a hundred feet of the creatures. One sniff of a dog and the rats melted away. Then the sound of their barking (and they always barked, for if the dark didn't do it for them there was no stopping them once they caught the scent of the rats) could be heard a street away and had the traps down on you faster than you could say beadle. You might as well stand under a grating and flash your lantern like a lighthouse as take a dog down the tunnels. It was an out-and-out invitation for trouble.

Red Joe knew that Tom knew this well as he did, given Tom'd been the one to teach it him in the first place, but he said it all the same, scowling at the dog that slunk at

Tom's heels. It was a mangy-looking beast and no mistake, downright decrepit with its ears sprouting in different directions and its fur stretched so thin over its body the skin showed through. It couldn't as much as look you in the eye. For the life of him Joe couldn't fathom why Tom had taken such a fancy to it. It had been weeks now. The first time Joe had seen them together he'd laughed out loud at the sight of them, side by side with their muzzles stuck up in the air and their mouths open so that they seemed to be tasting it, for all the world like a pair of chipped teapots ready to pour. He wasn't laughing now.

Tom squatted in the mud, pressing his fingers into the corners of a crate to test their sturdiness.

'We ain't taking it,' Joe said again, glowering at the dog as it cringed against Tom's leg. One of its ears was torn and its lip too and the reek of defeat rose off of it like steam. The rats would rip it to pieces soon as look at it.

Tom reached into one of his pockets for a curl of iron-wire.

'She won't bark,' he said with quiet certainty, twisting wire tight around the hinges of the crate.

'What you reckon it will or won't do

ain't neither here nor there. It ain't coming. And that's final.'

'She won't bark,' Tom said again and fondled the dog's head.

Joe wanted to kick it.

'They all bark,' Joe said mulishly. 'You learned me that, remember?'

'Not her. I swear it. Not so much as a whimper, not even in the thick of it in that cavern under Queen-lane. Silent as the dead.'

'You mean —'

'I took her down already, Joe. Five times since Sunday.'

'You done what?'

'She's a ratter. I had to see what she was good for.'

Joe gaped at him, his mouth round as a flounder's.

'She ain't bad neither,' Tom added. His lips twitched as he hooked an arm round the dog's neck and rubbed her whiskery chin. She tucked her head into Tom's armpit and looked steadily up at Joe with her pink eyes. 'She ain't half bad at all.'

Tom took a kind of satisfaction from Joe's astonishment but when he'd said the dog wasn't half bad he had to confess he wasn't being entirely truthful. The fact was that she was better than that, much better.

If he'd not seen her with his own eyes Tom would never have believed it. She didn't look like a ratter, for starters. And ratting wasn't something you could teach a dog. A beast either had the taste for it or they didn't, simple as that. If this one didn't have the stomach for it that was her business. Meanwhile she stayed and he found he didn't mind. He liked the warm indentation left on the blanket by her curled body, the way, when Tom had finished his supper, she slipped her muzzle without ceremony into his hand. He liked the company.

And then, one afternoon when the dog had been with him for close on a week, Tom had been obliged to bring back to his lodgings a crate of the beasts after the proprietor of the King's Head on Cock-hill welched on a deal for one hundred of them. The dog raised her head from the bed as Tom pushed open the door. He set the crate on the floor and clicked his fingers at her in greeting but she did not look at him. Her pink eyes were fixed on the crate, her nostrils wide and all aquiver. The rats could smell her too. Inside the packed crate they screamed and writhed. Filthy gobbets of fur pressed between the narrow gaps in the wire. Tom clicked his fingers again but again the dog paid him no mind. It was as if he weren't even there. Very slowly she raised herself up on to her front legs and ran her pink tongue over her lips. Her eyes were sharp, focused as a pickpocket's, and a silvery thread of saliva looped from her mouth as, with great deliberation, she pushed herself off the low bed and crept towards the twisting mass of rats, her belly low against the splintered floor. Tom stared. Then, without stopping to think, he plunged his hand into the crate and pulled out a rat, throwing it across the room. It was a big one, broad as a man's thigh but agile too, and it streaked away towards the corner of the room towards a battered three-legged stool. The dog was too fast for it. Before the rat had got halfway to the corner she had pounced, clamping it between her jaws. It tried to twist itself out of her grasp but she bit down upon it so hard that Tom heard the crunch of the rat's bones. It went limp. Carefully, without ceremony, the dog laid the rat at Tom's feet and waited.

That night she slaughtered twenty of the unsold rats. And every time, even at the last when Tom released ten of them together, the dog set about the task without so much as a sound. She had about her an air of precise purpose that made Tom think not of other fighting dogs or even of the brisk butchers at Smithfield market, but of men of business, the starched and bespectacled clerks with their chained bill-books and their rigid mouths that marched daily across London Bridge to the counting-houses of the City. The Old Lady of Threadneedle-street, he thought to himself and smiled. Though Lady'd do. When she was finished he took Lady on to his lap and, dipping a rag into a kettle of water that was cooling beside the crumbling fire, he gently wiped the blood from her face. That night she slept with her nose in the V of his arm.

Two days later he took her into the sewers.

They became a familiar sight, Long Arm Tom and the rum-looking dog that stuck like a silent shadow to his heels. In the taverns and coffee-houses he frequented it could always be found under his chair, its chin on his feet. For all that they couldn't warm to the beast the others got used to stepping over it. It didn't growl at you and bark like some of them, in fact it was silent as death, but it was an ugly mutt and un-friendly as they came. If you got yourself too close to it it would back away like a weanling to hide itself in Tom's coat. It wasn't unusual to see him share his dinner with the animal and slipping it some of the most succulent pieces of meat into the bargain. There were those that said such strong affection for a dumb animal was one of the sure signs that a man was preparing to turn up his toes. Well, when Tom's day came he'd be missed, they agreed on that. Tom was a quiet cove, a man not known for giving much in the way of quarter, but he was as much a piece of their part of London as the stink of the gully holes. When Long Arm Tom breathed his last it would mark the passing of something. There would be no more toshers like Tom to step into his shoes when he dropped them, for all the pair of them was worn down to slops. The city was changing and all of their lives were set to change with it. There were no two ways of looking at that.

VII

Polly was not altogether wrong about the significance of William's work upon his state of mind, although in the confusion of the Greek-street offices there was little routine and even less regular assurance of funds, at least in so far as public works were concerned. The Board had been established to transform the chaotic clog of London into a city of purposeful movement — of water, air, traffic, people and commodities — and their greatest priority was the construction of a sewer system that would provide a clean water supply and safely extract the city's waste. A grand plan indeed. But Parliament had not considered it necessary to endow them with the fiscal and administrative powers they required to force through so vast a project. Instead the Board was caught up in endless disputes with the city's vestries, whose approval needed to be obtained for all expenditure and over whom the Board wielded no direct authority. Proposals were issued, questioned, contested and withdrawn for reconsideration. Recommendations were blocked on the grounds of expense, of inconvenience, of principle, and frequently for the simple pleasure of saying no. Meetings were convened to contest the conclusions of previous meetings. Those plans that were eventually ratified found themselves bogged in a mire of politicking, endless circles of postponements, protocols and paperwork.

Meanwhile the senior members of the Board quarrelled amongst themselves. The most heated debate turned upon the necessity of a system that would allow for the conversion of the city's waste into manure, a system the Chinese people were claimed to have adopted with great success. One hundred and forty such proposals were invited and considered and, in the face of Bazalgette's arguments against such a notion, there was for a time intense pressure to replace him. But despite these obstacles Bazalgette remained calm and practical. Every day in Greek-street he presided over the painstaking assessments of depth and bore, of pressure and power, of tide and gradient, until there grew beneath the pencils of his draughtsmen the vision of a mighty new city beneath the old, a magnificent metropolis contained by iron walls with hundreds of miles of pipe-lanes and pipe-streets criss-crossed with pipe-rivers and, in three great swathes to the North of the river and two to its South, five mighty thoroughfares with buttressed ceilings as high as cathedrals. The four pumping towers were the underground city's spires, reaching up so far they pierced the cloud of ground level, with the pumping station at Abbey Mills, conceived in the Venetian Gothic style, its royal palace, presiding over all. It was a city of pomp and splendour, a place as far from the primitive labyrinth William knew as the new stucco squares of Belgravia were from the squalid piggeries and potteries of Notting Dale. Except that this city was for everyone. In this place there would be drinking-fountains where fresh water would be freely available. No one would have to dip their pail into the foul brack of a common ditch and drink. There would be no open sewers that bubbled up into the houses of the poor and poisoned the earth and the air. In this city there would be no festering cesspools, no open gully holes where the cholera and his monstrous cousins might crouch and wait. They would be borne away as the excretions of the people would be borne away, carried on an irresistible tide towards the sea. Disease would be all but vanquished, as it had been vanquished in Scutari. It would have constituted a miracle if William still believed in miracles. And in a way he did. His faith in a merciful and loving God had collapsed like ashes in a dying fire but there was still a faint heat in him that warmed his blood and it was kindled by that most earthly of saviours, sanitary engineering.

If Bazalgette's vision was the future William clung to, the rotting sewers they would replace were his refuge in the present. He had been away from London for fewer than twenty months and yet it seemed to him that the population of the city had doubled, trebled during his absence. According to the information furnished to the Board the population of the city was in the region of two and a half million souls, perhaps a little more. William was no more able to comprehend such a figure in relation to the London that he saw than he would have been able to understand from a figure of gallons the immensity of the seas. But he felt it and it overwhelmed him. The noise and the stink of the traffic as he crossed the river, heavy wagons, laden with bales and barrels, pushing and shoving for space with gigs, broughams, hearses, hansoms, knackers' carts, Barclay's drays and herds of pigs and sheep and foot passengers, left him dust-blinded and shaken. At night, in spite of the opium Polly assured him would help him sleep, the unholy chaos and clamour of the city sweated into the horror of his dreams. He would have been unable to countenance his work, the long walk to Soho and back through the elbowing screeching streets, the brusque demands of the senior engineers, the harried impatience of the clerks, had it not been for the tunnels. The other surveyors complained bitterly about the foul conditions underground. Their ventures into the system were hurried affairs, sufficient only to take the baldest necessary measurements. The flushers that acted as their guides, parish sewer-cleaners by turns scornful of and cowed by the presence of gentlemen in their private territories, were glad to be rid of them. Mr May was another matter. He lingered in the tunnels until they tired of the wait. Before long it was agreed that, once he had been taken to the correct part of the channel, he might be left alone there, a rope marking the route back to the nearest exit, as long as one of the flushing team remained above ground to warn him of adverse weather conditions and to guide him, if necessary, back to safety. When they first settled in the house in Lambeth Polly had suggested to William that he might begin a garden in the muddy slice of yard behind the cottage, a garden not just for vegetables but for the flowers he had always loved, a refuge full of colour and fragrance, as different from the dark stinking sewers as snow from soot. She brought home a seed catalogue and placed it beside his plate at dinner. He didn't open it. He couldn't bear to. A garden was impossible, utterly impossible. The dark stinking sewers, meanwhile, drew him like a magnet.

At first the sewers were no more than a private darkness in which to cut. The intensity of the cravings frightened and disgusted him but he could not smother them. They were stronger by far than he. They swelled and strengthened within him until they occupied him completely, obliterating all sense and feeling except this, his flesh on fire and screaming for the knife. And, as much as he dreaded them, he longed for them. Wherever he was working he concealed a knife behind a loose brick in the crumbling wall so that he might always be ready. He hid a roll of bandage in his pouch. Polly could not always fail to notice the bandages. She rebuked him lightly, teasing him for his carelessness with his tools, but in the face of his silence she quickly changed the subject. She had no wish to dwell on it or to spoil things. On the days he came home bandaged he was her William again. He was affectionate, even sentimental. He stroked her cheek and called her his little milkwort and the tears sprang easily into his eyes. He swept his son up on to his lap and kissed his golden head, trying not to flinch when the child wriggled playfully inside the circle of his arms. On those days they were happy.

Behind his back the other engineers called William the Sultan of the Sewers. Although they knew he was scrupulous in his habits, a few clamped their noses with their fingers as he passed them in the corridors. As a taunt it was light-hearted enough but there was no affection in it. The other men thought him aloof and resented it. Had William been born of high estate they would doubtless have respected his reserve as fitting to a man in his position but in the son of a humble shopkeeper such chilly pride was intolerable. There were many men in Greek-street with connections to the military and whispers circulated of a less than worthy service in the Russian War, of a dishonourable discharge, even of desertion. Before his appointment by the Board William's character and reputation had been burnished by the personal recommendations of Robert Rawlinson. Now the sticky dust of rumour settled over him and dulled his sheen. William knew it and, fearful of attracting any more attention, withdrew further. He kept his face close to the paper as he hunched over his table in his narrow wooden carrel and whenever it was possible he retreated into the private recesses of the sewers. He knew at least that his work could not be faulted. His inspections were detailed and precise, his recommendations judicious. In time it was suggested, to the considerable satisfaction of his fellow engineers, that he assume the burden of the Commission's routine inspections. After that he spent a part of every day crouched beneath the city's granite crust.

Months passed. And still the cravings came. William would feel them massing, stealthy and threatening, in the spaces between his ribs. When the blackness started, spreading like ink through the frills of his lungs and pressing its knuckles into the soft flesh of his throat, he made his way underground. There might have been other places he could have cut which he could have reached more easily and where he would not have been discovered. In the single tiled water-closet at Greek-street, for example, or in the midnight silence of the house in Lambeth while Polly and the child slept. But he went always into the tunnels. In the tunnels moral judgements were suspended. The strict and immutable precepts that governed the behaviour of those who walked directly over you, their feet striking the granite above your head, those rigid demarcations of right and wrong, of reputation and respectability, underground became fluid, elusive. The darkness accepted him without question or condemnation, receiving him silently into its embrace. The darkness had no curiosity and no memory. In the darkness there was only silence and solitude and safety and the extraordinary brilliant explosion of self as blade found flesh.

It was a warm May evening when William stumbled into the cavern. The city was drowsy and lit with a soft lilac light, the pale sky trimmed with flounces of gold and pale pink. William noticed nothing as he hastened towards the King-street sewer. His saliva was sour, bitter and metallic. His breath came in painful snatches. The muscles in his face jumped. The manhole at

Dean-street had been locked. He had spent some minutes struggling vainly to lift it, forcing the tips of his fingers under the iron cover and wrenching at it, but to no avail. Now the blackness gripped him, forcing its elbows into his chest, twisting his guts into knots. It prised open his arms, pushing rods of blackness along his fingers that pressed upwards with such hot insistence from beneath the restrictions of his filthy fingernails that William ripped at them frantically with his teeth. The taste of blood in his mouth lit such a flare of anticipation through his belly that he was certain he would scream. He broke into a run. The blackness crowded his head, narrowing his concentration to the next paving stone, the next. His heart and his boots beat out the frantic rhythm. The metal casing of his lantern banged painfully against his thigh but he barely noticed it. Closer, closer. Around the next corner. And there it was, the small hut of the flushers, set up like a sentry-box on the corner. William held the master-key. His hand trembled so much that he could hardly steady it sufficiently to enter his pocket. The key caught in the lining of his coat. Desperate, blind with urgency, William ripped it out and fumbled it into the lock. The door opened. William half-climbed, half-fell, into the opening, his feet insensible to the iron ladder set into the wall. The stink immediately flooded his head, the stink of shit and sea and rotting brick. He devoured it, the tears squeezing from between his clenched eyelids, as he pushed his way into the darkness, burying himself in its soft folds. When he had gone far enough he leaned against the oozing wall and fumbled for the knife. The water was high, nearly to his knees. It was of no consequence. He would not need to be here long. His hands no longer trembled. The knife was steady. He cut. For one eternal suspended moment his heart was perfectly still, caught in the perfect beauty of ecstasy, and then it burst. The blood sang out from his arm, clear and triumphant. Exultantly, William thrust the knife aloft, his fist clenched around the handle. The blackness hovered for a moment, like a scream echoing on the air, and then it was gone. Once more William was himself. He was free.

Some time later William lit his lantern and began to make his way out of the tunnel. This stretch of the sewers was unfamiliar to him. It was not long before he realized he was lost. This did not disturb him unduly. The King-street sewer had many exits, a number of them newly constructed with a trap which could be opened from beneath in situations of emergency. He had only to find one. The water was rising but he walked steadily and without alarm, treading carefully on the uneven floor. The light from his lantern glinted on the dark surface of the stream. When he reached a place where the tunnel branched in more than one direction, he paused only fractionally before choosing the likeliest-looking course and continuing on his way. He had been walking for perhaps ten minutes when the tunnel began to rise. Although the stream, to his surprise, seemed if anything to grow deeper, the air was notably less thick, the stink of excrement leavened by salt and the light kiss of circulating air. The echo of William's boots no longer throbbed against the narrow walls of the tunnel. He must be close to ground level. William looked upwards, searching the crown of the tunnel for an exit. Instead he saw only a black arch of stone, as though the tunnel had come to an end. There would be a grating beyond the arch. William scrambled towards it, holding his lantern as high as he could.

There was no grating. But William had

already forgotten that it was a grating he sought, for what he saw instead captivated him so utterly that all he could do was stand and stare. Before him lay a vast chamber, perhaps thirty feet in length, its roof soaring high above it like a cathedral's. The chamber had no floor. Instead, in front of William, there stretched a magnificent expanse of black water, as glossy and pristine as polished slate, elevated somehow so that it stood away from the chamber's walls and yet forming a perfect rectangle. Along its length on both sides the water murmured as it slid in gauzy silver ribbons down on to the cracked brick below. On one side of the lake the wall rose in great slabs of grey granite that glittered with tiny stars of mica. On the other they ascended in sweeping curves of brick, so slick with nitre that they looked as though they were cast from molten bronze, and adorned with a sequence of chamfered Gothic arches, each one set with panel of stone for a window. Dominating the chamber, set into the glassy surface of the water, were eight stone pillars, their hexagonal columns as thick and silvery as birch trees reaching out their branches twenty feet above the water into a forest canopy of arches. From these arches clusters of pale stalactites hung like pendants of flawless ivory, golden-white in the light of the lantern.

William stared and his breath caught in his throat. Apart from the whisperings of the water the chamber was perfectly silent and still. It wasn't real. It could not possibly be real. William stared and he knew he stared into his own heart. He knew already that he would never come back to this place. He knew that, if he tried to look for it, it would be gone or changed, lost to him in a way he would not be able to bear. But he also knew that he would hold it inside himself forever, this place which by its existence made his own existence possible.

As the months passed, William came increasingly to depend upon the tunnels as the one place where the world was steady. He never again tried to find the chamber. It was enough to know it was there. In the tunnels he breathed more deeply. He had never understood why some of the men found themselves nauseated by the stink underground. To his mind the odour was infinitely more tolerable down in the cold purity of the darkness than it was in the streets above him. In the sewers the smell was simple and direct. In the streets the stink of excrement was but one enemy in an ambush of torments. It knitted itself into the stench of fog and bodies and factories and refuse and the choked tangle of traffic and the never-ending racket and clatter to throttle the senses and make a man mad. In the sewers there was filth and the unpredictable anxieties of tide and weather but within that there prevailed a kind of order. In the sewers a man might feel himself measured by heights and spans and gradients. A man who had never ventured down into the bowels of the capital, be he a man of London all his life, could surely not imagine such a place. For the man who was there, alone in the darkness, it was London that was impossible to imagine.

William's work was largely a matter of routine but its methodical nature satisfied and soothed him. Slowly he grew to understand the shape of the old sewer system, to know his way through its maze of branching veins and arteries. And slowly, so slowly that he hardly dared permit himself to become aware of it, the cravings began to retreat. He went for two weeks without cutting, then three. Time spooled away smoothly and the calmness that settled on him after he cut prevailed in him for longer, persisting for a day, then several days, and on occasion as long as a week. When he returned home to Lambeth he found himself able to listen almost attentively to his wife's chatter, to play with baby William without snapping in frustration at his son's childish demands. Quietened by laudanum he slept at night and his sleep was soft and blank. When Polly rolled against him at night he no longer cried out in fear. Instead he arranged himself around the curve of her and slept on.

At the offices in Greek-street the talk of the other men no longer sounded as indistinct echoes in his ears. William attempted pleasantries and his lips formed them in the correct shapes. He smiled, tentatively perhaps, but at the appropriate moments. It was too late for warmth but little by little the coolness that the other men had determined to reflect back at him was brought up to room temperature. May would always be a queer fellow, on that they were all agreed, but his history, real or imagined, was no longer a subject for muttered discussion. He was an able chap, respectable and polite. He did the work that was required of him quietly and without ceremony. He was content to perform the tasks others disliked. By the time he had been there a year he had become as much a part of the place as the narrow mullioned windows that looked out towards the grey-green scrub of Soho-square, and, like the windows, the other occupants of the office would no doubt have felt the lack of him if one day he was no longer there. While he remained in place, however, they took him quite for granted.

Except for Bazalgette. On more than one occasion William's diligence and eye for detail had brought him to the attention of the Chief Engineer and he watched him with interest. The bulk of his men were competent and almost all of them were better educated and more thoroughly steeped in the theories of civil engineering than May, but no other man under his jurisdiction, engineer or surveyor, had so thorough a practical knowledge of the London sewers in their current state of disintegration. According to the logs, May had covered at least five times more of the network below ground than any other surveyor to the Board. His brick samples, removed from parts of the tunnel at various heights and in varying states of disintegration before being boxed and meticulously labelled in his careful hand, occupied almost a complete room on the fourth floor. When

Bazalgette became preoccupied with the problem of bricks and mortar and their mutual inability to withstand the absorption of water, he had his clerk place a table there where he could work, the samples laid out before him. There could be no drainage without flow of water, that much was clear. But there could be no mains sewerage, to Bazalgette's mind at least, for a city that would soon number three million souls, without bricks and mortar. Local sewers could be constructed from glazed earthenware pipe but they would need to flow into a channel capable of taking many millions of gallons of water every day. In order to accommodate such a flow the main drainage channels in even his earliest plans were twelve feet wide and up to fourteen high. No pipe in the world could be constructed to those dimensions. Stone was expensive and impractical. Only bricks and mortar provided the required strength with the necessary structural flexibility. But ordinary bricks and mortar were porous. They absorbed water and effluvium which caused them to crumble and rot so that they collapsed and caused obstructions. The maintenance required to keep them functioning would be expensive and dele-terious to the system's effectiveness. A different solution was required. Experiments had already been undertaken with Portland cement and its results had exceeded all expectations. Bazalgette had proved that it would provide not only a basis for a mortar that resisted water but one that would harden without needing to dry out. This left him only one problem. In the first short days of 1858, when the snowdrops in Soho-square were still pale green and shuddered unhappily in the windy chill, Bazalgette summoned May and two other engineers to his office and charged them, under the expert guidance of his deputy, Lovick, with the responsibility for developing a prototype for an affordable waterproof brick.

William stared at his supper and rubbed his damp palms on his knees. Though he wore only a cotton shirt the sweat gathered in his armpits and glued the thin fabric to his back. He had no appetite. The limp fish glistened on the plate, its mouth hanging open, as if it too were overcome by the heat.

'A penny for them?'

William blinked and then, recalling himself, smiled up at his wife.

'I was thinking about Staffordshire

Blues,' he said apologetically.

'Let me guess. I don't suppose those would be a kind of brick, would they now?'

'I'm afraid so.'

Polly giggled as she lowered herself carefully into a bentwood chair.

'Well, then, I'm keeping my money, thank you kindly,' she said, shaking her head. 'Your Staffordshires might be as blue as sapphires and a wonder of the world but I've already bought myself enough bricks these last months to build me a mansion.' Breathing heavily she leaned back and fanned herself. 'Oh, will you look at that! How many times have I told that girl to tend to the corners of the room? Ninepence a week and the spiders still have the better of her!'

Polly waved an irritated arm towards the cobweb that drooped from the ceiling but she did not stand. Tendrils of hair clung to her damp face. In the oppressive heat her ankles had swelled and her wrists and even her cheeks until, propped in the hard chair, she resembled an overstuffed doll. Every morning for six long weeks the waking city had stared up into the relentless white kiln of the dawn and wished the sun had already set. There was not the faintest breath of wind. Instead, an open window brought in only the stale sour exhalations of a million bodies in a thousand breathless lanes and courtyards and, more insistently still, of the thick brown putrefying river. The steamboats struggled up and down its soupy length, their wheels churning up its foul shallows and sending the stink slapping against the stone facings of bridges and buildings. In the streets passers-by clutched handkerchiefs to their mouths or wrapped their neckcloths over their faces and tried not to breathe. Everyone feared the cholera, its miasma swelling and thickening until it squatted over the city like a November particular. Those who could had long since left.

Polly's new dress had dark circles beneath the arms and there was a sore patch on her neck where the collar pinched her. She rubbed at it with a puffy finger. The dress had cost more than they could afford but she was a respectable woman now. It would not do to continue to wear the dresses she had worn in service. Besides, the pretty striped stuff had been irresistible. She stroked it fondly.

From upstairs came a low whimper as little William wriggled in his sleep, seeking out a cool place on the sheets.

'Poor lamb, his stomach's still troubling

him,' Polly said, tilting her head towards the sound. 'Godfrey's Cordial always worked a treat with George, especially if you added a little extra poppy-powder, but Sweetie won't take it.'

Her husband was silent. The bulky heat wadded the room. Even the walls sweated, damp patches spreading across the white-wash. When he finally spoke it was so softly that Polly didn't catch the words.

'*Dianthus barbatus.*'

Polly stretched.

'What was that, dear?'

'*Dianthus barbatus.*' He said it slowly, letting the words melt on his tongue. Then he raised his head and looked at her. 'Sweet William.'

For a moment Polly stared at him and her caramel eyes widened.

'You looked it up.'

'Yes.'

'Sweet William. You looked it up.'

The smile spread across her face and through her chest. She had almost given up hoping. His botany books had remained on their high shelf, untouched, their worn leather covers thick with dust. But how silly she'd been, to think he had forgotten. He had been busy with his important work for the Board, that was all. And besides, it hadn't been so long a wait. Baby William was barely three years old. When the time came to enchant him with the story of how his Papa had insisted upon giving them both, his own sweet flowers, their very own scientific names there would be no need to add that he had come by his a little late.

'I shall never remember all of that, you know,' she declared happily, letting her head fall backwards. The sweat slid through her hair, oiling her scalp. 'I shall have to make do with Di.'

'Di will do very well.'

Still smiling Polly ran her fingertips over the silky fabric of her new gown and shut her eyes. William pushed away his plate and contemplated his wife. Her flushed face sparkled and, where it met the curve of her forehead, the chestnut of her hair was stained dark as mahogany. It was unbearably hot. Quietly he picked up an old straw bonnet that hung by its ribbons from a hook by the door and fanned her with it. She touched his arm and murmured something, tipping her head back to catch any trace of coolness in the stirred-up air. Her closed eyelids were oyster-pale and traced with a pattern of blue and violet lines. He fanned her for a long time until her head lolled backwards and tiny snores started to snag in her throat. Then he picked up his botany journals and took them to the back step.

The sky had darkened into a deep blue across which lacy ribbons of pink and gold were sliced into scraps by a scaffold of dark chimneys. Between the step and the out-building that housed the privy the stretch of empty yard was baked hard and the patch of weeds that had flourished at the south end in late spring were bleached and dry. Treacle-mustard, mostly, and goosegrass. Soot had drifted into the corners like black snow. William scratched in the dust with a stick, a cross-hatch of lines. They made bricks from this London clay, yellow stock mostly, a sand-coloured brick flecked with black where the ash it was mixed with had burned into the bricks during firing. Yellow stock was cheap and plentiful but it was much too soft for sewers. It sucked up moisture like a sponge. What was required was for the bricks either to be naturally dense, like Staffordshire Blues which were expensive and in short supply, or to find a technique by which ordinary brick might be glazed, as Mr Doulton had so success-fully managed with earthenware pipes at the Lambeth potteries. But how to manu-facture glazed bricks, which were habitually used only for decorative purposes, economically and on the required scale? The new man, Hawke, claimed it could not be done, that London bricks, fired a little longer than usual, would be perfectly adequate. After all, there were brickworks aplenty in the city and Bazalgette's system would require tens of millions of bricks at the very least. But William had disagreed with him. There was only one place he believed might be able to do it, a Works in Strowbridge where the first-ever glazed porcelain baths had been perfected and manufactured. The baths had won a Gold 'Isis' Medal at the Exhibition in 1851 and were now in great demand from hospitals and public institutions. In order to produce them the firm had patented a series of ten kilns covering two acres of ground which, through an ingenious design and elaborate system of flues, managed to combine great size with economical fuel consumption which allowed for the production of hundreds of baths every week. If they could only expand their kilns or turn their entire production over to bricks —

A soft footfall on the flags of the passage recalled him. The light was almost drained from the sky and the little yard was striped with silver by a coin moon. If she asked he would tell Polly he had been thinking about the garden, he decided hastily. She would like that. But when he turned around it was his son who stared at him, his eyes drooping sleepily, his thumb jammed in his mouth. Tears had dried into salty tracks on his freckled cheeks.

'Hello there, little man,' William murmured, holding his arms open. The boy stumbled into them, already halfway back to sleep as William stood and carried him back up to bed. His bed was bright with moonlight as he laid him down and drew the sheet over him. His eyelids bore the same tracery as his mother's, William thought, as fine and complex as a leaf. Patterns of the kind he drew in the dust with a stick or on his blotter in Greek-street, patterns like —

Reflexively he stroked the underside of his forearm, tracing the lines beneath the thin cotton of his sleeve. There were no open cuts there, nothing but fading scars and clean pink lines marking where the last of the scabs had peeled away. The cravings came less and less often these days. Of course there were many days when he felt uncertain and awkward, carrying himself cautiously and with stiffened arms as though he were water in a flat dish that might spill at any moment. But he no longer felt that he was disappearing. At night he touched Polly's damp slippery summer skin with his fingertips and felt a responsive quiver in his groin. He held his son in his arms and felt the soles of his feet ache with love. He studied the design of a brick and felt his mind stretch and flex. On the best days, if he sat very still, something settled upon him that was almost like contentment. And on the bad ones, when he felt the dish of himself begin to quiver and slop, he took himself quietly into the sewers and remained there until the cravings withdrew.

He had not cut in almost a month. He hardly dared to hope it but in the back of his mind he thought that perhaps the last time had purged him finally of the blackness in his blood. That time the intensity of the experience had transported him beyond any place he had been before and in the exquisite ecstasy of relief he had abandoned himself completely. Time had rushed away. When at last the warning clang of the manhole echoed through the tunnel it took him some minutes to recall himself to the present. His entire being was suffused with a kind of white clean tranquillity across which the letters of his name repeated themselves into infinity. He was William. His thumping heart confirmed it: *William — William — William.* He was safe. He stood and fumbled in his lap for his knife but it was not there. It was not in the recess either. He could remember nothing but he supposed that at some point it must have fallen from his hand into the stream. It was of no consequence. He felt serene, composed. At ground level he pressed a shilling into the palm of the grateful flusher and walked slowly home. It was not until much later that he thought to bathe his arm. He bathed it briskly, hardly looking at it, and swabbed it with iodine. But when he took the pad away and glanced cursorily at the yellow-tinted flesh it was not the sharp sting of the antiseptic that made him draw in his breath. He blinked hard and shook his head to clear it but what he saw remained quite steady. It was unmistakable, the up and down cuts perfectly precise. Hurriedly he washed and wrapped his arm. He would not look at it again. He would think no more of it. It meant nothing. The cuts converged at their edges, that was all. It was a mere happenstance that, instead of the usual long parallel slices drawn across the flesh, he had carved into his arm the deep and distinct shape of a W.

It was another two weeks before the blistering weather broke. But, before it did so, the heat had managed to achieve for the sanitary administration of the capital what the Bengal mutinies the year before had done for the administration of India. The newspapers called it simply the Great Stink. Day after day, week after week, the Stygian pool of the Thames had stewed in the relentless sun and sent its putrid reproaches directly and powerfully into the House of Commons. It was claimed that no one who inhaled the sickening stench would ever forget it, assuming, that was, that he lived long enough to remember it. Sheets soaked in chloride of lime were hung in the riverside windows of the House but they were powerless against the river's onslaught. The stink pressed into the cracks in the mortar, through the painted wood of the panelled walls and upwards through the cellars. The Home Secretary himself was seen rushing from the chamber, his cheeks whiter than the handkerchief he held pressed against his mouth. Parliament could no longer ignore the parlous state of the city's drains. In the week before the summer recess Bazalgette's proposals were approved in full. The Board was endowed with all the powers necessary to proceed without recourse to the vestries. Most importantly an undertaking for the provision of three million pounds was accepted by Parliament, to be repaid by the levying of an extraordinary tax on the city's residents over the next forty years.

London would never be the same again.

VIII

It all changed in the tunnels after that terrible summer, and not for the better neither. For a time, when the heat lay over the city like a filthy blanket, things were quiet. Everyone was strained, weary, oppressed by thirst and terror of the cholera. Grown men fell in the street, unable to take another step. Healthy infants weakened and died. For days there was no water, for all they left the standpipe open day and night, just in case. And everywhere there was the choking shit-reek of the river, persistent as lice. It burrowed through the fibres of your shirt and into your skin. It set up home in your hair and whiskers. It occupied every inch of you, cramming itself into your ears and eyes and nostrils so that you carried it with you and could never get free of it. There was many as had to drink that filthy stream too, there being nothing else. It never rained.

Tom and Joe took Lady down the tunnels nearly every day. While it wasn't so much as cool down there at least you could breathe without the stink forcing your breakfast up into the back of your throat. Over the familiar stench of the stream the air smelled agreeably of wet brick and darkness. The rats were made stupid by the heat, giving themselves up to the crates easy as infants, but at the Badger business was slow. For a while Brassey even shut up shop, claiming that the weather had robbed both men and dogs of their appetite for the kill.

The rats they could not sell Tom put out for Lady. The heat didn't seem to bother her. Methodical as ever, she was, and a quick learner too. Tom taught her all he knew that summer. He showed her where to clamp the rat behind the head when she bit into it so that her teeth pierced its throat and killed it in a single movement. He showed her how to toss her head as she dropped it so that the corpse might be cast aside, out of the way. All the tricks of the trade. And every night he washed out her mouth with peppermint-water to stop the canker coming on and fed her with meat soaked in a little milk to strengthen her muscles. She lay across his legs and panted, her tongue pink as her eyes, Tom's hand upon her head. When he laid her on the bed to sleep his trousers were damp from the heat of her.

At last, as the days shortened, the rain came. As it pitted the brown surface of the river the people poured out of their cramped lanes and courtyards and flowed through the muddy streets. Bad as the rats they were, scrabbling and scrambling and pushing, not even knowing where they was going but bent upon going there all the same. And as for the sewers, why, they was almost as busy. Tom could barely believe what he saw. The rain stopped them for a while. You couldn't go down when the rain was heavy. But once the floods receded there were men of all kinds down there day and night. Small wooden sheds with tarpaulin lids sprouted over gratings and manholes. Often Tom caught the echo of voices and had to retreat into the darkness or take a different path. You couldn't rely on the flushers to help you out no more neither. There had been a time when the flushers had known what was what, when them and the toshers had rubbed along together well enough. One of the old gangers over Bermondsey way had even been on the tosh himself when he was a lad. It was only when his old man died and the business wasn't so good that he'd gone over to the flushing, tempted by the regular wage. The two of them weren't so different when it came to it, Tom reckoned, both of them making their livings by knowing the tunnels like the backs of their hands and sorting out what got itself stuck there, only because they wasn't in competition or nothing there wasn't no need for trouble. The same way the flushers helped the tosh by making sure the tunnels didn't block up or collapse, the toshers cleaned out the overflows and kept down the rats. It was true that the flushing had the advantage of being lawful but it wasn't as if flushers were the kind of folks that had much affection for the law. When it came to a choice between a tosher and a trap the sensible flusher knew whose side he was on.

Until now. Something about the elegant company they were suddenly keeping had gone to the flushers' heads. Or perhaps it was the newspapers, trumpeting on fit to bust about the triumphal glories of civilization and all that whatnot. Time was, you only had to worry about the peelers or the johnnies on the water. Now the flushers were worse than both put together. The boatmen and the coppers only got the whiff of you if you were fool enough to let them. They had to see your lantern from the river or through a grating, or spot you as you were slipping in and out. But the flushers were right there in the tunnels with you. If a flusher heard something suspicious he'd go after it. And any flusher worth his salt knew the tunnels well as you did. If he was fixed on finding you and had the time for it, you were in trouble. All you could do was to go slow and steady and hope to the Almighty that if you got too close they were with their fancy gents. There wasn't any flusher who'd risk leaving them alone with naught but a lantern for company. A gent'd scream bloody blue murder.

It was around the time of the shooting star they called Donati's Comet that Limping Gil and two of his men got hauled up and given three months in Millbank.

'The sky lit up like Moses & Son, folks on every bridge and street corner, and what does he do?' Joe scoffed when he heard the news. 'He couldn't have showed himself up more clear if he'd gone to Parliament and asked 'em directions.'

Tom laughed but he was uneasy. The back of his neck prickled, the way it did when something wasn't right. And then a week later the two of them almost got done for under Newgate. They were in the cavern where the rats bred, had their crates open and all. There was barely time to pull the basket into the shadows. The flushers had open lanterns and they swung them about, splattering light into all the safe corners. They'd have been fingered for sure except that all of a sudden the cornered rats had got it in their heads to fly at the intruders like a swarm of wild bees.

'Those dumb beasts don't know which side their bread's buttered,' Joe remarked dryly when he and Tom finally emerged on to the street. 'Taking our side? Anyone'd think they was after getting themselves topped.'

But they were both more cautious after that. They didn't say anything to each other but both of them knew what the other was thinking. Bit by bit the sewers were shutting themselves up tight as mussels and there wasn't nothing could be done about it. They might be able to eke it out for another year or two but, the way things were headed, with the sluice-gates and the gents and the flushers on the nab, it was only a matter of time before the business would be gone. It wasn't so bad for Joe. He knew a few men from his days on the pure, he might be able to find something in the way of work in the tanyards even it was just hauling skins. But

Tom was too old. He'd made good money in his day, from the rats especially, but it wasn't the way of toshers to be prudent with their haul or to hold something back for a rainy day. You went in, you got what you could, you spent it, and when your belly and your pockets were empty and the landlord needed paying you went back in. The sewers would always be there, that's the way the toshers had it figured, ready to give up their prizes to them that knew the game. Only now it seemed they'd figured it wrong.

Except Tom had Lady. The night after they burned the effigy of Guy Fawkes at Vauxhall Tom took her to the Black Badger. When he told Brassey he would be putting a dog of his own into the ring the proprietor merely shrugged. He was distracted. That day he'd had word that, after a long absence, the Captain was due to return. Hastily he scrawled Lady's name on a grimy piece of paper and nodded towards an empty bench.

'She's good,' Tom said quietly.

'Is it?' Brassey shrugged carelessly. His eyes were pinned on the door. 'Well, throw it up there when the time comes. It can go in if there's interest enough.'

'Ain't that pink beast old Jeremiah's

169

bitch?' one man asked another as the room filled up, jabbing a finger in Lady's direction. In his grubby choker and torn frock-coat he had the disgruntled whiff of a clergyman fallen on hard times. His face was veined with blue like Stilton cheese.

His associate, a costermonger who smelled strongly of tainted meat, shook his head as he squeezed Lady's paws.

'Can't be. Jerry hopped the twig more than three months back. Anyways his dog had nothing in the way of flesh on its bones. This one's a rum looker, I'll grant you, but there's power in them haunches —'

At this the costermonger threw a cautious glance over his shoulder and dropped his voice to a whisper.

A little later Brassey skipped over to the door. The Captain had arrived. Again he was accompanied by his narrow-faced friend who looked, to Tom's reckoning, even thinner than before.

'You'd better have some killers here tonight, Frank. Some fresh blood.' The Captain smiled, baring his teeth. 'I have no wish to be disappointed again.'

'Captain, Captain, disappointed? With the sport we have for you tonight?' Brassey oozed, his neckless head rolling in its socket. 'I hardly think so.'

His toad smile stretched wide. But when he spun round to seize his boy by the scruff of the neck, it shrivelled like it'd been sprinkled with salt. If the upstairs room was not open in two minutes, he hissed into the lad's ear, punishments would rain down upon his head like all the judgements of Hell.

Pointing the way with his toes, Brassey led the Captain to his box. But the Captain wouldn't sit. Instead, cheered by his companion who shrieked and clutched his handkerchief to his mouth like a lady prone to the faint, he climbed into the pit. Pushing Brassey's lad aside, he began to yank the rats one by one from their crate by their tails. The omnibus driver cautioned him against being bitten but he took not the least notice. When one of the creatures attempted to scramble up his leg he snatched it off and tossed it into the air.

'Get off of me, you varmint,' he snarled and, kicking out with a boot while the creature was still in mid-air, sent it flying across the pit where it landed with a dull smack against the far wall. A loud cheer went up from the Fancy. The Captain gave a bow and, kicking out at two more rats that sniffed at the cuff of his trouser, climbed out of the pit and snapped his fingers.

'Come on!' he growled. His face was flushed and he leaned so far forward over the pit that the gas-lamps lit flames in his dark eyes. 'Let's have it.'

The first dog wasn't up to much, nor the second neither, come to that. Angrily the Captain summoned a couple of dependable owners and demanded that they put their animals into the ring. Reluctantly they shook their heads, claiming their dogs to be out of sorts or not yet ready for such big ones. The Captain's face darkened. Grabbing his friend's cane he swung its round silver top hard at the milling rats. It wasn't long before he caught one on the skull. The creature staggered across the pit and collapsed.

'For Christ's sake! If *I* can do it —' he hissed at his friend, who sniggered and inspected the bloodstains on his cane, the point of his tongue thrust between his teeth as if he would lick them off.

Apprehensively Brassey had another dog put into the ring. Its face was set into a vicious sneer but it made only halfhearted moves towards its prey, starting like a child as a rat sprang into its face and backing towards its second. The second drummed his hands together furiously and barked at the dog to go at them but for all his efforts

172

the dog looked more anxious than blood-thirsty. It made a few feeble pounces but the rats had him rattled and they knew it. Together they advanced on the dog. Angrily the Captain kicked at the pit and called for an end to it.

'You waste my time, Brassey,' the Captain spat. 'I would have seen more sport at a Sewing Circle.'

'Come now, my friend,' Brassey soothed, the sweat greasing his forehead. 'Be patient. We have barely begun.'

The Captain jeered and snatched up his hat. Behind him his companion tugged at his neckcloth, a simpleton's smirk plucking at the corners of his mouth.

'Come, Henry,' the Captain barked. 'We shall not trouble ourselves again with so inferior a place.'

This *was* sport. The Fancy quietened down to watch.

'Gentlemen, gentlemen, please. Not so fast.' Brassey's little eyes darted around the room. 'Ah, Tom! Now, gentlemen, here we have a dog for your consideration. Never fought before.'

The Captain growled angrily and kicked over his chair.

'Not here, that is,' Brassey added hastily. 'But she's a champion in the Borough. Famous there, she is. A *phee-nomenon.* Right, Tom? Famous, you two is, in the Borough.'

He gave Tom's sleeve a sharp twist. Tom said nothing but his hand sought out Lady's ears. She rubbed her head against his palm.

'A phenomenon?' the Captain said contemptuously. 'That mongrel?'

A low rumble of laughter ran around the room. Brassey gulped and his toad eyes bulged.

'Assuredly. Laid good money on her myself, many a time.' He licked his lips as he made a show of setting the Captain's chair upright and brushing the sawdust from its seat. 'Go on, Tom. Show the Captain what she's made of.'

The Captain hesitated. Then with a shrug he tossed his hat back on his chair and folded his arms over his chest. He did not sit down.

'Well, go on then, mongrel man,' he drawled. 'Let the massacre begin.'

A fresh mound of rats was released into the pit. Very quietly Tom untied the rope from around Lady's neck and held her face between his hands. She stared at him steadily with her pink eyes. Then he held her over the wall of the ring.

'What are you doing?' Brassey hissed, his face scarlet. 'You's the second, ain't yer? You got to get in with her.'

But Tom shook his head.

'No. She don't like it.'

'For the love of God, man —'

Ignoring the publican Tom lowered Lady gently to the floor. The Fancy muttered, shaking their heads. The Captain glowered. For a moment Tom remained quite still, his hands around the drum of Lady's chest, his fingers slotted between her ribs. The Captain tapped a restless boot and drummed his fingers on the pit wall. Brassey clenched his damp fists and closed his eyes. Then Tom stood, folding his hands together. He looked steadily down at the dog. Lady paused, her own gaze set thoughtfully upon the squalling mound of rats. She looked small and very pink.

And then, without a sound, she set about the killing. One after the other she killed them, another and then another, barely pausing to take a breath. The Fancy stared, their mouths open. The Captain's fingers stopped drumming to grip the rim of the pit. His eyes sharpened with greed and delight. In hardly more than a minute a dozen rats with scarlet necks lay dying around the ring and the white paint of the pit was grained with blood. When time was called the corpses piled like dirty sandbags against the walls. Tom called quietly to Lady. Obediently she sat, every muscle taut, her eyes fixed on the few live rats that were left.

There was a moment of stunned silence and then the shouts erupted. The Captain beat his fists hard against the pit wall. His eyes flashed and his breath came in quick pants like a dog.

'More!' he urged. 'Give her more!'

Excitedly the Fancy took up the call. *More! More!* Fists full of coins punched the air. *More! Here! More!*

'Why not indeed!' crowed Brassey, dancing in delight as he spied the note slotted between the Captain's friend's fingers. 'Give the beast another round.'

Tom reached down into the pit and lifted Lady into his arms. Shouts of protest rang round the parlour.

'That'll do,' Tom said quietly.

'But Tom — Tom, come now, another twenty —' Brassey protested.

'She's done,' he repeated firmly.

'A fine killer.' The Captain spoke softly, leaning towards Tom. He reached a hand out to touch Lady's head but the dog drew her lips back from her teeth in a silent snarl. Smiling faintly the Captain reached into his pocket for a cigar. 'A fine, fine killer.'

'I told you, didn't I?' Brassey interrupted triumphantly, a lit match flaring from his fingers. 'A phenomenon. And Tom means to fight her here regular, ain't that right, my friend? Regular.'

The Captain inhaled and leaned up against the wall so Brassey was pushed out.

'I'm looking for a dog,' he said to Tom.

Tom waited. The Captain pursed his lips and released the smoke in a neat chain of rings.

'If yours can kill fifteen in a single minute I'll give you fifty guineas for her.'

'One hundred.'

The Captain choked on a mouthful of smoke.

'One hundred guineas?' he coughed. 'Are you out of your mind?'

'That's the price.'

The Captain looked Tom up and down. The tosher's hair was crusted into clumps and the reek of the sewers clung to his old coat. God only knew how bad he smelled to the dog who had her nose tucked right into one torn lapel. One hundred guineas! The old trickster must take him for a fool.

A tramp like that would take fifty and think himself the luckiest cove alive.

'It's quite impossible,' he said with a shrug. 'Fifty's the best I can do.'

Tom shrugged back.

'One hundred,' he said again.

The two men stared at each other for a moment. Tom's face held steady but the Captain's eye twitched and two spots of red burned in his cheeks.

'Seventy-five,' the Captain said at last.

Tom raised one eyebrow.

'Good night, Brassey,' he said quietly, nodding over the Captain's shoulder.

'Tom, come now,' urged Brassey, eyeing the Captain nervously. 'Seventy-five guineas —'

'Good night,' Tom said again.

The Captain must have had a long stride. He was at the parlour door as Tom reached out to open it.

'Eighteen in a minute.'

'One hundred guineas?'

'One hundred guineas.'

Tom thought for a moment, his hand caressing Lady's ear. Then he nodded.

'Tomorrow night?' the Captain demanded.

Tom shook his head.

'The dog needs rest. Give us a month.'

The Captain sneered but his eyes fixed on Lady as if she was a slab of steak.

'I thought she was supposed to be a *phee-nomenon.*'

'You saw her.'

'A phenomenon with no stomach for the fight,' the Captain snapped, jabbing at the dog's nose with the lit end of his cigar. 'You think I'm paying one hundred guineas for *that?*'

'So don't,' Tom replied with a shrug.

The Captain chewed on his cigar before spitting out a ball of smoke.

'All right. All right,' he allowed angrily. 'One month from today.'

'One hundred guineas,' Tom repeated slowly, savouring the taste.

'One hundred guineas.' The Captain scowled at the dog but greed softened the corners of his mouth. 'The beast'd better prove herself worth it.'

One hundred guineas. That night Tom carried Lady all the way home, hugged against his chest. One hundred guineas. Eighteen in a minute was a push but not impossible, not for Lady. She wasn't no ordinary dog. Tom'd get his one hundred guineas, there was no doubt of it. Who cared now if they built the Queen of England a palace down the tunnels? He'd not have to go down there again for nothing, not if he lived another dozen years. One hundred guineas! The price of thousands upon thousands of rats, years of rats even if they were still there for the catching — for just one dog. Someone had been smiling on him, the day he'd picked up Lady outside the Badger. Who'd've thought a man like him would have luck like that? *One hundred guineas. One hundred guineas!* It was nothing short of a miracle.

Back in his lodgings the two of them shared a dish of stew. Tom felt the first stirrings of anxiety. Perhaps he'd been wrong to insist on a month. It was time enough for the Captain to change his mind, for another dog to take his fancy. Tom swallowed firmly and took another bite of bread. Dogs like Lady didn't come along every day. And this way he'd have time to work her that bit more, so as to be sure of the prize. In a few weeks he'd have his hundred guineas — one hundred guineas! And the Captain, well, the Captain would have Lady. Tom's hand crept unbidden to the spot on the dog's belly where she liked to be scratched. She curled herself blissfully round it and closed her eyes. She'd have a good life with the Captain. A one hundred-guinea dog'd live like a queen, best cuts of meat at every meal. He tried not to remember the way the Captain had looked at Lady, greedily, like he might eat her. Most likely he'd have her sleep on his own bed, to keep her from thieves. One hundred guineas. He must've seen she'd be a champion.

Gravy slopped from the dish of stew on to the bare boards of the floor. Tom's knees were trembling. It was the weight of her, too heavy for his old legs. He put the dish down and Lady stretched out across his lap, contented as a cat. The candlelight made her look pinker than ever. She was a rum-looking beast, he thought to himself, and he felt something choking him, like a piece of meat had got itself stuck in his throat. He swallowed hard but it didn't shift. His nose prickled. Impatiently he rubbed it on his sleeve. He'd never needed nobody, not his whole life. Being alone was the way of things for him. He'd always liked it that way, no one to depend on him, to be a burden on him. He was too old for that sort of thing, these days. And Lady, well, Lady was going up in the world. It wouldn't be long before she'd have herself a fancy gold collar like the stuffed champion at the Badger, maybe even two collars. Her life'd be that flashy she'd never stop to think on her old master in his mean lodgings above the courtyard in St Giles. Like enough she'd think herself well shot of him. She was set to be a champion, this one, and he wished her well. All he could hope for was she wouldn't forget him, old Tom who'd set her on her way. He wouldn't forget her. He would never forget her. He wrapped his arms around her, so tight she snapped at him sleepily and wriggled out of his embrace. He did not move himself until the rush-light had burned itself out and the very last of her warmth had cooled from his lap.

IX

'Fifty brickyards right here in London and you tell me we have to go *where* for our bricks?'

'Strowbridge, sir. It's in ———shire.'

'How many times do I have to caution you on this matter?' Hawke snapped. 'Do you have any notion of the expense of transporting bricks more than one hundred and fifty miles?'

'Of course, sir. Here, I have detailed our calculations.'

Hawke snatched at the sheaf of papers that William held out to him. Glancing at the first page he smacked at it dismissively with the back of his hand and his face darkened. William bit his lip but he stood his ground. Hawke's anger was regrettable, since Hawke was not only his superior but wielded considerable authority with the Board of Works, but nonetheless in this instance William considered himself on safe ground. The brick specifications to which Hawke objected so strongly had been laid down by Bazalgette himself. In the tests that they had run upon them, the Strowbridge bricks had shown themselves to be ideal for the purpose. Indeed William had, in the course of the last months, come to suspect that Hawke's fits of anger, although frequent and excessively convincing, might not reflect his true state of mind. It was Hawke's job to account for every penny spent by the Board and to ensure that every possible economy and efficiency could be made. Intimidation was doubtless a useful tool in those negotiations. But even bullying could only achieve so much. Already arrangements were being finalized for the first sewer excavations to begin. Contracts with the brickyards would need to be drawn up before Christmas. Bellow and bluster he might but sooner or later Hawke would have to accept that, although more costly than he wished, the approval of the contract with the Strowbridge Works was as inevitable as it was justifiable.

'The assumptions we have made are detailed in the appendix,' William said evenly. 'Mr Lovick agrees that they are as accurate as can be expected at this time.'

Hawke glared at William, thrusting the fistful of papers into William's face.

'This is impossible! There are yards

right here in London that will produce bricks at half this price. Less than half. Alfred England's yard, to name but one. You will cease this nonsense about Strowbridge and work with those brickyards, with England's, damn you, or I will have you hauled up in front of the Board. Do I make myself clear?'

Wadding the papers into a ball, he tossed them in the direction of the wastepaper basket. William resisted the urge to retrieve them. A muscle in Hawke's cheek twitched as he leaned across his desk.

'Is it your expressed intention that this project founder, Mr May? Or perhaps you stand to gain directly from the Strowbridge contract? Is that it? They cutting you in, are they? How much, May, eh? Hundreds? More, surely? Thousands?'

William gasped. He understood the requirement for Hawke to press him on decisions of this nature, to ensure that the Board's money was properly spent, but to make so low a charge, to impugn not only William's judgement but his good name, his honour? The anger boiled in his chest. But at the same time he was certain that that was what Hawke hoped for, that he would lose control. He would not lose control. Clenching his fists, William took a deep breath.

'As I am sure you are aware, sir,' he replied carefully, 'the Committee has clearly stipulated that all contracts shall be awarded solely on the basis of merit. And, as we have discussed on a number of previous occasions, no London brickyard can meet the specifications required by Mr Bazalgette.'

'Do you take me for a fool, you insolent clod?' Hawke hissed. 'England's brickyard incapable of producing bricks?'

'Of producing the right bricks, sir.'

'Then, dammit, man, it's down to you to show 'em how!'

'That would be quite impossible, sir. You see, the methods used by the Strowbridge Works are protected under patent.'

'Under patent? If that is the concern — !' Hawke passed an incredulous hand over his forehead before permitting himself a small chilly smile of the variety proffered by schoolteachers to obstinately ignorant children. 'Let me tell you something, Mr May. Patents are — well, let us just say that there is no reason they should limit our operations. You have visited these Works, have you not? And you understand the principles of their production? Well, then.

England's is an established and reputable yard that is prepared to offer us extremely favourable terms. If we simply employ the Strowbridge techniques there I am sure that the necessary adjustments can be made to ensure we are not in — how can I put it? — direct infringement. Patents, Mr May, are notoriously difficult to protect. If that is the only obstacle —'

'I am afraid it is not that simple, sir,' William countered. 'Even if we were to disregard the patent, which I had understood to be in breach of law, the complex kiln system at Strowbridge has taken years to perfect. Even if we were able to copy so sophisticated a system it would surely be an impossibility in the time that we have to produce sufficient bricks of the required quality —'

'Enough!' Hawke slammed his fist down on to his leather blotter. Piles of papers shuddered in alarm. Very slowly, Hawke leaned over the desk until his face almost touched William's. His dark eyebrows were shiny with oil. He smelled sharply of sweat and taverns.

'You listen to me, May,' he snarled. Flecks of saliva gathered in the corners of his mouth. 'I have tried to reason with you. For months now I have tried to reason with you. But of course I wasted my time. Who after all can hope to reason with a lunatic? Oh yes, I know all about you. Did you think you were safe because Rawlinson kept his mouth shut? Well, I'm so terribly sorry to have to disappoint you. You see, I know everything. All of it. You lost your wits against the Russians, didn't you, you filthy coward? Went barmy, deranged, stark staring mad, off your head. God damn it, you loon, they should lock you up and throw away the key. You think I don't know what you do down there in those sewers when you think you're all alone? You're a deviant, May, a freak of nature. Do you hear me? You disgust me. You'd disgust any right-minded, God-fearing Christian. The members of the Board, for example. What do you think they would say if they knew about your perversions? Do you really think they would permit you to remain in employment here? Do you? Do you?'

Hawke's face was so close that William could see into the slick dark pinpricks of his pores. William clenched his hands in front of him. He said nothing. He felt pale, cold, as insubstantial as smoke. Then, abruptly, Hawke pulled away. When he spoke again his voice was as smooth as a blade.

'Tomorrow you will meet Alfred England. You will inform him in detail of whatever improvements he needs to make to his yards here in London in order to produce these bricks so beloved of Mr Bazalgette. And you would be prudent to ensure it is done to your own satisfaction because when the time comes for tenders to be put out you will personally endorse the quality of England's product. You will not support the Strowbridge tender because if you do so I will be obliged to share with the Board all I know. All of it. After that, well, we could hardly expect them to continue to offer you employment. Or indeed any other reputable business, come to that. It would be quite unthinkable, would you not agree? There is little hope for the future for a man whose good character has suffered so severe a setback. You will lose everything.'

Hawke's mouth twisted in grim amusement as he brushed imaginary specks from his sleeve. William stared back at him, his face ashen. Words whirled in his head and were gone. His tongue, his lips, they recognized none of them.

'I believe our business is complete. But I would reassure you that I am a man of my word.' Hawke's smile twitched. 'It would be inadvisable to put me to the test. Good day, sir.'

William did not remember how he found his way back to his cubbyhole or the hours that followed as he sat quite rigid, staring at the wall. His finger ran automatically down columns of figures and across sectional drawings but the pencil marks blurred and swayed and he made no sense of them. The fear and the self-hatred reacted together like yeast on dough, swelling inside him till he could hardly breathe. He had thought himself almost safe. He had not cut for weeks. Outside the November afternoon was already darkening. It had been a long dry autumn. Fallen leaves were pounded into coppery dust by the incessant traffic and in the early afternoons the melted-butter sun pooled on the sooty back step. Not that William was in Lambeth to see it. Now that Bazalgette's great project had begun the offices at Greek-street were frenzied with activity. Every day there were queries and calculations and contracts to be resolved. William was frequently at his desk before seven, not returning home until late into the evening. But on Sundays he had begun once again to sketch. He bought a new journal in soft tan leather in which he might record in ink and watercolour the flowers that flourished in the scrub ground around the railway line. At the same time he purchased a cloth-covered sketchbook and a quiver of coloured pencils for Di so that he might sit beside his father, his tongue jutting from his teeth as he formed his own ragged petals and leaves. In late September, William had brought home spoiled sheets of onion-skin on which he had started, tentatively at first and then with growing warmth, to plan the garden. There would be vegetables, naturally, but he thought little of those. He concentrated instead on the sunny southern strip of the yard. There he and Di would plant flowers for Polly. For Polly and the infant. For Polly was once again with child. Night after night, as she slept beside him, William cupped the swell of her belly gently in his hands and planned the cradle he would make for it. Di had never had a cradle. At the old woman's house in Battersea, Polly had told him, the children had lain wrapped in fruit-box rows like apples. But this baby would have a cradle, a rocking cradle with drapes and a tiny quilt, a cradle fit for a fairy tale. And William would open the door in Lambeth and the cradle would be set before a blazing fire and Polly would smile and hold her finger to her lips because in the perfect cradle the child would be sleeping, its tiny pink mouth curved in a tiny pink smile. And all would be as it was supposed to be. As they had dreamed it would be.

The fire in the surveyors' room had sunk and the ash sighed as it dropped into the grate. William's hands were frozen, tinged blue around the knuckles. He was quite alone. Hawke's vicious words blundered around his head but they were no more than black shadows that evaded him and made him dizzy. He had to confront them, even as he sat shivering in his cold stall he knew that. He had to grasp them, to bend them to his own will, or he would lose everything. *You will lose everything.* But, however stridently he repeated this terrible mantra it slithered away from him so that somehow he could not hold on to the truth of it. His mind was sealed shut. His heart shrivelled, clenched as hard as a walnut, and refused to allow it in. William saw this and he loathed himself for his weakness. He knew already that he would stand aside, watching the inexorable onslaught of his own ruin, and that he would do nothing. He would feel nothing. He clenched his fists, driving his knuckles into the flesh of his thighs as the blackness began to fill him, slowly at first, drifting like soot and then in an unstoppable flood of such intensity that it crushed the organs in his chest and poisoned the marrow of his bones. It crammed into his eyes until he could see nothing but blackness, wadding his head with a kind of incessant merciless screech. He could not breathe. The blackness choked his lungs and closed its sinewy tentacles around his throat. Discarded on his desk was a knife of the kind used for cutting newspapers. Its silver blade flickered, a slice of perfect light in the blind blackness. It was blunt but one edge of the blade was serrated so that if you bore down on it hard enough and sawed with sufficient savagery —

Afterwards he supposed he had walked around the city for many hours. His feet ached and the cuffs of his trousers were thick with dust. Shortly before sunrise he returned to the cottage in Lambeth for a fresh shirt. The sleeves of the old one hung in bloody tatters. He rolled it into a ball and concealed it in the narrow cupboard beneath the stairs. Polly and the child were not yet awake. In the kitchen he poured out water and washed. The ragged wounds in his arms were filthy and rough with cotton fibres but his hands did not shake as he cleaned and wrapped them and quietly left the house. He felt calm and very clear.

It was going to be another fine day. The sun was a freshly-washed lemon against the pale blue of the sky and the last of the brown leaves drifted from the low branches of the plane trees like wizened hands. As he crossed the river he looked downstream to where the first iron ribs of the new Westminster Bridge drew thick black lines against the sunlit lace of the river. Beyond it, alongside a vast trench dug into the north bank of the river, great heaps of scaffold jostled with wooden huts and piles of earth and clay and, presiding over the magnificent chaos, a giant crane, its mighty arm held aloft in triumph. Across the city, London was in a state of siege and barricade, fortifications bristling in every street as the mud was carted away and in its place the foundations laid for new and better buildings, faster railways, straighter, broader thoroughfares. The force of progress was constant and unstoppable. It drove tirelessly through the London clay, pushing upwards through the mud into colonnades and spires, downwards into tunnels and buried palaces. The most a man could

hope for was to harness that energy to re-
fine it, so that the spires might be glorious
against the morning sky, and the course of
the tunnels forever solid and true. And
long after the sordid stories of ordinary
lives ill-lived had been lost from memory
those spires and tunnels would endure.
And, although there might be no other witnesses, perhaps in time those spires and
tunnels might come to stand, in some unseen way, as a testament to the possibility
that something approximating to honour
might at last be coaxed from the broken
seeds of a dishonourable life.

Alfred England was a big man, broad
and aggressively be-whiskered, but he had
an unnaturally high-pitched voice and a
jumpy demeanour. Often during their en-
counter that day and on other days that
followed, his features would shift through a
number of expressions as though trying
them out before settling upon one.

Hawke, for his part, oozed an oily com-
plicity. He clapped William chummily
upon the shoulder when he effected the in-
troductions and spoke in smoothly confi-
dential tones of the partnership he hoped
to broker between the two men. William
shook the yard-owner's hand reluctantly.

He had hoped that he would have the opportunity to speak to Hawke earlier in the day and thereby avoid such a meeting altogether but, whether intentionally or otherwise, Hawke had proved elusive, making his own way to the brickyard and sending a hansom to bring William from Greek-street. The roads south were crowded and, despite the shouts of the driver and the skittish energy of his horse, the cab made slow progress. Inside the seat was dusty and smelled sharply of stale sweat. William set his feet wide on the floor as the vehicle jolted along Victoria-street, pitching steeply to avoid a sheep that had skittered away from the flock grazing outside Westminster Abbey. He felt cold and perfectly calm. Beneath its bandages his forearm throbbed comfortingly. England's brickyard would never be considered for tender. It specialized in the type of cheap brick used by speculators to throw up the back-to-back terraced housing that squeezed itself into the cramped spaces alongside factories and railway lines and which sucked rain and soot into their flimsy walls as greedily as a sponge.

A pair of tall wrought-iron gates bore the legend ENGLAND & SON across them. The porter yawned as he slowly dragged them open, displaying the half-chewed fragments of his lunch. Stepping down from the cab William took a yellow brick from a quantity stacked beside a wall and weighed it in his hand. It was as light and porous as pumice. Many others in the heap were obvious clinkers, bricks that had been severely burned or had cracked and warped during firing. The yard itself was oddly quiet. A few men lugged pallets of bricks to a covered wagon that stood at the far end of the yard and the chimneys of the kiln belched black smoke but there was none of the usual bustle and clamour of a busy enterprise. Against one wall a pair of heavy-shouldered men with the shaggy muscularity of carthorses leaned and stared at William as he picked his way across the rough ground. One of them held a pipe concealed behind his back. In the dry weather the mud had hardened into deep ruts and rising up from their serrated foundations the vast mounds of bricks looked as raw and desolate as abandoned dwellings.

'Business slow? Goodness, no!' England's glance flickered uneasily towards Hawke, whose face twitched into a frown as he gave a barely perceptible nod. 'There continues to be a great demand for our bricks.

This is England's, after all. We have one of the finest reputations in London. But we have slowed our production to enable us to concentrate exclusively upon the requirements of the Board.' England cleared his throat. 'We understand you need us to move with all possible speed.'

William had a sudden image of a woman, one palm cradling her swollen belly, the other clasping the hand of a small boy. The hands were rough with work and with the effort of holding on. Polly. And his mother. Both of them, distinct and yet indistinguishable, like the picture his teacher had shown him once that was both a bird and a rabbit depending on which you chose to see. He had never forgiven his father for dying, even though he had seen with his own eyes the grocer's desperate struggle to stay alive. Others in their small town had observed the same. It was generally agreed that the death of the shopkeeper, unlike some they could mention, had been managed in an exemplary fashion. And so, even in their poverty, his family had retained something of their old respectability. When they had been forced to accept the helping hand of charity it had proffered a lofty glove but never a punitive one. It would not be so for Polly. The disgrace would hang about her, layer upon layer, like mourning veils, stifling her light, trumpeting her forever as one apart, as untouchable. All that she had determined not to know would be known by all. Her husband would be proclaimed a coward, a lunatic, a mortal danger to himself and — the leap was small, little more than a step — to others. Who could know what terrors the madman concealed in their midst had intended? Hawke's whispers would carry on the wind, titillating London's parlours and clubs with their hints and intimations. Right-minded people would shun them, quivering with self-righteous disgust. Their merciless grind of poverty would be appropriate punishment, their shame God's will. What then? Where would they go? What would they do?

As he opened his mouth William prayed for Polly's blessing and forgiveness.

'Mr England, there can be no possibility of a contract between England's and the Board. Such a contract would be in breach of both the letter and the spirit of the work the Board has undertaken for the healthful future of London. I thank you for your time and wish you fortune in all your future enterprises. And now, if you will excuse me, I am afraid I must return to Greek-street immediately.'

Although William had hardly thought beyond the necessity of making his position perfectly clear, he realized when it did not happen that he had half-expected Hawke to hit him. As it was the man remained quite still, caught in the dusty beam of sunlight that sliced through the high window. His face was turned away from William, his shoulders set with fury or shock. It was England who leaped to his feet, his limbs jumping and twitching like a tangled marionette. His cheeks were an ashy white blotched with red and he raked his fingers through his bushy hair until it stood up on its ends.

'What is it that you *want* from me? More, is that it? You — you leeches! Would you see me — ?'

'Be quiet, you fool!'

Hawke slammed a hand down on the desk, palm flat, but his face was clenched with barely suppressed fury. Abruptly the door of the office banged open to reveal a burly-looking foreman in a canvas apron, his thick arms crossed across his chest. The sleeves of his shirt were rolled high to expose the faded blue outlines of a seaman's tattoos. William backed towards the door. The foreman braced himself, blocking the doorway and cleared his throat.

' 'Speriencin' any trouble, Mr England, sir?'

Hawke gave a little snarl. His nostrils were white with contempt. Slowly, his gaze never leaving England's, he raised his hand and closed it into a fist which he brought slowly upwards, pressing his knuckles fastidiously against the corners of his mouth. The brickyard owner smoothed his lapels. His hands trembled but the colour was returning patchily to his face.

'No trouble, Briggs,' he said. His voice was gluey and he cleared his throat before continuing. 'Although I think it would be appropriate if you remained in the outside office while I complete my business with Mr Hawke. There may be matters upon which I will wish to consult you.'

'Very good, sir.'

The door closed again. William inclined his head.

'If you will excuse me, gentlemen —'

'We are not yet finished.'

It was Hawke now who blocked the path to the door.

'You appear not to appreciate the gravity of your situation, Mr May,' he said. His voice was smooth, almost congenial, but his eyes flickered like a snake's. 'It is my opinion that we have reached a critical point in our negotiations. A wrong turning at this juncture would be ruinous for you, I fear.'

England watched William's face and his fingertips tap-tap-tapped in tiny movements against the polished wood of his desk.

'It would be sheer folly to leave this room, Mr May,' Hawke murmured. 'I commend you to consider your reputation, your responsibilities to your family. There can be no returning from this.'

William gazed steadily at Hawke and then, turning to England, he touched his hat.

'Good day, gentlemen.'

Perhaps it was the recognition of defeat that rooted Hawke to the spot. More likely it was simple astonishment. In the small anteroom outside the foreman half-raised himself from his seat, his neck straining against its collar like an impatient dog's, but no instruction came from his master. He could only watch as William walked briskly past him and out into the yard.

In the days that followed William waited for the summons to the Board. His belly crawled with the certainty of disaster. He saw Hawke only once, at a committee meeting to discuss the progress of excavations beneath the heath at Hampstead. Shortly before the meeting was brought to a close Hawke made a show of passing a hastily scrawled note to Lovick which Lovick placed unopened in the pocket of his coat. As William passed him in the shadowy corridor at the close of the meeting Hawke shook his head and smiled.

And so William waited. The days stretched into weeks and still there was no word from the Board. Lovick and his fellow engineers treated him as they always had, with a tolerant disinterest. He worked late into the nights preparing his formal recommendation to Bazalgette that the Board accept the tender of the Strowbridge brickyard. He assembled samples. He calculated measurements and drafted sectional drawings. He continued to make his regular visits into the sewers. At home he labelled his botanical drawings and added details to his plans for the garden. But he felt no urge to cut. A calmness had settled upon him, a calmness that both relieved and baffled him. He grew thin and pale but he didn't grow desperate. He watched as Polly ripened and slowed and complained contentedly of the idleness of the girl who helped in the house. He noticed with a squeeze of his heart how Di's hair had thickened and how his baby wrists had hardened and sprouted from the cuffs of his jacket, and he felt a deep quiet shame and regret. But the terrible blackness did not come. At first he did not trust its absence, probing for it, as a tongue will seek out the pain from a rotten tooth, despite itself. After all it had happened before, this slippage of time when the blackness had held off for days, weeks sometimes, but always it had come, darker and more warped by its delay. And still it did not come. William hardly dared believe it — that, just as Hawke was fashioning his trap, he might at last be free.

X

Only a fool'd have taken a man like the Captain at his word and Tom was no fool. Whenever the tides were right he took Lady down the tunnels. And at night, when there was a fight on, he went to the Badger, by way of keeping an eye on his arrangements. He didn't talk to the Captain, not at first, but he was careful to make sure the Captain saw him there. It wasn't that he said or did anything to draw attention to himself. It was enough in the beginning that the Captain saw him with the Fancy and understood he was a part of things here, part of a tight-bound order where fists carried more authority than fancy arguments and the constraints of law and conscience were as likely to stop the way things were done as the sun was to burn off a London particular. An order where outsiders did well not to try anything on.

Tom mightn't have had much in the way of a gentleman's polish or a gentleman's schooling but his sense of smell remained sharp as ever. It wasn't long before he found himself drawn into a discussion with the Captain's associates as the deal the pair of them had struck was described and marvelled over. It wasn't long before the Captain called for drinks to seal their agreement and the habitually word-shy Tom found himself encouraged to tell tales of the pit and of the violence that had been done there. The Captain's associates thrilled with shock and horrified excitement. And a little later, when the first rounds of fighting had been completed and the gentlemen leaned back in their chairs, sweating and glazed with bloodlust and their own audacity, it was Tom who let slip that, for a tosher, the life down the sewers beat into a cocked hat anything a man might see on the surface, if it were the thrill of danger he was after.

Straightways the gentlemen's eyes turned rounder than ever and they leaned forward, impatient for more.

'Well, well, well,' the Captain said, baring his teeth. 'I'll wager there's all kinds of evil doings down there. Murder and worse.'

Tom shrugged.

'You gets some strange happenings right enough,' he acknowledged.

'Tell us,' the Captain instructed, the two

words equal parts cajolery and threat.

'You don't want to know,' Tom said.

'Oh, but we do,' the Captain insisted. He glanced at the lascivious faces of his associates and his hand thoughtfully jingled the coins in his pocket. 'We really do.'

And so it began, Tom's trade in tales of the tosh. All of a sudden the man who'd never wasted a word in all his life found himself working through them as free and careless as any street huckster. Stories of corruption and cruelty, that was what was called for, stories that made the gentlemen's eyes sparkle and their breath come in quick slabs from their wide-open mouths. And the grislier the story the more they panted and the more the money slid out their pockets like it was greased with dripping. Tom was happy to oblige. He saw no reason to stay fixed to the actual truth, not if the gentlemen were satisfied. There was stories of what was and then there were stories of what could have been, if details were added in and imaginings let loose a little. Tom told tales of men taken with their hands and feet tied together to be thrown into the sewers at Newgate where fierce armies of rats would strip the flesh from their live bodies until nothing remained but their skeletons and two chewed-up loops of rope. He talked of a public house but a few hundred feet from the room where they sat, where men who had betrayed their friends to the law were murdered in the cellar and thrown through a trapdoor in the floor into the sewer below, never to be heard of again. He told of the stretch at old Grinacre in Southwark where the waters were thick with the unwanted limbs of cadavers cast into the open sewers by medical students done cutting them up, and to this almost-truth he added details of the murderers who, trying to cover up their crime, sliced up their own victims and cast them into the same stretch of shore so as to muddle up all the parts together.

'And the murderers, the perpetrators of these — these ghastly acts, surely they are caught when the bodies are discovered?' gasped one gentleman, licking his lips.

'Most of 'em ain't never found,' Tom replied carelessly. 'There's a thousand hiding places in the tunnels, sir, if you knows where to look. Places a man can stow a body and never get caught. You ever go down there you'll see the brickwork's bristling with bones and whatnot what got stuck in the holes and never worked their ways out.'

'Good God,' the gentleman said. 'And all right beneath our feet. It's worse than the horrors of Hell.'

He gave a shiver of satisfied revulsion and slipped a coin into Tom's outstretched palm. Tom nodded. He didn't see fit to mention that on the rare occasion that he or Red Joe found a dead body in the tunnels they passed it straight on to the dredgermen who in turn would land it at Rotherhithe where the inquest money was the best in the city. Somehow Tom didn't reckon the gentlemen'd like that too much.

At last, when Tom had exhausted his grim imaginings and the drink had begun to slow the men's tongues and their tips, he took himself off, the coins jingling a little tune in his pocket. It always gave him a stab of pleasure to open the door to his lodgings and see her there, sprawled on the blanket. As for Lady, she wasn't half so sure she was pleased to see Tom. Her eyes were so pink and she'd have such a drooping look about her shoulders you could almost believe she'd been weeping, and oftentimes she slunk away from him, pressing herself into the rotting floorboards so as to dodge his touch. Even when he took her in his arms she would hold her head up away from him, her nose stuck into the air like a goose, so as he would know for certain she was well affronted with him and wanted him to know it too.

And then, all of a sudden, she would give up being cross and she would rest her chin on his shoulder so that her whiskers tickled his ear, and the chewed rope of her tail would thump against his leg and he would hold her tight against his chest until the thumpings of their heartbeats caught each other's rhythm and became one.

XI

It was three days before the Strowbridge contract was due to be signed and submitted to the Board for final approval, and only nine days before Christmas, that William was summoned urgently to see Lovick. It was a little after ten o'clock in the morning. Outside it was snowing, the dirty flakes peeling away from the fog like old paint. For a moment William stared at the flimsy wooden wall of his carrel, unable to move. Some weeks before he had pinned there an article from *The Builder*, underlining the concluding sentence in dark ink. *For good or evil, the metropolis has entered upon a work of no common magnitude.* Every day, when he settled himself at his desk and he saw those words again, a quiet pride prickled the soles of his feet. Now the words blurred. Slowly he rose, his knees unsteady, and made his way through the familiar warren of rooms to Lovick's large office. He kept his hands thrust in his pockets. Despite the fires that burned in the grates the narrow chambers were cold and the air seemed thin, like the air on a high mountain, so that his breathing was shallow and laboured. William looked about him at the chaos of paper, the bowed heads, the flurry of clerks and messengers, and his heart ached. He would never step inside these rooms again.

When William was finally shown in, Lovick was not alone. With him was a short stout gentleman with a round pink face and a shiny pink pate fringed with soft down. Set upon so child-like a face his wire-rimmed spectacles looked as though they had been begged from an obliging uncle.

'Ah, May.' Lovick coughed. He was clearly ill at ease. 'Sit down, sit down.'

William sat and stared at his knees. Now that he was here he longed only for the interview to be got over as quickly as possible. Disgrace glinted above his bent neck like the blade of a guillotine.

'May,' Lovick said again. 'First of all, I would like to thank you for all the fine work you have done on behalf of the Commission. I would not wish what is to follow in any way to imply any disappointment in your work on either my or Mr Bazalgette's behalf.'

William nodded, his hands clenched at

his sides. Let it be done, he pleaded silently. Let it be over.

'May, as you know, you came to us with the warm recommendation of Mr Rawlinson, a gentleman I hold in the highest esteem. I have seen nothing in your work that would contradict his opinion of you. However —'

This was it. The breath died in William's chest.

'However, we are concerned that the — that the strains of the job may have exhausted you. This is Dr Feather.' Lovick gestured towards the gentleman in the window, who nodded, setting off a ripple that travelled through his plump shoulders and down across his belly. 'I have asked him here to examine you. I would appreciate it if you could assist him in any way he asks. Dr Feather? I believe matters have been arranged as you requested. Should you require assistance you have only to call.'

With that Lovick stood and left the room. Dumbly William looked up at the doctor. His was an unlikely face for an executioner, round and flushed pink with good living and so given to smiling that his cheeks were permanently dimpled. Their cheeriness mocked William and all the miserable squalor of his disgrace. There was nothing to hope for behind those glinting spectacles, nothing but the drawing-out of pain. In the employ of the Commission the doctor would find what he had been asked to find. In the flourish of a pen Hawke's threats would become official papers. Hawke had said he knew about the cutting. William wrapped his hands reflexively around his forearms, pressing the fabric of his sleeves against the damaged flesh. Once the doctor saw the scars his diagnosis would require no further substantiation.

But the doctor did not ask to look at his arms. Instead he perched himself on the corner of Lovick's desk, one portly leg swinging awkwardly off the ground, and proceeded to ask William a series of questions. In the questions themselves William could discern no obvious pattern. They ranged from demands for a detailed description of his daily routine to the names of European capital cities, from a brief history of his personal circumstances to his conclusions upon the mutiny in India and the chronology of the books of the Old Testament. After each question there followed a long silence during which the doctor, his forehead creased into fat folds, pondered William's responses before making jabbing notes in a small leather book. Each answer received equal consideration and was noted with equal care. William held the fabric of his coat close to his arms and endeavoured to keep his voice steady as all the while he waited for the pencil to be jabbed at his forearms with an instruction to raise his sleeves.

It never came. The doctor's question about William's outdoor pursuits led to a happy digression in which the doctor confessed to a particular affection for *Orchis hircina,* the lizard orchid, which had flourished along the sand dunes that fringed the garden of his boyhood home in Sussex.

'It has no perfume to speak of, of course, indeed I have always found it somewhat foul in odour. But when it comes to nature as theatre —'

When William admitted that, as a boy, he too had lain in wait for the enchanting moment when, one after another, the orchid released its long ribboned lips from the bud, the doctor nodded happily. And when William took his botanical journal from the pocket of his coat to show him the sketches he had made of *Spiranthes spiralis,* Polly's favourite because of its English name, autumn lady's-tresses, the doctor paused only briefly before scribbling a final note in his book.

'Very good, Mr May. Very good,' the doctor beamed, snapping the book shut. 'How pleasant to meet a fellow enthusiast. I believe that covers everything.' He went over to the door and opened it, a smile still pressing up against his plump cheeks. 'Do come back in, Mr Lovick.'

There was a murmur of voices from outside before Lovick entered the room.

'You have all you need?' Lovick enquired with a glance towards William.

'I most certainly do,' the doctor assured him, nodding happily.

'Good.' Lovick smiled. 'In that case I believe we need detain you no longer, Mr May.'

William stared from the doctor to Lovick and back.

'That is all?'

'That is all. Unless Dr Feather has anything further he wishes to add — ?'

The doctor shook his head, steadying his belly between his hands.

'Then we are quite finished. Now back to your work, if you please,' Lovick chided gently. 'These days we can ill afford to lose a minute.'

Nothing more was said. Shortly before

noon Lovick came to ask William for some papers. No mention was made of his interview with the doctor but, as William rummaged for them in his portfolio, Lovick's hand rested briefly upon his shoulder. Then he was gone. William was left alone.

It was over. Hawke could not touch him now. This dark December day that would have brought about his ruin had instead delivered his restoration. He had been examined by a doctor, an expert in the study of nervous disorders, of — to put it bluntly — madness, and pronounced sane. There had been no question of it. The diagnosis would be confirmed, documented, signed, filed. Somewhere — and always — there would be a piece of paper that would state it impartially, categorically. William May was sane. He was sane and he was safe. His family was safe. The nightmare that had begun on a blind November morning in Turkey more than four years before was over. He was sane.

Somewhere, locked inside himself, there was relief, he was sure of it, even joy, but in the thin grey light of a snow-tamped afternoon he felt only dazzled and exhausted. The ceaseless flood and ebb of clerks and papers ran in and out of his cubicle, sucking impatiently at him, turning him over and over like a pebble. He longed to get out. He longed for the tunnels, for the safe embrace of the darkness, but if he left Greek-street now he would be missed. There was too much work that needed to be done. And besides, he told himself, his impulse to view the tunnels as a kind of sanctuary was no more than habit, an inappropriate and injudicious habit it would behove him to break. He no longer had any need for sanctuary. He was sane, was he not? He was sane. The measurements he required for his calculations would not be needed for a few days. He would wait. It would be more prudent to wait. The afternoon darkened and still the tide of ledgers washed through his stall, tugging their clerks behind them by the leather-covered chains strung from their belts. From time to time William reached into his coat pocket to stroke the leather binding of his journal with his fingertips. It was as warm and soft as a cheek. A little after six a boy brought soup in an enamel basin. William lifted the plate that covered it and sniffed. It smelled good, rich and meaty. The saliva rushed into William's mouth. He had eaten nothing all day.

'Mr Lovick sent me for it, sir,' the boy said brightly, producing a hunk of bread and cheese wrapped in paper from his pocket. 'On account you was workin' late an' all.'

William ate it gratefully, carefully wiping his fingers on his handkerchief so as not to leave greasy prints on his papers. When he finally extinguished his light it was nearly eight. In Greek-street a vicious wind sliced at his face and whipped the cuffs of his trousers. Although it had stopped snowing, the streets, rutted and softened during the day by the bustle of feet, had begun to freeze once more and the going was treacherous. William picked his way carefully along Princes-street. He felt dizzy with exhaustion. Carriages loomed abruptly out of the yellowed darkness, the clatter of their wheels muffled by the carpet of snow, and the pale spheres of the gas-lights trembled on their iron stalks like dandelion clocks. The streets were empty and the few people William passed huddled into their coats, their heads lowered. William longed to be home. As he cut through a narrow courtyard towards the river he stumbled on the icy mud and would have fallen if a man had not caught him by the arm and hauled him to his feet.

'Mr May.'

The voice was low and hoarse. Startled,

William twisted round to look at the stranger's face. He wore a fur hat pulled low over his ears and breath veiled his whiskers in vapour.

'Mr England?'

'There has been a mistake. A misunderstanding. The contract —'

William shook his head. In a darkened doorway something scraped. William set his hands cautiously over the pockets containing his purse and handkerchief. This area was notorious for thieves.

'Mr England, there is no mistake. I have made my position quite clear. The matter is closed.'

With such briskness as the icy path allowed William began to walk away but England caught him by the wrist. His grip was tight enough to be painful.

'Oh, but it is not, Mr May. It is not.'

'This conversation can serve you no purpose, Mr England. The Board will not consider your tender. Nothing you can say or do can change that.'

'No?'

'Let go of my arm,' William said coldly. 'Or I shall call for the police.'

'Here?' England wrenched William's arm up behind his back. 'They say sewers are deathly places. From what I hear the tide can turn quite unexpected. Down there in the darkness a man wouldn't know what had hit him. Tide would batter him against the wall so brutally that by the time it was done with him even the bastard's mother wouldn't recognize him. So they say.'

'You do not frighten me, Mr England.'

'Then you are even more of a fool than you appear. You've got a little one, haven't you, May? A boy, that right? Terrible if anything happened to the little one.'

'Take your hands off me!'

'Still, you can't watch them every hour of the day, can you? And London's a shocking place for accidents.'

It was then that the glassy numbness in William's head smashed, flooding his head with blackness. With all the force he could muster he flung his head backwards into England's face. There was a dull crunch. England moaned and staggered, letting go of William's arm to clutch his face. Blood leaked between his fingers and spattered across the dirty snow. His eyes were round with shock. He cast around him, as though looking for someone in the shadows. William wheeled round, the blackness flooding his chest. England lunged at him but William was too quick. The blackness roared through his arms, his legs. He slammed his fist hard into the bloodied mess of England's nose so that the brickyard owner reeled backwards, striking his head against the brick wall. As he slid down the wall William kicked him in the stomach.

'Where are you?' England moaned. 'Help me, for God's sake!'

'You come anywhere near my family and I'll kill you,' William spat. The blackness crowded his nostrils, his throat, his ears. It pounded in his temples and filled his mouth with cold black saliva. It squeezed against his eyes, compressing the courtyard into no more than a narrow ribbon of faint light. 'I mean it. I'll kill you.'

A match scraped and flared orange in the shadowed doorway. William wheeled round. He sensed him then more than seeing him, the man who watched them, the smoke from his cigarette curling around the brim of his hat and upwards towards the dark sky. A Turk then? The man didn't move. You weren't supposed to, not until the next watch drew close enough for you to be certain of them. The orders were clear on that. There were words you were meant to say. William felt a flicker of panic. He could not remember the words. He scrabbled frantically through the blackness in his head but he could not remember the words.

'For pity's sake, man,' England moaned again, one hand straining towards the shadows. 'Get the bastard!'

William ran. He ran, stumbling in the snow, his legs jarred and twisted by the frozen ruts of mud, through alleys and courtyards, in and out of the light. There was nothing but the ache of the cold air in his chest, the laboured constrictions of his heart, the weight of his legs — and the blackness. He was compressed into blackness, thick and opaque but without shape, like the darkness of the night is without shape. Everywhere he ran he felt the eyes upon him, hot as coals. Relentlessly they followed him but also blindly, unable to make sense of what they saw. William knew it, so at the same time he was trapped and perfectly free. As long as he kept running. And so he ran.

When he stopped running he was underground. It did not occur to him to ask how he had come to be there or for how long. The tide was rising and he had no lantern but he was oblivious to the icy stream of shit that rushed around his legs, flooding his polished boots and dragging at the wool of his best trousers. He felt only the desperate, deafening need to cut. His right hand clenched in the darkness, every fibre of muscle in his fingers and palms screaming for the familiar weight of the knife. The cravings overran him, a monstrous, murderous army driving battalion after savage battalion into his skull and between his ribs to lay him waste and commandeer the very marrow of his bones. Every inch of his skin was alive with them, every tiny filament of hair blazing as though set alight. Their bayonets spiked every shallow breath he dragged into his throat as he slipped and stumbled down into the darkness, his frozen feet clumsy on the rotten bricks.

He was close now, he knew it, although he could see nothing. The cravings came faster and thicker, faster and thicker, peeling away the skin from his heart, filling his lungs until every breath was an agony and his chest quivered like a shell ready to explode. The darkness was so complete that he could not see his own hands. William closed his eyes, squeezing them shut. Abruptly the floor of the tunnel dropped away. He was almost there. Bent double, stiff and clumsy with cold, he scrabbled desperately with his fingers at the slimed walls. His whole body was screaming now, his fouled blood a thick black acid, eating away at flesh and bone. He could no longer feel his feet. He gasped as he stumbled and almost fell. Righting himself his knuckles knocked against the rough edges of his hewn-out recess. He had found the place.

The cravings roared and screamed in his ears as he tore frenziedly at the wall, ripping his fingers on the sharp rubble of mortar as he felt for the loose brick. It moved beneath his hand. The seconds it took to extricate it were unbearable. At last he hurled the brick across the tunnel, his other hand snatching frenziedly at the handle of his knife. There was a splash, a faint groan. The thick black stream swirled around him. It was almost at his thighs now. He ripped wildly at the sleeve of his coat. The stink of decomposition crowded his head, the stink of death. He could make them out now, strewn along the grey banks, the shrivelled black corpses of his fellow soldiers. Somewhere, muffled by snow or distance, a bombardment thundered. The darkness flashed with splatters of fire. His arm screamed for the blade but the fear was stronger, sucking his feet down into the thick mud of the trench. There would be no relief tonight, no leaking dawn to call him back. The enemy was all around him, steadily edging forward, edging forward, crawling towards him in their inexorable thousands, a clodded plough of grey, noiseless in the snow. They came from left and right, advancing on him from behind, from in front, their grey arms reaching out from the fog over his head, their bayonets slicing up through the earth beneath his feet. They had no object but him. They closed around him, tighter and tighter. There were columns of them now, advancing and advancing. There would be no end to them. William shrank back into the recess in the wall, his blade clutched in his arms like an infant. His breath came in tattered ribbons. He could not move.

They were on him now. William could hear their moans, the liquid suck of their breath. They had come for William, their bayonets drawn. He could see them as they moved relentlessly forward, ramming their blades again and again into the thick flesh of the night. William would die here, in this brutish hell of mud and ice. His corpse would be hurled with a thousand others into a pit and the mud would fill his mouth and press itself into his unclosed eyes. The fear choked him, twisting his guts and clutching at the flesh between his ribs. He did not want to die. He must not die. His hands clenched around the handle of his knife. Without breaking the skin he stroked the sharp blade very deliberately down his neck and along the flesh of his exposed arm. The Russians stumbled in the darkness. They were close now, very close. Someone cried out, a low gurgling noise like water sucked down a drain. William's fear crackled into the blade, setting it alight. All of a sudden his head was flooded with hot black blood. Throwing himself from his hiding place he stabbed blindly into the darkness. But he was no longer alone. Someone else was out there, in the darkness. The air was thick with the moans of the enemy as the ranks of slaughtered men collapsed into the stream, the splashes flashing silver in the dark night. They fell one on top of the other, blood spreading in black pools across the dirty grey of their coats. He was closer now. William pressed himself back into the wall. He saw him only for a moment, his face a faint white moon in the pale glow of his lamp as he pressed something into a gap in the sandbags that lined the trench. But William knew him. The relief watch. The soldier did not speak. Instead he turned away, moving swiftly up the trench towards the

guard post. William was saved. From behind him there came a long ghastly moan
as life leaked from a man's body like sand.
Exultantly, his eyes closed, William raised
his blade and thrust it down again and
again into the mass of corpses before him.
The silent scream of pain in his arm was a
cry of perfect victory.

At last, a black blizzard blowing itself
out, the clamour in William's head cleared.
Time had slipped. Dark blood congealed
in his hand, barely warm. But he felt none
of the sense of calm that always infused
him at these times. Instead he felt nauseous, dizzy, disturbed. There was too
much about this that was wrong. He was in
the sewers, he held a knife in his hand, his
arm throbbed. These things were familiar.
The blackouts were familiar too but not
like this. Always in the past he had mislaid
time, hours sometimes that he could not
account for. This time, in a way he could
not begin to explain, he had lost himself.
He shivered violently. He was half-frozen.
He wore not his sewer uniform but his best
suit of clothes. He had no light. The tide
was up to his thighs and moving so
strongly that he had to set his legs hard
against the pull of the current. Most unsettling of all, he was filled with a terrible

certainty that he had not been alone. He had to get out.

Thrusting his knife deep into his pocket he stumbled backwards, uphill, towards the exit, struggling against the downward pull of the rising water. He walked as fast as he could but the darkness was as thick as serge. He shook his head, too, but he could not dislodge the strange unsettling fragments that scraped beneath his skull like the remains of a dream. His feet shrieking with pain as he thawed them before a meagre peat fire, his fingers fumbling with the pencil as he completed the watch log. The back of his head alight with autumn sunlight as his brush traced the delicate violet veins of the pale toadflax. The splattered arc of blood on canvas as the blade of a bayonet tore through the wall of a tent. The walls of the tunnels crumbling around him, threatening to bury him alive. Hawke's voice slicing through the darkness, gleaming with menace. And through it all the relief watch, guardian angel and spectre of death, warm and ghostly as breath in the winter darkness.

At the top of the slope, where he was accustomed to straighten up, his head still grazed the low roof. Perhaps the rising tide affected the bed of the stream. He pressed forward. It was not far now. By his calculations the grating should be only a little further along, leading out of a broad tunnel on his right. He felt for the archway with his hands, forcing himself to endure the slimy flesh of the fungi that sprouted along the brickwork, but the wall was solid and there was not the faintest hint of light. The tunnel felt narrower than he remembered but then the darkness altered a man's perceptions, skewing his relationship with space and time. The channel was surely no more than a few yards further on. Biting sharply upon his lip he fumbled along the channel.

Abruptly it curved sharply to the right. William did not remember any curve. Had he missed the turning? He should have been able to stand easily in this part of the system but instead the crown of the tunnel lowered. If he held out his arms his fingertips touched both walls simultaneously. That was not right either. Even the grain of the course beneath his feet was unfamiliar. The mud was deeper than it should be here and tumbled with sharp stones. He struggled to keep himself steady. The stream rushed past him, so that he had to lean into it to remain upright. As he lowered his head a fine mist of frozen filth insinuated itself into his nostrils, his mouth. The stench of excrement and rotting seaweed was sickening. He felt the panic start to choke him.

The tide was rising faster now, he was sure of it. He had to get out before the river pulled him under, flooding his lungs with the city's ceaseless stream of excrement. He needed to head upstream, away from the sluice gates to the river where the force of the water through the iron flaps would surely crush him. On and on into the darkness he pushed. His foot struck a wall. He felt into the darkness. Brick. Solid brick. The end of the tunnel. He was trapped. Desperately he wheeled around, pushing back the way he had come. His legs were lead weights, exhausted with the effort of propelling him through the water. The maze of tunnels forked, curved, sloped, and William stumbled along them wildly, thoughtlessly, everything in him straining towards the idea of the light. But he found no light, no escape. The tunnels narrowed, their walls crumbling around him, their courses treacherous. William lost his footing, was carried backwards by the stinking stream, struggled to stand again and pressed forwards. The knife in his pocket slashed at his leg. He scraped his knuckles, his forehead, banged his shoulders and his knees. As though from a long way off he heard his own voice echoing in the darkness, strange and high-pitched, forcing forth a jumble of vicious threats and endearments. He prayed, shouting the words into the darkness, pleading with God to restore him to his faith as he cursed Him for deserting him. And still the tunnels lured him on, taking him deeper and deeper into the depths of the earth, the whole suffocating weight of the metropolis pressing down upon him, burying him alive. And still the tide rose. The darkness bulged with guttural knocks and echoes. William knew they were the forces of Hell sent to receive him. They were not far behind him now. He had almost nothing left for the fight.

The tide was almost to his waist. William stumbled onwards, his hands flailing paddles in the filthy stream. He made hardly any progress now. The cold had penetrated into the innermost parts of him. His body shook uncontrollably. With each step, tunnel blurred into trench and trench into tunnel. He was tired. He was so tired. If he could only make it till the next watch, to the grating, till the relief arrived. He was so tired. He moved his legs only with the greatest concentration of effort. But ahead of him — he stared. The darkness was lifting. The edges of night were streaked with the first watery filaments of day. There would be green coffee back at the camp if he had the strength to roast it. If there was enough wood for a fire. If he could only keep on walking. He had to keep walking. A soldier must never abandon his post. Then his foot struck a rock and he stumbled, falling forwards on to a heap of what he took for sandbags. He did not have the strength to stand again. But the light was brighter now. The sun — or was it the moon? — swung above him, round and white and blinding. It hurt his eyes to look at it. And beside the light, so bright that he seemed made up of the light itself, was the figure of a man. Light made man. The Almighty God, Maker of heaven and earth. Forgive us our trespasses. Beside him was a small white dog. Within its scarlet mouth its teeth were sharp as knives. William felt the terror rise in him. The light was a trick, a beacon to lead him towards the fires of eternal damnation. Father, Oh, Father, why have You forsaken me?

And then he saw the man's face.

'Mr Rawlinson?'

Robert Rawlinson seemed quite oblivious to the filthy river that coursed around him. His glossy hat shone and his starched neckcloth was crisp and perfectly white. The dog too was white, white as fresh Crimean snow.

'Mr May,' Rawlinson asked gravely. 'Do you mean to die?'

William gazed up at him, dazzled by the light. He wanted to weep with relief.

'Is — is it dawn?'

Rawlinson considered him thoughtfully. Then he placed his hands beneath William's armpits and hauled him up to stand. He was strong. He spoke to William although the words were lost in the roar of the stream. Then, slinging William's arm around his neck, he half-carried him along the surging torrent of the submerged trench. William let his head fall against Rawlinson's shoulder.

'We shall have to bury them,' William whispered. 'The bodies. We shall have to go back and bury them.'

'Hush now,' Rawlinson said gently. William was silent, his hand around the reassuring shape of the knife handle in his pocket. He had no strength for further questions. He barely noticed as Rawlinson bundled him upwards and on to a dirt floor. His tent? Perhaps. He was no longer in the river, that he knew, but he knew it distantly, without relief. Pushed now by Rawlinson's hand between his shoulder blades, he stumbled a few more steps. The air changed. The breeze on his sodden clothes chilled him so that he shuddered violently. Then his knees gave way. The ground was hard and uncomfortably rutted. Rawlinson bent over him for a moment, loosening his clothes, settling him to sleep. Then he was no longer there. Laying his head down on the frozen mud, May closed his eyes.

XII

The appearance of the stranger rattled Tom something proper. What with it being lateish and the tide on the up, he'd been sure the two of them'd have the tunnels to themselves. He'd reckoned on no more than a quick in-and-out, now that the fight was almost upon her. He wanted Lady fresh. But then he'd had the fancy of seeking her out a little something by the way of a good luck charm. The thought twined around him like a weed till it had him quite wrapped up. It didn't have to be something special. Perhaps a coin, strung on a length of ribbon around her neck by way of a medal. He wasn't about to go to any proper trouble. It was only when he got towards his former toshing grounds he figured it wouldn't hurt to have a rummage beneath some of the gratings, for old time's sake. There was time enough to spare, after all, and you learned to follow your instincts in a game like the tosh. You never knew your luck.

He was directly under the grating at the

east point of Regent-circus when he heard him. It was a tricky shaft with a long gully so that to get your fingers into the sludge you had to lay yourself on a sloping ledge with your arm buried almost to the shoulder. Lady lay silently on his back, settling herself afresh whenever he shifted about. He couldn't remember the last time he'd toshed here. There were usually decent pickings to be had — there was a cab stand at the junction with Coventry-street and the bits and pieces that got themselves dropped in the manure had a habit of getting overlooked — but you had to be careful to mind your step. The grating fell away direct from the street and if the peelers cared to have a peer beneath their boots you'd be lucky if they didn't stare you straight in the face. Any commotion in the tunnels would have them down on him hard as a cellar door. Meanwhile your boots was stuck right out in the tunnel beneath, clear as a bell and twice as tempting to anyone who might be coming along behind. It would be easy to miss hearing them with the clatter of the street echoing round your skull.

But you'd have had to be deafer than a stone to miss this one. Pulling out his arm with the slow twisting movement that kept the mud quiet, Tom slithered down the ledge into the stream, taking Lady into his arms. The water was high, too high. He'd let the gully get the better of him. Lady licked his ear but he shook her off so as to listen. They were lucky. The noise was coming from the west. Slick as a fish in the black stream he headed east, towards the cavern.

The cavern was a low raised space like a long step over the main sewer. Most likely it'd once been the outfall from a tributary stream. The story went that, years before, back when Tom was still a lad, one of the old coves had uncovered an anchor here, buried in the mud. They said it had made the tosher's fortune, that somehow or other he'd sold it to the government and they kept it in a glass case to this day, somewhere over Greenwich way where folks paid a shilling a time for the chance to get a gawp at it. Tom had his doubts about the truth of that story but he did know there'd never been a stream here in his time. With nothing to keep it occupied the outfall had half collapsed. You could only head up the tunnel a matter of feet before a tumble of masonry blocked it right off. In recent years another fall had good as closed off the entrance so unless you knew it you weren't likely to suspect there was anything there at all. The height of it meant you had to squat but it was dry, even when the tide was coming up fast. Tom knew they'd be safe there for a good while. He set Lady down and crouched against the wall. They were both breathing hard.

The man was getting closer. He made no effort to be silent, gabbling away to himself, his breath coming out in strange little groans like a sixpenny jade. Surely he couldn't be a flusher. Flushers always came down in twos or threes. Besides, you could always tell a flusher a mile off from the stretched-out suck of the sludge as they rolled their feet out of the mud. Seemed that to be a flusher you had to walk that way. Bill liked to claim it was because flushers, not being creatures of the smartest persuasion, put their dinners into their boots for safe keeping and lived every step in mortal fear of crushing them. But by the sounds of it this one wasn't worrying himself about where he was putting his feet. You could hear the splashes and the curses as he stumbled. He was getting closer all the time. Of all the nights, Tom thought angrily to himself. Extra bother tonight'd really foul things up. He cocked his head, listening. The words were clearer now, although there wasn't nothing much in the way of sense to them, and they tumbled over one another, for all the world arguing with themselves.

'Why do you leave me here? It's so dark, so bloody dark. Don't be afraid, William. Don't be afraid, my sweet William. I am with you. Though you walk alone through the valley of the shadow of death, God will guide and comfort you. The merciful Lord succours those who have done their duty. Have you done your duty? Have you? Fix your bayonet, May. Who knows where they may be hiding? You must never sleep. Oh God, why do you abandon me in my suffering? I am not afraid of the dark. In the light our deeds will be shown for what they truly are. It's so damned dark. I have done my duty. God and Empire. How can I march when the blood makes the going so slippy? There is no Heaven and no Hell, you hear me? Only darkness. Blood and shit and darkness for all eternity. Oh Jesus, where the hell are they? Where are the others?'

Tom could smell the voice now. Above the reek of the stream it carried the faint prickle of soap and laundry starch. The strange union of stinks set the hairs on

Tom's neck prickling sharp as pins. He placed a comforting hand on Lady's back.

'You did for them, though. There were a hundred of them, a thousand, but you had them. I was there. I did my duty. I had them, like that, like that. Didn't I? William would never run. Not my William, my brave, sweet William, my baby boy. Why is it so dark? Lord, have mercy! You have turned Your face away from me and cut out my soul! Is that what you call mercy? Answer me, damn you! Oh, sweet Jesus, there is so much blood. A river of blood. I am drowning, do you hear me? I'm drowning in blood. I can't breathe! You think you can frighten me? Almighty God, to whom all hearts are open. You want to take a look in mine? Too dark, you say? Damn you, do you hear me, damn you to hell! Will it never be dawn? Hush now, sweet William, hush. It was a dream. It is still night. It will always be night. In Hell there is no sunrise. The blood runs so fast I can barely walk. We had them, didn't we? We showed them. Like that. Like that. Why, why is it so terribly dark?'

There was a sharp splash and a thud. Tom heard a long low moan like a rabbit giving itself up to the trap. It faded and died, lost in the roar of the stream. The tunnel settled itself around the new silence. Tom crept to the mouth of the cavern. The stranger must have dropped his lantern when he fell. The tunnel was perfectly dark. Tom cursed quietly to himself. He'd heard tales of government gents who'd got themselves lost in the tunnels and fair lost their marbles. Or it might be a crusher, coming down on a tip-off. That was all Tom needed. If he was one of them, his cronies'd be down to fetch him out in the shake of a tail, sure as eggs. A battalion of them, most likely, with lamps and rattles and the devil only knew what else, stirring up trouble.

'My little milkwort. It's so dark.'

It was more a breath than words. The gentleman's head was clear of the water then. But he went on lying there and made no move to get himself back on his feet. The tide was rising faster now. If no one came after him it'd be over the gent's head within the hour. How many of them would there be down here then, on the lookout for the one who got himself drownded? Tom hesitated for a moment, Lady's nose against his back. Then he opened the shutter on his lantern.

It wasn't a trap. Tom breathed a little easier then. But whoever he was he was in a right sorry state, no two ways about it. He'd lost his hat, and his hair and whiskers might have been any colour, so caked were they with mud and shit. His face was ghostly white and streaked with slime. But the curious thing was how he was dressed. The gents coming down from the Parliament wore oiled leather head to foot for fear the faintest smear of shit might dirty their delicate hands. Not this one. Every stitch he wore was sodden and plastered with all the compliments of the tunnels but there wasn't no mistaking they were regular street clothes, from the woollen overcoat to the neckcloth, and nothing patched up about them neither. There was studs in the front of his shirt, proper studs, and a pin in his neckerchief. Gold by the appearance of it, Tom thought, sizing it up with his tosher's eye. Who the blazes was he?

And then, right out of the blue, the man opened his eyes and stared right at Tom, his gaze so pasted on to the tosher's face it was like he meant to fix every part of it perfect in his memory. Three months in Mill-bank Limping Gil had done. Tom felt the breath punched clean out of his throat.

'Mr Rawlinson?'

The words rang out clear as a bell. Tom hesitated. The voice was tidy as you like, a gent's voice, but there wasn't nothing else about this man that put you in mind of a gentleman. Not to put too fine a point on it, by Tom's reckoning the man was stark raving mad. Watching him as he smiled, all twisted up with his eyes rolling about, and the hungry way he plucked at the air with his hands, it wasn't a stretch to picture this creature chained up with the other lunatics in the dirty straw of the Bedlam.

'Is that you, Mr Rawlinson?'

The man caught at his sleeve. Tom grimaced. Surely there'd not be a soul alive who'd set any store by the ravings of a man like this, even assuming his addled head was clear enough to remember any of it after. The main thing was to get him out the tunnels, and quick. Tom paused for only a moment before nodding.

'That's right,' he agreed, bringing the lantern right up close to the man's face so as to dazzle him with it. You couldn't be too careful. 'Rawlinson. That's me.'

The man blinked in the bright light.

'Is — is it dawn?'

Tom smirked, he couldn't help it. The bloke was off his rocker, clear as day, more like to reckon Tom was the hippopotamus in the Zoo as hand him over to the traps. Hoisting the gentleman up by his armpits

Tom slung his arm around his neck. He wouldn't give Tom too much trouble at any rate, despite the weight of his wet clothes. There wasn't much more to him than skin and bone.

'Stay here, Lady,' Tom muttered, face close to hers. 'Good girl. I'll be back in a shake.'

Fast as he could he hustled the man along the tunnel. The man let his head fall against Tom's shoulder. They were up almost at the cellar when he spoke.

'We shall have to bury them,' the man said clearly. 'The bodies.'

Slow as a sleepwalker the gent reached into his pocket and pulled out a knife. Its blade was rusty with dried blood. Tom felt a kick of startled anger in his belly. Wrenching the knife roughly from the man's loose grip, Tom thrust the crazy bugger up through the gap, throwing him into the cellar. The madman collapsed on to the mud floor but Tom seized him by the ankles and dragged him up the shallow cellar steps and into the alley. His head bounced against the steps like a football. Tom hoped it hurt. He had to get the bastard far enough away from the cellar so as he'd never recall the place. Two corners and then the alley opened into a narrow yard. That'd do. The studs in the man's shirt caught the first glimmers of morning light. Quick as a flash Tom had them out and into his own pocket. As an afterthought he took the man's handkerchief too, although he tucked the bloodstained knife back into the pocket of his sodden trousers. If the bastard got himself picked up before he froze to death it'd like as not give him a spot of bother. There was satisfaction in that.

The moment Tom let go of him the madman curled himself up on the ground, knees to his chest, tight as a prawn. Tom spat disgustedly at the patch of ground near his head and hurried back into the tunnels to fetch Lady.

XIII

It was a pair of coal-heavers, cutting through the alleys on their way down towards the river, who came across William in the early hours of dawn. Even in the winter they were expected to be at work by five o'clock, humping the loads of coal on their backs from the ships to the wagons by the red light of hanging cauldrons. This morning was no exception. When they first saw William's huddled body, white with a light dusting of fresh snow, they took it for nothing more than a heap of rubbish. One of the men scuffed it with a boot as they passed. Roused, his pleas barely audible, William cried out for help. Usually the men would have paid no heed to such an appeal. It was not in the nature of either man to do something for nothing and William, filthy and half-frozen as he was, did not immediately present a prospect that suggested profit.

But William was fortunate. As they walked the two men had been engaged in a fierce debate as to which of the two was the stronger. It was the taller of the two, a giant of a man in a well-tarred short smock-frock and patched velveteen knee breeches, who suggested he prove his superior strength by carrying the injured man upon a single shoulder as far as the bridge. As was habitual for coal-heavers, the men had been paid their daily wage the previous evening not by the wharfinger but by his brother, the publican, who liked to keep the men waiting for their money while offering them something by way of refreshment on credit. The slighter man had little of his pay left in his pocket and a great deal of the publican's beer in his belly. There were, however, sufficient funds to cover a satisfactory wager and the bet was settled. Whistling cheerily to attest to the undemanding nature of the contest, the giant swung William on to his back with as little ceremony as if he had been a sack of coal. William's feverish forehead bumped clumsily against the man's back as he strode south, the slighter man quickening his step to keep pace. The snow fell steadily, lining the fan-tail of the giant's hat. If he felt any strain he made no show of it. At Thames-street, his blackened palm already extended to collect on his debt, the giant swung William down and looked for somewhere to deposit him.

'Git on wi' yer,' urged the slighter man, put out by his loss. 'We'se late, they'll be on us like fleas.'

The giant tipped back his hat slightly to scratch his head. While he'd walked he'd considered the burden on his back no more than a weight to be hefted, a deal lighter than the coal but otherwise no different. Now that he could see his face, that burden was once again a man, a man who, however unwittingly, had helped him to a fair taking. He was moaning steadily in the high and hopeless manner of a sickly infant.

'Can't just leave 'im 'ere, can I?' the giant said.

He cast around. In the swirling snow-globe light of a gas-lamp he made out a rickety flight of steps leading down to the riverbank and, beneath a notice warning passers-by to be decent, a narrow wooden bench. Sweeping the worst of the snow away with a huge hand he settled William into one corner of it. William's head slumped upon his chest and his legs sprawled outwards but he remained approximately upright. A smear of coal dust charred one white cheek.

'Git on wi' yer, then,' the giant said, suddenly as anxious as his friend to be gone, and together the two men disappeared into the night.

William was left on Thames-street, his body convulsed with cold and fever, but, although from time to time his eyes opened, their blank gaze recognized nothing of his surroundings. In his restless delirium William was back in Balaclava, pleading for the love of God for a drop of water as the mule he was slung over slithered through the frozen mud towards the harbour and the ship that would take him to Scutari. It was pitch dark and snowing and every jolting footstep echoed through his body in a thousand breathless whimpers of pain. The air was crowded with the desperate entreaties of the other wounded men. They settled on William as thickly as the snow, filling his ears and drifting down the back of his ragged coat. But the Turkish bearers seemed not to hear them. They smoked and jested with one another noisily in their unfathomable tongue, their swarthy faces swimming in and out of focus, their sticky laughter warm with the soldiers' leaking blood. When, at last, his mule fell and William was thrown to the ground, one amongst their number shoved him upright in the snow like a doll. The Turk was vast, the size of two men. He loomed over William, as if considering his prize, his black hands raised. His slack mouth hung open but beneath the crown of his hat his eyes were red with greed. William shrank backwards. Faintly he thought to cry for help but the world had somehow receded, the clamour and chaos of the harbour compressed into a fist that lodged at the back of William's skull, while throughout the rest of his deserted head the silence was broken only by the moan of a frozen wind, scattering shards of snow into the void. Here, there was nothing. Here, he would freeze to death and when they came afterwards to this spot there would be nothing. His very bones would be compressed by the nothingness until it too took on the characteristics of nothingness. Here at the edge of everything there was no God. There was no Devil. There was only oblivion. You could turn away if you had the strength. You could battle towards the noise and the throb of the light, slash and hammer at suffering with your bayonet and your bare fists until it opened up to take you in. Or you could lie down in the blackness and give yourself up to the wind. Its frozen breath would take away the pain and the fever and the intolerable thirst. All you had to do was to let go.

'Who are you?' the darkness demanded not unkindly, cradling his face in its frozen fingers. 'Do you have a wife? Will she not be wondering where you are?'

William thought of Polly, of the smooth coils of her chestnut hair and the mole on the back of her neck like a splatter of chocolate, and the pain twisted between his ribs. He turned his head so that the moaning of the wind might fill his ears. No more of anything. There was no longer a man by the name of William May. Was there ever? Perhaps, for a brief snatched moment, there was a patch of feverish heat in the cold darkness. Now, at last, he who was nothing would be returned to nothing. It was over. The darkness closed over his head like water.

When William finally opened his eyes again the glare of light dazzled him. Flinching, he squeezed his eyes closed and turned his head away. The movement exploded a shell of pain at the back of his skull. He shivered uncontrollably, although his face was intolerably hot. He was on his back and something held him down, pinning his arms to his sides so that his hands juddered like landed fish against his thighs. The light pressed against his closed eyelids, flooding them with a vicious red. His legs and his neck and the roots of his teeth ached and when he tried to press saliva into his parched throat his tongue was glued to the roof of his mouth.

'Water,' he muttered to the Turk. 'Water, I beg you.'

Abruptly something soft and pleasantly cool passed over his forehead and encircled his head, lifting it. A cup was held to his lips. William drank. As he swallowed, the water seemed to flow not only into his throat but upwards into his brain, soothing its scorched folds. The bloody undersides of his eyelids darkened to a pigeon grey.

'Tesekkur ederim,' he murmured. 'Thank you.'

Time passed. The light came and went. Vaguely, like half-forgotten dreams, dislocated noises tugged at his memory before evaporating into silence. In turn and together he shivered and burned, the relentless sweats crusting him with a skin of salt. And all the while impossible images swam in and out of his head. His mother's hand stroking his face, her fingertips seeking out the golden bead of a sunbeam on his cheek, as his son stared at him, his unblinking eyes given adult shadows by the smoky light of a rush-lamp. Polly's pink ribbon mouth curving itself around the soft Irish syllables of Meath, the one-legged soldier. Hawke, his whiskers flecked with spittle, sitting in his father's favourite chair, a green ledger of shop accounts open upon his knee. Alfred England, smiling solicitously and offering him a dish of cakes, each one a disc of burned London clay.

And always, in the far corner, smudged by a ceaseless dusk, Mr Bazalgette, his fingers steepled against his lips. *I beg you to recollect yourself, May,* the great engineer murmured. *From the turmoil of his natural instincts an engineer brings order. Order, May, if you please.* William could not make out his face but the hooded eyes fixed upon his as though they were only inches away, grave and dark with disappointment. *An engineer brings order.* My hands shake so, he tried to protest to Bazalgette, but his lips would not obey him. Instead, over and over, they repeated the great man's words: *an engineer brings order, an engineer brings order.* In the fevered confusion of his half-sleep the words repeated themselves with the steady rhythm of a steam engine but they brought him no peace. Struggle as he might William could not remember what it was he sought to make sense of.

XIV

Then the fever fell away and he woke. The square of the window was marbled with a cold grey light, splintered by black and leafless branches. Above the sill the paint flaked from the window frame. William looked towards the corner where he had become accustomed to see the figure of Mr Bazalgette, his head bowed thoughtfully over his fingers, but instead he saw only the curved washstand with its familiar basin painted with forget-me-nots and the sampler with its bunchily stitched promise of HOME SWEET HOME. A small fire burned in the grate. He turned his head. There was a faint smear of pain across the underside of his forehead as he moved but it held steady upon his neck, the skin almost cool. On the other side a bentwood chair had been pulled up to the bedside, a tartan shawl thrown over its back. A basket of mending sat upon the bare floor, a spool of thread abandoned untidily across it, and next to it the forget-me-not jug with its chipped spout, a white rag laid over it. From beyond the window he could hear the rattle of wheels over cobbles and the dispirited lamentation of 'Milk! Ha'penny half-pint!' from the street. A horse whinnied. Softened by distance, the drawn-out goose honks of the penny steamers scuffled with the higher-pitched remonstrations of a departing train.

He was home.

For a perfect moment the ordinariness of the bare room flooded him with peace. And then, into the still warm pool of his belly, began to leak the thin sour effluvia of elusive dreams and half-forgotten terrors. His stomach crawled uneasily and along his arms the hairs bristled.

'Polly?' he called out in a low voice, his tongue clumsy with disuse.

A moment later he heard the pad of shoeless footfalls on the bare boards of the landing. William swallowed and, with an effort, raised himself up on to one elbow. In the doorway Di stood hesitantly, his hair sticking up in a startled crown around his sleepy face. His eyes were round above the woollen blanket he clutched in his arms. The way he stared at his father set William's skin alive with agitation. He squeezed his eyes shut.

'Polly!' he shouted again, this time more roughly.

He did not open his eyes. He heard her as she murmured something to the boy and the rustle of her skirts as she crossed the room towards the bed. Her step was heavy and he could hear the laboured pull of her breathing. The touch of her hand upon his forehead made him flinch.

'William? Are — are you awake?'

William opened his mouth but the dread spun him in such circles he was too dizzy to speak. Instead he nodded dumbly, his eyes still tight shut.

'Water. You must take a little water.'

Her hand tilted his head until his lips touched the rim of a cup. He drank a little but the liquid caught in his throat and he coughed. Polly clasped his limp hand, pressing her lips to his palm.

'Oh, my love! How I've — but the fever is almost gone. All is well. All will be quite well.' Polly spoke cheerfully but there was a shrill note to her voice that grated against William's ribs. 'And you must eat, get back your strength. Some soup maybe? A little cheese?' William shook his head, clenching his eyes shut. Carefully Polly replaced his hand on the coverlet. 'Maybe later then. Oh, Di, my little lambkin, all will be well! But get along with you now. Your papa is quite worn out. We must let him sleep.'

William did not open his eyes again until he was certain they were in the kitchen. Di always jumped down the last three stairs, however many times Polly scolded him for it. The flimsy banisters rattled, then quietened. He wanted only to be alone, to lose himself in sleep. While he was awake his head crammed with questions and the ghosts of answers rose in a sweaty chill over his skin. There were certainties, he insisted to himself. Immutable certainties. He was in Lambeth. The war was over. He could not have walked the frozen trenches, it was impossible, however vivid their horrors. They were no more than dreams, fiery imaginings stoked by fever. He had a wife, a son, a modest but respectable position in the Metropolitan Board of Works. He was surveyor to the Commission of Sewers. Sewers. The word sent a terrible spasm of dread through his chest, dislodging fragments of memory: the rising tide, the weight of the water dragging at his trousers, the shape of the knife in his hand, the falling bodies of the soldiers . . .

Reflexively his hand sought out his arm. It throbbed, although until that moment he had not noticed it. Beneath the sleeve of his nightgown a thick bandage ran from wrist to elbow. William's fingers stiffened.

He faltered. It was best to leave the bandage in place, for if the wounds were open there was a considerable risk of infection. Perhaps though they were little more than scratches. It would mean something, would it not, if they were only scratches? It was possible.

Ripping roughly at the bandage William dragged it off. The fresh wounds were crusted with black scabs, jewelled with bright beads of fresh blood where William in his haste had torn at the edges. The skin, already tight and shiny with scars, had knit together awkwardly so that it puckered along the seams. The cuts were thickly clustered, so thickly that William could barely make out beneath them the fading pink of the letter W, and at least one of them was very deep, encircling the arm as if the knife had sought to wipe itself clean on fresh flesh. And between the slashes, clustered together in the middle, were perhaps twelve short cuts, each approximately an inch long. They were not healing well. The lips of the wounds were swollen and yellowed, weeping a thin pus. William winced as he ran a fingertip over them. They were deep, very deep. A knife held flat against the arm would not make a cut of this kind. It would be necessary instead to take the knife in one's fist and, with the point downwards, stab it and stab it and stab it . . .

William vomited on to the floor, so that splashes of the liquid caught in the wicker of the mending basket. There was nothing in his stomach but a little water but still he retched again and again, his abdomen clenched into a fist, the bile bitter on his tongue. When he heard Polly once again upon the stairs he dared not look at her. Instead he held out his damaged arm, his fingers extended in desperate supplication. The stained bandages lay in a jumbled heap upon the coverlet.

At the threshold of the bedroom Polly gasped and stopped abruptly, her wide skirts obscuring the doorway.

'Di, get downstairs.'

Startled by the sharpness of her tone the boy obeyed. They listened together to the thump as he leaped the last stairs into the narrow hallway. Then Polly closed the door, pouring water into the basin on the washstand.

'Bless me, what in heaven's name do you think you are doing?' she scolded her husband, snatching up the discarded bandages and twisting them tightly around his arm so that the tips of William's fingers tingled.

When she was finished she crouched beside the bed, bent awkwardly over her swollen belly, and mopped at the floor with a wadded rag. There were strands of white in the rich chestnut-brown of her hair and a reddish freckle stood out in its pale parting. William fixed his eyes upon the freckle, holding himself steady.

'What happened?' he whispered.

'You've been sick, dear, that's all. Once I've got the mess cleared I'll bring you some broth to settle your stomach. That nice Mr Mitchell threw in a couple of decent bones for me yesterday when he heard you were taken poorly.'

She scrubbed briskly at the wooden boards. She did not look at him. William felt a dark dropping sensation in his stomach, as if he were falling and falling through a sewer shaft.

'But before that,' he made himself ask. 'When — ? I — I have been here, in bed here, for some time, I think?'

'You've not been well at all,' Polly said cheerfully, rinsing the rag in the basin. 'Ranting and raving with the fever and all sorts. Still, that's behind us now. Best to forget it and fix on righting yourself.'

'But — ?'

'It was Tuesday morning when the constables brought you home, around five o'clock I suppose it would have been. Woke Di with the commotion, not to mention half the street likely enough with you all afire and jabbering on fit to bust.' Polly paused, the rag twisted in a fierce rope between her hands. Then she began mopping again with renewed vigour. 'Today's Saturday.'

Four days. He had lain here for four days. His disquiet eased a little, although he could not have said why.

'We have a great deal to be grateful for, all the same,' Polly went on in the same bright tone. 'Goodness knows what would have become of you if they hadn't happened along. Found you half-frozen to death by the river, they did, your clothes all torn and filthy and your face as white as a sheet. Not to mention your best studs ripped clean from your shirt.' Polly broke off from her mopping to shake her head. Her bark of laughter bristled like a mouthful of pins. 'What for the love of the Almighty were you thinking of, my pet, out like that and on such a bitter night? You're lucky you're alive!'

'Am I?'

He had not intended to ask the question aloud but somehow the words became entangled with a sigh and escaped him. At once Polly flung her rag on to the floor and snatched his wrists, her fingers digging painfully into the damaged flesh. Her pink mouth was pressed into a hard white line and the golden flecks in her eyes flashed with fury.

'You stop that this instant, do you hear me? I won't have talk like that, I won't, not while I'm alive in this house. I won't have you ruin us, you understand? I won't have it. I don't care if you've struck a pact with the Devil himself, I'm not going to stand by and watch while you get us throwed out into the gutter. What do you think will happen to us if you go and get yourself froze to death? If you keep on — you know, with that — that business you do to yourself?' Her voice cracked as she raised her head to stare towards the window. 'You think your precious Board's going to concern itself over whether we've a place to go or food in our mouths? Or trouble themselves with what's going to become of Di or the baby when it comes? Do you think there aren't one hundred men out there lining up to take up your position soon as look at you? You think they aren't there now, making up to your Mr Lovage while you lie here whimpering? Well, do you?'

She turned back and gazed into his face. Distress crumpled the smooth skin between her brows and, as she pleated the stuff of her apron roughly between her fingers, he saw the tears shining in her eyes. It blurred the hard golden flecks in her eyes to the colour of watery tea. Something clutched at the pit of William's stomach.

'Why, William?' she asked. Quite suddenly the fire had gone out in her and her voice was as soft and grey as ash. A single tear slipped down her cheek. 'We're happy. Aren't we happy?'

William gazed back at her hopelessly. He wanted to comfort her but his heart was hollow. There was not a scrap of comfort in him. Even his bones felt hollow, so brittle they might be snapped in two. At the base of his skull, like the scrabblings of a mouse behind the skirting board, the cravings stirred and stretched.

Polly squeezed her eyes closed. Then, scrubbing at her damp cheek with her apron, she swept up the basin of dirty water and pressed her face into a smile.

'Well, you've got some colour back in your cheeks, I'm glad to see. That'll be the sickness passing. I'll bring you up some soup and then it's time we got you up and about. I've pressed and patched your trousers though I'm afraid they'll never be as good as they was. Still, you'll be wanting to get yourself back to the Board on Monday, I'm sure. Not a moment to lose, isn't that what Mr Lovage always says? Besides, we'd like to see your face of an evening. Di and I have been quite dull without you.'

Without waiting for a reply she hurried out of the room. William closed his eyes. He heard her calling for Di from the top of the stairs and the muffled hiccup of his answering shout. He followed the complaints of the stairs as she descended to the kitchen. He felt nothing. His wife's harsh words struck at him but feebly, without conviction, and they faded like smoke as the black rush of the cravings surged at him and through him, packing his chest and his throat and each and every one of his brittle scraped-out bones with their voracious black heat. They scalded the soles of his feet and set the roots of his hair alight. His skin burned.

Shakily, William pushed back the coverlet. As he struggled to sit upright the room dipped and swayed around him, and he clutched the mattress to steady himself. Then, holding tightly to the iron bedstead, he swung his feet to the floor and stood, his legs trembling. The cravings tore through his body like a blaze of burning gas. His entire body was on fire now, every blackened fibre screaming for release. The coarse stuff of the bandage tormented his blistering skin. He ripped at his sleeve as he staggered across the room. The kitchen. There were knives in the kitchen. And then out of the fog of his memory came an image, perfectly sharp. The dark tunnel. The body. The splash of footsteps. His hand around the handle of his knife as he sheathed it in his trouser pocket. William wheeled around. But his trousers were not laid over the back of the chair as they always were. He had to find them. He had to find the knife. He flung open the door of the bedroom, lurching across the narrow landing. Before him the flight of stairs reeled and swam, dropping away from him in treacherous swoops. His legs buckled. The cravings made it hard to breathe.

Clasping the flimsy banister with both hands he dragged himself downwards. At the foot of the stairs he missed his footing and fell, striking his head against the sharp corner of the wall. A shaft of sunlight sliced through the coloured glass panel in the door, dripping spots of red and purple on to the scrubbed flags, on to the backs of his hands. He could feel the blood leaking into his hair. Blood. Its warm stickiness inflamed him. He pressed his fingers into the wound and licked them. The hunger exploded within him, the screams rising and rising, pressing up beneath his diaphragm, forcing his lungs into his throat. He tried to get up but his legs would not obey him.

So he crawled. When his nightgown caught around his knees he tore at it so viciously that the thin cotton ripped to his waist. His damp palms left grey shadows on the flags and his breath came in rapid pants, like a dog. He had only to make it to the kitchen. There were knives in the kitchen. Their blades flashed cool and silver as water. He fell against the kitchen door, his fingers scrabbling the raw pine, his wild eyes raking the dresser for the knife, for any knife. The dresser had a glass panel, he could break that if he had to, or there was the shattered edge of a plate, a dish. Something sharp, anything sharp. A cleaver glinted on the scrubbed table. A cleaver! He flung himself at the table, hauling himself up with his undamaged arm and stretching, stretching out with each of his fingers until at last they touched the cool, smooth metal of the blade. William could feel the certainty of ecstasy opening up within him, a brilliant pinprick of perfect light. Triumphantly he snatched up the heavy knife, holding it aloft. Each of his fingers pressed themselves ardently against its handle as he slid down against the table leg and pressed his lips to the blade. His breath bloomed in a brief cloud on the cold metal. Then, with delicate precision, he brought it down and sliced open the flesh of his naked thigh.

'Oh, sweet Jesus!'

Polly stood in the doorway, her hands clapped over her mouth as the wooden clothes pins clattered from her looped-up apron on to the stone floor. Her eyes were round with horror. In front of her, his head thrown back against the leg of the kitchen table, William slumped in a puddle of blood, his torn nightgown raised to his waist. A single deep gash ran across the ghost-white skin of his thigh. The blood had begun to clot, although a sticky stream still ran dreamily down the curve of his leg and on to the soft coil of his exposed penis. The dressing trailed from his arm, exposing the wrecked flesh, the curled underside of the bandage patterned with stiff dark stains set off with splatters of fresh scarlet. Where the skin was not scarred or scabbed it was marked with a twisted barley sugar pattern of faint pink lines where the too-tight dressing had pressed into his skin. His arms were flung out at his side and in his right hand, cradled loosely in his fingers, he held the meat cleaver. A curl of sandy hair clung to its bloodstained blade. His eyes were closed, his mouth slack, but his face shone like an angel's, flooded with joy.

The rage drained the blood from her veins, leaving her white and stiff and perfectly cold.

'Get up!' she snarled. 'Get up, do you hear me?'

Grabbing his ruined arm she twisted it painfully, kicking a stout boot into his side. William gasped and fell backwards, striking his shoulder against the table.

'Get up!'

She kicked him again, harder this time. The wound on his leg issued a startled spurt of blood. William opened his eyes and frowned at her, blinking, struggling to place her, to bring her into focus. Somewhere beyond him he could sense agitation, someone shouting, but it could not reach him. He was perfectly composed.

Polly snatched the cleaver from his hand. 'You want your son to see you like this?'

she screamed, shaking the blade in his face. 'Well, do you?'

She grabbed him by the collar of his nightgown and shook him, jolting his head. William barely noticed. But the rough movement dislodged something in his head and, as clear as if he stood before him, William saw a man. The shadowed crown of his hat obscured his features but his face was white and his eyes burned with the reflected flame of his lantern. In his hand he held a knife.

'There was someone else,' William said suddenly. 'In the tunnels. I saw him.'

Polly's face twisted and her hands fell slackly to her sides.

'Get out of here!' she implored him, her voice worn thin with desperation. The tears streamed down her white cheeks.

'Only for a moment. But I saw him.'

'William, listen to me, I beg you!'

William closed his eyes and listened. Amplified but impeccably crisp, a fragment of that lost night echoed through his head like the peals of the Sunday bells, part of a pattern but at the same time all separate, each chime true to itself. The scrape of brick, the squelch of mud and the slap of water, the sucked-in gasp and the grunt of effort, the mewling of a drowning kitten, the choked liquid gurgles, the dull thud of a boot against flesh, the flat plummeting splash of a heavy sack pitched into the stream, all returned to William in perfect formation like a sweet snatch of melody. He could even feel the slimed chill of the tunnel wall against the palms of his hands as he pressed himself back against it, the pitch of his covert breath in his chest, the uneasy stiffness of his legs against the pull of the stream. He had been anxious, afraid of being seen, of being heard. He had seen nothing, no more than the glimpse of a face snatched in lamplight. But he had heard. He heard it again now. The last desperate moan of a dying man.

He gasped, reaching out to clasp Polly's hands.

'He murdered someone,' he whispered, his eyes bright with certainty. 'Down there. I know it. He murdered someone.'

Polly crumpled. Her head fell forward so that her hair sagged in its pins, and her shoulders shook. Her hands in William's were cold and slack. William stared at her for a moment, his expression puzzled, before lifting her chin with his finger. She stared at him with her drowned red eyes. Gently, William stroked sticky strands of hair away from her wet face.

'Don't be afraid, my little milkwort,' William said tenderly 'We are quite safe here.'

From Polly's mouth there escaped a strange strangulated sob of laughter. Then, pressing one hand over her mouth and clutching the other hard against the curve of her swollen belly, she fled from the room, slamming the door behind her.

William sat for a long time on the cold stone floor, thinking. Through the open window there drifted the high chirrups of his son's laughter and the softer echo of his wife. Then, with his habitual meticulousness, he cleaned and dressed the wound on his leg and mopped the blood from the kitchen floor. The fever had weakened him so he had often to pause and rest. The wound in his leg throbbed. When at last he tipped away the dirtied water his whole body ached for sleep. Very slowly he made his way towards the stairs. At the doorway he paused, his hand on the porcelain knob, and looked back. The flags were still not quite clean. In places the blood had seeped into the grey mortar between the slabs, staining it brown. Tomorrow he would try again. Moving stiffly, bent over like an old man, he shuffled along the passageway to the stairs.

★ ★ ★

On several occasions during the week of his convalescence William tried again to speak to Polly of the murder he had witnessed but Polly remained perfectly deaf on the subject. She sang over his words with a vicious kind of gaiety or she called out to Di to bring her her sewing basket. Once or twice, when she was on her feet and thus able to manage her increasingly clumsy body with sufficient haste, she left the room. It was as though he had never spoken. With Di she was cheerful and loving as always, although the advanced state of her confinement left her tired and breathless. To William she spoke only when absolutely necessary and then only in a tone of brittle politeness that he did not recognize as hers. She was a dutiful nurse, straightening his sheets, bringing him soups and infusions of herbs, even reading to him when his eyes were too tired to follow the words. But she could barely bring herself to look at him. The golden flecks in her eyes were hard and dull, like tarnished brass. She locked the kitchen knives in a high cabinet along with William's razor and the paperknife. The iron key jangled from her belt like a jailer's. When Di tried to play with it she smacked away his fingers so sharply that he cried. Afterwards, when the boy crept into what remained of her lap and closed his eyes, she stroked his hair and the tears gathered in the corners of her caramel eyes. At night she slept with the key concealed beneath her pillow.

As soon as William could adequately stand she insisted he return to work.

'You have responsibilities, if you haven't forgotten,' she admonished him grimly. 'There's men biting off their own hands to take your position. You think they're going to hold it open for you while you swoon away like a lady?'

William leaned against the doorjamb. Negotiating the staircase had exhausted him and his knees trembled. He had lost a good deal of weight. His trousers sagged on his hips and the flesh beneath his cheekbones appeared to have been scooped out with a spoon. His hair stood up in startled tufts. He resembled more than anything the man who had been returned to her from the Crimea. Polly kept her gaze fixed rigidly upon the fireplace.

'I will have to inform them,' William said quietly. 'Of the murder. It is incumbent upon me as a servant of the Board. You do understand that, don't you?'

He started back as Polly wheeled around, her face dark with rage.

'What is wrong with you?' she screamed. 'Are you set on ruining us? Is that it? Well, is it?'

'Polly, please. Of course not. I have no wish to cause trouble for us. But the sewers are Board property. If there has been a *murder* —'

'Murder? You listen to me, you blind addle-headed fool. If there truly has been a murder you'd better bloody hope they never find out. You think they'll just thank you warmly and give you half a crown? You with your — your filthy cuts all over your body and your bloody knife in your pocket? I found the knife, William. I found it. It don't look too good, does it? And if you go trotting off telling them about some murder, who exactly do *you* reckon they'll think did it?'

XV

The Captain'd been vague but Tom was lucky. Him and Lady'd had to go no more than a few hundred yards before they'd happened on the body. Tom'd smelled it first. It was the smell of blood picked it out, powerful strong and with that sticky edge of sweetness that blood always got just when it set to drying. There was the stink of shit too. Before he copped it the cove'd filled his drawers. You wouldn't have thought you'd notice a stink like that down here, given you was already three foot deep in the stuff but somehow out of the stream it was different. More solid, somehow, and meatier, even though the body had been dead a while. Two days, Tom guessed, for all the cold weather had kept it fresh.

Apart from its hair the corpse was almost dry. A quirk of the tide had caught it in a bottleneck in one of the narrow tunnels that led off from the Dean-street stream, so as it was wedged clean out the water. Tom set his shoulder against the body and shoved. The body gave a little, like clay that wasn't yet hard, but it wasn't moving anywhere, forwards or back. This channel was deep and even at full tide the body wouldn't be under the water. There wouldn't be the force in the stream to budge him, not till the spring tides came in March. Tom smiled to himself. Make sure it doesn't ever get out, those'd been the Captain's instructions. So long as there wasn't no body for the traps to find they'd not be able to pin anything on his friend. But the Captain'd wasted his friend's money. The stream'd already done the job for him. If he'd chosen it himself Tom couldn't have jammed it in a safer spot.

Tom peered at the body. A gent, dressed respectable in a greatcoat over a dark suit of clothes. Well, he'd reckoned on that. What surprised him more was the state of him. He'd expected a bodge if he was honest, the way the Captain'd put it to him, shaking his head and frowning as if he wasn't too pleased at having to sort out another man's messes for him. An accident, Tom'd had it down as, perhaps a knock to the back of the head, maybe a single gun shot. But this body'd have turned the stomach of a sailor. For starters they'd cut his throat so deep the head was thrown backwards further than the lid on a pewter pot and the tips of its hair trailed in the stream, but that wasn't the half of it. The spread of his chest was a bedlam of blood and mashed flesh, the dark fabric of his vest pounded together with the stiff front of his shirt into a scarlet pulp. You'd have to stab a man fifteen, twenty times to do that kind of damage. Tom paddled his fingers in the man's ruined chest, hoping for a watch, but there was nothing but the cold oyster-meat of his flesh. He could have what he wanted, that was the arrangement, as long as any papers went to the Captain. The Captain'd been particular about that. He'd asked if Tom could read and when Tom'd said there'd never been much call for reading in his line of work he'd nodded and said that in that case he was to bring anything that looked like a paper, for all it was no more than a scribble. Not that his friend had reckoned there'd be anything important, the Captain'd said easily, but they'd be something by way of proof Tom'd done the necessaries. Papers aside, anything else on the body was Tom's to keep. It was one of the reasons Tom'd agreed to do it, though the Captain's terms weren't what you'd call generous. That and greasing the wheels of business. There was still a week or two to go until the fight.

The more a man's interests was tied up with another's, the more he was to be trusted. Tom'd learned that lesson early.

Tom wiped his hands dainty as a lady on the man's hair before yanking on a handful of it to lift the head. The face of the dead man was cold and yellow as dried wax, save for a splatter of blood beneath one eye, and the corners of its bloodless lips drew back like a dog's into showy black whiskers. Its eyes were pale and wide open and they started from their sockets, staring out in what Tom fancied was more astonishment than terror. Dim-witted beggar, Tom thought, tossing the head back into the stream. It bounced against the brick wall with a dull thud and something in the neck crunched and snapped, letting the head drift further down into the cold water. The tide left a bubbled brown scum on the stretched yellow skin of its forehead.

'You'd think a gent'd take better care of his appearance, wouldn't you?' Tom muttered dryly to Lady as he set her down on the shelf created by the dead man's legs.

With a practised eye he looked the man over. Not a man for jewellery then, which was a pity. No rings, no pin in what was left of the neckcloth. Cuff-links in the shirt cuffs, that was something. Good boots, if a little worn at the soles. Lady sniffed cautiously at the man's groin as Tom stripped them off, tipping the water out of them and shoving them toe-down into his pockets. The hem of the man's greatcoat, unbuttoned, trailed in the water. Tom rummaged through the pockets. Papers of some kind, not bank notes, too thick, scabbed with seals and whatnot. A letter or two. Gloves, a handkerchief marked with fancy blue initials. A pocketbook, similarly stamped in gold. He opened it. More papers and postage stamps and, tucked into the back, a five shilling note. You'd find more on a sailor. No snuffbox, neither, nor any of the trinkets you might've hoped for. Tom felt a prickle of vexation.

The tide licked at his hips. He had to get a shift on. He rubbed the cloth of the coat between his fingers. Worth taking. The man's arms had stiffened which made the job trickier than it might've been and he was lying with all his weight on the back of it, but it wasn't like Tom hadn't done it before. When he'd got the coat off he inspected it in the light of the lantern. It wasn't in bad nick, all things considered, the damage no more than a rip in the pocket and a button missing. He slipped his fingers into the man's trouser pockets. A leather purse, no markings. Tom opened it. A few more coins, none more than a shilling. Tom cursed to himself. If the tide hadn't gone and done the job for him he'd have reckoned himself properly out of pocket. As it was it was hardly worth the candle. Still, the trousers were decent, not as good as the coat, but decent. Cleaned up they'd fetch a bit of something from the Jew down Rosemary-lane. Hurriedly he fumbled the buttons open and lifted Lady into his arms so he could pull them off. With the dog in his arms it was awkward. The cloth was sodden and bulky with blood and sewer water and the dead man's doings and the legs were set stiff as posts.

At last he wrenched the trousers free and, shaking out the worst of it into the stream, he rolled them into the coat and bundled them around his waist. The stripped body lolled in the faint light of the lantern, the legs oddly hairless and white as sewer-eels. The gashed neck leered at Tom with its sticky black grin. He was done. Now it was time for the tide to do its part. A week or two and not even the gent's own mother'd be able to put a name to the body. Another week for luck and Tom'd come back for it. Between them he and the dredger-men would manage for it to be pulled out the water quite unexpected-like up Rotherhithe way. They was paying a crown and sixpence inquest money over at Rotherhithe these days, more than twice as much as any other place along the river, and, what with it being him what found it, Tom'd be sure of half of that at the least. The Captain'd never know the difference. Checking that the body was still firmly wedged in the tunnel and dampening his light, Tom took Lady in his arms and hurried away, against the tide, towards the main sewer.

It was late by the time he pulled himself up into the cellar, later than he'd imagined. The hollering and whatnot that seeped of an evening out of the padding-kens in the alley had settled into the flatter rustle of night. Tom took down one of the rat crates from the recess in the wall and stowed the man's clothes inside it. The cuff-links he slipped into the finger of a glove, tying the dead man's handkerchief around it in a bundle. There was a place he had in the tunnels no one knew about but him. They'd be safe there, at least until things had a chance to settle. You never quite knew. Traps was sharper these days, and they wasn't so unwilling to take a poke around the rookeries the way they had been at the start.

He pulled the papers from his pocket and opened them up. There was what looked like a letter written on sheets of paper as stiff as a fingernail and, tucked into its leaves, a couple of very official-looking documents, bristling with signatures and stamps and all the rest of it. The Captain'd asked for the papers back. As proof, was what he'd said. So as he could be sure Tom'd done what he'd been asked. Tom'd agreed, at the time. Now he considered the papers for a moment, feeling the heft of them between his fingers. There was initials on the pocketbook. That'd give the Captain his proof. The papers, well, Tom had lived a lifetime on the streets and his nose was sharp. If you was looking to do business with men like the Captain it was as well to have a little something set aside by way of insurance. He tucked them into the hem of his coat with the gloves and the handkerchief. He'd take them down soon as he could. The postage stamps and the change-purse he'd hawk to the Jew in the morning.

Lady lay quietly at his side as he worked, her nose resting on her paws. When he was finished Tom clicked his fingers and she rose, slipping the cold tip of her nose into his hand. Her whiskers twitched against his palm as she lifted her chin to look at him. He tugged at her ear, the lamby one that stood to attention; his other hand was clenched tight in his pocket, the knuckles sharp against his thigh. He stood like that for a moment, his fingers searching out the familiar shape and sense of her ear, the bump of the veins, the faint bristle of hairs along its edge, the curve of it neat as a lady's slipper. It was always unnatural hot, Lady's upright ear, even on a wicked night like this one. Tom shivered and then, clearing his throat, he banged his fist briskly against his leg. It was late and he was almost falling asleep on his feet. The pocket rattled. It was a moment before he remembered he still had them studs in there, the ones he'd skimmed off of the lunatic two nights earlier. What with all the palaver he'd forgotten clean about them.

Squatting beside Lady, he set them out on his palm. They weren't particularly fancy, no more than mother-of-pearl set into what looked like tin, but in the light of the lantern the shell glowed pink and orange, pretty as a sunset. Lady nudged them gently with her nose.

'You like 'em, lassie?' Tom murmured, watching her face.

Lady's pink tongue lolled out and her stump of a tail worried the cellar floor. Tom smiled at her and, lifting her chin gently, he touched his nose to hers. Her whiskers quivered against his upper lip.

'They're all yours,' he whispered.

Very gently, soft as a warm breath, Lady licked his cheek. Tom's fingers sought out the sensitive spot on her belly and scratched. Lady tilted her head back, stretching into his caress until the back of her head rested on his shoulder. Dropping the studs back into his pocket Tom wrapped his arms around her and drew her to him.

'We should get home,' he murmured but he didn't move. Neither did Lady. He held her close, memorizing the pattern of the hair along her skull, the black ripples of her gums, the bump of her shoulders and her spine as they pressed awkwardly against his belly. It wasn't long before the pain in his stiff knees was nagging at him, fearsome as a fishwife, but Tom paid it no heed. There was a dark hole inside his chest that had already started to open. He knew it would make him dizzy when he stood up. So he stayed where he was, his knees ablaze with the cramp, his arms wrapped around the dog. His hundred-guinea girl. The tears dropped on to the black velvet of her broken ear and quivered there, bright as diamonds.

XVI

The downstairs parlour at the Badger was fuller than Tom'd ever seen it. The din filled the place close as fog, so as you couldn't make out any particular sound until you was right up against it and even then you only had it a moment before you lost it again. Every last thought in your head was drowned out by the shouts and stamping of boots and the banging of pots and dogs whimpering and snarling and rattling their chains against the wooden forms, and the whole commotion all thickened up together by the smoke from the lamps and the candles and the fire and a hundred stubby pipes.

It was almost Christmas. Only a brace of streets away the grand shops draped themselves like a duchess's necklace around the great curve of Regent-street, their enormous windows aflame with gaslight and stuffed with silks of every colour under the sun. The pavements were crammed with elegantly dressed people, strolling and pointing and not paying proper attention to their belongings. It weren't no surprise that the mood in the small smoky room was high and rising, not to mention the racket. Tom bent down as Lady pressed herself against his legs, taking her into his arms. She rested her chin on his shoulder as the rumness of it all tugged at his belly and the stringy sinews of his thighs. That he was standing here, on the night he was to make himself a proper fortune, and wanting with all his heart to be somewhere else.

All of a sudden Brassey was at his side.

'Tom,' he said, peering at Lady with his toady little eyes. 'You better be ready. If you go and make me look a fool —'

He left it there, smiling his toad smile. Tom'd have liked to thump him but there'd've been no purpose in it. With the crush in the parlour the proprietor would've been kept upright even if Tom'd succeeded in knocking him clean off his feet.

'We're ready,' Tom muttered instead.

'Fancy collar the creature's got herself,' Brassey observed, his little eyes glinting. 'Hers, is it?'

Tom frowned. It rubbed his bristles up the wrong way, the way Brassey looked at him as though he was always on the dodge and it was only out of the kindness of his heart that he, Brassey, wasn't headed direct to the beak to see justice done. Every man in this parlour knew Brassey to be the slippiest man alive. Tom, on the other hand, had made a point of getting Lady's collar made up on the level. Somehow it had seemed right to have things done proper. So he'd paid a coiner he knew in Drury-lane the best part of a crown to have the madman's studs set into handsome links of melted Britannia spoon. His coins were always slummed with lamp-black and oil to take the gleam of newness off of them but the coiner's daughter had taken time to polish up the collar to a fine shine. It twinkled and glinted in the parlour's dirty light, bright as a beadle's chain.

'Course it's hers,' Tom replied tersely. 'Who's else'd it be?'

Brassey fluttered his eyelids, bowing slightly from the waist.

'Who else's indeed?' he agreed. 'Still, you must fancy your chances, a cautious man like yourself, parting with your winnings afore they're safe in your pocket.'

Tom glanced down at Lady. She peered at him through half-closed eyes and set her nose closer to his neck. He swallowed, loosening the knot in his throat.

'She'll win.'

'She'd better.' Brassey rocked backwards on his slippered feet and rubbed his hands together. 'She'd better.'

Tom looked around the room.

'Where's the Captain?'

Brassey licked his lips.

'He'll be here. Plenty of time yet. But he'll be here.'

There were to be several dogs brought up ahead of Lady with the intention of getting the Fancy's appetite whetted before the main dish was served. At nine o'clock on the nose Brassey had the men brought upstairs. The Captain was not yet arrived but Brassey was impatient to keep the tension rising, experience having shown him that excitable men were martyrs to thirst. Tom sat downstairs in the near-deserted front parlour, Lady upon his lap. The only other drinker was an old man with whiskers like sheep's wool snagged on a thorn bush and a sheep's doleful expression who stared into his dirty glass and occasionally expelled a snorting burst of air by way of conversation. Otherwise the room was silent but for the odd thump and scrabble of claws from the pit upstairs. Lady cocked her upright ear to catch it, her pink tongue quivering. It occurred to Tom with a sharp twist of his gut that she was excited.

They'd been waiting a good while when a dark-faced coster-boy staggered down the stairs, a bloodied bulldog in his arms. Dressed slap-up flash, his hair teased into six curls beneath a plush skullcap of the type the costers called a King's-man, he stood in the centre of the parlour and thrust the dog out in front of him, as if offering the animal to Tom for inspection. Lady lifted her head to oblige him, her pink eyes alert.

'Go well?' Tom asked, since the lad looked set on staying put till he did.

The boy scowled. Dropping the dog without warning on to the floor, he delivered a fierce kick to its ribs. It slunk beneath the settle. Tom fancied he felt Lady flinch.

'If I ever gets my fists on that devil what sold 'im me,' he growled. 'Told me it was a ratter born and bred, 'e did, like to bring 'em down a score a minute. That useless beast?' He spat scornfully on to the sawdust floor and wiped his hands on his tight breeches. 'Couldn't've deaded a singleton, not if the ugly little bastard'd lain there and offered it its throat for Sunday dinner.'

Tom shook his head.

'I's only glad there wasn't no one much

mattered up there to see it,' the coster-boy went on, more cheerfully. ' 'E'd've given me all sorts, that Cap'n gent, what with Brassey gettin' me to talk the bleedin' runt up something proper last time I seed 'im.'

Tom stroked Lady's head thoughtfully.

'Captain's not in, then?'

'Nah. Big to-do up Kentish-town way to-night. Prime chaff, they says. Reckon 'e fancied 'is chances over there.' The lad grinned broadly, revealing a wide gap in the space ordinarily given over to a pair of front teeth. 'Brassey's got a face on 'im sourer 'n week-old milk.'

He wasn't coming. Tom's hand moved up and over Lady's head, the veins twisted around the bumps of his knuckles like they was lengths of twine securing his fingers to his palm, and even as he watched it move it felt like it belonged to someone else.

The Captain's not coming.

He couldn't make sense of it. For nearly a month he had strained towards this moment and against it, counting off the days on his fingers and in the pit of his stomach, knowing all the while that on this day everything would turn. The last few weeks he'd all but forgotten his fear that the Captain would betray him. Too much water under the bridge, Tom'd reckoned. Too much he knew. When he'd handed over the pocketbook and told the Captain there'd been no papers on the dead man, Tom'd known the Captain didn't much believe him. There wasn't nothing the Captain could do, of course, Tom being so insistent, but from that moment Tom'd figured himself safe. And then, all of a sudden, without so much as a sniff of warning, the fight was off. Tonight was to be a night like any other. No worse than most, better than some, a night you'd be pushed to remember a week from now. Despite the wager, despite all that had passed between them, the Captain had not come. There would be no fight. There would be no one hundred guineas.

The chill ran like a streak of sweat down his spine. No one hundred guineas. For all he'd not yet won it that money'd squatted for weeks on the edge of things, spilling from its sack like golden corn. And now the Captain wasn't coming. Tom shivered, he couldn't help himself. The Captain had done him over and, like a cotton-headed dollymop, Tom was left with his drawers around his ankles and his ears ringing with a hundred empty promises. The rage and disappointment curdled the spit in Tom's mouth and stiffened his fingers so that

Lady shook her head to loosen his grasp. The Captain had needed a man of Tom's kind, someone to entertain his friends, to dispose of his friend's awkward doings. And Long Arm Tom with his terrier's nose for a dodge, who had reckoned himself so wide awake he'd thought there wasn't a trickster in all of the metropolis sharp enough to catch him out, Long Arm Tom had been hooked and landed like a fish, and all the time he was being reeled in he'd not thought to put up the slightest twist of a fight. He'd been a fool, a blind greedy old fool, and when he lay himself down in his crib tonight he'd have what he deserved. Nothing. Nothing but Lady.

'Fine collar your dog's got itself,' the lad observed admiringly, fingering his own brightly-patterned neckerchief. 'Champion, is she? Worth a flatch?'

Tom said nothing. Instead he pushed Lady to the floor and stood up. His legs were old and very tired and they shook a little as he straightened. The coster-boy aimed another less enthusiastic kick in the direction of his own dog and crossed the parlour towards the bar.

'She'd've been a champion,' Tom muttered but the coster-lad did not turn around. 'A true champion. Given half a chance.'

When Lady wriggled her nose into the palm of his hand Tom snatched his hand away, making a show of wiping it off on his coat. The dog stared at him with her pink eyes and then slunk away, her belly almost grazing the floor. Tom wanted to kick her and he wanted to take her in his arms, and he wanted both powerfully and at the same time. His chest hurt.

The outside door burst open. Into the parlour tumbled several gentlemen, wrapped in thick greatcoats and heavy scarves and bringing with them a burst of frozen air and the bosky bog stink of whisky.

'Brandy!' ordered one of them, thrashing at the air with a silver-topped cane. 'Let there be brandy!'

'But surely there's a mistake,' another one protested, his words misshapen by drink. 'Nothing doing here. Look you, there's no one here but an old man.'

'Why, Tom,' drawled a familiar voice and the Captain doffed his hat with a flourish, tipping it to Lady. 'Good evening to you.'

The Captain's face was flushed, the spots of red in his cheeks as bright as a trollop's. His lips were red too and glossy and the tip of his tongue flickered out to lick at them, over and over. The pores stood out black on his skin and the dark centres of his eyes were so unnaturally large there was room for only a thin band of colour around them. Tom sniffed but to his surprise he couldn't find it, the animal musk of fucking. Just whisky and the harsh reek of fog and snow, metallic as blood. Tom's eyes narrowed.

'Deal still on?' he demanded.

The Captain inclined his head.

'One hundred guineas?' Tom pressed.

'Was that our agreement?' The Captain's eyes glittered as he smiled, baring his sharp yellow teeth. 'Well then, naturally. One hundred guineas.'

Perhaps Brassey had been spying through the keyhole or perhaps he had the toad's instinct for a fly. Whatever it was he was in the downstairs parlour and flexing his slippered feet before his boy had time to set a bottle on the table. A number of dogs had already been in, he told the gentlemen, his head swivelling frantically on his shoulders, but there were a number still to be done with upstairs if the gentlemen fancied something by way of a warm-up. Otherwise he would have the pit cleared forthwith to accommodate the big fight. Whatever the gentlemen chose. His fingers rubbed at the slope of his belly, counting his likely takings.

As his companions fell upon the brandy the Captain gestured at Tom to place Lady upon the table so he might give her the once-over. In contrast to his companions who fumbled with their glasses, their eyes and mouths dazed with drink, the Captain's features were precise. His dark eyes glowed. His breath came fast. A smile twitched at the corners of his mouth.

'So you're a killer, are you, girl?' he murmured to Lady, his shiny lips scarlet against the black of his whiskers, and he squeezed her jaw so hard that she winced. 'Got the taste for it, have you? The taste for blood?'

Tom said nothing. He stared at the floor, his hands clenched in his pockets. When Brassey escorted the gentlemen upstairs, he did not follow them. There were to be three or four rounds before Lady's. The dog lay at his feet. He did not touch her. He hardly moved. He kept his hands in his lap and his mind empty. If he started thinking he wouldn't stop. So he stared at the smoky shadows on the wall, his hands in his lap, and he waited.

When at last they were summoned Lady was almost asleep. She blinked groggily at Tom as he roused her. Why hadn't he thought to keep her awake? Tom rebuked himself angrily. He should've sharpened her mind on something, so as to keep her alert. She'd be slower now, on account of dozing off like that. Tom felt flustered and unnerved. Upstairs he set the dog on the platform and stood back as the Fancy rushed at her, peering into her mouth and squeezing her paws. When they was done prodding and poking they sidled up to Brassey, muttering into his ear, and the proprietor nodded and scribbled their wagers on to a folded wad of paper. Though he tried for a solemn expression, as befitted the importance of the occasion, the glee was slapped across his face like whitewash. There were muttered exchanges, meaningful glances. The pit was smeared with blood. In one corner Brassey's boy wiped his nose on the back of his hand and threw rat corpses by their tails into a rotted basket.

In their box the Captain and his associates banged their hands impatiently on the rim of the pit. The sill of the box was a mess of bottles and smeared glasses. One gentleman's head hung oddly from his collar, like it was no longer quite fixed on his shoulders, and his cheeks glowed green as watercress. The Captain nudged him gently and, making a proper effort to hold his head steady and not look down, the green gentleman plucked a bill from his pocketbook and, as though it were the note itself was the cause of his afflictions, waved at the Captain to do him the honour of taking it away. The Captain smiled his wolf smile and, folding the note carefully, slapped the green gentleman upon the shoulder. The slap nearly lost the man his footing altogether. He stumbled against the wall, sliding as much by luck as calculation into the chair beside him, and closed his eyes.

Brassey's lad rang a bell to signify the closing of the betting. Brassey made a few last jabs at his paper. Then he nodded at Tom. The Fancy clotted the rim of the pit, shoving at each other to secure a good position. There were indignant curses as elbows were jostled and glasses slopped. Then Brassey clapped his hands and the room fell silent.

'And now, gentlemen, for the moment we've all been waiting for, the very pinnacle of this evening of delights, in which we challenge the champion dog of the Borough, known to us Fancy men simply as Lady, to the killing of eighteen big 'uns within the space of a single minute.'

He nodded at his boy who lifted the wire

crate of rats into the pit. They weren't
Tom's rats. According to Brassey the Captain had insisted on it, so as to keep things
on the level. Jittered as he was, it occurred
to Tom to wonder who Brassey'd got the
beasts from and for what price. The boy
opened the flap set into the crate's lid and
shoved in his hand, stirring the heaving
mass like a pudding. The green-faced gentleman watched the boy, his face creased
with horror, and then, very quietly, deposited the contents of his stomach into the
corner of the box. None of his companions
paid him the faintest scrap of notice. Instead they beat each other around the
shoulders, their elegant clothes in disarray
and their eyes wild for blood. Only the
Captain held himself quite still, his eyes
fixed upon the rats as they streaked away
from the crate and piled themselves into a
writhing wad of brown against the far wall.

'Twenty,' the boy declared, closing the
crate.

With a great show of ceremony Brassey
clambered up on a chair placed close to
the gentlemen's box and drew a pocket
watch from his vest, raising his other arm
to call for silence. The Fancy drew in its
breath all in a great wheeze together as,
Lady in his arms, Tom slung his leg over

the wall of the pit. The dog made no sound but at the sight of the rats the hair across her shoulders stiffened and her legs quivered like fiddle strings.

'Time — now!'

Brassey brought down his arm. Tom let Lady go. Like a streak of lightning she crossed the pit, thrusting her face into the mound and bringing out the first of her trophies. The rats were big ones, sure enough, their heads near the size of oranges, but they were no match for Lady's cunning and dash. The rats didn't know what'd hit them. She bit into the beasts and tossed the bodies behind her with all the steadfast swagger of a coster-boy going at a roasted fowl. Contained by the second's circle Tom had only to stand and watch. And still she didn't slow. Clamp and toss, clamp and toss. As the blood and the bodies darkened the floor, the shouts began to rise and the stamps grew harder and louder until the room shook with them. Tom didn't turn to look into the box, so set were his eyes upon Lady that he might have been looking out of her head himself, but if he'd thought to turn he'd have seen that, although the Captain stood perfectly still, his wolf eyes flashed and the sweat on his forehead sparkled like ice on a windowpane. At his sides his fists were clenched, each knuckle white with triumph.

'And time!' Brassey shouted.

The roar was deafening. Tom clicked his fingers and straight off Lady dropped the rat in her mouth with all the delicacy of a lady's handkerchief and sat back on her haunches, her paws set neatly together. All around her lay dark clumps of fur. There would be an official count, it was the way things were done, but Tom knew straight off that Lady'd done it. Twenty beasts they'd had in there. A minute later there was only one rat in the pit that still moved. It eyed Lady peevishly before sitting up in the far corner of the pit, setting about its whiskers with its pink paws. Quietly, just like they were alone together down the tunnels, Tom knelt and held his arms out to Lady. She wriggled into them and grinned at him, her tail making patterns on the blood-spattered floor. Tom closed his eyes. His heart was banging fit to bust clean out of his chest. They stayed that way as Brassey's lad worked around them, counting the bodies into his basket. They did not look over towards the box where the Captain was smiling and nodding and shaking hands with those of his friends still possessed of the necessary dexterity. They'd done it. Lady was a champion. She'd go home with the Captain and Tom'd go his own way, a rich man. The spit rushed into Tom's mouth and his eyes blurred.

'Nineteen!' announced the lad, tossing the final corpse into his pottle.

The Fancy erupted. It was a while before Brassey could silence the crowd. Proceeds would be distributed in the downstairs parlour, he announced. There was a clatter of boots behind him on the stairs while, around the pit, the remainder of the Fancy gathered in noisy groups, each alive with talk of the silent dog and the supposed fortune the tosher was to make from the Captain's wager and whether it was true that the dog was the self-same beast that had fared so poor for old Jeremiah who was now dead, and what might be the dog's bloodline and whether there were other animals out there that might be pressed into fighting to such remarkable effect. Amongst all this flurry there was only one man who was quite still and quite silent, his head bowed over so as you could see the knobbles of his spine poking out above the collar of his coat. In the curve of the old man's squatting body the dog was almost invisible.

'An impressive performance.'

The Captain stood over Tom, his feet set

wide apart and his hand out. Reluctantly Tom shook it but he didn't look the Captain in the eye.

'One hundred guineas,' Tom said. The words came out cracked in the middle. He cleared his throat and tried again. 'One hundred guineas.'

The Captain smiled his wolf smile and patted his coat pocket.

'It is a great deal of money,' he said smoothly. 'Best to settle things away from the crowds, do you not agree?'

Taking Lady in his arms, Tom followed the Captain down the stairs and into the parlour where Brassey had set himself up at a small table and was busy licking the stub of his pencil. When he saw the Captain enter the room he chivvied away the coster-men who clustered around him and made something of a ceremony of pulling out a chair and dusting off its seat with his handkerchief.

'Good, good,' the Captain murmured. 'Now, Brassey, as to this wager.'

'Yes, yes, the wager,' Brassey oozed. 'We must settle the wager.'

'One hundred guineas, Tom, is a considerable sum. A sum, as I said upstairs to Mr Brassey, too considerable to risk carrying upon my person in a tavern such as this one.' The Captain peeled his lips back from his teeth. 'I was at pains to point out, was I not, Mr Brassey, that the deplorable locality of your premises and the felonious instincts of your customers provide very little in the way of a guarantee of safe passage for any items of value?'

'Quite so, quite so,' Brassey agreed, bridling as if the Captain had bestowed upon him a compliment of the highest order.

'Besides, who ever heard of a wager of this magnitude paid out in a single transaction?' The Captain shrugged. 'I therefore propose that we resolve the issue as it would be resolved in more distinguished establishments than this one. I have here forty guineas. Forty guineas,' the Captain said again, as though to impress upon Tom and Brassey the significance of the sum, and he patted his coat. 'As a deposit it represents a fair sum, I'm sure you will agree. Tom will have this now and I will take the dog. The balance of the wager I will pay out in two remaining instalments of thirty guineas, the first due next week and the second the week after that. I trust that you will find an arrangement of that kind satisfactory?'

He tipped his head at Tom who frowned suspiciously.

'No,' he said firmly. 'No money, no dog. Them's always been my terms all my life and I ain't about to change them now. When I gets my hundred guineas, you gets the dog. Not a day before.'

'Tom, Tom, listen to yourself,' Brassey cajoled. 'The Captain's not one of your ruffian associates. He's a gentleman, with a gentleman's honour. Ain't that right, sir?'

'But of course.'

Tom set his shoulders and his face darkened.

'Once I got my money, you get the dog.'

'Tom,' the Captain said smoothly. 'Mr Brassey is right. A gentleman would never break his word. However, I believe, Tom, that you and I understand each other. This is not the first time we have done business, after all. My friend was much obliged to you for disposing of his — detritus, shall we call it? As a result, my friend would be most displeased with me if I were to give you the slightest cause for unhappiness. You are intimately acquainted with personal matters of his that he has every wish to remain private. Any betrayal of you, Tom, would therefore be a much greater betrayal of a man I have known all my life.'

The Captain studied Tom's face.

'You are suspicious,' he continued. 'I understand that. It would be unreasonable of me to expect a man of your kind to do business like a gentleman.' He patted the pockets of his coat and drew out a folded sheet of paper. 'To that end I have already made sure to have a schedule of payments, all drawn up and endorsed by a lawyer, to place our dealings on an official footing. It is quite simple. I sign it here and you, Tom,' he pointed, 'here. Mr Brassey will witness our signatures.'

Brassey nodded vigorously, his head spinning like a greased ball in its socket.

'It comprises nothing less than a written guarantee for payment of the full amount,' the Captain assured him. 'One hundred guineas, as detailed here. And naturally if you do not receive the money you may reclaim the dog. The contract stipulates that most clearly. Here, do you see?'

Tom peered suspiciously at the document that the Captain held out to him. There was fancy lettering at the top of it and a stamp and a seal, both marked with the same pattern. There were two parts to the writing, both done in thick black ink. Tom could not make head nor tail of it.

'I don't hold with no papers,' Tom muttered.

'Come now, that will have to change now you are a man of means,' the Captain said and the gaslight flashed on the sharp points of his teeth. 'The law is no longer an adversary to a fellow but must become his friend, when he has money. Is that not so, Mr Brassey?'

Brassey nodded, revolving his head in his shoulders, and the smile twitched across his face.

'Indeed it is, sir,' he agreed eagerly. 'Indeed it is.'

'I am quite sure Mr Brassey is familiar with documents of this kind. But perhaps you would prefer to look it over first on your account?'

Tom stared at the paper and the black letters jumped and scattered across its creamy surface like ants. Forty guineas! Forty guineas was a fortune in itself and he could see nothing suspicious about the papers, being as they were awash with stamps and wax and signatures and the like. But the back of his neck prickled and he held Lady tight, her solid warmth against his chest.

'I want my money,' he said again, doggedly. 'All of it.'

'Ah,' exhaled the Captain. 'Well, of course you do.' He weighed the bag of money in his hand. 'And naturally it must be your decision whether or not you accept my terms. Either you accept one hundred guineas over three weeks or — well, let us just say that I would consider very carefully whether I might not be able to strike a more advantageous deal with someone else.' He squeezed the purse one last time and made to put it back in his pocket. 'I am surprised you would consider passing up so considerable a sum. However, as I say, it is for you to decide.'

'Tom!' urged Brassey, his eyes swivelling. 'You're offending the Captain. It ain't a handful of ha'pence now. This contract was drawn up by proper lawyers, in a court of law. Watertight, far as I can see. Straight as a die. Look here, I'm for signing my part right now.'

'Good man, good man.' The Captain slapped Brassey jovially on the shoulder. 'Tom?'

Lady licked Tom's ear, her breath hot and metalled with blood. Sudden as you like, Tom thrust her out in front of him, half dropping her into the surprised arms of the Captain. The Captain recoiled and dropped her hastily to the floor. Tom didn't look at her. He couldn't.

'Take her. Just take her.' He thrust his

hand out and the Captain placed the purse upon it. 'I want them papers, mind.'

'Of course you do.'

The Captain signed with a flourish and passed the pen to Tom. He hesitated, the pen held aloft.

'And if you don't pay me I get her back.'

'Assuredly.'

Jabbing at the paper as if he'd run it through, Tom made his own clumsy mark.

'Excellent,' the Captain said briskly. 'I believe we are done here. Tom, I shall see you a week from today with the next payment. It has been a pleasure to do business with you. Brassey, take the dog. I shall send someone for it in the morning.'

Brassey caught Lady by the collar and, his toad's face compressed with distaste, made to pull her out of the parlour. She dug in her heels, staring at Tom with an expression of bewildered appeal. Tom turned away from her towards the fire, staring hard at the dusty figure of Beauty in her glass case. His mouth was dry as dust. He heard Brassey summon his boy and instruct him to install Lady in the scrap of yard at the back of the tavern but he did not turn around. There was the scrape of her claws on the wooden boards and at last the boy's heavy footfalls as he clumped along the stone floor of the tavern's narrow back passage. It seemed strange to him that he could hear any of it at all, so loud was the roaring in his ears. The weight pressed down upon his chest, leaden as a dead man, so he couldn't hardly breathe. And, all of a sudden, he was back there, at Cuckold's Point, barely more than a boy, and the Thames mud was sucking him down, sucking him down as he floundered and scrabbled for anything with the faintest purchase until the mud clamped his ribs together and pushed down on his shoulders and he was looking at the sky and tasting the mud and the shit in his mouth and waiting for the feel of it packing his nostrils and his eyes and pressing into all his private corners until it had taken every last trace of warmth and breath and life and filled him instead from front to back and top to bottom with thick and stinking muck, rotting him away from the inside until he was as black and cold and dark and rotten as ever it was.

The purse containing the forty guineas was heavy. He'd not held so great a sum of money in his whole life. He weighed it in his hand as the Captain had weighed it and it gave him a hot respectful little shiver in his chest. Forty guineas. He rolled the words around his mouth, savouring their cold sweet taste. Next week there would be thirty more. And the week after that. The candle flame in his chest grew brighter, pushing back the shadows. He squeezed the purse tightly in his fist until the coins pressed uncomfortably into the palm of his hand and then, as the Captain had done, he buried the purse in the concealed pocket of his canvas coat and patted it. The weight of it tugged at his coat and he could've sworn it gave off a faint golden glow, warming his old bones. The papers he secreted in another corner of the hem. He'd stash them down in the tunnels with the others, where they'd be safe. One hundred guineas. His face twitched into a smile. It was time to go home. Natural as breathing, he snapped his fingers and held out his palm. He had glanced impatiently at the floor before he remembered. His hand felt big and empty and foolish as he buried it deep in his pocket and closed his fingers tightly around the lumpy bulk of the purse. Then, together, he and the guineas made their way homeward.

XVII

In accordance with his agreement with Polly, William made no mention of a murder to the authorities when he returned to work at the offices in Greek-street immediately after Christmas. Indeed he said little of anything to anyone and instead hid himself in his narrow carrel, speaking only when spoken to. Even then it was often necessary to touch him upon the shoulder so that he might realize that he was being addressed. As he bent over his work, he pressed his pencil downwards with such force that the lead snapped and the blotter beneath his paper was carved with a perfect facsimile of his calculations. His face had a sickly pallor, save for the dark smudges that stained the skin beneath his eyes, while the eyes themselves were yellowed and bloodshot beneath their heavy lids. As Hawke remarked with interest to Lovick, the illness seemed to have aged the surveyor ten years at the very least. Surely, Hawke added, the burdens of May's position were now likely to prove intolerable to the poor man, particularly given his history of ill health and what might justly — and here Hawke trusted that this was a frank exchange between men of professional integrity — be called downright unsteadiness. Greek-street was not an infirmary, the Board hardly a charitable institution for convalescents. Should not some other surveyor be appointed in his place?

Lovick, who disliked Hawke and privately harboured grave doubts as to his professional integrity, was forced to agree. May was clearly unwell. He therefore had the surveyor discharged from his underground duties. He did not, however, dismiss him. Instead he reassigned William to the group of men responsible for the construction of the pumping station at Abbey Mills where all three northern intercepting sewers would combine. Bazalgette's careful ingenuity of design ensured that the high- and the middle-level sewers discharged to the east by gravitation alone but, in order for the stream from the lower-level sewer to converge with its fellows, its entire contents had to be pumped upwards more than fourteen feet to meet the other streams before the aggregate river could flow along an outfall sewer, to be built above ground across the marshes, to a reservoir just west of Barking Creek. To that end Bazalgette had commissioned James Watt & Co. to build eight vast beam engines to his particular specifications. He also designed a building to accommodate them and to provide access to the vast tunnel system required by the confluence of the three huge and separate sewers.

There might have been little difficulty in the design and construction of a structure that would adequately fulfil its practical function, although the sheer weight of the vast coal-powered beam engines would ensure it was the source of headaches amongst the surveyors and builders charged with its execution. A simple matter of walls and a roof would likely have sufficed, with ladders to provide access to the upper reaches of the engines. But, for Bazalgette and the Board, the pumping station was invested with considerably greater significance than a lodging house for pumps and gauges. London had committed more than three million pounds to the overhaul of its drainage system. A new threepenny tax had been introduced to finance the scheme. Every property owner in London owned a little stretch of the eighty-odd miles of new tunnels that had begun to bury themselves under the metropolis.

Along with its sister structure at Crossness, which would serve the southern sewer system, Bazalgette was determined that the edifice at Abbey Mills was to stand as a monument to the greatest and most costly feat of engineering that the world had ever known, but which almost no one in the world would ever be privileged to see, a magnificent emblem for a system that, by dint of its function, would always be unromantic, unattractive and underground.

Bazalgette's drawings for Abbey Mills depicted a magnificent building in the Venetian Gothic style, a cross-shaped brick-built structure crowned with a spectacular cupola and flanked by two vast chimneys, each over two hundred feet high. The brickwork was to be extravagantly patterned, employing three different tones of brick as well as stone covings intricately carved with fruits and flowers, while the interior was dominated by an octagonal structure of iron columns with richly ornamented capitals, supporting an elaborately wrought iron gallery. It would have been impossible for William not to be cognizant of the grandeur of the design but, unlike his fellows, he found himself quite indifferent to its charms. He concentrated instead on the logistical demands of the building. There was much to be calculated. In order to pump the stream efficiently it was necessary for the beam engines to be set directly over the tunnel system, which, given that the flywheels alone were proposed to weigh in at over fifty tons each, made for considerable difficulties. William set about his work with dogged determination but joylessly, as though the beam engines were an occupying army by whom he had been captured and enslaved. All the same he derived some consolation from the methodical columns of figures that marched across the page in front of him. In his carrel he was, if nothing else, safe. Outside, in the street, without the figures to hold him steady, he found himself frequently lost or confused. The wound in his leg had not healed well and he walked awkwardly, rickety on the rutted ground. The thick winter fogs panicked him. Faces loomed out of the darkness like the ghosts of murdered men. Once he wandered directly into the path of an omnibus and would certainly have been knocked down had a sharp-eyed crossing-sweeper not snatched at his sleeve and dragged him to safety. He purchased a knife for the gutting of fish from the Italian scissor-grinder in Broad-street and concealed it in a locked drawer in his desk. The cuts were shallow, barely more than scratches, but their patterns were frantic and he embellished them daily.

His new companions, claiming for themselves a considerably loftier position in the Commission's hierarchy than they allowed the tunnel crews, left him alone. It was their habit to take their midday meal together at a coffee-house on Dean-street but, after William declined their first reluctant suggestion that he accompany them, they were glad to be relieved of the obligation to extend the invitation again. Instead William ate his lunch alone and, every day as he ate, he forced his memory to walk again through the same sewers he had walked on that terrible night, his senses straining for every remembered sound and smell that might tell him something, anything, of what had happened. If he could remember, he told himself again and again, he was not mad. He would show Polly that he was not mad. And so he clung to memory, as a miner might cling to a rope, so that it might lead him safely out of the darkness. He no longer carried his botany journal with him. He hardly knew where it was. Instead he kept a leather-bound notebook in which he wrote down the faintest scrap of recollection. Soon he had covered almost half its pages with his closely scribbled notes. Very slowly, fragment by fragment, a picture was emerging. He looked at it aslant, through faltering eyes, at the same time thrilled and terrified by what he might be about to see.

He mentioned it to no one. There was no one he could talk to. He no longer had any wish to speak of it with Polly. Something in the way she had looked at him the night that she had spat at him to keep his mouth shut about the murder had cut him adrift from her. Each evening that followed, the gulf that separated them grew wider until William was certain that, even as they sat on either side of the kitchen fire, she with her head bent over her mending, he staring unseeingly at a book in his lap, he could have shouted himself hoarse and still she would have been unable to hear a single syllable. He could not forget the rasping bitterness with which she had rounded on him, the way the skin had stretched and tightened across her white face. That face. It loomed like a winter moon over the dark night of his memory, the eyes closed, the nostrils clamped and bloodless, the mouth and neck twisted away from him in disgust, as though the very sight of him was intolerable to her.

He revolted her. William had seen it quite clearly, scored into every rigid filament of that white face. He disgusted her and he frightened her. She thought his frailty abhorrent, a cowardly and deplorable submission to a foe that, with only a little grit and effort, he might have been able to overcome without difficulty. But at the same time she feared his strength, the terrible courage that drove him to plunge a knife into his own flesh. She looked at him and she could not bear it, that the rock upon which she had built her life had crumbled into sand. Her husband, who had represented for her all that was steady and grave and wise, who had, for the love of her, willingly borne the weight of both their worlds upon his shoulders that she might dance and spin through life unencumbered by anything more substantial than a flower tucked behind her ear, her husband had allowed himself to be broken. And he would take her with him because that was the way of things. It was not only, or even primarily, a matter of prosperity or good character. Polly had become used to the security provided by William's wages, to the comforts of their little home, to the elevated status that came with having a girl to do the worst of the work. She enjoyed her new-found respectability. But, no stranger to life's vicissitudes, she could have reconciled herself to the loss of it all, she could have withstood any number of physical hardships, as long as she might believe herself happy. All her life she had meant to be happy. She had thought it the easiest, most natural thing in the world. To Polly, happiness was like goodness. It always won. It might be tested, just as the virtuous children in stories were tested, so that it might prove itself true, but, like goodness, if those that upheld it turned their faces resolutely against those who would have it corrupted, happiness would invariably triumph.

The Russian War had been such a test. But Polly had waited and forborne until, as she had known they would, the warm rays of happiness and hope chased away the grey ghosts of William's war just as the sun burned off the early morning mist. They had been happy again, for a while. But now the misery drifted from him and around him like a poisonous black miasma, infecting all that it touched. Her laughter could not light it. Her sweet kisses were turned to soot. Her cheerful words and snatches of song were returned to her un-heard, stripped of merriment and meaning. It was too strong for her, and too cruel. And so her laughter hardened and her lips too, so that they might no longer shape themselves into kisses. The songs caught in the back of her throat and made her cough. In the shadowed darkness of his unhappi-ness she lost sight not only of her husband but of herself.

All this William saw and he wrote it all in his notebook. Every day he scoured the newspapers for information that might pertain to the events of that night. There were no reports of a body recovered from the sewers, no mention of a missing person. But William's certainty continued to grow. He was not mad. There had been a murder. In the tunnels that night a man had been killed. Somewhere in the system there would be a body. Given the change in his circumstances it would be difficult for him to find a legitimate reason to go down into the tunnels himself but there were others that might. There were pre-texts that could always be found, the checking of measurements or a house-holder who had complained to the Board of subsidence. He was still involved a little with the Strowbridge contract. Hastily he summoned Donald Hood, one of the apprentices, and instructed him to carry out a precise examination of the stretch of tunnels that extended from Regent-circus to Seven-dials. He wished for a written report by the end of the week.

By Thursday there was still no word from Hood. That night William sat in his carrel long after the last of the engineers had gone home and stared at his notebook. Somehow he had heard a man die. *Drowning?* he wrote first, and then, beneath it, *Strangulation?* It was considerably later, as he rehearsed the man's soft gurgle over and over in his head, that he understood he had made a mistake. Striking both words out he paused and then wrote in thick black pencil, pressing very hard, *Throat cut.* He underlined it twice.

For a long time he stared at the words he had written. More than anything, he wanted to hold time still, to sit here quietly, the voices silent in his head, and to defer forever the moment when he must rise and put on his greatcoat and go home to see once again the disgust and the horror etched into the soft curves of her face. But time would not be stopped and the voices would not quieten. At last, William picked up his pencil and wrote the words that until that moment he had not permitted himself to think.

She believes I killed him.

He sat for a long time, his pencil held over the paper, as the words that came next curled themselves into a fist in his head. His hand trembled as he touched the lead to the paper and the letters he wrote came out spidery and faint.

Did I kill him?

'May.'

William fumbled his open notebook beneath a pile of papers and scrambled to his feet. Lovick peered over the wall of his carrel, his half-moon glasses winking in the dim light.

'Sir.'

'Still here? It's late, you know. You should get home to that family of yours.'

William forced himself to smile. Yet again the thought of his son brought on in him a feeling of anxiety, bristling the hairs on his neck. Even the sight of one of Di's toys, abandoned on the floor, made him uneasy these days, although he could not say why. At home he was so filled with anxiety that he hardly wanted the boy out of his sight and at night he longed to have him sleep with them in their bed, but Polly kept Di determinedly away from his father. Whenever William spoke to him, he was sure he saw fear in the boy's eyes. His fear made William's agitation worse.

'Yes, sir.'

'Well, good night, then.'

'Good night, sir.'

William waited. He heard Lovick mutter his good nights to the clerks and his footfall on the stairs. Then, drawing the pile of papers towards him, he withdrew the notebook. A sheet of paper came with it. Across its head were emblazoned the words ENGLAND & SON. And suddenly, with a sharp stab of recollection, William understood. The swirling agitation in his belly hardened into a vortex that forced itself fiercely down into his gut. England had been there that night. There had been a fight. England had threatened his son. Di was in danger. William almost threw the notebook into the drawer and snatched the key from the lock. He had to get home. Dragging his bad leg in a limping run he was halfway down the stairs before it occurred to him. It had been more than two weeks since that night. The contract with Strowbridge had been signed perhaps two days later. Surely if England meant to hurt Di, to hurt any of them, then he would have already done it. The pressure of the vortex eased a little. Perhaps he had never had any intention of carrying out his threat. He had meant only to frighten William into giving him the contract. But the contract had gone elsewhere. Of what value would it be to England now to risk his own reputation to damage William's family? It was too late for that now. And his son was safe.

All the same, William paused, his hand upon the polished banister. Then, thoughtfully, he turned and went back upstairs.

Hawke's office was in darkness. By the dim light from the street lamp William wrote him a message, requesting an interview with him the following day at Hawke's convenience. Then he went home. He could hear Polly moving about the kitchen. Quietly removing his boots William crept upstairs. Di was asleep in his low bed, his hair rumpled and his arms flung out. William watched him for a while and then, careful not to disturb him, he lay down next to him. The boy's breath was warm with the yeasty smell of fresh bread. If anything happened to him — William could not bear to think upon it. When Polly found him there he too was asleep. Her first instinct was to shake him awake, to order him out of the room, but halfway to the bed her step faltered. William's arm encircled his son and Di's plump hand was splayed like a starfish upon it, holding him close. On the pillow, their hair tumbled together. Their chests rose and fell quietly together. Polly sighed, adjusting the quilt so that it covered them both, and went to her bed alone.

The next day Hawke sent word to William that he was ready for him shortly before midday. William paused only to comb his hair and straighten his neckcloth. When he reached Hawke's office, however, Hawke was busy and William was forced to wait for some considerable time in an uncomfortable chair placed there for the purpose. His hands jiggled restlessly in his lap. The young clerk who occupied the cubicle outside Hawke's door stared insolently at him, giving him several thorough up-and-down looks in between excavating his dirty nails with a paperknife. At last Hawke summoned William in. When the clerk closed the door behind him the slam shook the door jamb and stirred the papers on Hawke's desk.

Behind the bulk of his desk Hawke clamped his hands together and stared at William. He did not invite him to sit.

'What is it you want?' he demanded. There was not the faintest pretence of courtesy in the question.

'It — it's about England & Son,' William began.

Hawke stood. Against the light from the window William could not make out the expression upon his face but his shadow fell upon William like a threat.

'Oh, it is, is it?' he said quietly and his dark eyes flashed.

'Yes, sir. No doubt Mr England will have been most dissatisfied with the award of the tunnel contract to the Strowbridge yard —'

'What are you suggesting, May?'

The menace in Hawke's tone was unmistakable.

'I wished only to suggest that he consider tendering for the Abbey Mills contract, sir,' William rushed. 'There is a considerable requirement there for London brick and, given his competitive prices, England's yard would stand a reasonable chance of success.' He cleared his throat, looking down at his hands. 'I would do what I could to help him, sir. I should like him to know that.'

He was answered with a mocking bark of laughter. William's heart sank.

'You should, should you?' Hawke said with grim amusement.

He snorted again. William watched uneasily as Hawke straightened up and turned to look out of the window, stretching and pulling at his fingers. Beneath his dark whiskers a muscle twitched. William waited.

'Is it true that you threatened Mr England's life?' Hawke asked at last.

'No! If there were threats made they were on Mr England's side. Surely you don't think —'

Hawke waved away William's words.

'If I see him I'll be sure to let him know you wish to make amends. Although such overtures may by now be a little late.' His mouth extended into a strange stretched smile. 'I fear that your problems with Mr England may be just beginning.'

'I should like to hope, sir, that we might put our differences —'

'Should you? Well, I commend your optimism.'

Hawke tapped a brass bell set into the top of his desk and immediately the office door swung open and the clerk appeared. Hawke busied himself with some papers on his desk. His mouth twitched.

'Ah, Spratt, good. Bring me the month's

329

records,' he instructed without looking up. 'I am due to report to the Board this afternoon. Good day, Mr May.'

William hesitated.

'Good day, Mr May,' Hawke said again, sharpening his consonants.

There was nothing for it but to leave.

'Good day, sir,' William murmured.

Spratt the clerk smirked impertinently as William limped out of the office, and rested his inky hands on his heap of leather ledgers.

'He didn't give you so much as the time of day, then,' Spratt observed.

William didn't deign to reply. Haste had made him foolish, he saw that now. He should have known that Hawke would not forgive him for what he had seen. Although Hawke knew himself to be safe from May, given May's inferior position and the absence of any proof of misconduct, it was inevitable that Hawke would always regard him as a dangerous adversary and any interest in Hawke's business as hostile and unwelcome.

As soon as he was back in his carrel William scribbled a note. The content of the letter was direct and unambiguous. He had no wish for bad blood to persist between himself and the brickyard owner. He regretted the failure of England's to secure the original contract for the sewer project but considered there were a number of other opportunities within the aegis of the Board's work that Mr England might find to his advantage. He therefore suggested an interview at Mr England's convenience during which he, May, would be able to provide him with further details. Summoning a messenger, William instructed that the envelope be delivered to the Battersea brickyard at the earliest opportunity. Before the messenger had left the room he was tapping his pencil impatiently against his teeth, wondering how soon he might expect a reply.

'Your report, Mr May, sir.'

Donald Hood stood at William's shoulder, holding a sheaf of papers dolefully in one hand. Hood was a pale man with greasy skin who looked as though he had been moulded from candle wax. His nose ran like a long drip down the middle of his face and his shoulders drooped unevenly as if, during his manufacture, a draught had caused the candle to melt more on one side than the other.

'Well?' William demanded, swinging round to snatch the papers and searching the apprentice's face. 'Did you find anything?'

'As you suspected, sir, there is evidence of further subsidence.' Hood's voice had a nasal quality but otherwise it was quite without expression, and he gave every word he spoke precisely equal emphasis. 'Since the inspection carried out last June the condition of the western section of the tunnel has perceptibly deteriorated —'

'Yes, yes, but did you *find* anything? Anything of importance?'

'Well, yes, sir. Initial examination of deposits would appear to indicate that, in direct contravention of Board directives —'

'Did you carry out a complete assessment? Of *all* the smaller sewers?'

Hood's shoulders sank a little lower and his mouth slid downwards in mournful reproach.

'Begging your pardon, sir, but if you will permit me to draw your attention to the Board directives issued in September of last year, you will be as aware as I am myself that not even the flushers are now permitted to enter the minor sewers, them being of particular danger, sir.'

'So you are saying you did not?'

'Of course not, sir.' Hood blinked slowly, his waxy eyelids appearing to melt over his protruding eyes, and shook his head. 'It would have been in clear contravention —'

'Oh, for the love of God!'

William could contain his impatience no longer. He snatched the documents from the startled apprentice's hand and promptly dismissed him. There was no help for it. He would have to go down there himself. The ink was barely dry on the Strowbridge contract. If questioned he would claim that something in Hood's report pertaining to brick deterioration had aroused his concern. It would not be difficult to think of something. But he could not go down alone. If he was not to arouse suspicion he would need to follow Hood's precious Board directives to the letter. Besides, he would require witnesses. Seizing his coat he limped as fast as he was able up one flight of stairs to the set of rooms where until recently he had had his carrel and carefully peered in. The door to Hawke's office stood open but, to his relief, there was no sign of its occupant, or of the young clerk who served as his gate-keeper.

William crossed the room, nodding to the one or two men who raised their heads as he passed. They nodded vaguely in their turn and forgot him, as they had always forgotten him. Upon the opposite wall were pinned a substantial number of charts and diagrams, each representing a section of the scheme currently under development. William quickly found the one he was looking for. There was a team of flushers scheduled to enter the system at Regent-circus at a little after two o'clock. He checked his watch. That gave him less than thirty minutes. William hurried towards the staircase, almost bumping into Hawke's young clerk who was carrying a dish of something covered by a stained cloth.

'Looking for Mr Hawke again, sir?' Spratt enquired, his eyes glinting with curiosity. 'Bit of a glutton for punishment, ain't you?'

'My business with Mr Hawke is quite complete, thank you,' he replied stiffly. Straddle-legged in the doorway Spratt made no move to step aside. Instead he smirked as William squeezed past him, his sharp eyes watching the surveyor as he made his awkward descent of the staircase. At the landing William was forced to pause to catch his breath, one hand upon the banister. Despite himself he looked up. Spratt smiled slowly and, after wiping his nose luxuriously on the back of one hand, raised it in a languid wave. William felt his neck redden. Hurriedly he limped down the remaining stairs.

The small wooden shed had a tarpaulin roof and was one of a number erected for use by the flushers as a shelter and as a place to store the necessaries of their trade. This one stood at the north end of Regent-circus, tucked into the passageway known locally as Flower-lane, although as far as anyone knew no flower had ever been fool enough to try its luck in the alley's sour mud. When a sleepy-looking flusher answered William's knock William explained his requirements and was accordingly, and with some ill grace, provided with the necessary uniform for descending into the system. His coat and trousers the flushers hung unceremoniously from a rusty nail banged into the shed's wall.

'So, where's it precise-like you got to get to?' the ganger frowned when he arrived moments later. He was well acquainted with William and had a grudging respect for the surveyor's knowledge of the tunnels and for the composed poise he showed underground, but his arrival added an unwelcome burden to the day's responsibilities. 'There's rain expected and the tides ain't favourable.'

William repeated his story. In the course of his duties one of the apprentices had come across some brickwork of particular interest in one of the smaller tunnels. William was keen to see it for himself but the apprentice, unfamiliar with the layout of the sewers and anxious to be restored to ground level, had been unable to give William precise instructions as to the location. He would therefore be greatly appreciative if an experienced flusher might be made available so that he might attempt to verify the apprentice's report. The ganger sighed.

'One hour. That's yer lot. And if we drop the lid you scarper.'

William agreed. His scalp itched with excitement and dread. They would find the body, he had no doubt of it. Fastening his lantern to the front of his apron he followed the sleepy flusher down the iron ladder into the system.

Immediately he stepped into the stream his heart started up a frenzied thumping in his chest. Above him the iron hatch clanged shut, extinguishing the daylight. William stood in the pale circle of light from his own lantern and breathed in the foul dank air. Usually the smell calmed him, but this time he felt the nausea rising in the back of his throat. His hands trembled. He thrust them into the pockets of his apron and clamped the muscles in his legs so that they might move more decisively against the drag of the water. Upriver the flusher's light bobbed and swung. William rolled his feet through the mud, pushing on, trying to catch him up. Always in the tunnels he had pursued solitude but now he had a child's longing for the flusher's solid warmth beside him, for the comforting stink of his sewer-stiff clothes and the stale reek of ale upon his breath, for the reassuring pat of a hand upon his shoulder. But the flusher was too far ahead of him. He was so cold, that was the trouble. The damp chill crept into his bones and he ached painfully in the half-healed wound in his leg. His skin was alive with gooseflesh.

Up ahead the flusher stopped and waited for William to draw level. As the circles of light from their lanterns converged and thickened William felt the dread recede a little. Despite the brutish nature of his work and the smear of grime across one cheek the sleepy flusher had a gentle face. Together the two of them would find the body. And together they would return to ground level. There was nothing to be afraid of.

'This way?' The flusher jerked his head to the right. William nodded, pausing gratefully to catch his breath, but already the flusher had moved off again, his light striping the walls and glinting on the ploughed surface of the water. Between him and William, the darkness closed the tunnel like drapes. William struggled along the channel behind him, his breath coming in ragged gasps. His own light was dim and strangely smoky. There was something wrong with his lantern. Alarmed, he shook it and the flame guttered. A skittering plunge of panic dropped away inside him, so abruptly that he was certain he would fall through it. He clenched his face into a tight knot and gripped the handle of his lantern with his damp hand so that his knuckles stood up in yellowed points like teeth. He must not let himself look down. The body. He had to find the body. If he found the body he was not mad. If he found the body he could get out.

'Wait, please wait,' he called hoarsely to the flusher but his words were sucked down beneath the tumbling rush of the stream. His head dipped and swirled as the shadows around him dipped and swirled, dizzying him until he was certain he would vomit. It was so cold. He could not feel his feet, his fingers. He had to find the body. He had to get out of here. And now the old darkness started to fill those cold empty places, its desolate blackness rising like smoke up the chimneys of his legs. The cravings tightened his skin and dried his mouth, peeling his gums away from his teeth. His skin itched. The screams were rising in him, faster and more powerful than ever. They poured in their feral hoards from the darkest places in his soul and they could not be stopped. They slashed through his veins. They set his bones on fire. They pressed into his head as though they would smash his skull like an egg. He was powerless before their merciless onslaught. They were all he could hear and taste and feel and see. He had to let them out, before they destroyed him. But this time it was not the knife he longed for, not the knife that he knew would bring him relief. It was the body.

Further along the tunnel the flusher paused again, waiting for William to catch up. Ahead of him was a narrow channel, barely three feet high. The flusher's lantern swung as he turned to face William and as it swung the light snagged on something concealed a few feet into the tunnel. It was pale, almost white. And then it was gone, lost in the darkness. But the perfect image of its swollen fleshiness remained, scored

in great deep gashes into William's self.
The body. It was the body.

Frenziedly he pushed past the flusher
with such roughness that the man stumbled. Tearing the lantern from the front of
his apron he held it aloft. Then, with a
strangled cry of triumph, he sank to his
knees, so that the stream smeared its foul
contents across his chest, and forced his
way into the tunnel. The light bounced off
the walls, throwing back a white glare.
Fungi. The walls were padded with fungi,
bulging and bloating from the crumbling
walls. Their cold decaying stink pressed
into William's nostrils and swelled inside
his head. The body. He had seen the body.
Pressing his knees into the black sludge he
pushed further into the tunnel. The fungi
seemed to swell around him, deadening
sound, closing him off. Their puffy pallor
surrounded him, everywhere hinting at
dead flesh and yet concealing it. William
felt sickened and confused and then,
abruptly, wild with rage. Viciously he
struck out at the wads of fungi with his
lantern. The casing brought down lumps
of spongy flesh. Again and again William
struck, carving his way into the low tunnel.
And then, abruptly, the glass smashed and
the light went out. William was in perfect

darkness. He hurled the broken lantern away. The body was here. He had seen it. He plunged his arms into the stream, his fingers raking through the filth, and broken glass sliced into his fingers. The pain steadied him a little. Struggling on his knees, he pushed on into the black tunnel, ripping at the fleshy walls, thrusting his hands over and over into the mud beneath the stream.

'I know you're here!' It was his voice but it came from far away. 'I know you're here, you bastard!'

The hand closed over his mouth and pulled back his head. For a moment William was certain it belonged to him, to the dead man, and he felt the terrible thrill of triumph. But the hand was warm and it stank of shit and seaweed. It was hard to breathe. There was a wrench of pain as his arms were brought up behind him. He tried to struggle but he was caught off-balance and the grip that held him was too strong. The screams came still, up and up, but they were more ragged now, strangled and torn. Half-carried by the filthy stream William was dragged on his back from the tunnel. With a last muster of strength he kicked his boot against the tunnel wall, dislodging a crumble of brick. An arm hooked around his neck, crushing his windpipe. Someone shouted. The darkness deepened. Then, suddenly, it was pierced by a shaft of white light. Boots scraped against iron. Something lashed his wrists together painfully behind his back. Then, without ceremony, William was bundled upwards. The light hurt his eyes. He closed them, aware only of the terrible dark chill that gripped him and convulsed his limbs and neck in spasms of uncontrolled trembling.

'Get 'im out of 'ere,' growled the ganger.

A blanket was put about his shoulders. William felt its prickly pelt against his cheek as he sank into its greasy reek. Then, a door was opened and he was pushed through it. The light pierced his closed eyelids and flooded them with a painful red. He squeezed them shut as he stumbled forwards a few paces on the uneven ground, a hand pushing at the centre of his back. When at last he separated them a slit, they allowed beneath the shadow of his lashes only a slice of the dank wall of Flower-lane and, leaning against it, very close, the smirking countenance of a young man. The shiver clattered William's bones, penetrating each brittle shaft with a sharp needle of ice. As William lurched past him, his eyes fixed upon the ground, the youth let out a long delighted whistle.

'Like I said,' he whispered gleefully into William's ear. 'A veritable glutton for punishment.'

William pressed his eyes shut once more but it was too late. There could be no ridding himself of it. The dread and the blackness and the cold swirled together, draining in a ceaseless sucking vortex into the pit of his stomach, and at the centre of the vortex, leering with vicious satisfaction, was the gargoyle face of the young man. There was no way back. In the frozen darkness he knew it only as a terrible plunging feeling but he knew it all the same. He had reached the end and, where he had hoped to find comfort and peace, there was nothing. Nothing but his own terror and the terrible darkness, stretching into eternity, and the Devil's gargoyle smirk as he came to claim him. It was only much later that he was able to stand outside of himself and understand the terrible true simplicity of it. He had been forcibly removed from the sewers, a madman, shackled, shaking and thick with filth. And Spratt had been a witness to the entire spectacle.

XVIII

The following Saturday Tom showed up
early to the Badger, for all he'd meant to
keep the Captain waiting. He took Joe
along with him for the company. On the
way there he was sure he saw her pink face
grinning out at him from every shadow and
broken-down doorway. She'd shiver with
excitement when she saw him, of course,
the whole of her pink rump vibrating as she
wagged her chewed stump of a tail, her
snout cocked ready to fit into the palm of
his hand. All of a sudden there was a stitch
in his side so sharp he had to stop for a moment, leaning over, his hands upon his
thighs.

When he was fit to straighten up he
shook his head hard to dislodge the
thoughts of her. He was being fanciful, of
course. The Captain wasn't likely to bring
her along, not if he didn't mean to fight
her. He'd be resting her up. Right now she
was likely spread out in some fancy kennel,
nibbling on a juicy rump of beef. To drown
out the traces of her Tom embarked upon

a stream of idle speculations about the dogs he reckoned'd be up at the Badger that night. Joe listened, taken quite aback at the tumble of words pouring out from his habitually taciturn friend, and he scratched his head. It was a rum thing, a fortune, and no mistake. Joe'd never known a man come into a fortune before but from what he could tell it was like to take a man who all his life had been content to stand firm upon his feet and turn him fully upside down.

The Captain's box was empty when they arrived, although, from the way that Brassey had his boy go at the carvers with a damp rag, it was clear that he was expected any time. Tom leaned on the wall of the pit, to all appearances quite taken up by the fight, but his ears flexed and strained to catch the sound of footfalls upon the stair. In his pocket his fingers worked the corners of his contract till they were soft as a lady's glove. The brilliant glare of light upon the white-painted ring threw the extremities of the room into dim shadow which played tricks with him. Over and again he was sure he saw it, the door edging open a little and the tip of her pink nose twitching as she paused on the threshold to fill her nostrils with the pit's rich bouquet. Each time his heart squeezed a little and her name melted on his tongue. But the door never opened. It was only a twitching of the shadows that he saw, a guttering in the gaslight, the Fancy's stampings, perhaps, or the lick of a breeze through a broken sash. Each time the space inside Tom grew a little emptier and each time, like muck silting in a tunnel, the anger filled it a little more. Where was that slippery shit of a Captain? The bastard had promised him he would be there. He'd been late before, of course, later than this. But if he thought he could cheat his way out of this one —

Tom pinched the contract hard between his fingers.

They had watched four or five bouts, and Joe had secured himself a shilling or two in winnings, when Brassey declared the pit closed for the night.

'Of course, if you would care to repair downstairs for a spot of further refreshment —' he urged, the smile splitting his face in half like a rotten orange.

'Where is he?' Tom demanded of Brassey as the Fancy clattered noisily down to the lower parlour. 'He owes me. He said he'd come.'

'Come now, Tom,' Brassey's tone was

soothing but he hastened his pace and his eyes swivelled away from Tom's. 'A gentleman like the Captain has many calls upon his time. He cannot be expected to put himself always at the beck and call of ordinary folk such as yourself.'

'We had an agreement.'

'Naturally you did,' Brassey agreed. 'And I have every faith that the Captain can be relied upon to honour his debts.'

But Brassey's faith proved misplaced. The next Saturday Tom made his way once again to the Badger, his softened contract in his pocket, and again he waited. Again he strained for the sound of the man's step on the wooden stair, his hand upon the door. And again the Captain's recess remained empty. Tom did not let himself think what might have become of Lady. He did not notice that Brassey eyed him beadily from across the room, muttering something to his boy. Instead he sat in a corner and stoked the anger that was swelling inside him, taking over the space she'd left behind. He took a whisky and then another. His throat burned. Together the pair of them had been swindled, betrayed. Well, if that bastard reckoned Tom'd shrug and cut his losses he'd reckoned on the wrong man. Tom wasn't no martyr like those soft fools in the Bible, turning the other cheek. It wouldn't be long before the Captain'd wish he'd never set eyes on the tosher and his dog. Tom threw back another drink, soothed by the intensity of his anger, his overpowering urge for vengeance. Indeed, it would not've been stretching the truth much of a length to say that if the Captain had walked through the door at that very moment and handed Tom his thirty guineas all piled up and shiny on a silver tray there'd have been a part of him that'd have felt the disappointment keenly.

But the Captain did not come. On the third Saturday, when in due time the pit was closed and the boy busy with scrubbing down the blood-spattered paintwork, Brassey cornered Tom. He came straight to the point.

'You ain't welcome here no more. If you ever show your face again, I'll have you thrown out. Get it?'

Tom stared at him, less angry than astonished.

'It's the low types like you keeps the quality trade away,' Brassey went on. 'They don't want to be rubbing shoulders with the men what gets the rats. Besides, I got myself another supplier.'

'But the Captain —'

'Your business with the Captain ain't no concern of mine.' Brassey flexed his feet and his eyes swivelled in his head. 'All I knows is I got a business to run. You come here again, you'll have more'n a broken wager to concern you.'

It was Brassey's boy who pushed Tom out the door then, strong as an ox for all his slight frame. Tom thundered on the closed door until his arms ached. When at last he gave up shouting, the anger inside him was white hot. It lit him like a lantern. He would find the Captain. If the Captain was anywhere to be found he'd find him. And when he found him the Captain would wish to God he'd never been born.

XIX

All day Sunday Tom walked around the city, for all that snow had fallen again before dawn and the cold was brute enough to take your breath away. He walked through Soho to the river and then past the Tower to the Pool, where the air was heavy with ice and salt and tar and the wet-grass stink of rotting rope, and the masts stretched into forever like a forest of barren trees, and on beyond the Minories along Ratcliff-highway to the frozen swamps of Shadwell and Poplar. The Captain had Lady. The thought of it caught like a fishbone in his throat. But Tom'd find them. Even though he'd good as stolen her, she'd still cost the Captain forty guineas. He wasn't going to keep her as a lapdog, not at that price. He'd want to turn a profit from her, make good what he'd given. He'd want to fight her and soon, if he hadn't done so already. It was just a question of where.

He went first to the King's Head on Cock-hill where he was on good terms with the landlord, on account of Tom being one of Boggis's more dependable suppliers. But Boggis hadn't observed any man matching the Captain's description and no new dogs neither. The only other proprietor Tom contrived to cook up an exchange with that day was a one-time prize fighter, himself with a flattened fist of a nose, who owned what passed for a tavern in the remains of an old forge on the quaggy reaches of Mile-end. He drained the glass of rum-and-water Tom had stood him and scowled. He didn't have no need of Tom's business. He had his rats sent in from Clavering, over Essex way, and fine specimens they were too, sleek fat creatures you could make a coat of. He didn't have call for no more, specially not the low and filthy sewer-rat sort. His was a high-class establishment and his clients was picky. More than that Boggis was not prepared to say. A man of Tom's calling, throwing his money about, it didn't smell right. It was a fool's tongue found itself loosened by the bottle. He refused Tom's offer of another drink and wouldn't utter another word.

Discouraged, Tom made his way slowly back to his lodgings. More than once in the deepening gloom he caught a glimpse of a white dog and something in the way it held its nose up or wriggled its belly in the dust made his heart skip. More than once he called out her name. But it was never her. His feet ached. He who had always sought solitude, who had felt himself truly steady only when alone, now felt his lonesomeness drag heavy as a cloak at his shoulders.

On impulse, he turned down an alley and followed its twisting course to the river. Even on a Sunday the Docks jostled and shoved and the darkening afternoon echoed with shouts in a score of languages, jumbled together with splashes and hammerings and the doleful cries of animals and the rattle of chains. Between the layers of mud and salt and tar and sweat Tom could make out the harsh smart of strong tobacco, the sun-warmed fumes of rum, the rancid reek of hides, the exotic whiff of coffee and spices, the warm breath of wine, the yeasty stench of dry rot. At the water's edge a Sardinian brig was unloading its cargo and the quay tumbled with barrels and casks. Tom had to stand to one side as a row of its discharged mariners passed him six abreast, gold earrings glinting in their black beards, their red shirts caught at the waist with bright sashes. They smelled strongly of sweat and garlic sausage and their teeth flashed with more gold as they grinned and downed and filled the winter twilight with the music of their unfamiliar tongue. A little further along, in the shadow of a looming warehouse, a public house spilled its light on to the muddy ground. Above the clamour Tom could just make out the creak of a fiddle scraping out an Irish jig.

He went in. Sailors crowded the tavern, shouting in a dozen languages and all crushed around a fiddler in a red neckerchief who had been placed upon a table in the centre of the room. His bow sawed at his fiddle with such verve it seemed he might slice it clean in two, and he stamped his boot on the table's battered face until it jumped in time to the music. Around him the sailors sang and clapped and parted with their pay. A woman with matted hair and a weasel's watchful eyes tugged at her husband's vest, begging him to come home with her. He slapped her hands away, adding another to her cheek for good measure before swallowing himself up into the solid wall of his fellows. The woman spat copiously into the mass of men before, issuing a stream of curses, she stormed out of the tavern.

Tom found himself a corner where his

toes were less prone to trampling and, closing his eyes, let the music stamp and whoop through his head. Close by, two men, day labourers by the look of them, settled their pots on a ledge.

'Still, I catched meself a sight last night and no mistake,' one shouted to the other. 'Niver thought I'd see such a thing.'

His friend raised one eyebrow over the rim of his pot and sucked on his pipe.

'Up Spanks's place it were. Right peeculiar to look at but true as I'm standin' 'ere no murd'rer in 'istory was ever 'alf so eager. Took a score o' the varmints in a single minute — you'd not've believed it if you'd not seen it yourself. Silent as the tomb it was an' all — not so much as a whimper, start ter finish. I'd a-taken it for a spook if it hadn't a-been the property of a professional gent —'

Tom grabbed the labourer's coat.

'What the —' the fellow's friend began but Tom cut right across him.

'Where?' Tom demanded, his nose so close up against the labourer's own the two of them almost touched. 'The dog, where was she? Tell me, you bastard! Tell me or I'll rip your throat out, d'you hear me?'

The labourer shook him off. He was a heavily built man and his eyes were no more than slits beneath the jutting slab of his forehead.

'Well, I dunno 'bout that,' he drawled with a shrug. 'Worth a bit, I'd say, valuable hin-formation of that nature.'

Tom snarled.

'Sixpence.'

The labourer's face twitched. The rate at the Docks was fourpence an hour.

'A shillin'.'

Tom felt into his pocket for the coin and rested it on his palm. The labourer reached out to snatch it but Tom closed his fingers.

'Payment on delivery,' Tom growled and his heart thumped with anticipation. He'd've paid the shilling five times, ten times over for news of Lady but there wasn't any purpose in handing out more than what was necessary, even when you were newly into money. Old ways weren't easy to break.

The labourer kept his gaze fixed upon Tom's closed hand as he related what it was he knew. The dog he'd seen had been fighting up the pit they called the Bridge Tavern over Kensal way. It was a strange-looking beast, a jumble of breeds and so worn out in the coat that its skin showed through, but it was a champion killer, of that there weren't a doubt. Its owner was a gentleman, a doctor perhaps though he wasn't sure of it. The labourer didn't know his name or where it was he came from. He hadn't paid him much attention except to notice that he was dark about the whiskers and, unlike his animal, his coat was thick and of a fine quality. He was new to the Bridge, the labourer was sure of that. You couldn't fight a dog like that and not get yourself remembered. What with being new the gent'd not managed to catch himself more than a pound or two in winnings but he'd got the Fancy's appetite whetted good and proper. The labourer was ready to bet that at the next fight there'd be wagers of the heaviest sort. He might even put a shilling or two on himself, he added, his eyes narrowing to no more than a pair of lines as they glued themselves to Tom's closed fist. You never knew.

It was more than enough. Tom gave the labourer his shilling. It was hot to the touch. On Tom's palm it had imprinted a perfect shilling mark, so clear he might've coined from it. Tom raised the palm to his mouth and kissed it. His hand was trembling and his heart pounded in his ears. She was found. In a week he would see her again, and he would see the Captain, or the Doctor, or whoever the devil he was.

As to what he would do then, well, Tom was vague on the subject. It was a matter'd take some careful handling, he knew that, but he did not let it trouble him much. He'd found her. Besides, he had a week to think on it.

And think on it he did, turning it over and over, as those six days dragged themselves past. He knew there'd be no purpose in confronting him in the pit, of course. A slippery bastard like the Captain, he wasn't about to fall to his knees in front of all the Fancy and confess his treachery, any more than he was like to shake Tom's hand and give up the money he was owing. Red Joe counselled lying in wait for him outside of the tavern and snatching the Captain's winnings off of him under cover of night but that wasn't likely to amount to anything like the sum he was owed. Besides, the Captain had always been in the way of having associates about him, which would place Tom at a disadvantage. Gents didn't simply walk the streets like ordinary folks. They took cabs, carriages, and even if they wasn't with no one in particular they was seldom to be caught out alone. It'd be simpler to snatch back the dog, try and recoup his losses that way, but even if he was able to pull that off, what then? It'd take careful planning and first Tom had to see how the land lay. He was no nearer to a plan when, careful not to draw attention to himself, he entered the Bridge's pit through the concealed door in the tavern's cellar and slid unnoticed into a dark corner.

A little after ten o'clock there was a rap at the trapdoor. As it swung open the pit's proprietor, Spanks, a man beyond his middle years but with the beady eye and cockerel swagger of one with a good few more decades in him, raised his hand in salute and pursed his lips in a piercing whistle.

'How goes it, good Doctor?' Spanks declaimed, extracting the cork from a bottle of brandy with a triumphant pop. 'And may I prescribe for you a little tonic?'

It was the Captain, sure enough. He wore a plainer frock-coat than the one Tom was accustomed to seeing and he'd brought with him a leather bag of the type favoured by those in the medical profession but otherwise he had not concerned himself with anything in the way of a disguise. And of course he had Lady with him. Lady. Tom had to hold on to the table to steady himself, so strong were the feelings that flooded him at the sight of her. She looked well, Tom thought. He hadn't expected her to look so well, somehow, and relief and disappointment mixed queasily in his belly. She stood at the Captain's heels, her goose neck extended and her nose jammed up in the air. Tom's eyes devoured her, at the same time willing her to know him and beseeching her not to give him away. He needn't have worried. Already the Fancy in this part of town had got wind of something, and they crowded around the dog, jostling for a better look. The Captain set her upon a table and stood with one hand set possessively upon her shoulder, for all the world like her official owner. Tom had to clench his fists against his thighs and bite down hard upon his lip to stop himself from knocking the cheating swindler directly into the middle of next week.

As Tom had expected, the Captain had not come alone. He brought with him two associates, one of whom Tom recognized as the narrow-faced gent from the Badger, the other a brick-faced stranger with pendulous dewlaps that slapped against his stiff collar every time he took a drink, which was often. The Captain himself seemed in unusually expansive spirits, his face soft with wine. Slinging his feet upon a chair he poured himself a large brandy and took a draught. Careful to remain out of sight Tom crept closer to their table. From here he could see her better, or at least the back half of her, her pink-edged rump and the chewed stump of her tail. It took all the strength he had not to reach out and touch her.

The betting was soon under way and the Fancy clamoured about Spanks, laying their wagers. In the pit a wiry terrier danced around a score of rats like a nervous suitor. Only its second took any heed of it.

'So a beast like that'd cost you a pretty penny, I'll bet,' the brick-faced man muttered, nodding at Lady, his dewlaps all a-quiver.

'You do me a disservice,' the Captain replied, baring his teeth. 'Naturally I acquired her for less than half of what she was worth.'

The brick-faced man raised a purple eyebrow.

'Let us just say her previous owner was something of a simpleton,' the Captain drawled. 'A sewer-grubber of the lowest order.' The brick-faced man screwed up his mouth in disgust. 'Well, that has its advantages. For me, that is. It would appear that the atmosphere in those drains is so fetid it makes dung even of a man's wits.'

The brick-faced man laughed loudly and the Captain smirked. He was leaning back to say more when a bell sounded with a single urgent clap. The next moment the Fancy was draining from the pit faster than water down a pipe and Spanks's boy was in the pit, shovelling live rats back into their crate fast as his hands could manage. Spanks hurried over to the Captain.

'It's the peelers, gentlemen,' he muttered, jerking his head towards the ceiling. 'My apologies. Someone must've tipped 'em off. If you'd follow me —'

The Captain snatched up the brandy bottle in one hand and Lady's rope in the other.

'But what about the fight?' he snarled as Spanks steered him and the remaining ratters towards a second trapdoor set into the damp wall behind an iron grille. Tom kept his head down and his collar up. Lady, only a few feet ahead of him, raised her nose and sniffed at the air, her pink face puzzled and alert. 'Never mind that the wagers are nowhere close to what you promised. If you dare for one moment —'

'Next week, my fine doctor friend,' Spanks said smoothly, hurrying the last of the men out of the cellar. The Captain didn't see Tom as he slipped silently past him but Lady's nose was set to twitching in an instant. She strained at her rope as Spanks turned the key and slipped it beneath the tails of his coat. 'Next week. All bets stand.'

'You'd better be damned sure it's worth the wait,' the Captain spat through the grille and again the blacksmith clang of metal on metal echoed up the stairs. 'I want double the wagers, you hear me? Double!'

Quick as a flash, Tom turned around and winked at Lady, laying a finger upon his lips. With a strangled whimper she hurled herself towards him, her stump of a tail pumping fit to bust.

'Move it, man!' the brick-faced man called nervously from the alley. Tom slipped into a doorway as Lady plunged up the stairs, dragging the Captain behind her. In the alley she paused, tasting the air, her tail suddenly still.

'Come on, you stupid bitch!'

The Captain wrenched at her leash. Lady tried to resist him but her claws could get no purchase on the frozen ground. As he dragged her down the alley and the darkness blurred her white shape she kept her nose thrust into the air but her shoulders drooped. Tom could hardly bear to let her go. It was a long walk home. When at last Tom opened the door to his lodgings his head was clear. He had to get her back. There wasn't no money and even if there was he'd never get it. But he'd make bloody sure he got the dog back. And he'd get that swindling bastard of a Captain into the bargain, he'd get him if it was the last thing he ever did. Tom might not be an educated man but he knew how to play a hand, how to trust to more than luck to get a pack to fall out favourable. The Captain was about to find out he wasn't the only one who knew how to force a card.

XX

Spratt was thorough. On paper stamped with the Board's letterhead he took signed affidavits from both the ganger and the flusher. The surveyor had conducted himself inappropriately, both affirmed, and he had caused some material damage to the underground structure. And, yes, they also conceded, conduct of that kind could be mortally dangerous in the tunnels. Pressed further by the clerk, both men were forced to agree that the surveyor had appeared to be, as you might say, not in his right mind. Neither had particular objection to the term 'nervous hysteria'. To complete the picture, Spratt added a florid description of his own attesting to the surveyor's wild and filthy appearance upon his emergence from the tunnels.

The meticulous clerk did not stop there. Once the statements were complete he suggested to the grateful ganger that May be entrusted to his own custody. Then, to permit the testimony of any number of reliable and loose-tongued witnesses, he carefully steered the surveyor so that he entered the Greek-street offices through the clerks' room, the stinking blanket pinning his arms to his side in the manner of a straitjacket and the dung still plastered in his hair. Satisfied with the general air of disgusted commotion caused by the surveyor's appearance, Spratt let him go. His business was still not quite complete. Arranging his weasel face into an expression of grave concern he presented himself to May's superiors and made quiet enquiries as to the purpose of the surveyor's commission underground. Within a short time Spratt was able to ascertain that May had obtained access to the system by deception and that there appeared to be no legitimate explanation for his presence there. Thus armed, Hawke demanded an interview with Lovick.

It proved unnecessary. Frozen and exhausted, matted with shit and unable to master the frantic trembling in his limbs, William could fight no longer. He was defeated. The madness had wrenched and twisted at his brain until it had ripped the soft mass from its moorings. He had no desire at all to cut. Cutting would make him feel again. The thought of that was unbearable. He craved laudanum instead, chloral, anything that might bring sleep, that might dull the fear. With enough of it he might stop feeling altogether. He wanted that more than anything.

Gathering up what little strength he had left, William went to Lovick. The clerk in the outer office recoiled as he passed and, pressing a handkerchief to his mouth, commanded him in a muffled voice to wait. William did not hear him. He stumbled through the door without knocking. Lovick was deep in conversation with Grant, the two engineers engrossed in a plan spread out across the desk. Both looked up as William half-fell into the room.

'May, what the devil — ?'

William turned towards the sound of Lovick's voice. Although his eyes were open they had the unfocused numbness of a blind man. Lovick called sharply into the outer office for assistance as William collapsed to the floor, rocking and clutching his knees. Grant stared, his brow creased with disgust and astonishment.

'Help me.' William's voice was so low and cracked it was little more than a breath. 'Help me, I beg you.'

'What the devil — !' Grant echoed, at a loss. But Lovick had recovered himself. Immediately he instructed the clerk to remove Mr May to an adjoining room where he might safely be detained. Then he sent for Dr Feather.

The doctor arrived within the hour. He brought two burly attendants with him but in the event, and to their apparent disappointment, no coercion was necessary. William seemed to shrink a little and his hands jerked uncontrollably as he signed his name but he slipped his arms into the sleeves of the strait-waistcoat as though he were being fitted for it by a fine tailor. By the time Hawke thundered at Lovick's door, declaring the urgency of his business and insisting upon an immediate audience, William was already safely in a coach and on his way to Hounslow, a small town several miles to the west of the capital. There was a private asylum there which, because it did not require patients to be formally certified as insane, had long been favoured by decent families who wished to be saved awkwardness and embarrassment. It could therefore be relied upon, Feather assured Lovick, to show the utmost discretion in its dealings. There would be fees of course, and in the absence of family approval the Board would be required to underwrite a commitment to their settlement, but in the circumstances —

Lovick understood the circumstances only too well. Hastily, he agreed to Feather's proposals. He had been a fool not to heed Hawke's earlier warnings, of course. He had let his antipathy towards the man cloud his judgement and his mistake might cost the Commission dearly. Since its very outset the Board's work had been closely followed in the press and in Parliament. So far the response had been predominantly favourable, and Bazalgette and his fellows had been almost universally praised for both the rigid economy and stern prudence with which they were carrying out the work. But it remained early days. Any hint of scandal might tip the balance of public opinion in the other direction. Feather had assured him that securing an admission to one of the overcrowded pauper asylums might take weeks, longer if there were fewer than the usual number of deaths amongst current inmates. Who knew what trouble a lunatic might contrive to cause for the Board, given weeks? Hawke had been quite right to mistrust the man. He had been a juddering, stinking wreck. The sooner he was taken into custody the better for them all. Summoning a clerk Lovick requested that a message be taken to May's wife to notify her of her husband's situation and that interviews be arranged with suitable candidates to fill the newly vacant position. With work progressing at its current pace there was no time to be lost.

Feather took his own carriage to the asylum. The two attendants took up a position opposite William in a second, less elegant conveyance. Heavy iron rings were set into the walls of the coach at shoulder height and screens fashioned from cheap black cotton obscured the windows. The upholstery smelled of mildew and urine. In the gloomy half-light the men's faces were shadowy, cut into dark slabs, and their eyes glinted. They seemed hardly to sit upon the bench. Instead their feet pressed down hard into the dirty straw that strewed the floor and the muscles in their meaty legs flexed as though at any moment they might be ready to leap up and wrestle their charge back into place. From somewhere came the muffled rattle of chains. But William moved only when a particularly violent jolt dislodged him from his seat. Feather had given him a dose of something to render him quiet and in his hunger for it William had almost bitten the bowl from the spoon. Now the emptiness inside his head stretched as chill and blank as the winter sky. It did not occur to him to speculate upon what would become of him. He thought nothing of what it might be that Polly would be told or by whom. Thoughts of Di did drift vaguely across the emptiness but they were grimy tatters of thoughts, distant and insubstantial, a thin blend of longing and bewilderment, and an uneasy fear that even to think of him might besmirch the boy's purity with his dirt and disgrace. Then those thoughts were gone too. The draught that Feather had given him left his mouth gritty and dry. His tongue was clumsy in his mouth and his lips were pasted shut. He closed his eyes. The breath barely stirred within him as he shrank away from the edges of himself, shrivelling until he was nothing more than the cramped protests of his restrained arms and the grind of the headache in the soft hollows of his temples and the scope of all that was possible and all that would ever be was contained in the stink of mould and piss and the jolting sway of the darkened coach. Opposite him the attendants stretched their legs a little. One slid a flask from his coat and drank deeply from it before offering it to his fellow. The two men did not speak but occasionally, catching each other's eye, they laughed.

At last, the soot-stained London buildings gave way to flat grey fields and the leafless spikes of winter hedgerows. Their black fretwork patterned the shadowed windows. The road was rougher here and several times, unable to balance himself with his arms, William was thrown uncomfortably across the seat. Each time the assistants wrenched him upright by the straps of the strait-waistcoat with such force that his head jerked and the metal clasps bit painfully into his wrists. Some time later, when the interior of the coach was almost completely dark, the jolting finally slowed. The chains in their hiding place shifted and clanked. The coachman called sharply to the horses and while the coach was still swaying a knock came upon the window. One of the assistants lowered the sash and handed a sheaf of papers to a gatekeeper in a dark-coloured uniform who peered with undisguised contempt at William and sternly tapped the huge iron ring of keys that hung at his waist. Then, with a final jolt, the carriage juddered forward and came to a stop. William was hauled to his feet and thrust out into the night.

There was all sorts of commotion then, shouting and scurrying and the bright flare of gas that blinded William and made him flinch. He was taken into a bare room with stone flags like a scullery, he remembered that, and there he was given a bath and something was rubbed vigorously into his hair that set his scalp on fire. The attendants from the coach were gone but there were other men there, men with the same slabs of faces and the same readied muscles. He was given another draught of chloral, which he swallowed, and a basin of brown soup, which he did not. Dr Feather was there or perhaps someone else who looked like the doctor, and another physician with dark skin and heavy eyebrows who did not. Things were said, others were written down. Cold metal was pressed against his skin. A white light was shone into his eyes. He was dressed in an unfamiliar outfit of clothes, loose cotton garments of the kind worn by Hindu street-sellers that tied at the front with short strips of cloth. And then he was in a narrow crib, an ordinary bed almost except that the blankets were sewn to the mattress and his wrists were caught in canvas straps by his sides. There were other beds in the room, other noises, shuffles and bangs and the sound of soft weeping, cut into by sharp shouts from beyond the locked door. William's arms jerked and the restraints tightened against his wrists. Their unyielding rigidity calmed him. As they confined him so they confined the madness within him, pinning it down. He was safe in their embrace; he no longer had to be vigilant. And so for the first time in days he slept, drifting in and out of the noises and the shouts, across the dark unfamiliar room and through the tunnels and along the frozen trenches and past the shadowed faces that leered and wept and smirked until the noises became louder and more specific and the grey dawn forced itself tiredly through the barred window to present William with his new home.

The Hounslow asylum considered itself a progressive one. It was certainly small by the standards of county institutions. There were fewer than one hundred inmates, arranged in dormitories of eight, and although the rooms were deficient in warmth and general comfort, plastered walls being considered an unnecessary luxury for the insane, they were kept tolerably clean. Iron restraints were forbidden and, once a patient had demonstrated a satisfactory level of docility, even the canvas straps were seldom used and then only as a punishment for inappropriate behaviour. Difficult patients might be forced to wear strong-dresses, garments fashioned from canvas as heavy as slate that restricted their movement. The use of ice-cold shower baths was frequently effective in cooling the fevered heat of madness. But while some patients persisted with a course of passionate and often violent resistance, they were not in the majority. The asylum fostered an atmosphere of dazed tranquillity through a diet that was rich in sedatives and scanty in nutrition. Routine and regularity were all. Patients were given no access to pen and paper in case their usage should lead to overexcitement, and books and newspapers were strictly limited. It was expressly forbidden for patients to speak about themselves on the certain assurance that listening to a hysteric's utterances could only exacerbate his morbid sense of self-importance. And while there were strict rules governing the conduct of the attendants who were responsible for the daily care of the patients, men prepared to do the job were hard to come by and the asylum considered it reasonable, given the ratio of attendants to patients and the potentially volatile nature of their charges, to allow the attendants considerable latitude in their interpretation of these rules. There were, after all, only two physicians resident at the asylum and, while they made sure they were on hand to speak directly and with appropriate gravity to those responsible for meeting their patients' fees, their affairs frequently transpired to take them away from the hospital. They saw each patient perhaps for a few minutes each week. And so it was that the attendants were the true masters of the place and each ward became a miniature fiefdom in which the particular preferences of the attendants might be practised.

On his first morning in Hounslow William was slow to wake. The chloral had left a residue of grit inside his eyelids and upon the underside of his skull, and his arms in their restraints were heavy and numb. He breathed in and, despite the chill, the air tasted greasy and old. There were voices and the heavy sound of footsteps. Before he could open his eyes his head was lifted and a spoon thrust roughly between his glued lips, tearing at the skin. The metal spoon rattled against his teeth and was gone and he choked as he fell back upon the pillow, the tears starting from his eyes. Through the blur of tears he saw a man, half turned away. The man's shoulders drooped and his hair was powdered with grey. Then once again William slept.

Much later he woke again. The sleep had not refreshed him. The headache persisted at his temples and he felt at the same time fretful and drained. But his wrists were free. Very carefully, summoning his energy, he lifted his head. He was in a small room perhaps twelve feet square into which eight narrow cribs had been crammed. The walls were of sketchily whitewashed brick, set with a single small window striped with bars. There was no fireplace. Besides a comfortable-looking chair that took up a disproportionate amount of the small space the cribs were the room's only furniture. The chair was empty but most of the other cribs were occupied by men who lay quietly, their eyes closed or set upon the ceiling. Another man squatted in the narrow space between the beds, his hands clasping the iron bars of William's crib. Like the other men he wore a white tunic although his was grimy and hitched up around his waist. Beneath it he was naked. He was painfully thin. His nose jabbed out of his face like a hooked finger and his sallow skin was pitted with the knuckle-print scars of smallpox. But his eyes were a clear and brilliant blue and as he threw his head back the watery light from the window lit up his face. It was flooded with a kind of angelic ecstasy. Casting away the bars of the crib, he held his joyful arms aloft and rapturously gave himself up to the glory of Almighty God. As the words streamed from him in exultant adoration William felt a stab of loss so sharp he could barely keep from crying out and the darkness swirled giddily around him. He clenched his eyes closed, unable to bear the sight of this prophet who squatted before him. For shining from the man's face, lighting him up from within and flooding him with bliss, was all that William had lost, all that had died within him. The grief pierced William's heart and, pressing his fingers into his head as if he would crush his skull, he buried his face in his pillow.

The door slammed. The prophet's prayers became louder, more frantic.

'Oh for Christ's sake! You dirty little bastard, didn't I tell you — ? Jesus Christ. Peake, bucket. Now.'

There were footsteps, followed by the sharp crack of a slap and a more muffled crunch. There was a ragged groan. Then the prayers started up again but fainter this time, more breathless.

'You disgusting piece of scum, you'll

pick up every filthy little scrap of what you done or I'll have you lick it off the floor, do you hear me?'

There was another crunch, another gasp and the prayers ceased. William loosened the grip on his skull and lifted his face an inch from the pillow. Instantly he was assailed by the unmistakable stench of human excrement. Again something twisted in his heart. He thought he might vomit. Instead he bit down hard upon the raw skin of his lip. In the cot next to his a man with wiry white hair stared impassively at the ceiling, his hands folded across his chest. In the far corner of the room someone hummed tunelessly.

'I said, *pick it up!*' There was a sharp stamp and something cracked. Water sloshed across the floor.

'Oh my — Jesus, Mr Vickery!' A different voice, higher-pitched, squeaky with outrage. 'The sodding bastard has gone and bit me!'

There was another strangled gasp and then a thud.

'Get him out of here,' Vickery ordered. He no longer sounded so much angry as tired. 'Douche first, then solitary. Two weeks. He bites you again, make it four.'

The humming grew louder as something

bumped across the splintered floor. No one else in the dormitory moved. Then a key turned in a lock and the door opened.

'My God, My God,' whispered the prophet and his voice echoed in the empty corridor. 'Why hast thou forsaken me?'

'You stupid bloody sod,' Vickery said wearily. 'When will you learn to keep your fat mouth shut?'

The door slammed. Someone began to mutter a string of curses very softly to themselves, the same three words over and over. Another's feet thumped rhythmically against the iron bars of their cot. The feeling of oppression, of impending disaster, was so strong in William's chest that he wanted to scream out loud. He gripped the wrist restraints in his fists and pulled at them to calm himself. Then he felt a rap upon his shoulder. He turned his head. The man from the next bed leaned over towards him, beckoning him close with a finger. William started and his sense of dread strengthened. He had taken the man for an old one but, although his hair was quite white, his face was younger than William's own. His eyes darted about and his tongue flickered over his lips, again and again, like the tongue of a lizard.

'I pray for all the men in this house. Now

you have come I will pray for you.' He lowered his voice to a whisper. 'That's why I've been lodged here, amongst you. My father's friend Harrington requested I come here before I take up my parish duties. I'm to pray for the lunatics so that their suffering might be eased a little.' He smiled in William's direction but his tongue still flickered over his curved lips and his eyes never ceased in their restless darting about the room. 'I will pray for you.'

William turned his head away, the screams dying in his chest. The dread flattened a little, leaving a black scum of misery. He curled himself up, wrapping his arms around his knees, and called out for chloral to be brought. Over and over he called, in a voice as dull and rhythmic as the thump of his neighbour's fist upon the frame of his crib. At last, Vickery came. Matter-of-factly, as though he was following the conventions of medical practice to the letter, he slapped William hard across the cheek before thrusting the spoon between his lips. William swallowed and closed his eyes, pressing his hands into the churning chill of his belly. Then he waited for the darkness to pull him down.

XXI

It took close on an hour to ease the body out from the place where it was wedged. It'd made itself at home in its narrow cleft, its shoulders and hips swelling and softening into the brick, the skin a dark purple like it'd sucked itself full of the underground darkness. The rats had had a go at it, of course, and there was bits missing from the legs and fingers and anywhere else they'd found the room to squeeze around it but the salt and the cold had stopped the rotting going too fast ahead and the body smelled more of mud and seaweed than anything else.

Once they'd got it free, the tide favoured them, and for a deal of the way to the sluice they were able to let the river carry it, nudging it along by one of its stiffened feet when it caught in a gap in the brick. At the Temple steps, Tom had Joe go out first to scout things while he unbundled the necessaries from the tarpaulin on his back. It was a little before five o'clock in the morning and, though dawn was a good way off, the river was starting to get busy.

It was still too early for the steamers but the hay barges were out and the gardeners from upriver were taking their produce to the morning markets. Still, the early folks weren't much in the way of looking about them, not in Tom's experience. Besides, the moon was a young one, which was a piece of luck, and the clouds hung low over the city. Sticking as best he could to the darkest shadows along the river wall Tom let the body swing out into the river.

It bobbed face down, its gnawed fingers paddling at the water. Tom caught it by the ankle. With his head bent low over the dark water, he began to drag the body slowly downstream towards a stretch where there was a clutch of disused wooden barges moored several deep. Folks used them for sleeping sometimes but they was little more than hulks, their rotting hulls collapsing on to the mud at low tide. Tom wasn't much of a swimmer but he made his way out, half-walking, half-hauling himself along with the ancient tarred fenders that bulged along the barges' dark flanks, until he came to a place where the mooring chains met in a rough iron knot and a flimsy pier with tottering legs chopped up the flow of the river. The waterlogged corpse was heavy and hard to manage. Tom hooked his arms around its thick thighs so as to pull it along. It dragged reluctantly behind him, leaving a gentle V-shaped trail in the river. The water was icy cold. Tom shivered. It'd do for him the same as his companion, if he stayed here too long. Pushing the body ahead of him he ducked into the narrow space between the barges. He would not be seen here, not from the banks or from the river. The slice of sky between the two high flanks of the boats was grey now, the darkness dusty with dawn. Tom wedged the body in best he could and waited.

As the sky lightened the river became busier, noisier. The penny steamers honked and sloshed. On the banks, wagons and carriages rattled over granite slabs. Tom pressed himself against the rotten flank of the barge and willed the river towards the sea. And slowly, so slow Tom fancied it was doing all it could to defy the very fundamentals of its nature, it went. When it was only around Tom's knees he took an old coat from the tarpaulin bundle on his back and huddled into it, rubbing hard at his frozen arms. Still he waited. The tide drained away, so that the slice of sky shifted and the barges slumped into the slime, leaning down over Tom. He crouched lower, waiting for the water to puddle on the mud. At last it was low enough. Quickly as his frozen fingers would permit him, Tom pulled the old coat off his own back. Again he reached into his bundle. Into the top pocket he poked the man's handkerchief, firm enough so as it would stay but careful to let the ends with the man's initials bloom out with a dandy's flourish. Then he bundled the dead man's arms into the sleeves of the coat, wrenching impatiently at them when they wouldn't bend. A bone cracked. The coat would do, although it was no gent's garb. Tom could've used the man's suit, of course, he still had it, but it was a good one. It'd only be a waste to return it to a dead man who had no use for its quality and who'd be like to muddy it when he lay down. When the corpse was good as dressed Tom dragged it carefully to the top end of the barges. This was the riskiest part. The head had to be far enough out, after all, so as it would definitely be spotted before the tide came up again, but at the same time he didn't want it attracting attention afore he'd got himself a good distance away. Taking a deep breath he shoved the body out beneath the tangle of chains and up against the ramshackle pier. Then, fast as he could, using the cover of the barges and the river wall, holding himself in so thin he might almost have passed for invisible, he slipped away.

He came up the river stairs a few hundred yards downriver. Straight off, fearful in his wet clothes of freezing himself to death, he took himself into a coffee-house and there, in front of a sputtering fire and with his fists closed round a mug of hot tea and brandy, he steamed himself dry, filling the narrow room with the rotting stink of river. A little later he came out and made his way east along the river. A knot of people were standing on the bank, pointing. Tom looked out. A couple of dredgermen had pulled their splintery boat alongside the pier and were in the process of hauling something from amongst the chains of the barges.

'Oh my sweet Lord!' squealed one woman in horror and she stretched her neck for a better look. 'A dead 'un, for sure.'

'Fancy that,' Tom said and shook his head in surprise. 'Fancy that.'

He did not wait to see in which direction the dredgermen pushed off. They'd get a few bob for the corpse at most of the stops along the south side. His money, rightly, Tom thought as he walked slowly away, but he smiled all the same.

XXII

Other men in the dormitory resisted the doses Vickery forced upon them twice daily, pretending to swallow so that they might later spit it out or simply clamping their teeth against the spoon, but not William. The drugs nauseated and confused him. They dried his mouth and cramped his temples and smeared him with a film of greasy dread that shortened his breath and twitched at his eyelids. But they also deposited a sticky drift of dust across his consciousness, disguising him from himself. The madness felt closer, more real, as the chloral took hold. Twice a day the sedative drew him down into the darkness, separating him from time and place and flattening him out inside so that the lunacy might insinuate a little further and with a little more assurance into his most private crevices. When, in the cold grey of another exhausted dawn, the preoccupations and purposes of the outer world threatened to creep into his skull and cast their faint light upon the outer cortices of his brain, the chloral locked the shutters against them, barring their entry. He paid no heed to the other men with whom he shared the ward. He spoke to no one. He rose from his bed only when taken to the privy or to the dining hall for his sparse meals. He ate little, crumbling the coarse bread mechanically between his fingers. When he fumbled at his thoughts they crumbled too. He let them drop away. There was a hopeless satisfaction in it, in no longer having to struggle against it. With nothing to think of and no facility for thinking he preoccupied himself with a compulsive monitoring of his minor ailments: sores on his thighs and buttocks when, as a punishment, he had been left by Vickery to lie for a day in his own urine; the cramps in his legs; an earache; a persistent cough. He called often for tinctures and tonics and, when occasionally they were brought, he fretted upon their efficacy. He rarely slept but he drifted in and out of troubled dozes, waking from them cold and clammy and calling for choral. Held tight in the uneasy embrace of the drugs, blurred and dreary and bound by regulations and routine, there was, during the days at least, something approximating to peace. One morning, as the dishwater of another dawn leaked through the high window, the prophet was returned to the ward. The light extinguished from his face, he looked ordinary, exhausted. And so a week passed and then another.

While other inmates from time to time received correspondence, Polly sent nothing. William expected nothing. The madness separated them as absolutely and as irrevocably as death. Occasionally he had a sense of her, a shivery feeling of her breath upon the back of his neck as though he was the one still living and she the lingering spirit of the departed, but he knew it to be no more than that. They were no longer of the same world. The unborn child, however, haunted his ragged dreams. Night after night he stared in frozen horror as through the sprigged lawn of Polly's gown burst a terrible black demon infant, shrieking wildly and flailing not with tiny arms and legs but with one hundred lunatic tentacles, the perfect quintessence of derangement. Night after night he saw the terror in Polly's eyes as it leaped from her arms to scream and rage, clawing and throttling, stabbing and ripping, growing all the while to a terrible size and set upon devastation. Night after night it raged until at last, when all about it was destroyed, it turned its maddened red eyes upon William. All at once its hideous face softened and it reached out with its tentacle arms, yielding now and quiet, murmuring only one word, over and over. 'Father,' it said and its voice trembled with love. 'Father.'

The first time William woke the dormitory with his screams, Vickery shook him violently and had him spend the rest of the night with a rag bound over his mouth as punishment. In the morning Vickery made no mention of the incident but when he loosened the gag he had Peake bring William ointment for his sores. At breakfast, for the first time since arriving at the asylum, William tasted sugar in his tea.

As for Di, William would not permit himself to think upon him. It churned his belly into turbulent eddies and inflamed the ashy deadness in his chest. The briefest fragments of memory, the sweep of his eyelashes against his pale cheek, the dimples of his knuckles in his plump hands, the soft pink buds of his toes, each was enough to set the fretted skin on William's forearms prickling with longing, so that even beneath the sluggish weight of the sedative he could feel the cravings begin to stretch and flex in the pit of his stomach. He dug his nails into the palms of his hands and forced them down, waiting for confusion to blur their edges. It never took long. The sedative was strong, much stronger than was recommended for long-term usage, but then the asylum was understaffed. Chloral did the work of a dozen men and never complained of the work or arrived on the ward the worse for drink. There were very few attendants at Hounslow of whom one could confidently make the same claim.

William had been in the asylum for more than two weeks when Vickery gave him the newspaper. It was against the rules but William had passed a wretched night, wracked with dreams. When at last the monster called out to him with all its ghastly love and recognition William vomited in his sleep. Choking, barely able to breathe, William forced himself on to one elbow and vomited again. He could not stop. Again and again he retched, until all that was left was a thin bitter bile that dripped like drool down his chin. The vomit matted his hair and whiskers, and soaked his sheets. There was a pool of it on the floor. William called for water, quietly at first and then more insistently. In the bed next to William's the white-haired man woke and began to whimper, banging his head repeatedly against the iron bars of his crib. By the time Vickery stormed into the dormitory, his hair askew, three or four of the men were awake and agitated, cursing or weeping or thundering their fists against the wall.

'Silence!'

Vickery's voice rattled the bars of the window and for a moment the room was silent. When the mutterings and the weepings resumed they were more tentative, muffled by anxiety. His large body moving awkwardly in the narrow spaces between the cribs, Vickery fumbled and wrenched each man's wrists roughly into their canvas straps. Finally he came to William but instead of seizing his wrists he grabbed a handful of his hair and brought William's face up close to his candle. William felt the heat of the flame scorching his cheeks and he tried to pull back but Vickery tightened his grip, forcing the candle closer. The attendant's breath smelled of whisky and stale sleep. William stared in disbelief into the dark centre of the flame and then closed his eyes, unable to prevent himself from crying out as the heat blistered against his skin. Cursing, Vickery pushed him backwards so that William struck his head against the rails of the cot. He slid down into the bed, the darkness closing like water over his head, but before it could swallow him up he was hauled up by his tunic and thrown down on to the floor. He heard his own gasp as a sharp kick to his ribs knocked the breath from his body. Then a hand pressed his face down hard into the pool of vomit on the floor. It filled his mouth, his nostrils. He couldn't breathe.

'You want every freak in the whole damned madhouse ranting and raving, you bloody troublemaker?' Vickery spat. 'This room stinks. And don't fool yourself there's going to be anyone changing no bedding this time of night. Far as I'm concerned you can rot to death in it, you filthy bastard. And if I hear so much as a whimper out of you before morning it's the douche. Get it?'

The hand pressed down so hard that William was certain his nose would break. Then it was gone. The door slammed. William lay on the floor, the cold vomit congealing upon his face. It was a frozen moonless night and the room was dark and bitterly cold. William's limbs jerked and trembled and his ribs throbbed but his head, free of chloral, was clear as ice, thoughts caught in its frozen surface like fish. He stared at them and found himself at the same time troubled and lured by their perfect shape and clarity. He should call for more chloral. But he did not. Instead he reached out to touch them, turning them over. They did not crumble. There were no monsters lurking within them, no terrible swirling sense of foreboding blurring their edges. They were simple and coherent, ordinary thoughts with beginnings and ends where beginnings and ends might be expected to be. Thoughts of buildings, mostly, of the places he had known before. The shop in which he had spent so many boyhood afternoons with its dusty sacks of flour and smell of turning butter. The offices in Greek-street with their crammed carrels. The cupola and elegant chimneys of Abbey Mills, their reality so absolutely imprinted upon his memory it seemed to William impossible that they did not yet exist. The house in Lambeth. Very carefully, William stood at the bottom of the stairs, his hand upon the banister, and breathed in its familiar smells. He had not yet courage enough to look towards the kitchen or seek out his son. But he let himself think of Polly and the swell of her pregnant belly. He had a powerful longing to sweep them up in his arms, his wife and his unborn child. But perhaps the new baby had come. He felt

393

the soft tears starting to gather at the back of his throat and they eased the bitter bile taste that lingered in his mouth. Perhaps it was a girl. Lily Rose. Tomorrow, in the morning, he would ask someone what day it was. Perhaps tomorrow Polly would send word. Perhaps she might come. She would look at him without disgust and she would hold out her arms to him and hold him to her. She'd kiss his forehead, his eyelids, the palms of his hands, as she kissed Di when he sat upon her lap, and he would be forgiven. When at last William roused himself from the icy floor and sought to warm himself beneath his vomit-slicked blanket his face was crusted with dried vomit and blistered bubbles shone like white tears upon his burned cheek, but the space between his brows was smooth and his lips were curved, just faintly, into a smile.

In the morning Vickery as usual was yellow-faced with dark shadows beneath his bloodshot eyes. He administered the choral carefully, holding his head stiffly upon his neck as though he feared it might fall. When he came to William's bed he instructed him brusquely to stand. Peake would take him to the laundry where a warm bath had been drawn for him. Fearful that he was being taken instead to the douche, William stared at the bath in disbelief. There was even a worn cake of soap. He winced as he tore off his stained tunic. It was painful to raise his arms. Purple bruises bloomed down the right side of William's chest and his face stung when he splashed it with water. Peake surveyed the damage without curiosity before slouching against the wall and probing the upper reaches of his nostrils with a questing forefinger. Vickery came in just as the bath was losing the last of its warmth. Peake hurriedly wiped his finger on his trouser leg and stood to attention. Vickery dismissed him.

'Here,' Vickery muttered, not meeting William's eyes. 'I thought — if you're interested. Only in here, though. I see it in the dormitory, it's solitary.'

Already halfway to the door he thrust on to the one chair a dog-eared copy of the *Morning Herald*, its pages already cut and its print smudged with use. William picked it up. His eyes were unused to reading and he had to force them to focus upon the small print. He looked first at the date. 14th January 1859. A new year. Christmas Day had passed and he had had no notion of it. He was growing tired and was preparing to close the pages when his attention was caught by an article on page five.

INVESTIGATORS 'CLOSING IN' ON KILLER

Police officers investigating the death of Alfred England, the London brickyard owner whose body was recovered from the Thames two days ago, have confirmed that the businessman was the victim of a murderous attack. Although no details were given, a leading detective confirmed to this newspaper that Mr England's throat had been cut, thereby severing the man's windpipe. In addition there were found a number of other wounds to the chest and shoulders indicative of a violent struggle. The detective also disclosed that, subsequent to death, the body had been subject to considerable mutilation by rats, suggesting that it might have been at some stage concealed in the metropolitan sewer system. Indeed, the damage to the facial area was such that a positive identification of the body was made possible only by the laundry marks stitched into Mr England's shirt and undergarments.

Mr England, whose brickyard was

troubled by severe financial difficulties, was first thought to have fled from creditors when he disappeared without warning on the night of the 16th December. Scotland Yard expressed confidence that an arrest will be made without delay.

XXIII

'You know that dead cove they pulled out the river, the gent with the brickyard? The traps've only gone and found the one what did it. They've got him lodged down the Moor-street lock-up.'

'You sure they's got themselves the right one? Them crushers down that station couldn't catch themselves the cholera if they lived in a sink-hole and filled themselves to bustin' with the stink.'

Both men laughed and took another draught from their mugs. Tom, nursing a drink at the end of the counter closest to the fire, remained where he was but he turned his head slightly so as to catch their words more clearly.

'They're useless buggers and no mistake,' the first man agreed. 'Most likely the one they pulled in didn't do nothin' of the sort. Prob'ly some poor gudgeon they dragged out o' bed so as they looks like they's got things all sewed up and can get themselves off 'ome afore their dinner turns cold.'

The proprietor of the chop-house shook his head as he gathered up their mugs for a refill.

'It's the right one, all right. Not that them fancy officers of Scotland Yard 'ad much doin' in the way of an investigation. From what I 'ears from Eddowes, what runs the coffee-stall end o' Moor-street, the murderer told his missus the whole bleedin' story. Chapter and verse, in a letter. *A letter!* I mean, I ask you. What kind of lunatic writes down their crimes in a letter and hopes to get away with it, eh? They'd've 'ad more difficulty identifyin' a dog in a topper pickin' pockets on its back legs.'

'Who is 'e then, the murderer? Another gent, is it? They says the dead 'un 'ad a score o' debts and men all over London arter 'im for the payin' of 'em.'

The proprietor shrugged. Whatever else Eddowes knew, and in his line of work he heard it all, the identity of the murderous creditor remained a mystery. The first man scratched his head thoughtfully before thrusting his fingers into his ears and jerking them roughly up and down as though he was certain that, if he could only dislodge enough of the rubble, he'd have himself the answer right there in his head.

'So the missus went an' shopped 'im.' The second man snorted glumly. 'Charmin', that is. What kind of a world is it when yer wife squeals yer straight up to the traps? Used to be a man could expect proper loyalty and the respect 'e was due but what 'appened to that, I ask yer?'

Both he and his friend were silent then, both falling to thinking on their own women and giving them something in the way of a once-over, considering them in much the same way they were like to consider the merits and weaknesses of a dog or a horse. Neither came away much reassured by the certainty of a win. It put them both in poor humour. They were both occupied with declaring the universal perfidy of wives and children and police officers when Eddowes himself came in. The proprietor greeted him warmly, calling into the kitchen for a plate of liver and bacon and setting his usual mug of stout upon the counter.

'So I was just tellin' these gentlemen 'ere 'bout the traps pullin' in the brickyard murderer. 'Eard anythin' more on that score, then?'

'Bless me, what a tale that one is,' declared Eddowes, leaning back and taking a long draught of stout. He shook his head as he drank, his belly stuck out before him and one hand placed proudly upon its swell as though it were full to bursting with delicious morsels of news. 'What a tale!'

'Go on then,' the proprietor urged, propping his elbows on the counter. 'What tale?'

'Ah!' Eddowes took another drink and very slowly set his mug down upon the bar, wiping his mouth with the back of his hand. 'It's a tale, I'm tellin' you. A tale an' a half.'

'What tale?' the proprietor demanded again. Tom edged closer, careful to keep his mouth shut. It didn't pay to call attention to yourself.

'What tale?' the proprietor asked for the third time. This time he couldn't keep the edge of exasperation out of his voice.

'Steady yerself, my friend,' drawled Eddowes. 'Fetch us another of these and I'll tell you. It's a tale, though, there's no mistakin' that.'

Sucking contentedly on his teeth, Eddowes moved along the counter and settled himself so that his wide behind drew most of the warmth from the fire. Tom moved up a little to give him room.

'So.' Eddowes spread his hands on the counter and admired them. The proprietor cleared his throat briskly by way of encour-agement. 'So.'

Eddowes stretched his story with as much sighing and shaking of his head and spreading of his fingers and rinsing of stout and liver around his mouth as he could manage but the heart of the tale was this. The murderer was indeed a gen-tleman, and a right fancy one too by the sounds of it, from a grand family. Some-thing high up in Parliament or some such. The shame of it, Eddowes sighed happily, shaking his head, and the other men shook their heads too. The shame of it, they echoed, barely able to contain their glee.

When they had had their fill, Eddowes continued. It was true that this gent had written a letter which had been taken to the police but the letter had not contained a confession, not a jot of it. No indeed. On the contrary, it was what you might call an out-and-out denial. What the letter had claimed, and here Eddowes was so gen-erous with pauses and reflective sucking of his teeth that his audience was convinced he knew a great deal more than he was prepared to tell, was that it was someone else done it and that the lunatic knew who. When the men around him demanded to know who it was he'd tried to finger,

Eddowes just smiled mysteriously, a veritable sphinx, and repeated what he had already told them. What he would say, and this he was certain of since it had raised many an eyebrow and more than one disbelieving chuckle amongst the officers who frequented the coffee-stall, was that the murderer himself had had the nerve to suggest in his letter that he might be of considerable use to Scotland Yard in pursuing their investigations. Why? Because he'd been there. He'd not done nothing, of course, not touched no one. He was innocent as the infant Christ himself. But he'd been there and he'd heard the whole thing!

'What? 'E told 'em 'e was there? The cove's got to be some kind of lunatic!' marvelled the proprietor, rolling his eyes.

Eddowes looked at the proprietor with undisguised dislike. He had no intention of being upstaged. Shaking his head like a beak about to pass sentence, he took a mouthful of liver and chewed slowly, patting the delicious tale in his belly.

'Story'll keep, o'course. P'raps I ought'a be getting along,' he said at last, pushing away his plate.

Hurriedly, the proprietor placed another mug in front of him, compliments of the house, and apologized for the interruption.

'Go on, then,' urged his audience.

Eddowes paused a little longer, till the men was positively frothing for it, and then he told them. The gentleman murderer was indeed a lunatic. He was being held in a private gents' asylum somewhere west of the city.

'An asylum? Wouldn't 'e be locked up then?'

'Must've escaped, mustn't 'e? 'E escaped, right?'

Eddowes sighed and was silent. A dish of gooseberry pie was brought. A leather-armed chair was provided for the coffee-stall owner's greater comfort. Tom moved further away from the fireplace so that Eddowes could enjoy the warmth uninterrupted. And at last the story continued. They'd only had the lunatic locked up a matter of days before he wrote that letter. Of course, writing it was all the proof you needed that he was a lunatic, in Eddowes's opinion, because of course the physicians wasn't about to let no letters go out without having a read of them, was they? Matter of procedure. And natural enough they took this one straight to the traps. It wasn't what you might call a difficult case after that. Turned out the man was crazier than a crateful of March hares. Once they found out he was a long-standing enemy of the dead cove, what else did they need? Turned out he'd been rampaging round Parliament or whatever for months, terrorizing the clerks, frightening the life out of all the other gents. There'd been bribes, dodgy business dealings, threats, all sorts. The dead 'un wasn't the only one, just the one that got it in the neck. Literally. Eddowes permitted himself a chuckle at his own wit before continuing. Through some devious plot the lunatic had lured his victim down the sewers where he'd proceeded to cut his throat, thinking the body'd never be found. When they pulled him in he'd been covered in cuts all over, result of the struggle. And they reckoned it weren't the only time neither. Again Eddowes waved his hands, suggesting a wealth of secret information, before lowering his voice. The police reckoned there might be hundreds of bodies down there, hidden in the tunnels, all rotting away, all victims of the one maniac. Eddowes shook his head. They'd taken him out of the asylum, of course, got him down the lock-up. He was going to be held in Newgate, that was the word, till they could bring the trial. But it'd be a formality. The officers who came to the coffee-stall was already talking about the hanging.

'We'll be taking the room over your brother's place, o'course,' Eddowes said to the proprietor who nodded hastily. 'Best view in the 'ouse that's got, and I'd challenge anyone who tried to tell it otherways. You'd have to be standing on the scaffold itself to get better.'

'Ah, but there you're like to have a cloth over yer 'ead which ain't goin' ter improve your eyesight any,' joked one of the men, jabbing his friend in the ribs with his elbow.

Draining his mug Tom slipped out unnoticed. He walked the long way home but still he couldn't figure it. A favour for a friend, the Captain'd said. Well, naturally Tom'd nodded and sucked his teeth and known exactly what was meant. There were friends like that strewn all through the rookeries, friends who didn't have a name but had a way of getting themselves into a nasty bit of trouble and needing a hand out of it. Men who wouldn't spit on you if you was on fire suddenly came over all self-righteous for friends like that. Oh yes, Tom'd caught the Captain's meaning sure enough. Except now the traps'd gone and banged someone up for the killing, by all accounts an open-and-shut case. Surely this friend the Captain had put himself out for, the friend in a fix for whom he'd shown such regretful sympathy, surely this friend couldn't really exist? What were the chances? Tom'd sensed the slipperiness in him from the off. He'd been certain that the Captain had to be the last man in the capital to do another a favour, out of the goodness of his heart. He'd counted on it. It was Tom's insurance, the only reason he had for trusting the bastard. And yet, was this the one time that the double-crossing maggot had troubled to tell Tom the truth? It seemed impossible and yet Tom could find no other explanation. He'd set his trap and he'd caught a madman while the Captain walked free. Tom could barely credit the injustice in it.

The bastard still had Lady. No doubt he'd turn up at the Bridge Saturday next, one hand on her back like she was his fair and square, and the other held out for the winnings that were rightfully Tom's. Tom huddled beneath his blanket and inhaled the faint memory of her hayfield smell. After a while his hand crept out from beneath the blanket to seek out the empty space behind his knees. She had liked to wedge herself there of a night, tight in the snug curve of his legs, her nose resting on his ankles. Her claws had snagged the rough wool of the blanket into little loops. He stroked them, and fancied he felt through the wool the shape of her skull. There was a hole inside him tonight and its raw edges ached. There wasn't any comfort for an ache like that, not in the heat of rage nor in the cold clink of money neither. Lady'd grinned when she saw him, always, like he was the only thing in the world she wanted. Tom turned on his side, dragging the blanket up to his chin. He had to find another way. There wasn't any point to any of it otherwise. No point at all, if he didn't have her.

XXIV

The inspector in charge of the investigation into Alfred England's murder had refused to enter the room in which William was to be interviewed until the prisoner was placed in restraints. He could not risk the lunatic becoming violent during questioning, he had said, pushing up his spectacles with a spinster's pinched distaste. And so once again William placed his arms into the sleeves of the straight-waistcoat and allowed Peake to tighten the straps. The waistcoat pulled painfully against his damaged ribs but he bit his lip and did not flinch. His stomach fluttered and the saliva rose in his mouth. He could still taste the extraordinary elation that had filled him when he first wrote the letter, the hope that had filled him when he sneaked it to Peake. Peake would take it to Polly. He would be free. His hopes had not been in vain. There was to be an investigation. He would be exonerated, apologies would be made. Naturally enough the police were constrained by procedure in these matters. He would not

409

refuse the straight-waistcoat if they required it. In all matters he would be the very model of cooperation, of courtesy. This was his one chance. He would not squander it. If this interview proceeded favourably, if he could persuade the detectives of the veracity of his story, he would be free. His hands trembled with the effort of holding the anticipation in check.

At the police officer's instruction, another attendant set out a table and chairs for the inspector and his two associates and, towards the back wall, so that the space loomed emptily between them, another lower chair for the prisoner. William waited quietly, Peake at his side, keeping his gaze straight ahead. He forced himself to breathe quietly, evenly. Inside his skull his mind twisted and flailed, exhilaration wrestling with gloom, apprehension with conviction, seasoning his saliva with their powerful flavours, but William remained perfectly still, his face impassive, breathing in and out, slowly and calmly, the breath of an innocent man, a sane man. The waistcoat caused his hands to touch behind his back. Working to keep his face steady William clenched his fists, digging his nails into his palms, and bore down with all his strength upon the frantic roiling in his head. He had to think clearly. One by one, he stabbed his thoughts like settled bills on to the spike of his spine.

He had told the truth in his letter. *Stab.*

He had witnessed a murder but he had not committed one. *Stab.*

The fear and confusion had oppressed him till he had thought himself mad, had wished himself mad, even, but he was not mad. Exhausted, frightened, but not mad. Not mad. *Stab.*

He had been acquainted with Alfred England professionally but he had no reason to wish him dead. *Stab.*

There had been another man in the tunnels that night. *Stab.*

And William was certain he knew who. *Stab.*

But he fumbled then and immediately the clamour began again in his head, not just voices now but image after image of Hawke's face the day that William had tried to speak with him of the Abbey Mills contract. Hawke had known then that England was dead. Weeks before they found the body, Hawke had known. And he had set William up to take the blame. *I fear that your problems with Mr England may be just beginning.* Hawke had smiled then, knowing what would follow. The bitterness flooded William then and it took all his effort to keep his face blank. It would do him no good to make accusations now, he knew that well enough. He bit his lip, concentrating on steadying his breathing. If he was steady all would be well. *Regular in his habits, steady, disciplined, methodical in his problem-solving.* Methodically he resumed his inventory.

He would do all that he was able to assist the police with their investigation. *Stab.*

When Polly understood she would no longer look at him with those eyes. They could begin again, somewhere far from the city, far from the sewers. *Stab.*

He must not lose control. *Stab. Stab. Stab.* DO NOT LOSE CONTROL. There was no glass in the asylum but he knew what he must look like to the freshly laundered detectives, with his blistered face and his unkempt hair and his shoulders wrenched behind him in the grip of the straight-waistcoat. They had dressed him as a lunatic. They wanted him a lunatic. The fear prickled his unwashed scalp. If he was to struggle in the waistcoat, even for a moment, they would have him guilty. But he was innocent. In an English court of law a man was presumed innocent until proven guilty. And he had not yet been so much as arrested. There would be questions but William would be offered the opportunity to give his answers. These men held no grudge against him personally. They sought the truth. He had only to stay calm, to speak only when spoken to and then with courtesy, considering each question with care and answering each one gravely, directly, and they would see that he was one of them, a professional man, an honest man, no more a lunatic than they were themselves. The British constitution respected the rights of every man, at least when he was a man of standing and of character, a respectable man as he himself was, or had been, until so very recently. He had only to retain control, to behave as a sane man would behave, and to speak the truth. Justice would be done.

Slowly, almost ceremoniously, the police officers took their seats, the inspector at the centre. The inspector removed his hat and smoothed his hands over his wiry grey hair, for all the world as if it were a judicial wig. Then he pulled his spectacles further down his nose so that he might study William over their rims. He scrutinized him for a long moment and then abruptly, recalling himself, he pushed his spectacles back to the bridge of his nose and brought his gaze back to the papers in front of him. Pressing his lips together disapprovingly, his eyes down, he gestured at Peake to escort William to his chair. Restrained as he was with his arms behind his back William could only perch upon its edge. The inspector straightened his papers and looked up.

'Let us begin.'

The policeman at his right hand leaned on his notebook, licking his pencil expectantly. William tensed, waiting for the first question. He could see a slice of pale blue sky through the dirty window, a bird wheeling carelessly on the breeze. Calm, care, courtesy. He had pretended to swallow his chloral this morning but, when Vickery moved away, he had turned his head and let it drain from his mouth into the straw of his mattress. Perhaps he should have taken it, he thought suddenly. Perhaps it would have quietened the terrible thrashings in his head. He moved his tongue nervously in his dry mouth, his fists still clenched behind his back. His stomach pitched. Calm, care, courtesy. Think carefully before you speak. Be reasonable, thoughtful, polite. Do not lose control. When the inspector leaned forward, William cocked his head in an attitude of attentive cooperation. But the inspector did not ask a question. Instead he muttered something to the detective on his left. The man nodded and went to the door.

There was a pause, the sound of low voices, and then Vickery entered the room, followed by the asylum physician with the heavy eyebrows whose name was Pettit. They did not look at William. The inspector gestured at them to take another pair of chairs that had been set for them close to the table. The five men nodded at one another. From his chair across the room William watched them and the fear twisted in his throat. His stomach tightened, his bowels turned to water. In all of them, in varying degrees, he saw severity and censure and disgust and, in the twist of the mouth of the policeman with the pencil, something close to salaciousness, but in not one of the faces around the table was there the faintest trace of curiosity.

The inspector directed only one question to William during that interview, and it demanded of him only that he confirm his name and place of residence prior to his incarceration in the asylum. For the remainder of the hour that he was present in the room he outlined the case against the prisoner, occasionally requiring confirmation by Vickery or Pettit of a point of detail. Various gentlemen attached to the Metropolitan Board of Works had been extremely helpful in constructing the case against the prisoner. Of course much of it was already proven. May's presence in the asylum was more than enough proof for any jury of the prisoner's unsound mind. The prisoner had known the dead man. He had confessed in writing, and here the inspector thanked Pettit for his bringing the letter to Scotland Yard's attention, to being present at the murder. What was more, there was clear evidence of motive. Mr Hawke, May's superior at the Board, had testified to frequent violent arguments between the prisoner and the victim. Both men had threatened the other. On one occasion Mr Hawke had been obliged to intervene to prevent a fight. Would Dr Pettit confirm that the prisoner was indeed a violent man?

Pettit did not hesitate in agreeing. Why, only recently Mr Vickery had been forced to resort to brute force to bring one of his attacks under control, was that not true, Mr Vickery? Yes, that was absolutely true Vickery agreed emphatically, keeping his back turned firmly to William's chair. May had proved to be one of Vickery's more difficult charges. Vickery was also able to confirm that the prisoner had numerous marks upon his arms and thighs consistent with knife wounds and a murderous struggle. In fact, Vickery added, striking the table to add emphasis to the words, it would not come as a surprise to him to discover that England had not been May's first victim, given the age of a number of the scars.

There was a universal intake of breath then, a shifting of bodies yet further away from the part of the room in which the prisoner sat, without expression. No, Pettit confirmed, of course there were no plans to release May from the asylum, although there had been suggestions that he might in time be placed in a county institution when the Board's patience and benevolence came to its inevitable end. Since arriving at the asylum he had shown no interest in his surroundings, spending the vast part of every day without moving from his crib. In Pettit's professional opinion, the prisoner's insanity was advanced and well-established. He had reassured the Board that there was no danger of the prisoner ever being well enough to leave full-time medical care.

And what of the letter? In it the prisoner made claims of innocence. Was that simply deviousness or was such delusion consistent with his lunacy? Pettit sighed. It might be either, he conceded. It was possible that the prisoner, in his madness, believed himself innocent. In a case such as this one, where the prisoner himself had confessed to suffering from blackouts, where delusions of an advanced and violent nature had been witnessed not only in the asylum but beforehand, in the prisoner's place of employment, he might have no recollection of committing the murder. Pettit had come across such cases before. He had even encountered lunatics who, in the fevered heat of their imagination, had insisted upon fixing another man with the crime, so that they might more effectively ease themselves of the burden of their unacknowledged guilt. But had there not been discovered amongst the prisoner's papers at Greek-street a notebook in which the prisoner himself acknowledged that he might indeed have committed the crime? There could be no more unreliable witness than a lunatic. The most important thing, therefore, Pettit stressed, was to give the prisoner's own accounts no credence whatsoever. The police were to pay no need to anything that the prisoner claimed, however strongly he pleaded his case. His testimony was quite worthless.

Newgate being temporarily closed as a result of a chronic outbreak of dysentery, William was taken directly to a prison-ship moored at Woolwich, a massive and verminous hulk that had previously been used to transport convicts to the American colonies. There he was to await trial. Despite the concerns of the detectives, who were unnerved by the prisoner's outburst as they concluded the interview, his straight-waistcoat had been removed before he left the asylum, Pettit being unwilling to subsidize the penal system with contributions of his own. Instead they secured his hands in heavy iron cuffs. The windowless transport to Woolwich contained a heavily barred cage into which he was locked. Immediately upon arrival at the ship, leg irons were fastened around his legs. Although they were not to be chained together until William reached his cell, they made walking difficult. William concentrated his attention on shuffling his feet forwards a few inches at a time, allowing himself to think only of the uneasy balance in his feet, the pain in his shins. It was a relief to have so firm a purpose. The noise and the stench on the main deck were overwhelming. There were scores of narrow cells running along each side of the ship and yet more like a spine along its centre, each intended to accommodate a single prisoner but in many cases the prisoners were expected to share. Men roared and cursed and rattled at the doors of their cells as William passed, accompanied by three attendants. The voices pelted him like rocks, from all directions. William stared ahead of him, refusing to hear them. Some of the prisoners were secured by their arms which were passed through holes in the walls of their cells and secured on the other side by iron handcuffs shaped into a figure of eight so that they were required to kneel or lean against the ship's side. Another was held in the open corridor. At first it appeared that he was stooping to retrieve something he had dropped but on closer inspection it was clear that his neck was fastened to an iron bar while his feet were secured in a kind of stirrups. He attempted to spit at the gaolers' legs as they passed but his mouth could summon up only a wisp of saliva. Automatically, as though his arm was simply conforming to prison regulations, one of William's escorts delivered the prisoner an equally unconvincing strike across his shoulders with the flat of his hand. Their business completed, the procession moved on.

At the end of the main deck, William was bundled into a metal cage suspended upon a system of metal ropes and pulleys. It was too small to hold them all and only two of the guards squeezed in with William, nodding at the remaining warder to slam the door closed. There was a jerk, so that William stumbled forwards, and then the cage began slowly to sink downwards. The darkness grew thicker, the stench stronger. The cage descended past another deck without stopping before, with a startled groan, it jolted and stopped. The door was dragged open once more and William pushed into the gloom of a deck buried deep in the ship's belly. There he was placed in a cell much smaller than the ones on the upper deck, a space perhaps the size of a large press. It being in the centre of the ship there were no windows and the air tasted foul and used up. It itched in William's hair as though it were jumping with lice. There was no crib, no chair, nothing save a bucket in one corner and a little straw upon the floor. When his leg irons had been fastened by chains to iron rings upon its rusting wall the gaolers locked the door behind them and left. William stood in the centre of the cell for a long time after their footfalls had faded. It was quieter down here, the clamour from the upper decks muffled in the coagulated air, but it was not the tranquil hush of empty space. Instead it quivered and pulsated like a simmering soup, its bubbles occasionally bursting into cries or snarls of fury but most of the time issuing no more than a malodorous vapour of exhaustion and misery. William had a sudden impression of thousands of other men crammed together, piled one upon the other, each one nailed for eternity into his coffin of a cell. Thousands of men buried alive, sucking at what little air remained. He mustn't think like that. He mustn't think at all. If he allowed himself to think —

Determinedly William took a step forward so that his hands touched the door. Then he turned round. The chains that fixed him to the wall clamped painfully around his legs, pressing the irons into his flesh. He turned back again, staring at the floor. Beneath the small iron trap in the cell door the plank floor was worn into a shallow trough by the ceaseless tread of feet. The sight of it clenched his heart into a fist. He closed his eyes. Without the chloral his head was clear and without pain. Sounds were crisp. Very slowly he slid down the wall into a squat. He had to preserve his energies. He would have a lawyer, they had told him that. It was his right. Together he and the lawyer would get him out of here. He was innocent. It was Hawke who knew what had happened to England, Hawke who had somehow conspired to frame him for the killing. William was innocent. He was. Wasn't he?

XXV

The lawyer assigned to William's case was a nervous young man named Sydney Rose. After a long pupillage punctuated by extended periods of enforced leave during which his father could not be prevailed upon to settle his fees and during which Rose occupied himself with agonizing over his aptitude and suitability for a career in the law, he had finally been admitted to the Bar. William was his first client.

Although he came from a family that had for generations managed to obscure the extent of its financial difficulties beneath a determined veneer of respectability, Sydney Rose was not a man of prepossessing appearance. He was very thin with the fine colourless hair of a new baby and, although he was not particularly tall, he had legs and arms of unnatural length which, in the absence of much in the way of central government, had become adept at operating quite independently of one another. Rose responded to their unpredictability with a kind of startled deference. Indeed the young lawyer gave the impression of being in a state of almost permanent discomposure. He had a prominent Adam's apple that scraped against his collar when he swallowed, which was often, and protruding eyes with pink rims and eyelashes so pale that they were barely there at all. When he was nervous they bulged. His hairless cheeks had the blue-white pallor of skimmed milk. Only his hands were red, raw-boned and large, with bitten nails and savagely scrubbed knuckles. His suit was clean and tolerably pressed but it had been sewn for a man of more regular proportions and his wrists projected from the cuffs like knobbly flag-poles from which his red hands hung awkwardly, as if discomfited to find themselves so publicly displayed. To ease their embarrassment he had a tendency to clamp them behind his back as he spoke, gripping them together so tightly that they became redder and rawer still. When even this became too much for them they took refuge in his pockets, which the tailor had set inexplicably low in the seams of his trousers. Even accounting for the length of Rose's arms, this gave him a hunched and furtive look. It did not inspire confidence.

The detectives made no attempt to disguise their contempt when Rose first came to them to discuss the case. To their mind the case was open-and-shut, the Sessions no more than a formality. The gangling lawyer with his bulging eyes and his scarlet hands they dismissed as the cheapest means available to the Crown of conforming to the mandates of due legal process. They allowed Rose less than half an hour, giving one word answers to his questions while their fingers tapped restlessly upon the table. As for evidence that they might rely on in court, they were able to produce only a slim Manila envelope of papers for his inspection, comprising statements from two men at the Metropolitan Board of Works, a Mr Hawke and a Mr Spratt, and a further two men at the Hounslow asylum, a Dr Pettit and a Mr Vickery. There had been other evidence recovered, they conceded, but it had been misplaced. When it became available they would provide copies for Mr Rose's reference. Less than half an hour after his arrival Rose found himself once more on the street.

Although he was tempted to put off his visit until the following day, Rose went directly from the police station to Woolwich. He had never before visited the prison-ship moored there and the uproar and the filth appalled him. The stench made him nauseous. He crept through the bowels of the ship, his Adam's apple rasping like a cricket against his stiff collar, his hands clutched behind his back, wishing for all the world he could shut his bulging eyes and find himself magically transported back to the shabby quietude of his lodgings in the Temple. When at last they reached William's cell the gaol attendant did not open the door. It was not considered safe to permit Rose to enter the prisoner's cell. Instead the attendant unlocked the iron trap in the door habitually used for the passing through of the prisoner's daily allowance of bread and water, and motioned to Rose to squat so that he might talk through it. The gaoler gave Rose an iron bell with which he was to summon help if the prisoner gave him trouble or when he wished to leave. Someone would then show him out. Rose nodded and, when the attendant was out of sight, he bent down. From his side the prisoner would be able to make out only the visitor's eyes but the flap afforded Rose a full view of the defendant. It did nothing to raise Rose's spirits.

William lay shackled to the wall. He still wore the cotton pyjamas from the asylum, although they were dirty now and torn, and his sandy hair stood up like clumps of tussocky grass around his head. His eyes were closed. He put Rose in mind of the lion at London Zoo, the old moth-eaten one that the visitors grumbled about for it never moved or roared or did the things that lions always did in picture books but only stared at them unblinkingly with its baleful eyes, wishing them all dead. The prisoner stank like an old lion too. Rose extracted a handkerchief from his pocket and inhaled its comforting pear drop smell.

'Mr May?'

William opened his eyes, sliding them guardedly from side to side. They were not eyes that wished anyone dead, Rose thought suddenly, despite the prisoner's violent reputation. Rather they had the un-promising flatness of his Manila envelope.

'Here, through the trap. They won't let me in, I'm afraid, but I'm to represent you. At the Sessions. Sydney Rose.' The lawyer cleared his throat, his Adam's apple catching on his collar. 'Glad to make your acquaintance.'

Clumsily, uncertain of the appropriate etiquette for so singular a situation, Rose thrust one of his red hands as far as he could through the trap. The metal was cold against his bony wrist. Rose waited for a moment, his fingers twitching awkwardly, but there was no answering hand from the other side of the door. Perhaps he could not reach. Then again, Rose thought suddenly, he was a prisoner, a maniac. He felt a sudden agonized pang of vulnerability. A man like that would likely bite a fellow's finger off soon as look at it. Quick as he could he wrenched his hand back through the trap. Just too late he felt the ghostly touch of the other man's fingers against his.

'Mr Rose,' William said, very quietly.

Rose hesitated, rubbing the scraped knobbles of his wrist. The madman's voice was tarnished with disuse but controlled, educated. Less the voice of a madman than the voice of a clerk. Then he put his face back to the slot, so that his pink eyes gazed out from their metal surround as they might have through a medieval helmet. He made for an unconventional knight.

'Mr May,' he said. 'We have only a few days to make your case. I think you had better tell me everything.'

The words were careful but the voice was kind. William rubbed his hands over his eyes. He understood his rights. They were required to provide him with a lawyer, he knew that, but they were not required to provide him with an able lawyer. In the long empty hours he tried to hope for no more than a man who had a modicum of human decency and enough of a reputation for sobriety to remain upright through the trial. This man's eyes had the red-rimmed droop of a drinker. But he had placed his hand in the slot. He had wished to shake William's hand, to touch him. He had spoken to him with a tentative courtesy, a deference even, that William had not heard for weeks. He had spoken to him like a gentleman. William felt the tears prickle at the base of his nose and, beneath his diaphragm, an unfamiliar flicker. A flicker of hope.

Dragging his chain he moved as close to the door as he could and squatted. The men's eyes were no more than a foot apart. William wanted to reach out and touch the man's face, to feel the certainty of another's flesh beneath his fingers, but he kept his hands at his sides. Do not lose control. *Stab.* William licked his lips. He was not sure how his voice would sound. He had not used it for days.

'I — my bucket, Mr Rose.' William swallowed. 'I'd like it emptied.'

'Of course.' Rose nodded. 'Of course. I'll see what I can arrange.'

There was another long pause. Rose waited.

'I am not mad, Mr Rose,' William whispered at last. 'And I did not kill Alfred England.'

The lawyer's eyes bulged.

'Well, that's good,' Rose stammered.

'I did not kill him,' William said again, and the unshed tears pressed at his cheekbones. 'You believe me, don't you?'

Rose blinked unhappily as the prisoner leaned towards him as far as his shackles would allow. Close up, his eyes were not the flat buff that Rose had first supposed but lit with bright flecks of green and yellow. He'd been a surveyor once, they'd told him, a professional man, before he lost his mind. He had a family.

'Well,' he said and faltered. Behind his back his scarlet hands clamped together, the raw knuckles pressing like molars through the roughened skin. 'Look, Mr May. It is my job to defend you. Acquittal would be — naturally — an ideal result from my point of view as well as yours. But I've never — the case against you is strong. Very strong, from what I have seen. But, you know, we will try. We will try.'

William gazed into the pink eyes and bit his lip.

'You are all the hope I have, Mr Rose. They will hang me.'

Rose forced himself to return the prisoner's gaze. Was it intelligence that illuminated those lion's eyes, lighting them gold, or was it lunacy? How was one supposed to tell the difference?

'I will do what I can for you, Mr May,' he muttered softly. 'But I will need all the help you can give me. You — let us just say, it does not look good. For you. Do you understand? So I will need to know everything. Anything. From the beginning.'

And so William started from the beginning. At first the words came slowly as though he was dragging each one like a rock out of his chest. There were long pauses. May ground his wrists against their irons as though he might rub his way free. Rose's knees ached. He made notes, stretching each letter of each word into elaborate loops so as to fill the extended periods of silence. He strained not to hear the ghastly clankings and groanings from the other cells. He remained like that for several hours, his spirits sinking with the afternoon sun.

'I will have to leave soon, Mr May.'

William lifted his head and stared at Rose through the iron slot. Then he shook his head, slowly first and then violently as if he wished to cast it from his neck. The shudder spread through him until it possessed his whole body. His dazed eyes sharpened with desperation and on his bloodless cheeks there bloomed two vivid spots of red.

'No, no, please — I . . .'

William struggled to his feet. He did not look at Rose. Instead he paced the limits of his cell, two short steps in one direction, then two back, two forwards, two back. The irons on his legs clanked against their chains. Still he shook his head, clutching at it with both hands as though to shake the truth out of it. Perhaps that is indeed what happened. For suddenly and without warning the words began to cascade out of him, faster and faster until they thundered like an avalanche from his lips and Rose could barely hold himself steady against the onslaught. Outside the afternoon fog darkened until the rusting hulk was no more than a great slab of black against the charcoal sky, but Rose remained where he was, his face pressed up against the metal trap, and his hand moved frantically over the pages on his lap.

William seemed barely to know what he was saying but still the words came. He kept his eyes fixed upon the worn plank of the floor, upon the ghostly footprints of the ranks of prisoners long since gone, and he told the lawyer everything. He spoke of the horrors of the Crimea, of the nightmares that had followed, the blackouts. He told him all he could remember of his dealings with Hawke, of his own refusal to sign papers that Hawke had drawn up without the proper authorizations that would give England a valuable contract. He told him of Hawke's attempt to bribe him and then to intimidate him. He told him of England's desperation, of the brickyard owner's threats and his own continuing refusal to change his mind. He told him that there had indeed been a fight between the two of them, that he had struck England, but that afterwards he had run away. He told him that he had sought refuge in the tunnels as he had always done, and that the chill had given him a fever, from which he was slow to recover. But despite that, despite the heat of the fever, he had known, he had always known, that, in the darkness, he had been witness, albeit blindly, to a murder. He had repeatedly said as much to his wife but she had dismissed it, thought it no more than the fever talking. Which was why when, weeks later, he had heard of England's death, he had felt it so important to write to her, to offer through her his assistance to the police. He told Rose of his certainty that Hawke was somehow involved in England's death. He had agreed to grant England a contract in exchange for money but he had failed to secure that contract. England's yard was on the verge of bankruptcy. England was desperate for money. Had England threatened him in some way, tried to blackmail him? If Hawke had feared exposure, then —

'Mr Hawke?' Rose interrupted. 'He is the controller of finances for the sewer project, that is correct? A position of some pre-eminence on the Board?'

'Yes! He has a reputation for making the most stringent of economies. It was brilliant, don't you see? No one who knew Hawke would ever have guessed that he was all the while directing funds into his own pocket. But he was. He said as much to me. He offered me a share in it in exchange for my cooperation, if I made sure that England won a major contract.'

'Were there any witnesses to that proposition?'

'No, of course not. Hawke is not a fool.' Rose's eyelids lowered a little. William could hear the scratch of pencil against paper as he made another note.

'He was well known to be an adversary of yours, I believe?'

'Hawke? No more mine than anyone else's. Or at least not until the business with England.'

'But you were known to be at odds? It was at his insistence that you were first seen by a doctor, is that not the case?'

'He wished to discredit me,' William protested. 'Can you not see that?'

Rose was silent.

'It was on my recommendation that the contract went to another yard,' William persisted. 'Two days later England was dead. It was weeks before they found his body but Hawke knew it. He knew it then. When I went to him to suggest England for Abbey Mills, he laughed. Because he knew it was too late. He knew that England was already dead.'

Rose pressed his lips together and he tried not to sigh. His feet prickled with pins and needles and cramps clamped his shoulders. He shifted position, glancing down as surreptitiously as possible at the watch he had withdrawn from his vest pocket. He had been in the gaol, kneeling at the trap, for almost three hours and he still had nothing. There was nothing that the prisoner had told him that would stand up to cross-examination, even if he was permitted to take the stand. Which he would not be. As a certified lunatic his testimony was worth precisely nothing. The best Rose could hope for was that he would turn up something or someone to verify May's story. But what? Who? Hawke was hardly likely to volunteer his help. And the Board would close ranks, of that there was no doubt. Their position was already awkward. They would have no wish to see another of their number implicated in this ugly affair.

Besides, what chance was there that May was telling the truth? Or that what he believed to have happened had indeed happened? Rose could find himself upon a thousand wild goose chases seeking corroboration for a story that was no more than the product of a fevered imagination. The man was prone to vivid nightmares, to blackouts. He saw things that were not there. He claimed he was not mad but he had had himself committed to an asylum by his own signature. No one else doubted that May was guilty. Why should he? He flexed his feet, feeling the life creep painfully back into his calves, and closed his notebook.

'It's late,' Rose said and his pink eyes slid sideways. 'I must go.'

'You'll come back, won't you? To-morrow, when you've been able to talk to Hawke, to Lovick?'

'Perhaps,' Rose replied evasively.

For a moment William stood perfectly still. Then he sank to his knees. The leg irons dragged at his legs but William did not seem to notice. Instead he fixed his gaze on the trap in the door and all the bones in his face seemed to strain forward, sharp with intent. He cupped his hands, one on top of the other. His lion's eyes gleamed gold. In his dirty white clothes, with his tussocky hair, his ragged beard, he looked to Rose like an ascetic from the Old Testament, one of the prophets obliged to endure unbearable suffering in the name of a capricious and vengeful God. Not a lion after all but Daniel, scraping up the courage and the faith to venture into the den.

'I didn't kill him, Mr Rose.'

Rose blinked unhappily, forcing himself to hold the prisoner's gaze.

'We will do what we can,' he said again. 'I can promise no more than that. Good night, Mr May.'

Briskly he rang the bell provided to summon an attendant. William watched as the eyes withdrew from the trap. Through the narrow slot he could just make out the lawyer's raw red hands as he brushed ineffectually at his trousers, the hem of his coat. The cloth was grimy, rimed with dust and fragments of straw.

'One last thing,' William said very softly through the trap. 'Please take a message to my wife. Tell her I'm sorry for all the trouble I have caused. Tell her I love her, that I will always love her.'

The hands stopped. There was a pause before the fingers sought each other out, clasping each other in a tight embrace.

'Of course,' Rose murmured. 'Of course.'

'Tell her I am planning her garden. It will be a beautiful garden. Tell her —'

His words were trampled beneath the harsh footsteps of the attendant. Rose spoke in a low voice to the gaoler before wishing William a good night. In an urgent voice William begged the lawyer to lower his ear to the trap. Reluctantly Rose bent as William whispered something. Puzzled, uncertain he had heard correctly, Rose asked him to repeat it but the second time William could do little more than mouth the words. Exhaustion leached the marrow from his bones. He closed his eyes, slumping against the iron door of the cell as Rose was led away. *We will do what we can. We will do what we can.* William had thought to derive a little comfort from the words but they repeated emptily in his skull until their edges melted and their meaning seeped away. When at last he slept, his head on the hard pillow of his knees, he dreamed only of pink protruding eyes, framed with rusting metal, and when he woke, in the dark frozen hour before dawn, he was filled with a terrible certainty that, much as the lawyer had wished to find himself convinced, he had not believed a single word of William's story.

XXVI

The Crown's lawyers sent word to Rose's chambers the following morning. The investigating officers had the previous day carried out a search of May's carrel at the Board's Greek-street offices and, concealed beneath a loose floorboard under his desk, they had turned up a bayonet blade of the type used by private soldiers in the Russian War. They were certain it was the weapon with which England had been killed. The blade was scabbed with dried blood and, caught on the underside, were two black whiskers, of a length and colour consistent with the whiskers of the dead man. The discovery completed the prosecution case. Given the abhorrent nature of the crime and the dangers inherent in holding a lunatic on board a prison-ship for any longer than was absolutely necessary, the Crown wished to move with all speed towards a guilty verdict. The judge had therefore given his authority for the case to be moved to the first day of the Sessions. May would be tried on Monday, six days hence. Rose had till then to construct the prisoner's defence.

He would object, of course. They could not spring the trial on them in so high-handed a manner. But it was not that that preoccupied Rose as he set the kettle on the fire for tea. He thought instead of May, crouched and shackled in his lightless cell. So he had done it, after all. May had murdered Alfred England. Rose folded the message and set it among his papers, surprised at his own disappointment. As the kettle began to rattle upon its stand he stared into the flames, his elbows set upon his knees and his red hands clasped together. Disappointment was natural, he told himself briskly. No one wished to see their first client hang. But, later, as he took his hat and walked slowly through the Temple and along the river towards Lambeth Bridge, he knew it was more than that. There was something about May that had attracted Rose despite himself, although he could not precisely put his finger on what it was. It certainly wasn't that May's story was compelling, although the prisoner's belief in it had seemed sincere. It was more that, despite the filthy clothes and the matted hair and the kennel of a cell, there was something uncorrupted about him, something honourable. As though the body that contained it was soiled and verminous but, inside it, his soul remained perfectly pure. Well, it showed how wrong you could be. It must have been the trappings of gentlemanliness that had deceived him, for prisoners were rarely so courteous, or perhaps he had mistaken for virtue the meaningless innocence of the insane. Rose sighed. If he was ever to become more than a mediocre practitioner of the law he would have to become more adept at penetrating his clients' fictions.

On the bridge he paused, looking down at the brown water. The river was busy with coal barges and brightly coloured hoys, laden with straw, stately as little swans beside the great steamers which, despite their size, seemed always to be engaged in racing one another, their bells ringing and their wheels churning frantically while, all the while, their funnels belched smoke as though they were panting for breath. Above their racket, carried on the strong westerly breeze, came the shouts of the labourers and the striking of metal as the men toiled on the new Westminster Bridge. The river was choppy, whipped up by wind and paddle. The clouds were gathering in dark fat worms along the edges of the sky, there would be rain before nightfall, but for now the red winter sun glinted on its churned surface, so that it sparked and flashed like a black-smith's anvil. He had written May's message down, so as not to forget it, and the envelope was heavy in his pocket. This morning he had thought to post it but the news of the bayonet had changed his mind. May would hang next week, his name a synonym for wickedness to be whispered with greedy disgust in taverns and coffee-houses and drawing-rooms across the metropolis. His wife deserved more than a hastily scribbled note.

York-street was a narrow uncobbled street of terraced cottages squeezed on the diagonal between two noisy thoroughfares. It was as if, Rose thought, the houses had been nailed and glued into their rows before being brought here, only to discover upon arrival that the calculations had been inaccurate and they were too long for the space originally allotted them. Naturally there was not a builder in London who would have allowed so finicky a detail to deter them and so the street had been wedged in all the same, triangles of rough ground sprouting at either edge like fraying cloth where the seams did not line up. For the most part the houses were small but respectable, their paintwork fresh and their front steps scrubbed. But towards the far end of the street there was something of a commotion, shouts and tea chests spilling out on to the street. As Rose drew closer he saw that the door to number eight stood open, and two boys with faces Rose would have been unsurprised to see peering over the rim of the dock ran to and fro, boxes and crates balanced precariously against their narrow chests. Already there was a stack of possessions set upon the pavement. A bentwood chair accommodated a chipped china jug without a bowl and a sampler bearing the words HOME SWEET HOME. Rose hesitated, his fingers very lightly tracing the silky knots of the words.

'What the blazes d'you think you're doing?'

Rose looked up guiltily. A woman stood in the doorway. Her chestnut hair straggled around her face and her caramel eyes were ringed with purple shadows. An apron held in the waist of her shapeless dress. Behind her a small boy sought refuge in her skirt, his little hands kneading the sprigged cotton into balls.

'Mrs May?'

The woman narrowed her eyes suspiciously. 'Who are you?'

445

'Rose. Sydney Rose. I'm representing your husband.'

The woman frowned, placing one hand on the boy's blond head and drawing him closer to her.

'I'm his lawyer,' Rose added. 'I saw your husband yesterday. He asked me to come. With a message.'

He fumbled in his pocket. The woman's mouth tightened as though it had been pulled together with a drawstring.

'Message isn't much good. It's money we need. Don't suppose he sent any of that, did he?'

'I'm afraid not.'

'Go on then,' the woman said brusquely, not moving from the step, but Rose was sure that she trembled. 'What's the message?'

'Might I come inside?'

'Hardly seems necessary with most of what we got out here,' she said but her voice had lost its sharpness and she stood aside to let him in before showing him into a small parlour. There was no furniture. The floor had been swept but the walls were marked in places where candles had left their sooty traces. Rose stood awkwardly in the centre of the room, his red hands clamped behind his back. The little

446

boy had followed them into the parlour. While he did not relinquish his grip on his mother's skirt he no longer hid his face. Instead held his head stiffly erect, his feet set slightly ahead of his mother's as if he hoped to shield her from the force of whatever Rose might say, and he stared at Rose unblinkingly. He had the same wide-set toffee-coloured eyes as his mother, Rose thought. She must have been a pretty woman once, before she grew old and lost hope. Rose cleared his throat, his Adam's apple catching uncomfortably on the starched rim of his too-tight collar. The woman plaited her fingers together and stared intently at them, her bottom lip caught between her teeth.

'Your husband asked me to tell you that he loves you,' he rushed, without preamble. 'That he's sorry for all the trouble he's caused.'

'That's it, is it?' The woman did not look up.

'Not quite. He said he was planning you a beautiful garden. Something about milkwort, I think, and sweet william, although I fear I misheard.' Rose grimaced apologetically. 'I'm afraid I am a terrible ignoramus when it comes to flowers.'

For a moment the woman stood so still

Rose was alarmed she might have fainted. Then she covered her face with her hands. Her shoulders shook. Rose took a step forward and placed one of his red hands gently beneath her right elbow.

'Mrs May, I'm so terribly sorry —'

He waited for her to compose herself, to look up, but her hands remained pressed over her face. She made no sound. The little boy gazed up at her intently, stroking her leg through the shabby cloth of her skirt.

'Mrs May, perhaps you should sit?' Rose cast around for a chair. 'Perhaps on the stairs?'

Gently he steered her out of the parlour and into the narrow hall. From the room at the back of the house came a thin high cry, like the wail of a kitten. The boy glanced anxiously towards the noise but his mother paid it no heed. She sat on the stairs silently for a long time. The boy laid his head in her lap. Then, at last, she took her hands away from her face and, wiping her eyes on her apron, sent the child to the kitchen.

'They'll hang him, won't they?' she asked when he had gone, her voice soft but almost steady.

'I think so.' Rose faltered, twisting his

fingers painfully behind his back. 'They've found the knife, you see. Hidden beneath his desk in Greek-street.'

'No.' Polly shook her head, her forehead creased with disbelief. 'No. That's not possible.'

'I'm sorry —'

'But you don't understand. It's not possible.'

'I know how difficult this must be for you, Mrs May —'

'No!' Polly's head jerked up. 'They can't have found the knife. I — I — it's not the knife. It can't be.'

'Why not?'

'Because I have it.'

Rose stared at her.

'I beg your pardon?'

'I have it. William's knife. The one he had with him that night. It was in his pocket when those policemen brought him home. I found it. I — I was afraid. In case they came back. I buried it. In the flour bin. I didn't know what else to do.'

'And you still have it?'

'Yes. After that I locked up all the knives. So — so he'd be safe.'

'Might I see the knife? Please?'

Polly nodded. She tried to pull herself up by the banister but suddenly the blood drained from her face and she doubled over, clutching at her stomach.

'Are you quite well?' Rose asked anxiously.

Carefully, Polly straightened up.

'Come with me,' she said.

The kitchen was not yet entirely packed up, although the small space was crowded with boxes and baskets. The boy was staring into one, poking its contents with a finger. Polly thrust her hands into the flour bin. The dust rose obediently, settling on her arms and whitening her already pale face.

'Here.'

She handed him something wrapped in an old handkerchief. Flour sprinkled his shoes as he unwrapped it. A knife. Flour clung to the blade. Rose made to brush it off.

'There's blood on it, Mrs May.'

'He used to cut himself.' Polly glanced towards the boy and swallowed. Her voice was almost inaudible. 'I don't know why.'

'Did he ever use a bayonet?'

Polly closed her eyes, steadying herself on the edge of the range.

'Mrs May, I shouldn't —'

'He could not have taken a knife back to Greek-street, Mr Rose. He came straight here from the sewers that night. That knife was in his pocket. After that I kept all of our knives locked up. As for a bayonet —' Polly's face softened at the memory. She was still pretty, thought Rose. And hardly older than him. 'We threw his into the river. Together. A few months after he came home. We might have got something for it, if we'd sold it, but he said that knowing it was rusting at the bottom of the Thames would help put that terrible time behind him. He was getting better, you see. He was almost well.'

Again the thin reedy cry. The boy pulled his hand hurriedly from the basket.

'She's hungry, Mother.'

Polly reached into the basket and lifted out a bundle, crooning gently. The cry came again. Polly began to sing very softly, a lullaby Rose had never heard before. He felt a tug at the leg of his trousers. He looked down into the boy's caramel eyes.

'That's my new sister,' the boy said. 'Her name's Edith. She's coming with me to live with my Uncle Maurice. In Kent. That's in the country.'

'Is she now?'

The boy nodded.

'Mother's coming too, soon as she can. So we can be all three together. Three's a lucky number, Mother says.' He gazed at the baby, his eyes wide with fear and pride. 'That's why the baby has three names. Not just Edith. Edith Elizabeth Violet.'

It was raining hard by the time Rose left York-street. The two boys scrambled to pile the last boxes into the waiting wagon but the bentwood chair was still where they had left it, a bead of rain lingering uncertainly on the spout of the chipped jug. The silk threads of the sampler bled faint streams of colour into their linen ground. Rose pulled up his collar. All along the river, as the grey rain flung itself into his face, he practised the words, addressing himself with stern intransigence. This time he did not intend to be brushed off.

The policeman grumbled under his breath as he heaved the box of papers on to the table. The papers were nothing but routine, he said. No one had thought them worth keeping. They contained only information that might easily be verified by any number of gentlemen at the Board. That said, they was private papers and the policeman was not at liberty to release them into Rose's custody. They were to be returned to the Board's offices the following morning.

'Then I shall deliver them there myself,'

Rose informed him, lifting the box. 'Once I have satisfied myself to their contents.'

'Look here, you can't just —'

'Oh, I think you'll find I can. Thank you, sir. You have been most helpful.'

The policeman's moustache twitched but he made no move to stop him. Rose folded himself around the carton. It was heavy and unwieldy and Rose was not a strong man. But as he walked down the steps of the police station, the rain dripping from his nose and running in cold streams down the back of his coat, Rose's step was unnaturally light.

XXVII

Prisoners were not given chloral. The first two days without it were terrible. William's heart had raced, his limbs twitching and jumping in their iron fetters. His tongue was a wad of wool in his parched mouth. He was tormented by pain, by elusive terrors that, if he ceased for a moment in his vigilance against them, crept upwards through the soles of his feet and breathed their cold black breath down the nape of his neck. His head screeched and throbbed. He dared not sleep. The scrabblings of the rats in the straw made him start up in fear. Much of the day he spent hunched over, squatting over his rusty bucket, clutching desperately at the cramps that twisted his gut as his skin oozed a cold greasy sweat that stood out upon his forehead and congealed in his hair. No one emptied the bucket. No one spoke to him. His meals, such as they were, were passed on a bent metal dish through the trap in the door. At first William could not stop himself from calling out to the attendant, begging for a dose of the sedative, but there was never a reply. The trap opened, the food was pushed through, the trap was shut. If William tried to speak it was slammed. Three times a day this ritual was repeated. The food was meagre and consisted mostly of hard bread and a thin flavourless soup but William found himself longing for it, not so much because he was hungry but because he found himself comforted by the familiar blunt shape of the dirty hand that held out the dish. In those first days it was the only contact he had with another human being.

On the third day, or perhaps it was the fourth, he had woken to the clank of a prisoner being taken in irons from the cells. It was morning, he guessed. He had slept, perhaps for several hours. His head felt clear, the pounding headache no more than a fading bruise behind his eyes. If he kept his head still he might almost imagine it gone. His heart pumped quietly, evenly, in his chest. He held his hand in front of his face. It did not tremble. Carefully William took a deep breath. The stench from his bucket choked him. When his breakfast came William called to the attendant and asked for it to be emptied. The trap slammed shut. But an hour later it opened again, the familiar blunt hand folding itself over the iron slot. Each ragged nail was finished with a perfect curve of grime. William raised his head a little from his knees.

'Well, well. You got a visitor.'

Polly, he thought, and the thought exploded like a scarlet firework in his chest. He strained for the first sound of her sweet voice. Instead he heard the tentative voice of a young man and saw, through the slot, another hand, clean this time but red and raw, all knuckles and joints. Sydney Rose. His lawyer, courtesy of the Crown.

'Good luck to yer,' he had heard the attendant mutter with a low laugh. 'Gawd knows yer's goin' to need it.'

That afternoon William had talked until he was hoarse. The lawyer had seemed competent enough. But after the lawyer left he had felt hollow, the underside of his ribs bruised with misery. Dread too. He hadn't been afraid before. The asylum, the gaol, even the gallows, they had held no terror for him for all the fear he felt had been for himself, for what he might be capable of. He had believed himself mad. He had known himself mad. There was a devil within him, a devil that had buried itself in the darkest corners of his heart, a devil that poisoned his blood and stopped his eyes and ears and stole his hands so that it might commit crimes of unbearable horror in William's name. He had seen the certainty in other people's eyes, the detectives and the doctors and the lawyer too behind his iron mask. They stared at him and the disgust and the moral outrage and the fascination had combined to stretch their eyes and flood their mouths with saliva. They none of them had any doubt that he had killed Alfred England.

Chained in his cell as his body screamed out for chloral, William had struggled to smooth out the shaking sweating wreck of his thoughts but they slipped and jerked beneath his fingers, refusing to hold their shape. He would remember, he told himself, and he implored himself to believe it. He would remember if he had killed a man. At Inkerman he had killed a man, two men. The Russians had crept up on his tent in the thick fog and stabbed their bayonets through the canvas. The engineer who slept beside him had woken to find a blade penetrating his neck. Still stupid with sleep William had stumbled outside and, in his underclothes, had stabbed a Russian soldier between his shoulder blades as he crouched to reload his musket. Later, much later, he had killed another man but by then the carnage had distorted things so incomprehensibly that it had seemed almost ordinary. The first, that was different. William remembered every detail of it still, the pull on his shoulders as he raised the bayonet, the dull thud as he thrust the blade through the man's grey greatcoat, the way the man's back jerked, the gurgle in the man's throat, the force required to wrestle his blade free, the blood that bloomed like a flower across the rough cloth as the Russian fell sideways on to the mud. The man's thin ordinary face had been twisted with astonishment, his scabbed lips parted. He looked no different from a thousand British soldiers. William had vomited then, but hurriedly, wiping the blade of his bayonet on a tussock of grass as he doubled over. The screams and curses were all around him, lumps of sound in the fog. Blindly William stabbed, plunging his bayonet over and over into the man's chest. The blood ran between his fingers. The memory of it curdled William's stomach and he dug his nails into his palms, forcing it away. He could not have killed England, he pleaded with himself over and over. He could not possibly have forgotten.

The day the lawyer came was the first day his thoughts lay smoothly, without rucking and tearing beneath his fingers. They were flimsy but they held their shape, hemmed with the first threads of certainty. In the asylum the chloral had dulled his senses, suppressing thought and appetite. Now hunger shrivelled his belly but it prised open the fissures of his brain, letting in light. Letting in fear. For the first time since he had been brought to the ship he understood that he did not want to die. He longed to move unfettered, to breathe untainted air, to wash the matted grime from his hair. He thought of Polly, of Di, and, as he longed for them, he twisted his chains into tight knots, grinding his shins and his wrists hard against the rough edges of the irons. They were too blunt to draw blood but the pain calmed him.

He had asked Rose to return the following day. All that morning William waited, laying out his memories one by one and turning each one over and over, just as he had done in his notebook in the days after the murder. This time there was no possibility of paper and ink but as he forced himself to remember, his head tipped intently, he laid out a straw for each recalled scrap of sound, laying them like the rungs of a ladder on the floor next to him. When the Russian memories threatened, and the sucking thud of knife in flesh rose in his ears, he thrust them away. He had only to focus on that night. There had to be something he had forgotten. Something hidden inside those husks of sound, in the scrapes and the splashes and the squelches and the groans. Something that would hold.

It was some hours after the hand had taken back his lunch plate that he heard footsteps along the iron passage. They were lighter than the footfalls of the gaol attendants and more urgent. William felt the hair rise on the back of his neck. A moment later the iron trap opened. It was Rose. This time the lawyer did not waste time on courtesies.

'I think we may have something,' the lawyer rushed. 'Not enough, not yet, but something. Something that might incriminate your Hawke.'

William cried out in spite of himself. He stared at the eyes framed by the iron slot and for a moment he felt that his heart had burst open, flooding the hollow of his chest with warm sticky blood. His head swam so dizzily he was sure he would faint.

'I —' he managed.

'The contract you spoke of, I have found it.'

It had taken till four in the morning. In

the cold quiet hours of the night Rose had worked his way methodically through the box of papers he had taken from the police station. A great deal of it was concerned with the day-to-day business of a brickyard and Rose's head swam with figures, column after column of them: tunnelling, 6s.6d. per cubic yard; Portland cement, 13s. per cubic yard; brickwork, £14 per rod; stock bricks, 35s. per thousand; day labourer, 3s.6d. If there were secrets hidden in these accounts then they remained obscure to Rose. It was only at the bottom of the box that he had come across the contracts. A thick stack of them there were, tied together with ribbon inside a buff-coloured cover. Most were for small amounts, agreements with building speculators, the occasional minor vestry project. Most were more than a year old. Only one was dated December 1859. A contract for the supply of bricks to the Board by the undersigned, Alfred England of England & Son, Battersea. Hawke's signature was there, a serrated blade of black spikes, and England's too, in a soft childish hand with fat looping characters. Where May's signature was required there was nothing but a pencil cross, so harshly executed that the lead had torn the paper. Rose had stared at it so long, willing it to give up its secrets, that the words had ceased to have sense or meaning.

'Oh Mr Rose, oh my God —'

'I have your knife also,' Rose continued. 'It is reasonable to guess that the weapon found in your office was planted there to implicate you. But it's extremely circumstantial. It would not stand up in court. We need more. Something that places our man there, in the sewers, at the time of the murder. Something definite.'

Very slowly William brought his hands up to cover his face. He remained like that for several minutes. Then he raised his head. His eyes were bright, whether with hope or tears Rose could not tell.

'You believe I did not kill him,' William whispered.

It was not a question and Rose did not answer it.

'We do not have enough to convince a jury,' he said instead. 'I want you to go over your story again. Every detail.'

Again William covered his face. His roughened lips scraped the palms of his hands and his breath was hot between his fingers. In his chest the rush of blood cooled and congealed. He must not be afraid. On his forearms the scars swelled and burned. He had to retain his composure. He bit his lip, pressing the sharp tips of his incisors into the chapped flesh with such savagery that he drew blood. He sucked at it, letting the familiar metallic taste bead upon the tip of his tongue, then pressed it like mortar between his teeth. His tongue would bleed too, if he bit it hard enough. It was not necessary, not yet. But it calmed him. The roar in his ears quietened a little. Carefully he took up the straws he had laid out earlier, one for each sound, and, tearing them as though he would rip from within them the most insignificant of their secrets, he forced himself to remember.

When he was finished he looked up. The eyes in their iron slot slid away.

'It is not enough, is it.'

Again it was not a question.

'A legal defence is like one of your sewers,' Rose said quietly. 'Correctly constructed it can withstand any onslaught, however unpleasant. If, however, any of the bricks one has used is rotten or poorly fired or placed incorrectly in the structure it runs the risk of collapse. And if you have insufficient bricks —'

Bricks. The scrape of brick on brick. It meant something, that sound. It had a shape to it, a familiarity, just as the shrill protest of metal and the drip of water had in childhood always denoted washing day. Long after his mother was gone William would hear the sound of a mangle and think it Monday. In the same way this noise brought with it tastes, feelings. William closed his eyes. The scrape of brick on brick. The weight of the knife in his hand. The taste of blood in his mouth. A cold dank smell in his nostrils. Darkness. Stabbing, stabbing. A white face, eyes like dark holes. No, no, not that. The tunnels. The darkness of the tunnels. The wonderful throb of pain in his arm. Outlines sharp, hands, face, heart, solid and cool, present. Clarity. Peace. William heard himself as he cried out, gasping with sudden longing. Desperately he tried to wrap himself around the feelings, to hold them steady, but they were already gone, shadows lost to the light. William did not open his eyes but his teeth sought out the damaged part of his lip, driving down towards the warm taste of blood.

'Mr May?' Rose asked anxiously through the slot. 'Are you ill? Do you need water?'

William opened his eyes.

'He hid something,' he said. 'He hid something.'

'Who? Hawke?'

'Yes. He hid something. In the wall.'

'He did? What?'

'I don't know. But I know that's what happened. I used to — I hid things too. The bricks were rotten. They came out easily. You could hide something down there and be sure that no one would ever find it.'

'So you're saying —'

'He hid something down there. Perhaps something important. Something he didn't want discovered.'

'The weapon?'

'Perhaps.'

'Papers?'

'I don't know.'

'No. But something.'

'Yes. Something.'

'You're certain?'

'Quite certain.'

Rose's face was pressed so hard up against the iron door that its rim pressed painfully against the bridge of his nose.

'You can tell me where?'

William nodded.

'The gangers, they know the tunnels —'

'They'll take me down?'

'Perhaps. If you pay them.'

'Pay them. Yes.'

It was a long shot and Rose knew it. But the trial was scheduled for the following

Monday. He had only a few days left. He could not confront Hawke, not yet, not with what he had. But if there was something down there, well, it might change everything. It might not be enough to implicate Hawke in the murder but that hardly mattered now. He had only to cast sufficient doubt upon the prosecution's case against May to ensure the jury would be obliged to acquit. He would be the barrister who got the madman off. They'd take him seriously then, even his father and his hunting cronies who cared nothing for city professions except that they might provide a useful source of income when things were a little tight. They'd sit up and take notice of him, thrusting their red fingers at his name in the pages of their periodicals. He'd have made it then. There he goes, they'd say, as he strode through the Temple in a new suit on his way to the Old Bailey, there goes the famous lawyer who defended the indefensible. You never saw anything like that one, they'd say. If one thing is certain, it is that Sydney Rose QC was born to the law.

William coughed, a spasm that shook his frame and rattled the chains on his legs. The clank of the irons recalled Rose from his reverie. Pride was a sin, he reminded himself sharply, his face flushing at his own ridiculousness. He listened attentively to what May told him and took precise notes. But he felt a tickle of anticipation still, running like a stream of bubbles along his vertebrae. Don't fear it, he told himself, and this time he was gentler with himself. Without it you send a man knowingly to the gallows, a man with a wife and two children, a man who might be innocent. Never be afraid of hope.

XXVIII

The answer was no, the ganger said, and he shrugged his powerful shoulders. More than his job was worth, and that was the truth of it. Ever since it'd come out that the body of the brickyard owner'd been dragged out the tunnels there'd been a fair flood of folks interested in having a poke around underground, mostly men from the newspapers, of course, their noses twitching like bloodhounds. Then there was all them snooper types who could always be relied upon to take a special interest in happenings of a grisly nature. Rose wasn't the first one to beg a tour, not by a long chalk. There'd been winks and nods, the ganger and his boys'd been offered money and sometimes fair sums of it. But they wasn't having none of it. They was in the employ of the Board now, answerable direct to no less than Parliament herself, and the Board's orders'd been plain. There wasn't a soul to go down without their particular say-so. Now, of course, if Rose wanted to take things up with the likes of Mr Grant or

Mr Lovick, obtain the right paperwork, get things above board, then it'd be a different matter altogether. Then the ganger'd be happy to take him all the length and breadth of the system. Until then, he was sorry, sure enough, but rules was rules.

'But you don't understand. I have to get down today, tomorrow at the very latest,' Rose insisted, fumbling clumsily in his pocket for coins. 'For pity's sake, a man's life depends upon it.'

The ganger frowned. The whys and the wherefores of Rose's personal affairs were none of his concern, he said sharply. He'd said it once and he'd say it again. There wasn't no one to go down without the proper authority. Far as he was concerned that was the end of it. Meantime, he had work to get on with. He picked up a lantern and fiddled with its shutter.

'Will you go?' Rose asked suddenly. 'To watch, I mean. When they hang him.'

The ganger grimaced, discomfited.

'Dunno. Might, I s'pose. Hadn't thought.'

'But you knew him?'

'Course,' the ganger conceded.

'What did you make of him?'

The ganger shrugged.

'Dunno. Quiet sort. Polite.' The ganger shook his head, remembering. 'Kept himself to himself. Happy as a rat in the tunnels, though. Struggle to get him out it was, some days, he was that wrapped up in it. I'd never've believed it of him, not if I'd not seen it myself, him all to pieces and striking out like —' He looked up at Rose who nodded encouragingly. Abruptly, the ganger's face snapped shut. Rose waited but the ganger remained silent, his eyes intent upon the lantern in his lap.

'He says there's something hidden down there,' Rose said at last, very quietly. 'Evidence that would exonerate him. If only it could be found.'

Still the ganger said nothing.

'It would be terrible if they hanged the wrong man,' Rose murmured. The words settled around him, soft as dust. Very slowly he began to gather his possessions, settling his hat, pulling on his gloves, reaching for his umbrella. The ganger clamped his lips between his teeth and sucked at them, the lantern untouched in front of him.

'Still, rules is rules,' Rose conceded, almost to himself. 'Rules is rules.'

Tipping his hat to the ganger he picked up his portfolio of papers and walked towards the door.

'There is a bloke might do it.' The

ganger's voice was gruff. 'He'd want paying, o'course.'

'Where do I find him?'

The ganger named a tavern in the lanes north of Regent-circus.

'Ask around. They'll all know him.'

'And his name?'

The ganger shrugged.

'Everyone just calls him Long Arm Tom.'

The boy left him at the end of the lane in St Giles, pointing with a dirty finger. He couldn't take him no further but if Rose turned left at the end and then straightways right, almost back on himself, he'd find the place they called East-court. Then he was gone. It was unnervingly silent, although the afternoon was not yet dark, and Rose saw no one as he picked his way through the churn of muck. He kept his hands clenched tightly behind his back. He had never seen so wretched a place. The lane was barely more than a fissure between the buildings, throttled with filth and the putrid stink of excrement. On every side the houses crumbled and rotted, their broken windows patched with rags and paper, their splintered doors slumped on their hinges. Colourless rags slapped from clothes lines strung above his head, barring what little remained of the sky. The lane was ankle-deep in refuse, puddles of slops and decaying vegetable matter that had rotted in the mud. On more than one occasion Rose stumbled upon an ash-heap and choked as the stifling stench rose from its depths. It could have been no more offensive if he had wandered into the sewers themselves. The mean houses seemed to crowd in upon him like beggars, their foul breath hot upon his neck. He saw no one but all around him darkened doorways and low-pitched archways bristled with threatening shadows. Rose swallowed, keeping his eyes fixed straight ahead, but still he was certain that he caught glimpses in each one of the whites of lurking eyes, the flash of a knife or a garrotter's wire. He hastened his pace as his stomach churned, the nausea souring his saliva. It was madness that had possessed him to come here alone, unprotected. The proprietor of the Black Badger had as good as said so, even as he had offered him his lad as an escort. Wouldn't want him to miss the place, he'd said, his head swivelling on its shoulders as he'd shaken it, taking in Rose's pressed suit, the polished leather of his shoes beneath their crust of mud. He didn't wish

Tom no trouble, he'd said, his eyes bulging greedily from his head. He'd licked at his wide mouth as he studied Rose's card as though he might find traces of gravy still left there from lunch. A lawyer, was he? Most interesting. Well, the publican was not a man to get in the way of the due processes of the law. He wasn't giving away no secrets if he told him that Tom might be found always at East-court, left side as you stood in the entrance, two floors up.

The entrance to the court was through a slit of a gap between two houses that leaned treacherously in towards each other, their sagging walls black with soot and decay. It opened into a space barely wider than a clothes-press, so that by extending his arms Rose might have touched the two doors on either side of it simultaneously. It resembled more a narrow cliff-chasm than a place of human habitation. The reek of drains and unwashed bodies was sickening. Rose felt a powerful urge to run, to get away from the place as fast as he was able, but something held him there, less a determination to complete his errand than a sense that if he fled, the ganglion of interlacing alleys and lanes would close in around him, all the time darkening and shifting so that, however frenzied his efforts, he would never find his way out. Clenching his hand into a fist he banged hard upon the door. Then, tentatively in the dark silence of the court, he called out Tom's name.

Through the broken gap in the window Tom could see the crown of the man's hat. Cursing under his breath he waited. The man called out again. His voice was high, a girl's voice you might almost've said, and it rattled in his throat like a spoon in a tin cup. He didn't sound like a peeler, that much was for sure. Tom peered through the window. The man tipped his head back, sudden like, looking upwards, and Tom ducked into the shadows. He was taller than Tom, you could see that, but for all his gentleman's clobber he had an undernourished anxious look about him. Tom reckoned he'd have to do no more than spit on the man's hat for the weight of it to knock the bugger flat.

'Please,' the man begged, thumping again upon the door. 'I beg you, if you are there, come down. Mr Harker, the ganger, I've come from Mr Harker. He sent me. He said you might help me.'

Tom hesitated. Harker'd been a decent sort of bloke, before the Government got a hold of him and silted up his head with rules and regulations. Tom and him'd known each other a score of years or more. For all Harker was a Board man now he'd not've set out to land Tom in trouble.

'I'd pay you. Tom? Can you hear me? Name your price. You are my last hope. Tom?'

The voice was despondent, downright pitiful. Tom peered down into the court. The man raised his fist to beat one last time upon the door but it was like something got the better of him because he never struck the wood. Instead he let his arm fall to his side. He glanced up a final time at Tom's window and turned away, his shoulders slumping as he squeezed himself through the gap in the wall. All that was left in the churned muck of the yard were the neat imprints of his feet.

Tom slipped out the back. He cut across the gent's path just as he reached the end of the alley. The man started at the sight of him, his hands clutching at his mouth. The hands were red but his lips were white as ash and his eyes fair started out of his head. He looked to Tom like he might weep with fear.

'Calling for Long Arm Tom back there, were you?' Tom asked.

The man swallowed, his face stretched tight with fright.

'It's just he's a friend of mine,' Tom said offhandedly. 'So I thought, maybe I could take him a message.'

'A friend?' Rose managed to stammer.

Tom nodded. Rose swallowed again, attempting a smile. His red hands shook.

'A friend. That — that's — wonderful. Could — could you take me to meet him?'

Tom shrugged.

'Mebbe. Depends on what's the nature of your interest. In trouble, is he?'

'Oh, goodness me, no, absolutely not.' Rose shook his head vigorously 'Nothing like that. I wish only — I need his help. I would pay him, naturally.'

'What kind of help?'

'I'm afraid that would have to remain private between your friend and myself.'

'But you'd pay him.'

'Of course. I'd pay you too, if you took me to him.'

Tom thought for a moment.

'What is it, then, your line of business?' he asked.

'I — I'm a lawyer.'

Even in the fading light Rose saw the suspicion bloom in the old man's eyes.

'Your friend is not in trouble,' he in-

476

sisted. 'I swear it. The case I am working on has not the least connection with him. But I am told he could help me. That is all.'

Tom peered at him closely, sizing him up. A lawyer. What were the chances? The Captain's contract dragged at his hem, insistent as a brick.

'You don't look like a lawyer.'

'Well, I am one. In a highly regarded chambers, for that matter.'

'You alone?'

Unease prickled at the nape of Rose's neck. He nodded.

'All alone,' Tom mused, shaking his head. 'Asking for trouble, it is, a gentleman like you venturing into the rookery on your own. There's men wander in here don't never come out. You'd think a man of your profession'd know better'n that. Still, stroke of luck for me, you might say. A lawyer, are you? Who'd've thought?'

With that Tom smiled to himself, showing black stumps of teeth. His eyes flashed white in the thickening dusk. All around them the shadows bristled with menace. Rose swallowed the bitter saliva that rose in his mouth.

'Thank you.' His voice was shrill as he fumbled a half-crown from his pocket. He could turn and run, he supposed, but the darkness pressed in so thickly that the alleys closed over like scabs. He was trapped. He felt dizzy with dread. 'You have been most helpful. Now if you will only let me pass —'

The old man did not move. Instead he spat on the coin before rubbing it vigorously on what remained of his sleeve. Satisfied, he slipped it into his cuff.

'I thought you was after meeting Tom?'

'But —'

'Waste of half a crown other ways.'

It was the wink that settled it. Surely a man could not wink at you in that merry way and then the next moment set about dispatching you. At least that was how Rose was later to explain it. At the time, he felt barely connected to his feet as he allowed himself to be led through a twist of alleys and into a broader lane where the red smoky flame of an old grease lamp illuminated a dingy lodging house. On a blanket in front of it, dressed in a welter of rags and filth, a family huddled around a collection of dusty bottles and iron chains. They stared at Rose as he stepped over them, their eyes sunken and dull. One of the smallest children whimpered and reached out for the hem of Rose's coat but it cowered backwards as Tom growled, threatening it with the cracked toe of his boot. A few steps further on the tosher ducked through a low entrance, where the heavy wooden door was held ajar by a leather strap. Rose hesitated for a moment and then followed. The tavern was gloomy inside and quiet, no more than a few plain tables and benches set upon a sawdust floor. The ceiling was draped with a grey-green lace of mould. Tom slung a leg over a low seat in a corner and gesticulated at Rose to do the same. But instead Rose stood, clenching his hands behind his back.

'I understood we were to meet Tom,' he said fiercely.

'So we are.'

Rose looked around him. There were only a few men in the tavern, mostly sitting alone. They had looked up when he came in, as cows fix upon a stranger in a field, but now they had returned to their glasses. They drank as they stared, with a kind of stolid intensity.

'Well, then. Which one is he?'

'You's talking to him.'

'But —'

'Can't blame a man for caution.'

Rose hesitated. He had no idea whether the old man was telling the truth. But perhaps it didn't matter. All that mattered was getting into the tunnels. A woman with a square red face and a grimy apron brought mugs of porter. Tom nodded at Rose who dropped coins into the woman's outstretched hand.

'Very well,' Rose said reluctantly.

'Mebbe we can help each other out,' Tom added.

'Perhaps.'

'So what is it you want?'

Rose gave only the briefest necessary explanation. There'd been a murder. Tom had most likely heard talk of it. A gentleman, killed in the sewers. Tom shrugged but already he heard the warning bells in his head. By the time Rose was done with his story, Tom had a knot tied tight in the pit of his belly. The lawyer hadn't mentioned the Captain, not even so much as in passing. Still, there was a chance the Captain wasn't out of the woods, not if the lunatic got off. The thought of trouble for the Captain prickled like the smell of roasting beef in his nostrils. But his hands were tied. The lawyer here, talking to him, knowing what he looked like and where he lived? It was too close. Too close by half.

'Ain't going to be able to help you,' Tom said, and he shrugged. 'Don't go down the tunnels no more. Haven't been in years. 'Gainst the law it is, these days.'

'Surely there must be ways? Legal or otherwise. I'd pay you.'

Tom shook his head firmly.

'No way of getting in, not now they've closed off the river sluices.'

'So —'

'So that's that. Nothing to be done about it.'

Rose gazed pleadingly at the old man for a moment. Then he let out a long breath, like he was the air balloon at Cremorne letting down, and stared miserably at the table. Tom took an impatient gulp of beer.

'Something you could do for me, though,' he said quickly. 'As you're here.' He felt in his hem. 'I got a legal document here. By way of a contract. Only I don't rightly know how to get what's due to me.'

Rose ran a fingernail disconsolately along a scar on the table and said nothing.

'Here.' Tom opened up the papers and pushed them across the table.

Rose pressed his fingers against his eyes. The beginnings of a headache ran down his neck to clamp his shoulders. When at last he opened his eyes he glanced without interest at the papers in front of him.

'What the — ?' Rose gaped at the papers.

'Where on earth did you get these from?'

'They's nothing more than my due,' Tom said defensively, gripping them more tightly. 'Sold a man a dog, all above board. Only now he's not for paying me what it says here in the contract and now I wants my dog back. Simple as that.'

Rose frowned.

'This contract is for supplying sand.'

'No. A dog. There was a witness. Look —'

'Five tons of sand for the making of cement. To the Metropolitan Board of Works, dated 12th December 1858. Witnessed by a Mr Badger.'

Rose pointed to the place where Brassey had signed.

'But Brassey — Jesus Christ, the double-crossing bastard —'

But Rose wasn't listening. Rummaging inside his own coat he pulled out another set of papers which he laid on the table beside Tom's.

'It is him. The same letterhead, do you see? And the same style of signature, here. The names are different but —' Rose looked up at Tom, his eyes urgent. 'Who did you say you sold your dog to?'

'The Captain's what they call him round here. But I never catched his name.' Tom cleared his throat. 'Hardly knew him meself.'

Rose laid one paper over another so that the signatures almost overlapped. His eyes shone.

'He signed himself Smith. But the hand is the same, there's no mistaking it.' Rose pointed, his eyes shining. 'The way the letters tilt backwards, the spikes on the M here, and here on the W? He's cheated you out of your dog, him and Mr Badger.'

'That's what I said, ain't it?'

'Well then,' Rose said, triumphantly, seizing the old man's sleeve. 'You want your money, don't you?'

'Rather have me dog back,' Tom muttered.

'Really?'

Tom scowled at Rose's surprised expression, yanking his arm away.

'Very well,' Rose said hastily. 'The dog, then, if that's what you want. But I need to know everything, if I'm to help you. You have to tell me everything you know about the man you call the Captain. You see, I know him too. But his name isn't Smith, I'm afraid. His name is Hawke.'

XXIX

The tide was on the out. Tom waded to the recess and squatted there in the darkness as the stream leaked away, its solid leavings huddled together in the bricks where the tunnel made a sharp turn. There was a space beside him where Lady'd liked to sit, so familiar to him he could swear he could still see the outline of her, pale as a ghost, long after he'd shuttered his lantern. There'd always been comfort in it, the feel of her head beneath his hand. But tonight he clenched his fist, locking his arms between his knees and he squeezed his eyes shut, so as the white of her was lost in the explosion of dark red behind his eyes. Down here, there was room to think. Down here, in the darkness, he'd see things straight.

The lawyer'd asked him all sorts about the Captain, or plain old Mr Hawke as he'd insisted on calling him. Turned out the swindling bastard'd never been a Captain at all, nor a Doctor neither, though he'd had some kind of yellow-bellied grocer's job in the army in the Russian War, tucked up warm and cosy away from the fighting counting out coats and rations of meat. No doubt he'd skimmed a fair whack from them and all. Not that it'd hurt him. Now he was some bigwig in the Metropolitan Board of Works. No doubt he'd've had himself a chuckle over that, buttering Tom up to do his dirty work while all the time he was busy taking his livelihood away from him. If Tom'd known it he'd never've had nothing to do with him. Too close for comfort it'd been all along, too close by half.

Too late now. Even though he'd not set a foot wrong, far as he figured it, not done a thing that'd call attention to himself, a lawyer'd still turned up on his doorstep asking questions Tom had no intention of answering. It was just as well that the boy was green as raw cabbage. Tom'd thought straight off the lunatic didn't have much of a chance, not with a tenderfoot like that the only person to stand between him and the full weight of the law. Everything that one thought was written clean across his face, or in the twisting of his great red hands. When he was nervous or not sure of how you'd take something the lump that stuck out of his throat jumped up and down like it was out to get your attention. So Tom reckoned he was safe to believe him when the lawyer said he didn't reckon Tom had nothing to do with the murder.

But for all that, for all his greenness, he'd found Tom. Somehow there he was, that lawyer, twisting his hands and blinking his great bulging eyes and pressing Tom for answers, so nervous you could see the sweat standing out across his forehead. But there was something dogged about him all the same. And now he'd got Tom and the Captain linked together. Tom might be out of the way of things for now but it wouldn't be long before the bad smell coming off the Captain began to cling to Tom too, he didn't have no doubts about that. Like as not the next thing the lawyer'd do was to set about asking the Captain what he knew of Tom. And the Captain'd shop him, soon as look at him. Make most of it up, most likely, but they'd believe him. A man like that, slippery as a stinking eel, he'd wriggle out of anything, given even the faintest chink of a gap. Come up smelling of roses, he would, while he slapped you with the shit. He'd smile at you, showing his pointed teeth, and shake his head and walk off, your money in his pocket, your blood on his hands. Your dog at his heels.

Lady. Day or two before, Joe's boys'd gone and brought him a pup, a terrier with startled fur and bright button eyes who snarled at Tom, straining at its length of rope. A right bloodthirsty little bugger, they'd said, for all it was no bigger than a man's fist. Schooled up, they'd said, they reckoned it could be a proper little earner. Teeth like needles and not averse to using them neither. Tom'd thanked them, of course, they'd meant well enough, but he sent them away, and the dog with them. There'd be someone else'd have a better chance with it, he told them. As for Tom, he was too old and tired to start over again. That night and the last one he'd dreamed of her. She sat very still, half in the shadows, close enough so as he could hear the quick tugs of her breath, smell the warm yeast of her. Tom'd smiled at her, he'd clicked his fingers, held out his palm, but she just went on looking at him, her head on one side, never blinking her pink eyes. In his dreams he'd felt it then, the uneasy churn as the happiness soured in his stomach. He shouted at her then to come to him. He couldn't stop himself. Long after she'd vanished he was still shouting, so hard he woke himself up with the force of it. As he clutched his knees to his chest, struggling to steady his breathing, the pain'd pierced his throat like a knife.

In the darkness of the tunnels Tom swallowed. He'd been right. Down here you did see things straight. He bent his head as the tunnel sloped upwards, bringing the roof down to shoulder level before opening up again. The package was there, tucked in behind the granite slab, just where he'd left it. Only way with a man like the Captain was to play him by his own rules. Throw everything at him, everything you had, even if you wasn't sure exactly what it was, and hope it stuck. Bury him so deep in his own shit he was drowning in it before he so much as saw you coming. And then run like hell.

There was a place Rose and Tom had agreed on, a small coffee-house near the Temple, where the lawyer'd said the tosher could leave messages, if anything came back to him. He'd suggested his chambers first, which was the name fancy lawyers gave their offices, but something about Tom's face then had changed his mind. So he'd suggested the coffee-house instead, it being open all hours for the river trade. Tom could leave word there and Rose would meet him wherever, whenever. Any time of the day or night.

It were Joe who took the papers, wrapped in an old cloth and tied with twine. At first Tom'd thought to leave them there secretly so that the lawyer might find them in the morning, a gift from a nameless well-wisher, but they was all he had. He wasn't in the way of giving something away for nothing, even if that something turned out to be nothing but tailors' bills. But if it wasn't? He wasn't about to serve himself up to the law as an accompaniment to the main dish, neither. At Tom's insistence Joe darkened his copper hair with soot and muffled himself near to the eyes, just so as the lawyer'd be sure not to know him again, but his eyes twinkled above the grimy scarf and he brushed away Tom's repeated instructions like a cloud of troublesome flies.

'I got it, you daft bugger,' he grinned. 'Not hard, is it? Show this Rose cove the papers. If he's interested tell him they're his. Soon as you get your dog back.'

XXX

The stranger's thumbs were black against the creamy paper. For all that it was written on formal stationery, with the name of the business engraved in handsome black capitals at its head, it would not have pleased a schoolmaster. The writing was cramped and smudged and so hastily conceived that in places the words were strung together by loops of ink. In one or two places the pen had leaked. There was no envelope. The outside of the paper was marked with streaks of rusty brown and speckled with the first dark peppery dots of mould. It was clear that the letter had been much handled. The folds in the paper were deep and soft and showed up grey in the smoky light of the oil lamp. The rag in which it and the other correspondence had been wrapped was stiff with dirt and smelled unpleasantly of drains.

The boy from the coffee-house had banged on the door a little after one o'clock in the morning. Earlier that evening Rose had instructed the proprietor to alert him immediately if there was any message, any message at all, certain that he would be unable to sleep. But before he had even reached his lodgings the excitement had begun to ebb away. True, it had been an extraordinary coincidence. But he had discovered precisely nothing. Hawke had acquired a dog by deception. Or so the tosher claimed, and frankly Rose doubted whether he was a man who concerned himself overly with the finer details of the truth. With its shrewd eyes and broken teeth, his was far from an honest face. Hawke had not signed the contract in his own name. Rose might be able to point up the similarities between the style of the two hands, might even be able to persuade a jury that Hawke had signed an illegal contract, but what then? The most it proved was that Hawke dabbled a little in the seamier peripheries of the city. That might sit somewhat uncomfortably with his position at the Board of Works but it was not in itself illegal. The trail ended there. And still Rose had turned up nothing that might incriminate Hawke in the murder of Alfred England.

Rose had sat in the darkness, poring over the few facts he had gleaned until, like words read too many times, they became no more than meaningless shapes, stripped of any consequence. A little before midnight, as his little fire crumbled into the grate, he had fallen into a cavernous slumber. The barrage of the boy's fists upon the door had insinuated itself threateningly into dark dreams of the rookeries so that Rose woke to a fearful alertness, his heart thumping fast in his chest. His heart still thumped now and he sweated beneath his heavy coat in the thick fug of the coffee-house. Excitement tugged impatiently at his belly as he read the letter again.

Dear Mr Bazalgette,
  It is my unpleasant duty to inform you that Mr Charles Hawke, currently in your employment at Greek-street, is right under your noses selling contracts for Works' business to the highest bidder. No doubt as an honest man this will come as a shock to you, Mr Bazalgette, but all the time he claims to be driving the hardest bargain for the good of the Board, Mr Hawke is busy taking a rake-off for himself. I don't doubt he's already a rich man. And all in the most underhand manner imaginable.
  How do I know? Mr Hawke first ap-

proached me on the 4th September 1858. In return for the sum of one hundred guineas to be paid to him in cash, Mr Hawke would propose our company for a contract which he <u>guaranteed</u> would carry a minimum value of five thousand pounds. On signature Mr Hawke would take ten per cent of the contract or one thousand pounds, whichever was the greater. There is no need to concern you with the details of the financial difficulties in which England's has found itself in recent years, for all they claim the market has taken off. Suffice to say we understood the unlawful nature of Mr Hawke's offer but we felt we had no choice but to accept it.

As it went there was no contract. It is too late to seek others. The bank has foreclosed on its loan. The brickyard is to be sold. It is over. But, as I close England's doors for the last time, I feel I must set things straight. For myself, I am ashamed of my part in the whole shabby business. I was desperate and allowed myself to be persuaded into desperate measures. No doubt my confessions in this letter expose me to the full force of the law. It hardly matters now. But as for Mr Hawke, I could not stand aside as he cheated his way to a fortune. If you care to look you will find that at least three of the current suppliers to the Board 'purchased' their contracts from your Mr Hawke. He is a cold and calculating confidence trickster who is ruthlessly using a position of privilege to line his own pockets. If this letter does its part in bringing him to justice I will consider it worth the writing, whatever trouble I bring down upon my own head.

I am, sir, your humble servant &c.
ALFRED ENGLAND

So William May had told him the truth. Hawke had accepted bribes. If he had known England was to expose him he would doubtless have wanted him dead. Rose assured himself it was relief he felt then, relief and the effervescent rush of renewed hope, but he knew it was astonishment. He bit his thumbnail savagely as he pulled out the documents he had taken from the police station and spread them across the narrow table. England's handwriting was unmistakable, the swollen unsealed manner in which he formed his 'o's, the foreshortened stems of his 'b's and 'd's, the childish sprawl of his signature. The letter was unquestionably his. More significantly still he had marked it with the date. 16th December 1858. The last day England had been seen alive. Rose turned the page over and inspected it closely. The streaks of brown. Was it possible — could it be that they were England's blood?

The stranger smelled of unwashed linen and old fires. He watched impassively as Rose read the letter a final time. Then he took it back and tucked it into the greasy folds of his coat. Rose could hardly bear to watch it disappear. How Tom had come by it was anybody's guess, although one might be certain it had been unlawfully. Perhaps he had robbed the body. Perhaps he had been an accomplice. It did not matter. Even if, in the event of a miracle, he was able to convince the old man to testify, Rose could hardly put a sewer-hunter in the witness box. No, Tom was unimportant. It was the letter that counted. With the letter Rose finally had something. If he had the letter.

'I's takin' it you's interested,' the stranger said, scraping back his chair. 'From the look on yer face.'

Rose hadn't realized the size of him till

he stood. His head brushed the low ceiling, leaving a sooty smear on the damp plaster. Biting his lip, Rose nodded.

'What are Tom's terms?'

Joe shrugged.

'Tom? Don't think I knows a Tom.'

Rose took a deep breath.

'Of course not. Tom has nothing to do with it.' Rose paused but only briefly. He had nothing to lose. 'Tell him to meet me here tomorrow night, seven o'clock. I'll have the dog.'

XXXI

Dawn came at last, reluctantly prising up the darkened lid of the city. As soon as it was tolerably light, Rose took a message to the watchman's gate and instructed that it be delivered without delay. He had not slept. His eyes ached and his mouth tasted sour but for all that he twitched with a kind of frenzied energy. It would be several hours before he could reasonably expect a reply. He should use them constructively, he told himself firmly, to prepare his argument, to put his papers in order. Instead he paced his cramped room, his toes clenching in his boots, and behind his back his hands clamped and unclamped, chafing their chapped winter skin. The thundering of boots on the bare boards of the staircase outside his door rattled the glass in its peeling sash. He tried to make a fire for tea but the kindling was damp and mouldy and would not catch. The dank smoke stung his eyes. He would go to the coffee-house for breakfast as soon as he had received a reply. Anxiously he peered out of the window. On the patch of scrubby grass beneath him blackbirds pecked gloomily at the mud, ignoring the knot of barristers in black gowns that flapped past them. Rose bit his nails. Surely he would hear something soon. It was Thursday. The Sessions were scheduled for Monday. It was still possible that he might be able to secure a postponement. After the early morning flurry the lodging house was empty. In the silence the clock on the mantel ticked fussily to itself, its eager hands leaping to mark the minutes. Rose thought of William May, shackled in the filthy straw of his prison cell, and of the faceless Hawke, who walked free. He sat down, his hands dangled between his knees. He stood. He paced. And in between he stared at the path beneath the window, his hands twisting behind his back. He waited.

The messenger came a little after ten o'clock. Mr Bazalgette's clerk acknowledged receipt of Mr Rose's request but regretted that, given the extent of his commitments, it would be quite impossible for Mr Bazalgette to meet with him before February. However, given the urgent nature of his request, it was suggested that, if he could present himself at Greek-street at noon, Mr Bazalgette's deputy, Mr Lovick, would do his best to grant him a short interview.

Abruptly, Rose was thrown into a fever of anxious anticipation. He cast his papers frantically around, shuffling together the documents he had taken from the police, the hastily scrawled version of England's letter that he had written from memory as soon as he had returned from the coffee-house the previous night. Still it was a slim sheaf, no more than a few sheets. As for the dog — he was no closer to establishing what he might be able to do about the dog. There was no time for breakfast. He had thought to take a cab to Soho but near Westminster the road was up and the narrow streets were knotted with traffic. He arrived at the Board's offices painfully short of breath, his pale hair standing away from his head. The clerk who took his name raised an eyebrow and stared at him through spectacles that gave his eyes the hard sheen of polished pebbles. Left alone, Rose licked his palms surreptitiously and ran them over his scalp. The hard chair provided was low and uncomfortable. Rose perched on its edge, hugging his briefcase to his chest. Around him on the walls were displayed architectural drawings for what looked to be churches or palaces, all soaring towers and domes and enough fancy decoration to put a Byzantine mosque to shame.

There were no pictures of sewers but then why would anyone want to look at sewers? The palaces were attractive. The architect had drawn trees around them, and people in the foreground. A woman in a white dress walked along a path, a parasol held in one tiny hand.

The clerk cleared his throat.

'You may come up now, sir.'

Rose's stomach churned as he followed the clerk up a narrow staircase and along a corridor. At a closed door they stopped. The clerk knocked and opened it a crack.

'A Mr Rose to see you, sir.'

'Ah. Show him in.'

The small office was dominated by a huge mahogany desk. Like a ship in a bottle, Rose thought, and he glanced distractedly behind him at the doorway, wondering how it had possibly been squeezed through the narrow space. Mr Lovick sat behind it, frowning at some papers. He did not trouble to look up but instead waved a hand at the clerk, dismissing him. Rose hovered uncomfortably, eyeing Lovick's profile as he read. He was a dark man with thick black whiskers without a trace of grey. Beneath them his face was severe, an origami face folded into sharp points and edges. Rose swallowed.

'Mr Rose.' Lovick looked up at last, the frown still etched between his dark brows. He did not suggest that Rose sit down. Rose wrung out his hands behind his back. 'How can I help you?'

'Firstly, Mr Lovick, I want to thank you for seeing me. I know you are a very busy man.'

Lovick twisted his bloodless lips into a smile.

'Ah, a charming speech but unfortunately expressed to the wrong person. Mr Lovick has been called away on urgent business which will detain him for the remainder of the day and tomorrow too, I fear. In his absence I suggested to the clerk that perhaps I might be able to oblige you.' He inclined his head, watching Rose's face. 'My name is Hawke.'

Rose's eyes bulged and his Adam's apple scraped painfully against his collar.

'But —'

'You are Mr May's lawyer, I understand.' Hawke shook his head ruefully but still he fixed his eyes intently upon Rose. To his agitation Rose felt the flush rise in his neck.

'Excuse me, Mr Hawke, but I think it would be more appropriate if I —'

Hawke gave no sign of having heard him.

'It hardly seems necessary to go to the expense of a lawyer,' he observed instead. 'Given the circumstances.'

'And what circumstances would those be, Mr Hawke?' Rose demanded, patches of red blotching his pale cheeks.

Hawke's smile stretched a little.

'An open-and-shut case, isn't that what they call it?'

'Only when it is one,' Rose retorted. He glared back at Hawke, determined to keep his nerve.

Hawke's smile did not falter but his eyes narrowed.

'Oh?'

'When there is written evidence to the contrary, evidence that incriminates another, they call it something quite different,' Rose said, clutching his portfolio to his chest like a breastplate. 'They call it reasonable doubt.'

'Do they?'

'Oh yes. Particularly when that evidence is written in the hand of the dead man himself and stained with his own blood.'

'How very ghoulish. So might I see this fascinating document?'

'I don't have it with me. But I wouldn't make any assumptions quite yet, Mr Hawke. Not if I were you.'

'You don't have it at all, do you, Mr Rose?'

'But I will have. And now, if you'll excuse me, I've a witness to interview. Interesting character, actually. A fount of fascinating information. Appears to know the sewers like the back of his hand.'

His heart pounding victoriously in his throat, Rose marched to the door. On the threshold he paused and then turned around.

'I don't suppose the name Long Arm Tom means anything to you, does it, Mr Hawke?'

'Nothing at all.'

Hawke's answer came smoothly, without hesitation. But his eyes flickered as though he had been struck. Rose clenched his fists in triumph as he clattered back down the stairs. It was only when he stood outside, and the raw morning chill cooled the flush upon his neck, that he began to wonder what on earth it was he had gone and done.

XXXII

It was Brassey who told Binks, the proprietor of the chophouse, who told Tom that there was rumours doing the rounds that the Captain was planning to take Lady to the fight that Saturday night. Blustering like an autumn gale Brassey had been, Dawson said to Tom, his eyes fair popping out of his head and spluttering about how he'd thought of not letting the cheating scoundrel so much as put a foot through the door. According to Binks the Captain'd not showed up at the Badger for months. There was all kinds of debts unsettled, wagers not paid out. If the Captain thought he could just walk back in there, cool as you like, as if there'd been nothing awry, he had another think coming. Having said that, Brassey'd conceded he'd have a better chance of getting back his money if he let the bastard through the door. Principles was all very well in their place but sometimes a man had to give a little ground to get back what he was owed. Same was true of Tom. Brassey wasn't saying he'd been wrong, not exactly, but there was things he'd gone and done back then that he'd do different these days, knowing what he knew now. He wanted Tom to know that. And if Tom wanted to come back to the Badger, so as he could see justice done in the matter of the dog, then Brassey wasn't going to stop him. He wasn't a man to bear grudges. He might even think about taking up the rats again, he'd added casually then, shrugging his round shoulders. Business was still business, if the price was right.

Tom smiled then, a dry little twist of the mouth. So that was Brassey's game. Tom'd heard rumours about the lads supplying the Badger, how they was always bringing the crates at the last minute and then pushing the prices up, when it was too late for Brassey to get himself a load of the beasts anywhere else. It came as no surprise that the publican was dangling the lure of the Captain so as to get Tom back through the door. No doubt these days a penny a rat didn't seem so poor a bargain after all.

But for all his scorn of Brassey's clumsy methods Tom felt a flicker of excitement. The lawyer'd said to Joe that he'd have Lady for him at the coffee-house on Narrow-lane, seven o clock, but Tom'd not let himself believe it. It didn't seem possible, somehow, that gawky youth mustering the full strength of the law to bring the Captain to book. Lads like that, all knuckles and scarlet ears, there were lads like that in the rookeries too, from time to time, lads who'd thought to find themselves a future in the city. Lads who was always looking in the wrong direction when trouble came creeping up on them. The Captain'd only have to sneeze and the force of it'd send a lad like that blowing clean off course. But now it didn't matter. Tom didn't need the lawyer no more, not now. He could twist and turn in the wind as frenzied as he pleased. It wasn't no concern of Tom's. Tonight Lady would be at the Badger. A few hours and he'd see her. He'd touch her. His stomach squeezed.

He'd see the Captain and all. It was time Tom took negotiations into his own hands. The letters were back where they belonged, safe and sound in their hiding place in the tunnels. But Tom had every intention of making them work for their keep. Joe'd said the lawyer's face'd lit up like Moses & Son when he saw the letters. One in particular he'd read over and over, his eyes blazing and the colour standing out on his cheeks for all the world like it was a billy-doo from his sweetheart. Joe had stretched his fingers then, cracking his knuckles and laughing. His hand'd fair exhausted itself holding the paper up so as the lawyer could keep on a-gawping at it, he told Tom, and there was more than one time he'd had to place a steadying hand on the man's shoulders so as the lawyer might recall himself and lay his own greedy hands back flat on the table the way they'd agreed. If Joe'd let him he'd've been out the door with them before you could say sewer. As it was the lawyer'd thought them worth the dog, without so much as a hesitation. How much more valuable would they be to the Captain? Surely a dog and forty guineas? Cheap at the price.

Tom went to the coffee-house at seven o'clock. Not because he expected the lawyer to have Lady, because he didn't, but because the more he knew, the harder the bargain he could drive with the Captain. He did not take the letters. They were safer where they were. The moment he ducked through the low door he saw a white dog curled up under a table in the corner. Straightways, his breath stopped and his heart knocked sharply against his ribs, straightways before he'd even looked at it right and seen it was a sour-faced bulldog that bore not even the faintest resemblance to Lady. Cursing to himself he spat on to the sawdust floor and waited.

The lawyer was late. And he was alone. Although he'd known it all along Tom scowled at the lawyer and swallowed down the bitter taste in his mouth.

'You came,' Rose said.

'Alone, are you?'

'Yes.'

Rose twisted his hands together. He'd almost forgotten about the dog. All afternoon he had squirmed uncomfortably, guilt and anxiety smearing his stomach and prickling greasily in the roots of his hair. A man like Tom had a pauper's mistrust for the law, likely with good reason since he seemed hardly the kind to trouble himself with its strictures, but he had sent the letter all the same. He had acted upon his conscience to save an innocent man, trusting Rose to serve him well in return. Rose had betrayed that trust. Hawke would surely not let it pass. He would come after Tom. And it would be Rose's fault.

'I'm sorry,' Rose mumbled. 'I — things have been more difficult than I had hoped.'

Tom waited.

'I can do nothing without the letter,'

Rose blurted abruptly. 'Please. I beg you. If I have the letter we have a chance of getting your dog back. Without it — without it I have nothing. Which means I cannot help you.'

'What letter?'

'Please. Let us not play games. There is so little time.'

Tom blinked, his eyes round.

'Don't think I understands you, mister.'

'For pity's sake, man, stop this! I beg you.'

'I think you must've mistook me for some other cove, mister. I don't know nothing about no letter.'

Rose could contain himself no longer. The words came out in a rush, tumbling over one another.

'Tom, it's too late for this. He knows, do you understand me? Hawke, your Captain, he knows. He knows I'm on to him. That we have written evidence. And he knows about you. That I have talked to you. It's too late. We can't turn back now. But if I have the letter we have a chance. We can get him. I know we can get him. If I have the letter I can take things further with the Board. At the very least we could get him for corruption. He'd go to gaol. The man cheated you, Tom. Surely you want him in gaol. And if you were to take me down the tunnels, if we could find the evidence my client claims is hidden there, then perhaps —'

Tom held his palms upwards, playing for time. His head spun.

'This letter — it's bad for the Captain?'

'Bad? It exposes him as having accepted bribes in exchange for contracts. It was never sent. The man who wrote it is dead. Do you not see? It could hardly be worse.'

Tom saw and his heart skipped. So that was what the letter had contained. And now the Captain knew about it. No wonder Brassey'd been so careful to make sure Tom knew about the fight. Things happened at places like the Badger that no one ever found out about. But there was always two sides to every coin. The Captain could lay any trap he liked but it was Tom still had the letter. A letter like that, it'd be worth a dog at the very least.

'I'd like to help you,' Tom said, his face studiously blank. 'Gaol's too good for a rogue like that. But I think you mistook me for someone. I don't know nothing about no letter. And I told you — I don't go down the tunnels no more. It's against the law.'

Rose stared up at Tom as he stood,

wrapping his ragged coat around him.

'But —'

'I hope you finds the cove what's got your letter. Good night to you, mister.'

'No!'

Rose reached out to try and seize Tom's sleeve but the tosher was too fast for him. By the time Rose reached the door of the coffee-house the old man was gone.

XXXIII

The Strand was lurid and frantic, caught in the glare of the gas-lights. The shop windows screamed in one thousand garish colours and the doors of the theatres stood open, their gold and scarlet mouths inhaling a swarming mass of people. The road was locked with vehicles. Cabs jostled for position. Horses skittered, their harnesses clattering, their heads lost in glittering white clouds of their own breath. Drivers bellowed to one another, a pandemonium of pleasantries and rebukes. Streetwalkers plucked at Rose as he walked, begging for a glass of gin or a little something for the rent. Beside him an omnibus driver hied at his two horses, urging them forward, while the conductor beat ferociously upon the brightly painted green roof. Rose huddled into his coat, his eyes on his boots, as the wilful brightness buffeted him, paddling its fingers gaily in his misery. As he turned down King-James-lane a group of swells in fancy evening dress almost knocked him off his feet. Their rowdy laughter echoed in his ears, sharp with mockery.

A brazier lit up the small window of the watchman's hut with a cosy glow but the lodging house was dark, its sooty façade set into its habitual disapproving scowl. Rose hesitated. His heart was as cold as a stone in his chest. The Abbey Dining Rooms would be warm. They served boiled mutton on a Friday, and jam pudding. He had not eaten since breakfast and he suffered from severe headaches when he went too long without food. Rose knew it would be prudent to eat. But instead he walked towards the river, following it east. At Waterloo Bridge he paid his halfpence to the man who sat muffled to his nose in the tollbooth. He wanted to keep on walking, to walk and walk until he walked clear of the city and the miserable sooty chill of another failed day. He did not have the letter. Likely he would not get it. He had not even succeeded in gaining access to the tunnels. Huddled in his coat as he leaned over the stone parapet of the bridge Rose felt the hopelessness of the enterprise bearing down upon him. Even if he had managed to persuade someone to take him into the sewers, what then? For pity's sake, neither he nor May had anything but the vaguest notion of what it was he was supposed to be looking for.

May's map was still in the pocket of his trousers. He fingered it. He had folded and refolded it until it was barely larger than a postage stamp and the corners were sharp. There was almost no traffic on the bridge. The vagrants used the bridge at Southwark where there was no toll. There, even on a night as bitterly cold as this one, they crammed themselves into the recesses in the walls, huddled together for warmth until the police moved them along. But here there was only a single hansom, the coachman so swaddled in his blanket that only the tip of his nose could be seen beneath his hat. He hurried his horse on, his whip cracking like breaking ice.

Rose sighed, looking down at the river. The tide was running out and the wet slopes of the mudflats glistened stickily, exhaling their winter stink of salt and rotting turnip-tops. The chill insinuated itself up Rose's sleeves and down his collar, pressing itself through the worn fibres of his coat. Hurriedly, he tightened his muffler around his throat and thrust his hands back into his trouser pockets. The folded square of paper jabbed a little at the pad of his thumb. He turned it over in his pocket as he leaned out. A breeze had got up. It played down the length of the river so that the water was chased into little overlapping waves. As the moon slid out from behind a shawl of cloud, casting a pale silver light on the water, they glistened and squirmed. A gigantic black sea monster, Rose thought, that was the Thames, slithering through the city's ditch towards its lair beneath the open sea. A grotesque beast that devoured and half-digested the waste of the largest city in the world, its open maw ceaselessly swallowing its rotting vegetation, its excrement, its dead. Its appetite was voracious, indiscriminate, its tentacles stretching even into the city's bowels to lick at their squalid deposits. A scrap of paper would not trouble it at all. All Rose had to do was to open his fingers and let the square fall on to its powerful back. It would be gone, with a flick of the river's meaty spine, swept beneath London Bridge and alongside the Pool, past the rusting prison-ship at Woolwich. The cells had no windows. It would pass quite unnoticed to the sea, its fibres softening and melting until it was no more than the water itself. Or perhaps Fate, with its taste for the penny dreadfuls, would adhere it to the mouldering underbelly of the prison hulk itself, a letter returned unopened to its sender, addressee unknown. Perhaps it would still be there, clinging to the rough dark metal, when they took May away to Newgate to be hanged. *Tell her I am planning her garden.*

Rose shivered. He was chilled to the bone and a headache nudged his right temple. The muscular writhings of the river made him nauseous. Stamping his feet, burying his hands more deeply in his pockets, he walked back the way he had come. The paper was still sharp against the palm of his hand. He clenched it more tightly, finding solace in the discomfort. This time he walked briskly, without thinking. It was with considerable impatience that he encountered a knot of people blocking the narrow lane just short of Inner Temple. The gas-light above them had been turned up so high that it roared and its brutal glare scored the faces beneath it with inky lines of shadow. Muttering to himself Rose made to skirt around them but his attention was caught by a thickset man in a fan-tailed leather cap and high leather boots who stared down between his feet, frowning, a thick disc of iron propped against his leg. Beside him stood a policeman holding another lantern. Rose paused, then pushed a man in a top hat to one side. The policeman held up a warning hand. His palm was square and seamed with grime.

'Not too close, sir. This ain't a tourist attraction, you know.' He glared at the group of curious onlookers who had already begun to drift away. 'We don't want any accidents.'

Rose looked down. The round hole in the cobbles measured perhaps twenty inches across. Bolts of iron set into a vertical brick shaft led downwards into the darkness. Rose had a sudden image of Tom, lying in the darkness, his dead body bobbing like a bony white turd in the filthy underground stream, and he felt a twinge of horrified remorse.

'What — has something happened?' he asked.

The policeman shrugged and rubbed his lump of a nose with the back of his hand.

'Constable saw a light through the gratin' up by Kings-court. Obliged to go down after the blighters, ain't we. Regulations.'

Rose stared at the policeman.

'The police have access to the sewers?'

'It's them flushers go down,' the policeman corrected, screwing up his face. 'Gawd 'elp 'em.'

'But you have the authority to send them down? Any time? You don't need permission from the Board of Works?'

' 'Ow else we s'posed to enforce the law?'

The policemen involved in the May case were more than a little put out by Rose's demands. After the bruising criticism that had accompanied a string of unsolved crimes, the newspapers had been full of praise for the swiftness with which the perpetrator of this particularly grisly offence had been detained. It was late and they wished to go home. Rose's persistence was both unanticipated and unwelcome. The sewer regulations were in place to prevent unlawful entry to the system, they informed Rose loftily, not to facilitate public access. But Rose was importunate, his determination to secure his legal rights as the prisoner's attorney set into stony intransigence by the headache that stabbed at the back of his eyes and by the discomfiting realization that he should have known of them from the outset. For all that the police officers considered his demands as meaningless and as irritating as the buzzing of a horsefly, they had obligations as officers of the law, however onerous and tiresome they might be. When at last they understood that Rose was not to be swatted away, they agreed, with considerable sighing and shaking of heads, that, if Rose settled with one of the gangers upon an appropriate time to enter the system, they would provide two sergeants to accompany him. It cheered the inspector a little to select two of his least favoured men for the unsavoury duty.

The next morning Rose went as arranged to the excavations at the corner of Hyde Park. He was required to wait for over an hour before the ganger he was to meet emerged from underground. The western end of Piccadilly was closed to traffic and all around him cabs and carriages jostled for space as they tried to find their way through the narrow Mayfair lanes. Where the road had been there was now a rough gash the width of several men, criss-crossed with planking and set all about with a pandemonium of vast scaffolds and beams and cranes. An army of navvies and barrows and horses and steam engines swarmed over and around great heaps of earth and clay and bricks and planks, brandishing pickaxes, spades and hammers, their shouts and clanks lost beneath the thunderous clamour of a machine that appeared intent upon burying itself in the frozen ground. May's world. As the living embodiment of London's engineering preeminence it might have raised Rose's dreary spirits but instead the fortifications put him in mind of a giant guillotine, presiding over an open grave. The previous night he had dreamed that, still alive but unable to speak or move, he had watched in frozen horror as an undertaker bound his motionless body in a shroud. He had woken to find his sheets twisted as tight as a tourniquet around his legs. Everywhere, it seemed, he was surrounded with the presentiment of death. He sighed, his heart heavy, chafing his arms with both hands. Around him the houses sagged wearily against their huge timber props as though they could hardly find the strength to remain upright. The chilly air tasted of earth.

Rose had expected Harker but the ganger he met was a wiry man with skin weathered to the rough brown of roof shingles. Close on ten of them there were, he told Rose, working all over the city. Naturally he'd do what he could to oblige but there wasn't no chance of getting down till the next day, not now the tide was on the up. You could argue with Parliament itself, if you had a mind to, but you couldn't argue with the tide. Rose bit his lip and his heart sank lower still. Noon on Sunday would hardly leave him time to prepare his case for the Sessions. He would never get into the tunnels now, whatever he did. And, if by some miracle he managed it, there would be nothing there. The entire endeavour was doomed, he understood that now. The realization hardened his resolve. There were two tides daily, he said mulishly to the ganger. Surely they could go down that night. A man's life was at stake. He pulled the scrap of paper that May had drawn upon out of his pocket and handed it to the ganger. The ganger hesitated then. He tipped his leather hat back and rubbed his forehead. Rose crossed his arms, his jaw set with the unflinching obduracy of those who have quite lost hope. The ganger took a long drag of air, his hand cupped over his mouth as though he was pulling on a cigarette. When he nodded it was no more than a jerk of his head. There'd be a supplementary charge to the boys on account of the inconvenience, of course, payable prior to the arrival of the police officers, but it could be managed. Eleven o'clock. Regent's-circus. Any later and they wouldn't wait.

XXXIV

'So.' Tom thrust his hands into the cavernous pockets of his coat. A scrawny dog nosed around the ash-heap, its thin grey coat sucked between its protruding ribs. But when it cringed from his boot it was her white face that looked up at him, her snout that sought his palm, and the hole inside of him stretched and ached like hunger. Tonight. Perhaps it would be tonight. He didn't know if he had it in him to wait it out. Beneath his feet the plank bridge bounced a little. 'I hears from Dawson the Captain's expected here tonight.'

'Mmm. So they say.'

'Queer he'd come back. What with him in hock to you and all.'

'Wants to fight the dog. Who can blame him? He'll pay me when he wins.'

'Cosy.'

Brassey arched an eyebrow.

'Shame I can't make it,' Tom added.

'No?' Brassey's toad eyes narrowed a little. 'That is a shame.'

'By my reckoning the Captain'll be gutted.'

Brassey licked his lips uncomfortably.

'What you talking about? The Captain wouldn't hardly dare show his face if he expected you there, would he? Not given how things stand. Far as he's concerned you're barred.'

'Oh! So it's us against him, is it now? Well, ain't that nice.'

Brassey gave a modest little shiver, flexing his slippered foot.

'Us ordinary folk, we got to stick together, right, Tom? Tell you what. By way of setting things straight I'll even give you the rats back. Penny a pair. What d'you say to that?'

'You'd not set that in a legal document, now, would you? I got myself a bit of a taste for papers, with all their fancy stamps and signatures and whatnot. After all, rats or sand, what's the odds? Between ordinary folk, that is.'

Brassey's smile flickered uncertainly.

'You hear this, Brassey.' All trace of congeniality was gone. 'I ain't coming nowhere near this place tonight. If the Captain wants what I got, he can meet me at the entrance to Adams-lane at midnight. And he'd better bring the dog. You got it?'

Brassey's head slid forward.

'Anyone else with him, that's the end of

it. You can tell the Captain there's a Mr Rose interested if he ain't. Close as ticks, me and Mr Rose. And Mr Rose'd bite his right hand off for what I've got. If the Captain don't show.'

'Mr Rose,' Brassey echoed in a whisper.

'You tell him that, Brassey. Get this right, who knows? P'raps I mightn't come after you for what you done to screw me, you filthy lump of sewer shit!'

Tom stepped off the end of the plank.

'Course, I wouldn't reckon yourself out the woods just yet,' Tom added thoughtfully. 'You can't be sure of nothing these days. Not even a lawful covenant.'

Lifting the plank, he hurled it to one side, leaving Brassey stranded on the threshold behind a sea of mud.

'By the way. You send anyone with the Captain, or try any tricks on, I'll hack your fingers off one by one and feed them to those rats of yours.' Tom's smile stretched wide as a bulldog's over his dark stumps of teeth. 'I'd even charge you for the pleasure. How does a penny a pair sound to you?'

XXXV

William lay on his back in the filthy straw, his fettered legs twisted awkwardly beneath him. It was bitterly cold. Hunger clamped his belly and gnawed at his bones. It made him dizzy to stand. Without his leg irons holding him down he had the strange sensation that he might float upwards, dissipating into the contaminated underwater air like smoke. Since the lawyer's visit his entire body had been given over to imagining the lawyer's investigations, the character references he would elicit on William's behalf, the evidence he would uncover. The justice he would see done. William had gorged himself on hope, ravenously, not knowing that hope was like tainted meat, alive with worms that would in turn sate themselves upon him. But the lawyer had not come back. Now William's chest, his legs, even the bowl of his skull felt quite empty. Far away, out of reach, thoughts moved like distant twists of cloud that cast faint moving shadows and were gone. Even his dreams were thin, tentative things, frail as cobwebs, yielding without protest to the insistent slap of the tide against the ship's hull or the scream of chains as the iron cage was lowered or raised. When in the deathly hours before dawn the ship lapsed into uneasy silence, he talked quietly to himself, drawing comfort from the familiar cadence of his voice, the steady certainty of words. Tongue, breath, sounds, they could not rob him of those. They might chain him like an animal, tethered in his own filth, but he spoke like a man. He murmured the words into his cupped hands, stringing them together like beads, his eyes closed and his breath warm upon his fingers. They bore him forwards, rhythmic and repetitive as the rattling wheels of a steam train. *I am alive. All will be well. All will be well. I am alive. William May. William May. William May.*

The lawyer did not return. In the grey gruel half-light of the lower deck, William slid between sleep and wakefulness, barely able to tell one from the other. Time slipped. He heard the clang of the bell that signalled the distribution of bread at noon and knew it to be dawn, or midnight. He did not know what day it was. The lawyer sent word that his investigation continued, that he was cautiously hopeful of progress.

William was not permitted to see the letter. Instead it was read out to him by a warder who stumbled over the words, taking a breath between each one as though he were instructing the grocer's boy. William listened and the hope twisted in his belly, turning his bowels to water. He no longer found it possible to imagine a trial. They would bring him up from his iron dungeon into the daylight and the glare of the white winter sky would blind him.

He was not mad. But memories and dreams folded themselves into the empty submerged hours, printing their bright shapes upon his solitude. Late one evening, or perhaps it was morning, he could not tell, he turned and for a fleeting moment he was sure that he saw Polly's caramel eyes framed in the slot of his rusting door, heard the soft murmur of her voice above the animal cries of the other prisoners. But when he called out her name the only reply was the sharp strikes of the warder's boots as he marched along the iron corridor. The cravings rose in him, so suddenly that a scream was forced from his throat and the roots of his hair burst with black fire. The wall of the cell was rough with rust. William pressed his knuckles against it, his cheek, grinding them up and down as the cravings exploded in every part of him. Ripping his nails with the urgency he hauled himself to his feet, grinding and scouring his legs against their fetters until the metal burned against his skin, but still he did not bleed. He closed his eyes. The longing was so strong that he could almost feel it, the cool perfect curve of the knife handle in his fist. He picked it up and stabbed, and stabbed and stabbed. The face looked up at him then, its eyes black holes in its ghostly white face. Clenching his fists at his sides William bit down upon his tongue. For a moment he tasted only the black soot of his saliva. And then, in a beautiful red rush, his mouth filled with blood. He bit again and again until, bubbled with saliva, the blood spilled out from his lips and ran triumphantly down his chin.

Polly heard the scream as she hurried ahead of the warder but she said nothing. She kept her handkerchief pressed to her mouth. She could hardly stop herself from crying out with impatience as the warder fumbled clumsily with the cage's barred door. There was a stain on the hem of her carefully sponged dress. Her best dress now. She should never have come. All she wanted was to be gone, to be lost in the busy bustle of the day so that she might forget all that she had seen.

'You sure you don't want me to rouse 'im?' the warder asked again, frowning as the cage shuddered and began to grind its way upwards.

Polly shook her head. Something about that lawyer, the way he'd talked, it had haunted her. Till he came along she'd been fine. She'd closed down the past, like she'd closed down the house in Lambeth, removing herself piece by piece until it was empty and quite dark. But the lawyer had put something back, a tiny flickering rush-light that wouldn't go out. And so she'd come. The way he'd looked at her, like a wild animal, she could hardly bear to think of it. She pressed her fingers into her eyes, forcing another picture there, of William in his chair in Lambeth, Di set upon his lap. The oil-lamp flickered, casting its smoky light on to the pages of the picture book he held for the boy. She touched his shoulder and he looked up at her, his face calm above his white starched collar, and gently he smiled. Behind him the girl kneeled in front of the fireplace, blacking the grate.

The cage jolted, throwing her off-balance, and she clutched at the bars to steady herself. Despite the handkerchief the sickening stench of the prison caught in her nostrils. Beside his wooden plate William's excrement had puddled in an uncovered bucket. He'd turned over, his chains clanking around his legs, for all the world like one of the filthy bears they kept at the Zoo, and the way he'd looked at her, it had been like he wanted to devour her.

'Long way to come,' the warder said, with a shrug. 'For nothin'. Usually folks leastways want to say goodbye.'

Polly was silent for a long time. When at last she spoke the warder had to strain to hear her.

'I just did,' she said.

XXXVI

The ganger descended first, holding his lantern aloft so that Rose and the sergeants might find their footing on the iron rungs of the ladder. His eyes glinted in the lantern light, as opaque as a lizard's, as he gestured at Rose to begin his descent. Rose placed a tentative boot on the first rung. Already the stink coming up from beneath him was almost unbearable. It rushed into his nose as Rose lowered himself into the shaft, so overpoweringly that his gorge rose and his mouth flooded with sour saliva. He clamped his nose, breathing through his mouth in disgusted sips. He was certain he could taste it on his tongue, the nauseating stench of night soil. He stepped into the stream. The dark water reached to his knees and unspeakable lumps of brown matter nudged at his boots and swirled past him. The ganger directed him with a jab of his thumb towards the south before indicating to the first of the policemen to come down. The light from Rose's lantern made little headway in the foul thick darkness of the tunnel but around him he could make out crumbling brickwork, shiny with some kind of noxious grease. Beside him, where a rib of bricks jutted outwards from the curve of the tunnel, a putrid deposit of excrement slopped in a steep soft mound against the rotting wall and pale mushrooms sprouted with hideous fecundity across the tunnel's crown. Rose closed his eyes, clasping his fists at his sides. Thick sludge sucked sickeningly at the soles of his boots and he swayed. At the thought of falling headlong into the filthy stream his heart constricted. He opened his eyes, lowering his lamp so that he might stare into the darkness beyond. In its circle of light the water had the appearance of churned mud. A dead rat floated past, its fur slick against its narrow body and its naked feet stiffened into hooks. Rose swallowed. He could think of no punishment on earth, short of wading the River Styx itself, which might prepare a man for the horror he might find in the sewers of London.

The second policeman stepped into the stream with a dull splash. The ganger muttered something and, thrusting his lantern out ahead of him, pushed past Rose to lead the party south. Rose flinched, hunching his shoulders so that he might not brush accidentally against the vile brickwork. Knobs of floating debris nosed softly at his boots as he walked but he did not permit himself to look down. Behind him the sergeants coughed and spat in the darkness, their breathing shallow with revulsion. Several times the ganger indicated to Rose to wait so that the policemen might not get left too far behind. They had walked for what Rose estimated to be about a quarter of a mile when the ganger unhooked his lantern from its pole and held it above his head.

' 'Ere's where,' the ganger said laconically. His panelled face was expressionless but his eyes glittered in the lamplight.

Rose looked around him. The tunnel curved away, heading down into darkness, but at the crook of the curve there was a bulge which had perhaps been built originally as a storm drain and now formed something like an antechamber to the main tunnel. The tide did not scour this part of the channel and the stinking sediment coated the walls and banked its corners in dreadful heaps. Although the roof was not high enough for the taller of the two sergeants to stand upright, it was broad and the stream shallow. Along its walls the brickwork was badly eroded, patterned with mould and poisonous-looking fungi. Fallen bricks scattered the floor. There were a hundred possible hiding places here, a thousand. Rose wanted to weep with revulsion.

'This is it?' he asked, attempting briskness. 'The place on the map?'

'Yep.'

'Good.' The prospect of touching anything compressed his guts into cold heaves. 'How long have we got?'

The ganger shrugged.

'Hour. Hour and a half tops.'

'Then we'd best get going.'

Rose looked around at the two sergeants. The shorter of the two looked distinctly unwell, his pale face an unhealthy shade of green, his thick eyebrows and moustache limp with sweat.

'We ain't touching nothing,' his fellow officer said sharply. 'We're here as witnesses, nothing else. That's our orders.'

He glared at Rose, challenging the lawyer to object. Rose did not object. Instead he requested that both officers at least hold their lanterns up to assist him in his search. Then, as systematically as he could, trying to keep his mind empty, he began to feel his way along the slimy wall, sliding his fingers into the rotting mortar around each brick and tugging it to see if it would come away. It was awkward work in gloves. Rose persisted for perhaps fifteen minutes before, rigid with disgust and frustration, he tore them off. The feel of the foul bricks beneath his bare hands twisted his stomach and caused his throat to tighten. Several crumbled in his hand. One came out whole. With a rush of hope that swept away abhorrence, Rose thrust his hand into the hole. It was damp and filled with slime and fragments of crumbled brick. The sludge pressed between his fingers, insinuated itself underneath his nails. Blindly Rose threw down the brick and moved on down the wall, wrenching, twisting. Up and down, pressing, pulling, trying not to think, not to feel. He couldn't rush and risk missing one. Twenty minutes passed, thirty. The ganger watched him in silence. Still nothing. Rose scrabbled more frantically at the bricks, pulling and yanking at them, tossing the loose pieces into the stream. His hands were filthy, the tips of his fingers scraped and sore. His nails were torn. And still he ripped at the walls, his fingers pressing into the mortar, his hands twisting and tugging. For the first time a faint smile pulled at the corners of the ganger's mouth.

'Reckon 'e won't be 'appy till 'e's buried us all alive,' he said dryly.

The green-faced sergeant inhaled raggedly and closed his eyes, fanning himself with one hand.

Rose reached the end of the bulge in the tunnel. The other wall. It must be the other wall. He splashed across the filthy stream and began to work his way back. He worked without speaking until he reached a patch of the wall that was in shadow. He had assumed it was simply a trick of the light but now that he looked more closely he could see that it was in fact a recess set into the tunnel wall running from knee to shoulder height and perhaps two feet across. The bricks seemed looser here, the recess patterned with holes and blackened stubs of brick like the mouth of an old crone. Rose called to the ganger to bring his lantern closer. He pressed his fingers around the misshapen bricks, twisting and tugging. And then he found it. The brick was almost whole, its corners not yet rubbed away, but its surface bore several deep scratches. Rose pulled it out. Behind it was a hole, dark with shadow. A hole much larger than a single brick. Rose felt his heart clench. This was it. He was certain of it. Trying to keep his hand from trembling he reached in, stretching out his fingers. More sandy mortar, more brick. And then his fingertips brushed against something smooth. His heart thundering in his ears Rose closed his hand around it and pulled it out. A book, a leather notebook. Whatever he had expected to find it was not this. Rose turned it over in his hand. Embossed on the front were the initials WHM. And staining the tan leather, a large dark patch of ink. No, not ink. Not ink at all. Blood. Rose's mouth was dry.

He opened the book. Pictures of flowers, each one beautifully executed in inks and watercolour and meticulously labelled. Then, in the centre of the book, blank pages, some unintelligible doodlings in the same hand. Rose turned to the back. The page was filled with a single word, written in capitals. Rose felt dizzy, the sweat like cold grease across his forehead. He turned the pages, crumpling them, tearing at them. Page after page, the same word, the same hand. The pencil had been pressed down so hard that the paper had ripped right through. And spattered across the pages dark brown stains, like thick ink. Or blood. The same, page after page.

KILL. KILL. KILL.

The loathsome reek of the tunnel pressed into him and against him, forcing itself up into his throat. Rose closed his eyes, tried to swallow the nausea. The leather binding of the book stuck to his hands. His heart sucked at his ribs, taking up the refrain. KILL. KILL. KILL. It was the green-faced sergeant who noticed the light on the water at the far end of the tunnel. Immediately he straightened himself up, gesticulating in silence and with all the authority he could muster to the ganger. The ganger shrugged but, emboldened by the resumption of his official duties, the sergeant shook his head sternly and shook his finger at the light. The ganger hesitated. Then, rolling his eyes upwards and shaking his head, he closed off his lamp and indicated to the others to do the same. Rose staggered backwards slightly, oblivious, striking his elbow painfully against the wall of the tunnel. It was the green-faced sergeant who seized his lantern out of his hand, slamming its shutter. It was quite dark but still Rose saw the words, repeated over and over, stamped in fiery red dust on the darkness.

KILL. KILL. KILL. KILL.

★ ★ ★

The voices were low but, amplified by the acoustics of the low tunnel, they carried plainly downstream.

'The letter.'

And then again, in the same harsh murmur, 'You cannot think me such a fool that I'd follow you any further. The letter.'

'Anxious, are we?' The second voice was rougher, with the misshapen vowels of a London tradesman. There was no mistaking the threat in it.

'If you don't give me my letter I will kill the dog.'

'Patience, patience.' There was a faint splash then, and the scrape of brick against brick. 'Now, what have we here?'

'Give that to me.'

'Very interesting letter, this one. Very interesting indeed.'

'Listen, you filthy —'

'I ain't no lawyer but I'm betting a letter like this one could get a man into very hot water.'

'Give it to me.'

'Her first.'

A short pause.

'Well?'

'All yours. Pleasure doing business with you.'

The rustle of paper was barely audible above the rush of the stream.

'That's my girl.' The second voice was softer now. You could almost hear the smile in it. 'That's my sweet girl. Let's get you home.'

And then, more roughly, 'This way.'

The lights flickered. There was the soft splash of footsteps. Without making a sound the ganger began to slide along the tunnel in pursuit. Suddenly there was the whisper of metal against metal. The ganger froze.

'Oh, I don't think so, do you?' hissed the first voice.

'I'd not do that.' The second voice was hoarser than before but still it quivered with menace, taut as a garrotter's wire. 'Not if I was you.'

'Ah. But you are not.'

'I'm warning you, you so much as scratch me, she'll rip your throat out.'

'Not if I rip hers first. Feel this blade? Sharp, isn't it? Does the job very well, as it happens. It doesn't take much, to cut a man's throat. A flick of the wrist, a little more pressure. Like cutting meat. Or gutting a dog. Of course, they don't always die immediately. England, now England even tried to run. But down here, who's going to hear a man scream?'

'For the last time, I'm warning you —'

'Mr England, now, he wept like a baby —'

The shriek that followed pierced the tunnel like a blade. The green-faced sergeant gasped. Fumbling the truncheon from his belt, he pushed his way towards the light. The ganger followed, Rose behind him. Where the tunnel turned, a lantern had been hung from a hook in the brickwork. Behind it loomed a vast and terrible cave, buttressed and becolumned in the darkness like the underground palace of the Devil himself, hung about with vast spikes of nitre. The black floor shimmered, like a trap. And, caught like a stunned rat in the bright glare of the light, sprawled a man. In one hand he held a knife. A single ruby of blood glistened on its silver blade. With the other hand he clutched at the side of his neck. The blood gushed between his fingers in crimson streams. He was quite alone. The sergeant stared at him, his eyes round with horror.

'What the — sweet Jesus!'

The man looked up, his eyes frenzied in his bloodless face. Then, with a sudden burst of desperate strength, he twisted on to his feet and hurled himself into the stream. The sergeant was caught off guard. He stumbled and almost missed his footing but the ganger was faster. He seized the man, twisting his arms around behind his back. The man flailed madly, the blood from his savaged neck splattering the ganger's face with scarlet.

'Mr Hawke,' the sergeant said, and his voice was sonorous with regret. 'Mr Hawke. I'm afraid you're under arrest.'

XXXVII

You never saw nothing like it, the day of a hanging. Though the prisoner himself weren't due on to the gibbet till eight the following morning, the crowds started gathering from midnight, boys and girls most particularly but men and women of all ages among them, all set upon securing for themselves a fine view of the proceedings. There was a smell about them, Tom thought, like tom-cats on a summer's night. Through Holborn and up Snow-hill they came, past St Sepulchre's and along towards Newgate, jostling and pressing, their eyes darting about in the darkness and the eagerness rising off them like steam. All along the way the gin-shop owners had abandoned their beds and taken their shutters down and were doing brisk business. From time to time the company appeared, all in a mass, to see how the workmen got along with their knockings and hammerings before the thirst forced them back inside for further refreshment.

In the lanes the yellow globes of the gas-lamps were all swathed about with early morning mist and pipe smoke. People sauntered up and down the crowded streets and gathered in knots around those who fancied themselves authorities in the way of executions and who provided assurances to all who might listen about which way the prisoner would face and how the drop would be managed and at what point in the proceedings the noose would be secured around his neck. A barrier held the crowds back from the gallows itself, although there was already people crushed up against it by five o'clock and more than a few women who had fainted had to be passed back through the crowd, their dresses all disordered, so as to allow them some air. Atop a fair number of the houses in the vicinity rows of seats by way of a gallery had been set out on the roofs and, between trying to keep themselves steady on their precarious perches, all manner of bawdiness was called down from the occupants to the crowds below. When at last the grey dawn swilled like dirty water along the lanes, you could barely make out the bells sounding out the hours, so shrill and excitable were the screeches and the yellings and the singing-out of all kinds of lewd verse. You could hardly make out the words but you couldn't help but hear the name of Hawke thrust gleefully into every chorus, no matter if it didn't have nothing whatsoever to do with the song.

With all the carry-on and commotion around it the scaffold itself had a quiet look about it, no more than a stump of black with a chain jutting out from a little door in the black wall of the prison, its cross-beams like shoulders hunched away from the clamour. It seemed meagre somehow, hardly worthy of the great occasion.

Tom threaded his way through the crowd, Lady at his heels. He'd been careful to lay low after that night, staying away from East-court and keeping to the dark secret corners of the rookery where outside folks never ventured. At night he'd bedded down on a sack in the cellar, Lady pressed warm against the back of his knees, listening for footsteps above the gentle rumbling of her snores. That night in the tunnels, they'd come from nowhere, three or more of the bastards, without so much as a warning shout. Tom'd had no more than the blinking of an eye to melt himself into the darkness. Even then he wasn't sure if they'd not seen him go. Straight off he'd reckoned it'd been Hawke'd set them up, for protection. But then he heard. They'd hauled the Captain off to gaol. Turned out they had him fingered for the death of that bloke in the sewers after all. There should've been satisfaction in that but it set Tom on edge. There wasn't any telling what the Captain'd tell the law once he got to thinking about the noose tightening around his neck. For days Tom's shoulder had twitched, anticipating the weight of the hand bearing down on it, the wrenching up of his arms behind his back. But time passed and still nothing happened. Tom'd not been back to East-court in more than a week but according to Joe there'd been no eager trap'd come banging at the bolted door or turning up down the taverns asking questions. Even Eddowes, the coffee-stall proprietor who knew everything, hadn't heard no mention of Tom in all the sorry tale. Still Tom'd waited. Perhaps they meant to flush him out, to jump him just when he thought the coast was clear. But today the bastard was to hang. Today, at last, even cautious Tom considered himself safe. Lady, bless her, might've left the Captain with enough throat to sing but, even if he'd tried it, it'd seem there'd been no one to hear him. And now the job was to be finished for him, official as you like. No less than the full weight of the law, Parliament and Her Royal Majesty Queen Victoria herself, taking up where Lady left off. There was something very satisfactory about that.

By seven o'clock Tom and Lady was cosily settled in a nook in the brick wall with a straight view of the proceedings. The jokes and laughter of the crowd filled the air and the throng heaved and swayed and pushed, a dense sea of people far as the eye could stretch. Beyond Tom a man made a wild grab at a drainpipe and tried with all his strength to pull himself up on to a narrow ledge above the crowd but the shopkeeper whose ledge it was had a grip on his legs and had no intention of letting him loose. The crowd was straight away all attention and from all sides there issued shouts of encouragement so ferocious and intent you might've taken them for the Fancy at the pit. The thought made Tom laugh out loud. Above him the windows of the shops began to fill up with people. A fat tailor and his wife sat side by side in the room above the hatters, sipping complacently at cups of tea.

Meantime a party of traps paced about at the barrier, their faces so blank you'd've thought they were perfectly deaf to the hail of coarse remarks that rained down on them from the pert coster-boys and girls at the front of the crowd. The mob'd grown so dense by this time it was hard to stay on your feet. Tom sharpened his elbows so as they didn't jostle Lady curled up in his arms. He shouldn't't've brought her, really, she'd be crushed beneath the crowd's feet in an instant if he set her down, but it seemed only right she be here too. She'd a right to watch him swing as much as anyone and a deal more than most. There wasn't twenty of them gathered here this morning who'd've known the Captain if he came up and shook them by the hand. Lady, now, she'd know him all too well. There was a fresh wound beneath her left shoulder, a ragged curve, dark and livid against her pink skin. He'd bathed it with peppermint water but it still had an angry look about it he didn't like. If the truth were to be admitted, it were that that brought him here as much as anything. Whenever he looked at that wound, or for some reason it came into his head, it gave him a sour boiling ache in his belly. The bastard couldn't just steal her, oh no. He had to try and break her too. If he'd ruined her for the fight —

He felt the twitch of her ear against his

lips as she raised her head to lick his chin. He'd have her back. She'd be one of them dogs immortalized forever in a glass box, held up to all and sundry as one of the greats. For now though it was just the two of them, there to witness the bastard Captain's walk into Eternity. He'd grown soft, he told himself, tightening his arms around her, and despite himself he smiled. Long Arm Tom, older than the hills and soft as butter.

Once the sheriff's carriages had passed by the time slipped quickly away. As the quarters sounded the crowd began to grow more eager but at the same time quieter, craning and stretching for a view of anything that might indicate the prisoner was on his way. A ladder was brought out and taken in through a side door. Those who had the room raised their arms and pointed and then had the struggle of trying to place them back by their sides. A sole workman put the finishing touches to a beam and was cheered and heckled by the crowd. Above the heaving sea of people windows were slid open and people sprawled out over slates and ledges, all excitement and anticipation.

And then, at last, the clock began to sound out the hour. Immediately, as though the chimes were a steamer driving its great wheel through the sea of people, the crowd began to bob and sway and a terrible feverish shrieking began to build among the mob. Tom strained his neck. At first there was no movement on the platform. The black scaffold of the gallows huddled all alone on its stand, its back turned on the clamour. It put Tom in mind of a beaten child who dreads himself seen. And then the black prison door opened and a head emerged. The crowd gasped, thousands of mouths breathing in all together. It was as though, along with the breath, they'd sucked in all the noises of the street, so there was almost total silence. The head rose up, and showed itself as the head of William Calcraft, the Newgate executioner. Behind him came the Captain.

His black suit looked new and the bandage around his neck had the crisp white shine of a gentleman's stock. His wrists were tied in front of him but still he walked as though he swung them by his sides, with the hint of a swagger. He looked out over the crowd, his eyes dazed and screwed up against the brightness of the morning. A few of the coster-boys called out to him but mostly the crowd was quiet, their mouths open. They stared as the prisoner raised his arms together in a gesture Tom couldn't quite make out. There was a murmur through the sea of people then, like a wave. Those near the back craned their necks for a better look. Then the man who followed the Captain pushed the prisoner forward so that he stood directly beneath the beam. Calcraft drew a black cloth from his pocket and pulled it tightly over the prisoner's head and face. There was no pity or softening in the raised faces of the crowd. Instead they rose themselves on to the tips of their toes, their open mouths red and wet, and the sinews in their necks stood out like ropes. It was impossible to hear the words the clergyman mouthed but you couldn't miss seeing how his greedy eyes didn't fit with the solemn set of his mouth. Then the plank was pulled away and Hawke fell. From his elevated spot, Tom saw the executioner's hands reach up from beneath the platform to grip the Captain's ankles and pull them down with a hard tug. The body twitched and bounced and then, heavy as a sack, hung perfectly still.

The man was dead.

For a moment the crowd was silent and then the roar filled the place, so loud and jubilant that the very bricks of Newgate seemed to shake in their cold mortar. Tom didn't cheer. But he held Lady's face against his, inhaling her warm blanket smell. He hadn't stopped to take breakfast but all of a sudden his stomach, which had been taken up with complaining to him for an hour or more, no longer felt empty. Instead he felt warm and satisfied, as though he'd eaten a loaf of bread straight out the oven. There'd be many a poor man who'd be happy to know the smell of a dog could fill a hungry stomach, he thought dryly to himself. He was glad Joe wasn't here to see his face. All these years and soft as a girl. Joe'd laugh at that fit to bust and Tom'd never hear the end of it.

The hangman was joshing around with the dead body now, pretending to shake its hand. The crowd cheered. Tom smiled, burying his face in Lady's coat. It was time he took her home.

XXXVIII

Two days later William and Polly left London.

They took a little money with them. Although some of the Board had questioned its necessity, Lovick had succeeded in securing for William a small settlement that might allow sufficient funds to provide for his family's immediate requirements for the duration of a brief convalescence. It was never suggested that he might once again take up his position with the Board. Indeed, the letter that accompanied the details of the pension made it clear that this act of generosity was to serve not as an indication of a continuing relationship between May and the Commission but instead as a conclusion, the final curtain, as it were, coming down once and for all and with as little fuss as possible upon the entire unhappy episode. Hawke had quickly been replaced and a team of first-rate men assigned to his successor. Despite the scandal, the Commission continued to have the vigorous support of Parliament and of the people of London. Their work would continue without delay. And without William.

Polly did not attempt to conceal her indignation. The frown lines that had begun to etch themselves into her sallow cheeks darkened and deepened. William had done nothing wrong, she insisted to anyone who might listen. Hadn't the law itself said so? William had been no less a victim of Hawke's wickedness than England himself and, like England, he deserved not punishment but retribution. Thanks to the evil schemings of that monster her husband had been declared insane and locked up. She, who had once had a house and a servant, who had been a respectable woman of some position, had been reduced to a single room in a lodging house where she might take in what sewing she could simply to put food in her children's mouths. At the very least there should be a public apology, an acknowledgement of the terrible wrongs done to William, to them both, and the permission to resume his old position, his old life. Should there not? She wrote in a furious scrawl to Rawlinson, William's old benefactor, but received only a brief reply from his secretary, sending the engineer's best wishes to her husband for a prompt recovery and informing her politely that Rawlinson had the utmost respect for Bazalgette and the Metropolitan Board of Works and that he wished her to know that he supported entirely any conclusions they saw fit to arrive at in this matter.

When Polly received Rawlinson's letter she slapped at it angrily with the back of her hand, brandishing it at William and demanding he share her outrage, but he only shrugged anxiously and held out his arms. He held her a great deal in the weeks following his release, clutching at her hands whenever she passed him and burying his face in her apron. When she moved about their room his eyes followed her restlessly. He could not bear to be left alone. The landlady permitted use of her kitchen by her lodgers on Sundays and he liked to sit there with her, in a rocking chair pulled up close to the range. He liked it best when she baked bread, even though the baker called daily and there was no need of it. He sat in his chair, his eyes fixed upon his wife and his head full of the smell of it. He could not get enough of it, he admitted to her, the hot floury vigorous aroma of baking bread. He didn't tell her that when the bread was baking there was a respite from the stink of the prison, a stink that seemed to have taken up occupancy in his nostrils and which at night swelled in grey-green clouds of fog to take on monstrous forms that stalked his dreams. Instead he sat in his chair and played like Di with fragments of Polly's dough, twisting and pulling at them so frantically that they turned grey and remained resolutely flat when baked. He looked so solemn and despondent when they came out from the oven that Polly's stern face relented and she laughed, not in giddy peals as she had once laughed but in tight little snorts, as though she had little laughter left in her and wished to eke it out. Then William smiled too. Since leaving the prison-ship he smiled often, twitchy tentative smiles that clutched greedily at their faint reflection in his wife's face. My little milkwort, he murmured longingly, clasping her hands in his and breathing in her sweet musky smell. My most precious milkwort. And she brushed her dry lips across his forehead and for a moment the frown lines eased a little and in her caramel eyes something of the old golden sparkle caught the light.

He did not cut. He did not dare. He dreamed of it, his fingers closing around the familiar shape of the handle, the silvery flash of the blade as it plunged into his skin, and he felt his heart explode and his blood sing with ecstasy and his spirit cry out in exultation to the sky, but still he did not do it. His eyes followed her around the room, watching the tilt of her shoulders as she crouched to poke the fire, her fingers as they drove the needle in and out of the cloth. He smiled at her, his cautious desperate smiles, and she saw him and she smiled back. If he cut himself she would see. She would look at him with those eyes and she would not smile and his heart would shrivel and his blood would run cold and his spirit would be broken, naked and in chains. Nothing would be left when she was gone, nothing but the dark cold press of fear. He could not cut. He would not cut. He was sane, wasn't he? They had, after all, pronounced him sane. Sane and innocent. The words were as solid and authoritative as stones. They could not be denied. Fears and dreams might prowl in their shadows but fears and dreams were powerless to change the immutable nature of stones. In the meantime, if he moved little and thought less, he could concentrate on holding the bowl of himself almost steady in his lap.

The day after Hawke was hanged Polly's brother Maurice arrived at their lodgings as arranged. He had a little business he was obliged to conduct in a village only a few miles from Lambeth and so it was agreed that it would save an expense if he brought his empty wagon to transport what few possessions of Polly and William's remained to his house, where the family would stay until their future was decided. Polly went down to the street to meet him, leaving William fretfully watching her from the window. As she greeted her brother the mail coach clattered down the street and a parcel was placed in her hands. She glanced at it and then up to the window. William smiled anxiously back, willing her to hurry. She disappeared from view. A moment later he heard her tread on the stairs, followed by the heavier step of her brother.

'A package for you,' she announced, placing it in her husband's hands.

William glanced at it. He did not recognize the handwriting. His fingers were clumsy with the string and Polly was obliged to fetch a knife for him, covering the small cupboard with her skirts so that Maurice might not see that she kept the cabinet locked. She was no longer certain it was a necessary precaution but she did it anyway. If William noticed he passed no comment.

'Here,' she said. He held out his hand for the knife but instead she kneeled in front of him and cut through the string herself, slipping the blade into a pocket in her apron. William unwrapped the paper. The package contained a leather notebook and a short letter, written in black ink in a cramped hand that seemed unwilling to stand upright but at the same time unable to decide whether to slope to the left or to the right. Polly took up the paper.

'It's from that lawyer,' she said. 'Sydney Rose. It's your botany journal. Now why did you give him that? What earthly use could it've been to him?'

William shook his head. He had no recollection of giving Rose his journal. It had been months since he remembered last holding it. He weighed the notebook in his hands. Its leather cover, though badly stained, still felt soft and warm to the touch. As Polly directed Maurice towards their meagre heap of boxes she dropped the letter back on his lap. It was very brief.

Mr May,

By the time you receive this you will, I am quite sure, be enjoying life once more as a free man. To this day I can hardly trust my own memory of the extraordinary series of events that led to your exoneration. I can only imagine you will thank God for them for the remainder of your life.

Your obedient servant, &c.

Sydney Rose

It was the first time William had heard from Rose since his release. He'd half expected him to be there when they finally let him out of Woolwich. Even now he found it difficult to connect the hand pushed clumsily through the iron slot of the cell door with this compressed and stilted missive. It made him uneasy, though he couldn't have said precisely why. Putting the letter to one side he opened the notebook and flicked through the pages. Polly saw him frown.

'What's the matter?'

'The most recent pages, they've all been torn out,' William protested. 'Why would someone do such a thing? All my work, everything I was considering, it was all there. Now it's gone, forever.'

Polly peered over his head, resting one hand on his shoulder. He clasped it in both of his, pressing it to his lips.

'Your beautiful botany drawings,' she sighed into his hair. 'Poor love. That's a crime.'

'Botany? That's flowers, ain't it?' Maurice asked curiously.

William nodded.

'So you's a bit of a gardener, then?'

William shrugged, closing the book.

'A bit.'

Maurice turned to Polly.

'Why didn't you say so, you foolish girl? There's always gardeners needed up the Hall, blokes who know one end of a rose from another.' He turned back to William. 'Her Ladyship's mad keen for it. She's got a hothouse makes the Crystal Palace itself look like a cucumber frame. All the colours of the rainbow her garden is, come June time.'

'Maurice!' Polly rebuked stiffly. 'William's hardly interested in being a common gardener. He has a profession.'

Maurice shrugged.

'Well, all's I'm saying is, you won't want for work down our way if you can turn your hand to a spot of — what is it you call it? — botanizing.'

'For the love of peace —' Polly snapped.

She crossed her arms, shaking her head angrily at her brother, but William smiled. He did not notice that Polly frowned at him too, provoked by his silence. He looked at his lap and he smiled. The smile came from somewhere deep inside him and it pressed upwards through the dark winter earth of his chest with the pale determination of a snowdrop. Tinged with green, like seasickness, and fragile as paper. *Galanthus nivalis.* The first bloom of spring.

Author's Note

It was not until I returned to London after four years living in New York City that I realised how much I had missed the sprawling unruly profusion of the city in which I had been born and raised. I also understood, after years of discovering the secrets of another place, how little I knew of London's history, of the stories behind its familiar streets. I had always wanted to write a historical novel and it did not take long to decide that I should focus my research on mid-nineteenth-century London, a time of unshakeable faith in progress, when building was at its apogee and the city was the largest of its kind in the world.

At first I thought I would find my story amidst the railways, whose pitiless march into the heart of the city displaced so many lives and was to have so profound an effect upon the structure and appearance of the modern city. But the more I read about the railways the more distracted I became by quite another monumental construction, at least as remarkable. In 1860 the price of bricks in London doubled. In large part this was due to the building of structures, such as bridges and stations, required by the railway system, and the cheap back-to-back housing thrown up to accommodate those whom the railways had displaced. But mostly it was because, beneath the pavements of London, another, perhaps even more audacious building project was progressing. An entire network of sewers was under construction, over eighty miles of tunnel that, thanks to the ingenious designs of Joseph Bazalgette, would transform London's drainage system into one of the engineering wonders of the world.

During the 1830s nearly half of the infants born in English towns died before their fifth birthday. In London, by 1850 a city of two million souls, the statistics were worse still. Epidemics of diarrhoea, dysentery, typhoid, and the recently imported cholera swept regularly through the capital. Much of the city's drinking water was taken from the Thames, into which the city's waste was also dumped, turning the river into a huge open sewer. The Victorians believed that disease was spread through 'miasma' in the air, the presence of poisonous droplets evidenced by appalling stench. It is hardly surprising, therefore, that Parliament regarded the overpowering reek of the river during the hot, dry summer of 1858 as truly a matter of life and death. Within eighteen days of its first reading they passed the Act to allow Bazalgette's comprehensive works to begin.

Bazalgette emerged from my research as not only an engineer of great skill but also a man of vision, a workaholic who, when given six months off to recover from the rigours of the London sewers project, managed only one before rushing back to the office. And yet, when I sought out his memorial in London, I found only a small bust set into a dark corner beneath the railway bridge at Charing Cross, on the Thames Embankment that he designed and built. Beneath the bust runs the Latin text *flumini vincula posuit:* he placed chains upon the river. For the brilliance with which he pioneered systems copied subsequently throughout the world, he deserves much more.

One of the men who was later to implement Bazalgette's ideas in other cities was Robert Rawlinson, to whom I have also given a walk-on role in the book. Rawlinson was not the Commission's most senior engineer but remained in Turkey when the Commission's chairman, John Sutherland, returned to England to ensure that the necessary sanitary reforms were carried out. Rawlinson had stood against Bazalgette for the post of Chief Engineer to the Board of Works in 1851 but remained a close friend and ally of Bazalgette's for the remainder of his life.

By contrast, the researcher finds very few extant accounts of men of the status of William May, those who executed the ideas and instructions of other, greater men. However the diaries of H. Percy Boulnois, *Reminiscences of a Municipal Engineer*, gave me something of an insight into the precarious livelihoods of ordinary men. There is even less evidence of incidences of self-harm, which I took to reflect the taboo nature of the subject. The only example I was able to track down was the story of a woman, incarcerated in Bedlam, who regularly broke her windows and used the shards of glass to cut herself. Her guards commented that she failed to kill herself because she did not cut deeply enough or in the right places, attributing this to her derangement. To me it was evidence that they had quite failed to understand her intent. Throughout history the letting of blood has been a ritual of purification, a cleansing of a body fouled by sin or by disease. Modern-day accounts by self-harmers, such as those included in Marilee Strong's *A Bright Red Scream*, speak to the intense human pain that drives its sufferers to such extremities.

Any study of Britain in the mid-nineteenth century cannot fail to include the Russian War, fought between 1854 and 1856. Although it began as a religious quarrel between Russian Orthodox monks and French Catholics over precedence in the holy cities of Jerusalem and Nazareth, the Crimean War, as it was later to become known, was sparked when the Russians invaded part of the Ottoman (Turkish) Empire. Alarmed that they would take Constantinople and cut off routes to India, a vital part of the British Empire, the British agreed to join with the French and the Turks to eject Russia from the region. The conflict was Britain's only European war between the ending of the Napoleonic conflict in 1815 and the opening of the Great War in 1914, and quickly became a byword for poor generalship and logistical incompetence.

It was from the outset a conflict of appalling losses, first to cholera (ten thousand Allied soldiers died before the first shot of the war was fired) and then during a series of chaotically mismanaged encounters with the enemy. The battle of Inkerman, in which William sustains his wounds, began when the Russians invaded the British camp early one foggy morning while most of the men were still asleep; the battle that followed was a ramshackle affair fought with bayonets at extremely close quarters.

The Victorians were not ones for emotional analysis but, to a modern sensibility, it is all too easy to imagine the terrible psychological damage sustained by the young men who fought there. One nurse mentioned briefly in her journal that many junior soldiers 'became imbecile and it was believed that this affliction was often caused by fright'. Many more were invalided home with the loose diagnosis of 'low fever,' Victorian code for depression. On returning to London, there must have been many who found that the repressive certainties of Victorian society, the rigid definitions of what it meant to be a respectable Christian and gentleman, demanded so much of them that they were forced to act, in secret, in desperate and drastic ways.

As for Long Arm Tom, he walked almost whole from between the pages of Henry Mayhew's *London Labour and the London*

Poor. As the London correspondent for a large-scale survey of Britain's working poor, sponsored by the *Morning Chronicle* newspaper, Mayhew's unflinching reports upon the lives of London's poorest citizens were shocking and controversial. Unlike most Victorians, who approached the poor in the guise of moralists and missionaries, Mayhew interviewed the occupants of London's grimmest slums directly, reporting their speech verbatim and providing clear and impartial accounts of what they wore, how they lived, and how they scraped together a living. He talked to prostitutes and costermongers, toshers and street sweepers and flower girls, to all the vast ranks of the disregarded and the dispossessed, and his efforts have furnished the historian with what is arguably the finest oral history of his period.

Acknowledgments

While the historical events upon which this book is based are true, and a handful of real people have walk-on parts, William and Tom, and the story that connects them, are fictional. Any errors of fact are entirely my own.

I have plundered innumerable books for both information and inspiration but particular tribute must go to Henry Mayhew's seminal work, *London Labour and the London Poor* (1851), from between whose pages so many of this book's characters have emerged. John Hollingshead's wonderful *Underground London* (1862) proved equally indispensable, as did Hippolyte Taine's *Notes on England* (1872) and Sala's *Gaslight and Daylight* (1859). Other more contemporary but similarly invaluable sources include Peter Ackroyd's *London: The Biography* (2000), A. N. Wilson's *The Victorians* (2001) and Eric de Maré's *The London Doré Saw: A Victorian Evocation* (1972).

For information about the work of Joseph Bazalgette I am indebted to both Stephen Halliday's *The Great Stink of London* (1999) and Trench and Hillman's *London Under London* (1984), as well as many contemporary accounts, notably H. Percy Boulnois's *Reminiscences of a Municipal Engineer* (1920). I would also like to thank the staff of the local history section of Battersea Lending Library for allowing me access to their extensive collection of minutes from the meetings of the Municipal Board of Works.

In all matters concerning the Russian War I could have found no better sources than Paul Kerr's *The Crimean War* (1997) and John Shepherd's study of the medical aspects of the conflict, *The Crimean Doctors* (1990). I relied heavily upon *The Illustrated Flora of Britain and Northern Europe* (1989), by Marjorie Blamey and Christopher Grey-Wilson, for botanical detail. And I would have had only a fraction of the insight required for this book without Marilee Strong's remarkable study of self-injury, *A Bright Red Scream* (1998).

There are also large numbers of people without whose hard work and unstinting support this book would never have been written. Specific thanks go to Clare Alexander, my wonderful agent and friend

571

whose idea it was in the first place, and Mary Mount, my brilliant editor, and all of her team at Penguin, not to mention Sally Riley, Susan Miles, and the indefatigable staff at Battersea Library, Chelsea Library, and the British Library. I also want to thank Jill Sterry and her colleagues at Thames Water who provided me with first-hand experience of a London sewer.

Most of all I want to thank my children, Charlie and Flora, for sharing me so un-complainingly with my laptop, and my husband, Chris, without whom it would hardly be worth getting up in the morning.

About the Author

Clare Clark was born in London in 1967. A senior scholar at Trinity College Cambridge, she graduated with a double first in history. *The Great Stink* is her first novel. She is married with two children and lives in London.